Praise for the

"Between the four-legged fa ___ :n vying for Brie Hooker's favor, the ___ ......g her aunt's innocence, plus the villain's attempts to end her life, this book is a thrill-a-minute read."

— Cindy Sample,
National Bestselling Author of *Dying for a Donut*

"Grabbed me at chapter one and refused to let go until the very last page...Lovely offers up a charming setting that's so real you can almost smell the hay, a story that's laugh-out-loud funny, and a mystery that will keep you up past your bedtime."

— Annette Dashofy,
USA Today Bestselling Author of *Uneasy Prey*

"How vegan Brie Hooker balances cheese loving carnivores, more than one romantic interest, and murder in Linda Lovely's *Bones to Pick* is a humorous delight. A well-crafted series debut."

— Debra H. Goldstein,
IPPY Award-Winning Author of *Maze in Blue*

"Packed with suspense and action and some spicy romance. Its excitement wasn't the only thing that kept me flipping pages. The characters are funny and sweet and I look forward to getting to know them better in future books. I ate up every morsel."

— Dorothy St. James,
Author of the Southern Chocolate Shop Mysteries

"An entertaining mystery with a cast of colorful characters, a delightful Southern setting, and plenty of action. Spend time with Linda Lovely's Brie Hooker—a gutsy, smart heroine with a sharp eye and refreshing sense of humor—and you'll want to return to Ardon County and the Udderly Kidding goat farm again and again."

— Wendy Tyson,

BONES
TO PICK

The Brie Hooker Mystery Series
by Linda Lovely

BONES TO PICK (#1)
PICKED OFF (#2)

BONES TO PICK

A BRIE HOOKER MYSTERY

LINDA LOVELY

HENERY PRESS

Copyright

BONES TO PICK
A Brie Hooker Mystery
Part of the Henery Press Mystery Collection

First Edition | October 2017

Henery Press, LLC
www.henerypress.com

Cover art by Stephanie Savage
Author photograph by Danielle Dahl

Trade Paperback ISBN-13: 978-1-63511-259-7
Digital epub ISBN-13: 978-1-63511-260-3
Kindle ISBN-13: 978-1-63511-261-0
Hardcover ISBN-13: 978-1-63511-262-7

Printed in the United States of America

To My Critique Partners Near and Far
Our Shared Laughter Sweetens Every Book

ACKNOWLEDGMENTS

I had a blast doing the research for *Bones To Pick*. Many thanks to the owners of Split Creek Farm in South Carolina and Morning Glow Farm in Wisconsin. They provided tons of fun information about raising goats and making cheese. Thanks also to the folks at another fine South Carolina company, Palmetto Moonshine, for my legal moonshine tutorial. Of course, tastings of moonshine, goat cheese, and goat fudge were mandatory.

Dr. Glen Quattlebaum, our vegan family physician, deserves a special salute for his role in inspiring Brie Hooker's dietary choices, while all of my cheese and ice cream addicted kin contributed to Aunt Eva's menu leanings.

As always thanks to my husband, Tom Hooker. While I didn't change my last name to his—Linda Lovely Hooker, really?—I did give his surname to my main character. Because I had so many animals to name, I offered family members a shot at picking which animals they wanted named after them. This turned out to be a fun and surprising exercise. Tammy the Pig is actually named after my very attractive niece. Maybe I should plan a relative-animal match game for my website.

Paramedic Steve MacLeod provided valuable input on emergency medical responses, while Lorraine Q. Shumate schooled me in the ways of pedicure. Amazing where research takes you. Thanks for answering my questions.

Grateful shout outs are due Rachel Jackson, my sharp-eyed editor, who identified a variety of ways to improve my manuscript, and artist Stephanie Savage for the cool cover. Thank you, too, to Fara Driver, a beta reader, who had some keen observations about the ages of various characters.

Finally, major thanks to my critique partners for their support, excellent suggestions, and, most of all, their friendship. We've been together for years. That's why this book is dedicated to these six talented authors: Donna Campbell, Danielle Dahl, Charles Duke, Howard Lewis, Maryanne Romano, and Robin Weaver. Love you guys.

ONE

Hello, I'm Brie, and I'm a vegan.

It sounds like I'm introducing myself at a Vegetarians Anonymous meeting. But, trust me, there aren't enough vegetarians in Ardon County, South Carolina, to make a circle much less hold a meeting.

Give yourself ten points if you already know vegans are even pickier than vegetarians. We forgo meat, fish, eggs, and dairy. But we're big on cashews, walnuts, and almonds. All nuts are good nuts. Appropriate with my family.

Family. That's why I put my career as a vegan chef on hold to live and work in Ardon, a strong contender for the South's carnivore-and-grease capital. My current job? I help tend four hundred goats, make verboten cheese, and gather eggs I'll never poach. Most mornings when Aunt Eva rousts me before the roosters, I roll my eyes and mutter.

Still, I can't complain. I had a choice. Sort of.

Blame it on the pig—Tammy the Pig—for sticking her snout in our family business.

I'd consorted with vegans and vegetarians for too long. I seriously underestimated how much cholesterol meat eaters could snarf down at a good old-fashioned wake. Actually, I wasn't sure this wake was "old fashioned," but it was exactly how Aunt Lilly would have planned her own send-off—if she'd had the chance. Ten days ago, the feisty sixty-two-year-old had a toddler's curiosity and a twenty-year-old's appetite for adventure. Her death was a total shock.

I glanced at Aunt Lilly's epitaph hanging behind the picnic buffet. She'd penned it years back. Her twin, Aunt Eva, found it in Lilly's desk and reprinted it in eighty-point type.

"There once was a farmer named Lilly
Who never liked anything frilly,
She tended her goats,
Sowed a few wild oats,
And said grieving her death would be silly."

In a nod to Lilly's spirit, Aunt Eva planned today's wake complete with fiddling, hooch, goo-gogs of goat cheese, and the whole panoply of Southern fixins—mounds of country ham, fried chicken, barbecue, and mac-and-cheese awash in butter. Every veggie dish came dressed with bacon crumbles, drippings, or cream of mushroom soup.

Not a morsel fit for a vegan. Eva's revenge. I'd made the mistake of saying I didn't want to lose her, too, and hinted she'd live longer if she cut back on cholesterol. Not my smartest move. The name of her farm? Udderly Kidding Dairy. Cheese and eggs had been Eva's meal ticket for decades.

My innocent observation launched a war. Whenever I opened the refrigerator, I'd find a new message. This morning a Post-it on my dish of blueberries advised: *The choline in eggs may enhance brain development and memory—as a vegan you probably forgot.*

Smoke from the barbeque pit permeated the air as I replenished another platter of shredded pork on the buffet. My mouth watered and I teetered on the verge of drooling. While I was a dedicated vegan, my olfactory senses were still programmed "Genus Carnivorous." My stomach growled—loudly. Time to thwart its betrayal with the veggies and hummus dip I'd stashed in self-defense.

I'd just stuck a juicy carrot in my mouth when a large hand squeezed my shoulder.

"Brie, honey, you've been working nonstop," Dad said. "Take a break. Mom's on her way. We can play caterers. The food's prepared. No risks associated with our cooking."

I choked on my carrot and sputtered. "Good thing. Do you even remember the last time Mom turned on an oven?"

Dad smiled. "Can't recall. Maybe when you were a baby? But, hey, we're wizards at takeout and microwaves."

His smile faltered. I caught him staring at Aunt Lilly's epitaph.

"Still can't believe Lilly's gone." He attempted a smile. "Knowing her sense of humor, we're lucky she didn't open that epitaph with 'There once was a lass from Nantucket.'"

I'd never seen Dad so sad. Lilly's unexpected death stunned him to his core. He adored his older sisters.

Mom appeared at his side and wrapped an arm around his waist. She loved her sisters-in-law, too, though she complained my childless aunts spoiled me beyond repair.

Of course, Lilly's passing hit Eva the hardest. A fresh boatload of tears threatened as I thought about the aunt left behind. I figured my tear reservoir had dried up after days of crying. Wrong. The tragedy—a texting teenager smashing head-on into Lilly's car—provoked a week-long family weep-a-thon. It ended when Eva ordered us to cease and desist.

"This isn't what Lilly would want," she declared. "We're gonna throw a wake. One big, honking party."

Which explained the fifty-plus crowd of friends and neighbors milling about the farm, tapping their feet to fiddlin', and consuming enough calories to sustain the populace of a small principality for a week.

I hugged Dad. "Thanks. I could use a break. I'll find Eva. See how she's doing."

I spotted her near a flower garden filled with cheery jonquils. It looked like a spring painting. Unfortunately, the cold March wind that billowed Eva's scarlet poncho argued the blooms were false advertising. The weatherman predicted the thermometer would struggle to reach the mid-forties today.

My aunt's build was what I'd call sturdy, yet Eva seemed to sway in the gusty breeze as she chatted with Billy Jackson, the good ol' boy farrier who shod her mule. Though my parents pretended otherwise, we all knew Billy slept under Eva's crazy quilt at least two nights a week.

I nodded at the couple. Well, actually, the foursome. Brenda, the farm's spoiled pet goat, and Kai, Udderly's lead Border collie, were competing with Billy for my aunt's attention.

"Mom and Dad are watching the buffet," I said. "Thought I'd see if you need me to do anything. Are you expecting more folks?"

"No." Eva reached down and tickled the tiny black goat's shaggy head. "Imagine everyone who's coming is here by now. They'll start clearing out soon. Chow down and run. Can't blame 'em. Especially the idiot women who thought they ought to wear dresses. That biting wind's gotta be whistling up their drawers."

Billy grinned as he looked Eva up and down. Her choice of wake attire—poncho, black pants, and work boots—surprised no one, and would have delighted Lilly.

"Do you even own a dress?" Billy laughed.

"You're one to talk." Eva gave his baggy plaid suit and clip-on bowtie the stink eye. "I suppose you claim that gristle on your chin is needed to steady your fiddle."

He kissed Eva's cheek. "Yep, that's it. Time to rejoin my fellow fiddlers, but first I have a hankering to take a turn at the Magic Moonshine tent."

"You do that. Maybe the 'shine will improve your playing. It'll definitely make you sound better to your listening audience. After enough of that corn liquor even my singing could win applause."

A dark-haired stranger usurped Billy's place, bending low to plant a kiss on the white curls that sprang from my aunt's head like wood shavings. *Wow.* They stacked handsome tall when they built him. Had to be at least six-four.

Even minus an introduction, I figured this tall glass of sweet tea had to be Paint, the legendary owner of Magic Moonshine. Sunlight glinted off hair the blue-black of expensive velvet. Deep dimples. Rakish smile.

I'd spent days sobbing, and my libido apparently was saying "enough"—time to rejoin the living. If this bad boy were any more alive, he'd be required to wear a "Danger High Voltage" sign. Of course, Aunt Lilly wouldn't mind. She'd probably rent us a room.

I ventured a glance and found him smiling at me. My boots were suddenly fascinating. Never stare at shiny objects with the potential to hypnotize. I refused to fall under another playboy's spell.

"How's my best gal?" he asked, hugging Eva.

"Best for this minute, right?" my aunt challenged. "I bet my niece will be your best gal before I finish the introductions." Eva put a hand on my shoulder. "Paint, this young whippersnapper is Brie Hooker, my favorite niece. 'Course, she's my only niece. Brie, it's with great trepidation that I introduce you to David Paynter, better known as Paint, unrepentant moonshiner and heartbreaker."

Eva subjected Paint to her pretend badass stare, a sure sign he was one of her favorite sparring partners. "Don't you go messing with Brie, or I'll bury you down yonder with Mark, once I nail his hide."

Paint laughed, a deep, rumbling chuckle. He turned toward me and bowed like Rhett Butler reincarnated.

"Pleased to meet you, Brie. That puzzled look tells me you haven't met Mark, the wily coyote that harasses Eva's goats. She's wasted at least six boxes of buckshot trying to scare him off. Me? I'll gladly risk her shotgun to make your acquaintance. I've heard a lot about you."

Eva gave Paint a shove. "Well, if that's the case, go on. Give Brie a shot of your peach moonshine. It's pretty good."

"Peach moonshine it is," he said and took my arm.

A second later, he tightened his grip and pulled me to the right. "Better watch your step. You almost messed up those pretty boots."

He pointed at a fresh pile of fragrant poop, steaming in the brisk air inches from my suede boots.

"Thanks," I mumbled.

Still holding my arm, he steered me over uneven ground to a clear path. "Eva says you're staying with her. Hope you don't have to leave for a while. Your aunt's a fine lady, and it's going to be mighty hard on her once this flock of well-wishers flies off."

His baritone sent vibrations rippling through my body. My brain ordered me to ignore the tingling that remained in places it didn't belong.

He smiled. "Eva and Lilly spoke about you so often I feel like we're already friends. 'Course head-shaking accompanied some of their comments. They said you'd need to serve plenty of my moonshine if you ever opened a vegan B&B in Ardon County. Here abouts it's considered unpatriotic to serve eats that haven't been baptized in a vat of lard. Vegetables are optional; meat, mandatory."

Uh, oh. I always gave relatives and friends a free pass on good-natured kidding. But a stranger? This man was poking fun at my profession, yet my hackles—smoothed by the hunk's lopsided grin—managed only a faint bristle.

Back away. Pronto. Discovering my ex-fiancé, Jack, was boffing not one, but two co-workers the entire two years we were engaged made me highly allergic to lady-killers. Paint was most definitely a member of that tribe.

"What can I say? I'm a rebel," I replied. "It's my life's ambition to convince finger-lickin', fried-chicken lovers that life without meat, butter, eggs, and cheese does not involve a descent into the nine circles of hell."

Paint released me, then raised his hand to brush a wayward curl from my forehead. His flirting seemed to be congenital.

"If you're as feisty as your aunt claims, why don't you take me on as a challenge? I do eat tomatoes—fried green ones, anyway—and I'm open to sampling other members of the vegetable kingdom. So long as they don't get between me and my meat. Anyway, welcome to the Carolina foothills. Time to pour some white lightning. It's smoother than you might expect."

And so are you. Too smooth for me.

That's when we heard the screams.

TWO

Paint zoomed off like a Clemson running back, hurtling toward the screams—human, not goat. I managed to stay within a few yards of him, slipping and sliding as my suede boots unwittingly smooshed a doggie deposit. Udderly's guardian dogs, five Great Pyrenees, were large enough to saddle, and their poop piles rivaled cow paddies.

As I neared the barn, I slipped on wet straw. To slow my slide, I grabbed for the branch of a bush. I missed. My palm collided with weathered barn siding.

Ouch. Harpooned by a jagged splinter. Blood oozed from the sensitive pad below my right thumb. I stared at the inch-plus spear. Paint had kept running. He was no longer in sight.

The screams stopped. An accident? A heart attack?

I hustled around the corner of the barn. A little girl sobbed in the cleared area behind Udderly's retail sales cabin. I recognized Jenny, a rambunctious five-year-old from a nearby farm. Her mother knelt beside her, stroking her hair.

No child had produced the operatic screams we'd heard. Maybe Jenny's mother was the screamer. But the farm wife didn't seem the hysterical type. On prior visits to Udderly, I'd stopped at the roadside stand where she sold her family's produce. Right now the woman's face looked redder than one of her Early Girl tomatoes. Was the flush brought on by some danger—a goat butting her daughter, a snake slithering near the little girl?

I walked closer. Then I saw it.

A skull poked through the red clay. Soil had tinted the bone an absurd pink.

I gasped.

The sizeable cranium looked human. I spotted the grave digger, or should I say re-digger. Udderly's newest addition, a Vietnamese potbellied pig named Tammy, hunkered in a nearby puddle. Tiny cloven hoof marks led to and from the excavation. Tell-tale red mud dappled her dainty twitching snout. The pig's hundred-pound body quivered as her porcine gaze roved the audience she'd attracted.

A man squatted beside Tammy, speaking to the swine in soothing, almost musical tones. Pigs were dang smart and sensitive. Aunt Eva told me it was easy to hurt their feelings. The fellow stroking Tammy's grimy head must've been convinced she was one sensitive swine.

"It's okay," he repeated. "The lady wasn't screaming at you, Tammy."

Tammy snorted, lowered her head, and squeezed her eyes shut. The pig-whisperer gave the swine a final scratch and stood, freeing gangly limbs from his pretzel-like crouch. Mud caked the cuffs and knees of his khaki pants. Didn't seem to bother him one iota.

The mother shepherded her little girl away from the disturbing scene, and Paint knelt to examine the skeletal remains. "Looks like piggy uncovered more than she bargained for." He glanced at Muddy Cuffs. "Andy, you're a vet. Animal or human?"

"Human." Andy didn't hesitate. "But all that's left is bone. Had to have been buried a good while. Yet Tammy's rooting scratched only inches below the surface. If a settler dug this grave, it was mighty shallow."

"Probably didn't start that way." I pointed to a depression that began uphill near the retail cabin. "This wash has deepened a lot since my aunts built their store and the excavation diverted water away from the cabin. The runoff's been nibbling away at the ground."

Mom, Dad, and Aunt Eva joined the group eyeballing the skull. Eva looked peaked, almost ill. I felt a slight panic at the shift in her normally jolly appearance. I thought of my aunts as forces of nature. Unflappable. Indestructible. I'd lost one, and the other suddenly looked fragile. Finding a corpse on her property the same day she bid her twin goodbye had hit her hard.

Dad cocked his head. "Could be a Cherokee burial site. Or maybe a previous farmer buried a loved one and the grave marker got lost. Homestead burials have always been legal in South Carolina. Still are."

For once, the idea of finding a corpse in an unexpected location didn't prompt a gleeful chuckle from my dad, Dr. Howard Hooker. Though he was a professor of horticulture at Clemson University by day, he was an aspiring murder mystery author by night. Every time we went for a car ride, Dad made a game of searching the landscape for spots "just perfect" for disposing of bodies. So far, a dense patch of kudzu in a deep ravine topped his picks. "Kudzu grows so fast any flesh peeking through would disappear in a day."

Good thing Dad confined his commentary to family outings. We knew the corpses in question weren't real.

Mom whipped out her smartphone. "I'll call Judge Glenn. It's Sunday, but he always answers his cell. He'll know who to call. I'm assuming the Ardon County Sheriff's Department."

Dad nodded. "Probably, but I bet SLED—the South Carolina Law Enforcement Division—will take over. The locals don't have forensic specialists."

Mom rolled her eyes. "You spend way too much time with your Sisters in Crime."

It amused Mom that Dad's enthusiasm for his literary genre earned him the presidency of the Upstate South Carolina Chapter of Sisters in Crime.

Mom didn't fool with fictional crime. Too busy with the real thing. As the City of Clemson's attorney, she kept a bevy of lawyers, judges, and city and university cops on speed dial. However, Udderly Kidding wasn't in the same county as Clemson so it sat outside her domain.

"Judge Glenn, this is Iris Hooker. I'm at the Udderly Kidding Dairy in Ardon. An animal here unearthed a skull. We think it's human, but not recent. Should we call the sheriff?"

Mom nodded and made occasional I-get-it noises while she clamped the cell to her ear.

"Could you ask them to keep their arrival quiet? Better yet, could they wait until after four? About fifty folks are here for my sister-in-law's wake. I don't want to turn her farewell into a circus."

A minute later, Mom murmured her thanks and pocketed her cell. "The judge agreed an old skull doesn't warrant sirens or flashing lights. He'll ask the Ardon County Sheriff, Robbie Jones, to come by after four. Since I'm an officer of the court, his honor just requested that I keep people and animals clear of the area until the sheriff arrives."

Andy stood. "Paint, help me bring some hay bales from the barn. We can stack them to cordon off the area."

"Good idea." Paint stood, and the two men strode off. No needless chitchat. They appeared to be best buds.

I tugged Dad's sleeve, nodded toward his sister, and whispered, "I think Aunt Eva should sit down. Let's get her to one of the front porch rockers."

Dad walked over and draped an arm around his sister's shoulders. "Eva, let's sit a while so folks can find you to pay their respects. This skeleton is old news. Not our worry."

Eva's lips trembled. "No, Brother. I feel it in my own bones. It's that son-of-a-bitch Jed Watson come back to haunt me."

THREE

Jed Watson? The man Eva married in college? The man who vanished a few years later?

Dad's eyebrows shot up. "Eva, that's nonsense. That dirtbag ran off forty years back. You're letting your imagination run wild."

Eva straightened. "Some crime novelist you are. You know darn well any skeleton unearthed on my property would have something to do with that nasty worm. Nobody wished that sorry excuse for a man dead more than me."

"Calm down. Don't spout off and give the sheriff some harebrained notion that pile of bones is Jed," Dad said. "No profit in fueling gossip or dredging up ancient history. Authorities may have ruled Jed dead, but I always figured that no-good varmint was still alive five states over, most likely beating the stuffing out of some other poor woman."

Wow. I knew Eva took her maiden name back after they declared her husband dead, but I'd never heard a speck of the unsavory backstory. Dad liked to tell family tales, including ones about long-dead scoundrels. Guess this history wasn't ancient enough.

Curiosity made me eager to ask a whole passel of none-of-my-business questions, though I felt some justification about poking my nose here. I'd known Eva my entire life. So how come this was the first I'd heard of a mystery surrounding Jed's disappearance? Was Dad truly worried the sheriff might suspect Eva?

I was dying to play twenty questions. Too bad it wasn't the time or place.

I smiled at my aunt. "Why don't I get some of Paint's brew to settle our nerves? Eva, you like that apple pie flavor, right?"

"Yes, thanks, dear."

"Good idea, Brie," Dad added. "I'll take a toot of Paint's blackberry hooch. Eva's not the only one who could use a belt. We'll greet folks from those rockers. Better than standing like mannequins in a receiving line. And there's a lot less risk of falling down if we get a little tipsy."

Aunt Eva ignored Dad's jest. She looked haunted, lost in memory. A very bad memory.

I hurried to the small tent where Magic Moonshine dispensed free libations. A buxom young lass smiled as she poured shine into miniature Mason jars lined up behind four flavor signs: Apple Pie, Blackberry, Peach, and White Lightnin'.

"What can I do you for, honey?" the busty server purred.

I'm still an Iowa girl at heart, but, like my transplanted aunts and parents, I've learned not to take offense when strangers of both sexes and all ages call me honey, darlin', and sweetie. My high school social studies teacher urged us to appreciate foreign customs and cultures. I may not be in Rome, but I'm definitely in Ardon County.

I smiled at Miss Sugarmouth. The top four buttons of her blouse were undone. The way her bosoms oozed over the top, I seriously doubted those buttons had ever met their respective buttonholes. No mystery why Paint hired her. Couldn't blame him or her. Today's male mourners would enjoy a dash of cleavage with their shine, and she'd rake in lots more tips.

"Sweetie, do you have a tray I can use to take drinks to the folks on the porch?"

The devil still made me add the "sweetie" when I addressed Miss Sugarmouth. She didn't bat an eyelash. Probably too weighed down with mascara.

"Sure thing, honey."

I winced when the tray slid over the wood sliver firmly embedded in my palm. *Suck it up. No time for minor surgery.*

As I walked toward Eva's cabin, crunching noises advertised some late arrivals ambling down the gravel road. On the porch, Dad and Eva had settled into a rhythm, shaking hands with friends and neighbors and accepting sympathy pats. Hard to hug someone in a rocker.

I handed miniature glass jars to Eva and Dad before offering drinks to the folks who'd already run the gauntlet of the sit-down receiving line. Then I tiptoed behind Dad's rocker.

"I'll see if Mom wants anything and check back later to see how you and Eva are doing."

"Thanks, honey." He kissed my cheek.

I returned to Paint's moonshine stand and picked up a second drink tray, gingerly hoisting it to avoid bumping my skewered palm. Balancing the drinks, I picked my way across the rutted ground to what I worried might be a crime scene.

Mom perched between Paint and Andy atop the double row of hay bales stacked to keep the grisly discovery out of sight. The five-foot-two height on Mom's driver's license was a stretch. At five-four, I had her by at least three, maybe four, inches. My mother's build was tiny as well as short—a flat-chested size two. I couldn't recall ever being able to squeeze into her doll-size clothes. My build came courtesy of the females on Dad's side of the family. Compact but curvy. No possibility of going braless in polite society.

Mom's delicate appearance often confounded the troublemakers she prosecuted for the city. Too often the accused took one look at Iris Hooker and figured they'd hire some hulking male lawyer to walk all over the little lady in court.

Big mistake. The bullies often reaped unexpected rewards—a costly mélange of jail time, fines, and community service.

Mom spotted my tray-wobbling approach. "Are these Paint's concoctions?"

I nodded.

"Well, Daughter, sip nice and slow. Someday I may file charges against Magic Moonshine. Paint's shine is often an accomplice when Clemson tailgaters pull stunts that land them in front of a judge."

Paint lifted his glass in a salute. "Can I help it if all our flavors go down easy?"

Mom turned back to me. "Have you met these, ahem, gentlemen?"

I suddenly felt shy as my gaze flicked between the two males. "I met Paint earlier. This is my first chance to say hi to Andy. I'm Brie Hooker. You must be the veterinarian Aunt Eva's always talking about."

Andy rose to his feet. "Andy Green. Pleased to meet you, ma'am.

Your aunts were my very first customers when I opened my practice."

He waved a hand at Tammy, the now demure pig, wallowing a goodly distance away. "I'm really sorry Tammy picked today to root up these bones. I feel partly to blame. Talked your aunts into adopting Miss Piggy. It aggravates me how folks can't resist buying potbellied pigs as pets when they're adorable babies, but have no qualms about abandoning them once they start to grow."

Andy's outstretched hand awaited my handshake.

I held up my palm to display my injury. "Gotta take a rain check on a handshake. Unfortunately, I already shook hands with the barn."

Andy gently turned up my palm. "I'll fix you right up, if you don't mind a vet doing surgery. Give me a minute to wash up and meet me at my truck. Can't miss it. A double-cab GMC that kinda looks like aliens crash landed an aluminum spaceship in the truck bed. I'm parked by the milking barn."

As Andy loped off toward the retail shop's comfort station, Paint called after him. "Sneaky way to hold hands with a pretty lady."

Andy glanced over his shoulder and grinned. "You're just mad you didn't think of it first."

Paint chuckled and focused his hundred-watt grin on me. "Bet my white lightning could disinfect that sliver. Sure you don't want me to do the honors?"

I couldn't help but laugh. "Somehow I doubt honor has anything to do with it."

The moonshiner faked an injured look.

Mom rolled her eyes. "Heaven help me—and you, Brie. Not sure you're safe with the wildlife that frequents this farm. Forget those coyotes that worry Eva, I'm talking wolves." She looked toward the porch. "How's Eva holding up?"

"Better." I wanted to grill Mom about Jed Watson, but I needed to do so in private. "Guess I should steel myself for surgery." I took a Mason jar from the tray I'd set on a hay bale. "Down the hatch." My healthy swallow blazed a burning trail from throat to belly. Before I could stop myself, I sputtered.

"Shut your mouth," Paint said.

Yowzer. My eyes watered, and my throat spasmed. I coughed. "What?"

"Shut your mouth. Oxygen fuels the burn. You need to take a swallow then close your mouth. None of this sipping stuff."

"Now you tell me." I choked.

Mom laughed. "That's the best strategy I've heard yet to shut Brie up."

I wiped at the tears running down my cheeks. "Your moonshine packs more punch than my five-alarm Thai stir fry."

Paint's eyebrows rose. "My shine is smooth, once you get used to it. You want a little fire in your gut. Keeps life interesting."

A little too interesting. I'd been at Udderly Kidding Dairy just over a week, and I already felt like a spinning top with a dangerous wobble.

FOUR

"Afraid my operating theater's a little dusty." Andy whisked dirt off a spot on his open tailgate and spread an Army blanket he'd retrieved from the cab. "Hop on up."

What do you know? A gentleman. I wasn't about to complain that the white dog hairs coating his blanket would jump on my black wool slacks like fleas on a Bluetick hound. The realization I could identify a Bluetick hound testified to my ten-year immersion in Southern culture.

"Eva tells me you grew up in Iowa. How did your whole family wind up down South?"

"Despite rumors to the contrary, our family wasn't banished from Iowa. Aunt Eva moved to Ardon when she married, and Aunt Lilly came to help her with the farm. My folks were surprised they both stayed."

"Did your folks move at the same time?"

"No. Mom and Dad didn't move south until I was in college. Dad was a professor at Iowa State University when Clemson offered him the head of the horticultural department. Living near his sisters was a bonus. I was a short drive away, too, in the MBA program at Wake Forest University."

Andy's eyebrow twitched up. "You got an MBA to be a cook?"

Cook? The vet just lost points.

"After I got my MBA, I worked for a mortgage bank. Had my mid-life crisis early, in my late twenties. Realized I hated my job and decided what I really wanted was to be a chef—a chef who catered to vegans and vegetarians."

Andy opened one of a bevy of aluminum drawers in his truck's rendition of an animal ER. The instruments would have looked at home in a torture museum. I scrunched my eyes shut. When I opened them, I carefully fastened my gaze on the hazy top of a distant mountain.

"Won't take a minute," Andy said.

I'm a baby about blood and sharp objects poised to rip into my flesh. Perhaps that's why I'm the only thirty-three-year-old I know with virgin earlobes. Some friends sport three studs per ear. I'm too squeamish for even one piercing. A tattoo? I don't think so.

Andy gripped my wrist to steady my hand. Icy liquid oozed over my splinter. I kept my focus on the horizon, biting my lip in anticipation of a big ouch.

A teensy pinch.

"Got it," Andy said. "Good to go."

"Thanks. Painless. You'll be my first call if my puppy needs a vet."

"You have a dog?" He sounded downright gleeful.

"A Teacup Morkie. She's a toy cross between a Maltese and a Yorkie." I laughed. "Guess as a vet you know that."

"Yep, Morkies are cute," Andy said. "How did you pick her?"

"Like my aunts, I'm a sucker for orphans. My pup comes courtesy of a ditzy waitress who wanted a dog that fit in her purse. One day she couldn't gush enough about her teeny-weeny pet. The next she blew town and decided her puppy wasn't a great travel accessory."

"What's your dog's name?" Andy asked.

"Cashew, 'cause I'm nuts about her."

He smiled. "Is she here with you?"

"Yes. Though she seems a mite confused by her new companions. Eva introduced her to Udderly's guardian and herd dogs to make sure they understood Cashew wasn't a light snack. I think my pup confounds Udderly's cats more than the dogs. One old Tom hisses like Cashew's an overgrown mouse every time she comes near."

I inspected the small bandage decorating my right palm as my vet doctor closed his instrument drawer.

"Your aunts talked about you all the time—terrific chef, triathlete, organic gardener." Andy smiled.

"Don't put too much stock in the advance billing. It's biased."

"Yeah." He snickered. "I got that. You look more like your aunts than your mother. Eva bragged that she and Lilly named you."

"They did. Mom lobbied to christen me Bridgette, her mother's name. Dad wanted Marie, his mom's name. The twins insisted I deserved my own unique name and combined my parents' choices—Brie. Lilly took pride in coming up with a name no one could shorten. Said it was cruel to stick a kid with long ones that encouraged nicknames like Bunny and Marg."

Andy smiled. "So your childhood was nickname free?"

I snorted. "You kidding? With Hooker as my last name? By middle school, the boys whispered plenty. When I groused, Aunt Lilly told me to suck it up, and said, 'Just be glad we didn't name you Ima.'"

Andy laughed and his green eyes twinkled. "Sounds like Lilly."

"Lately I've been kidded about Brie as often as Hooker. 'Pretty cheesy name for a vegan.'"

Andy grinned. "Sounds like something Eva might say. You two must have fun planning meals."

"Lucky for Eva, I'm not evangelical. I believe it's a healthier lifestyle, and it makes more sense for the planet. But I consider diet a matter of personal choice. I don't make squinty-eyed faces or retching noises when friends stab into a bloody steak, though I may avert my eyes."

Andy chuckled. "Good. I love burgers. You'd have a hard sell convincing me to give 'em up."

When the vet grinned, he reminded me of Brad Pitt in his *Thelma and Louise* days—that is if Brad had been put on a rack and stretched. Andy looked to be as tall as Paint.

"I try to win vegan disciples through bribery and deceit," I replied. "I avoid dairy in my desserts but spare no chocolate. And I excel at camouflaging tofu. I can make it disappear completely in my vegan version of meatloaf, the one Dad calls 'moatloaf.'"

Andy took my arm to help me down from the high tailgate. My pants snagged and I freed the catch with my unbandaged left hand. "Thanks again. Time to check on the buffet and see if it needs replenishing."

"Need help?"

"Thanks, but no. People dropped off tons of food yesterday. Never seen so many casseroles. I just need to keep an eye on the line and switch out dishes as they empty. I'll bet Mom and Paint would like some company though."

"Not sure about that." Andy chuckled. "Paint thinks he's a stand-up comic, and he has a captive audience."

"Sounds as if you two know each other pretty well. Friends?"

"I've known Paint since he tried to corrupt our Sunday school teacher. Think we were six."

I laughed. My reward? A mischievous smile. Andy might be pre-programmed to greet women with "ma'am," but he clearly had a sense of humor.

For the next hour, I bustled between my aunt's compact kitchen and the two picnic tables jammed together to hold the feast. Though busy, I snuck frequent glances toward Mom and her fellow guardians of the grave. No sign of the sheriff. Good.

The chilly breezes didn't favor lingering. Most people paid their respects, filled a plate, ate, and boogied down the road. By four o'clock, only family and my aunt's closest friends—Paint, Andy, and Billy—remained.

At ten minutes after four, an Ardon County Sheriff's cruiser bumped down the rutted drive. Followed by two unmarked cars. A big black hearse rumbled in their wake.

FIVE

A man exited the cruiser. He turned and waited for the two men who'd arrived in unmarked cars to join him. The threesome then ambled toward Eva's front porch where we'd congregated post-wake. Mom, Dad, Aunt Eva, and Billy, Eva's farrier sweetie, occupied the four rockers. I sat on the dust-coated front steps with Paint and Andy. The moonshiner and vet had taken a proprietary interest in the skull they'd been guarding and weren't about to leave until the bones were claimed.

As the lawmen approached, my fellow stair-warmers and I stood. I made a half-hearted attempt to dust off my rump, certain the black pants covering my hiney now sported a colorful mix of white dog hairs and finely ground red clay.

The newcomers advanced in Southern slow-mo style. Mom said she'd met Sheriff Jones but didn't know if his reputation as a slacker was deserved. The driver of the cruiser matched her description of the sheriff. His pocked face topped a thick neck totally in keeping with a fireplug build. The sheriff's khaki uniform looked as wilted as romaine lettuce in a day-old Caesar salad. He clutched a cowboy hat in his left hand. A big honking gun hung from a thick leather belt with a coiled snake on the silver buckle.

Neither of the men who joined the sheriff wore uniforms. Based on the camera hanging around his neck, I figured the middle-aged dude in black slacks and a blue sweater had come to document the skull's location in case it was a crime scene. The other gent wore dirty jeans and a flannel shirt. An off-duty deputy?

No one exited the black hearse cozied up behind the unmarked cars. The final slumber wagon squatted on the driveway like a fat cockroach mired on a sticky pest strip. Its occupants—assuming they were all among the living—seemed content to wait until they were summoned to a grave.

Dad walked down the stairs. Mom suggested he handle the meet-and-greet with the sheriff to avoid any later claim of interference from an officer of the court in another jurisdiction. Dad had that hangdog look he got when he had a distasteful chore. I'd seen that face plenty as a kid when I'd been naughty and he needed to scold me.

Paint, Andy, and I shuffled to the side so we wouldn't impede Dad's march. He seemed determined to intercept the authorities before they reached Aunt Eva's homey cabin. Dad succeeded, greeting the men about five feet short of the front porch.

"You must be Sheriff Jones. I'm Howard Hooker." He kept his voice low. I figured Dad wanted to spare Aunt Eva more grief. Like that was possible.

The sheriff didn't bother to introduce his sidekicks.

"I'll show you where the skull was uncovered," Dad said. "This is my sister's property, but we just held a wake for her twin. Surely there's no need for her to be present at the excavation?"

Sheriff Jones peered up at the porch. The sun, low in the sky, reflected off the cabin's tin roof with laser-like intensity. I doubted he could make out the faces of the porch sitters huddled in deep shade.

"No need for Eva to be present." The sheriff's voice sounded like Paint's white lightnin' tasted—raw and potent. "We can interview her later."

"You know my sister?" Dad sounded surprised.

"Yes." He didn't elaborate. "Tell me again who unearthed the skull."

Dad gave a succinct account of Tammy's big pig dig. He didn't mention Eva's conviction that the skull belonged to one Jed Watson, a man she apparently had an excellent motive to murder.

"All right. Let's see what we have," the sheriff said.

Dad waved up at the porch-sitting contingent. "Iris, why don't you take everyone inside? It's a mite chilly. These gentlemen have everything they need. No point staying out here."

"Sheriff, do you mind an audience?" Paint asked. "Kind of curious how you go about gathering up old bones. Promise not to get in the way."

The sheriff glanced at his silent helpers. The jean-clad man and the camera guy both shrugged. "Don't care. Long as they stay a ways back, out of the way."

Andy smiled. "Good. I'd like to watch, too."

Excellent. Since the vet's comment prompted no objection, I saw no need to ask permission to tag along.

Dad led the sheriff toward the site, and the three of us looky-loos followed at a respectful distance. The procession had only advanced a few yards when Camera Man peeled off and headed for the hearse. He rapped on the slumber wagon's front door. The two men who emerged weren't dressed like pall bearers. One wore jeans a tiny step up from threadbare. His soiled shirt's rolled-up sleeves revealed bulging muscles and a "Mom" tattoo. The other gent sported overalls atop greying long johns.

I'd fallen behind while checking out the hearse crew and scurried to catch up. Dad, Mr. Dirty Jeans, and the sheriff crouched over the pinkish skull. Paint and Andy sat atop the hay bales they'd moved a few yards back to provide orchestra seats. Close enough to see all the action, far enough to stay clear of any flying shovels. Andy patted the empty spot of hay awaiting my tush. Nice and cozy between two attractive hunks.

I climbed up.

"The man in the jeans is the coroner," Paint whispered. "The camera man's Deputy Lawson. Don't know the gravediggers, but that fella with the Mom tattoo on his forearm looks kinda familiar."

"The guys with the shovels are the Webster brothers," Andy chimed in. "Their wives drag them to our church twice a year at Christmas and Easter."

The vet nodded at the men who'd just dumped shovels, a gurney, and a pile of black bags on the ground. "Last week, they buried a mare I had to put down at the Gage farm. Used a front loader for that job, not shovels."

I shuddered at the image. Why were we so intent on watching these bones be unearthed? Did I really need to know if the skeleton matched the skull's same absurd shade of pink—the color of white undies washed with a red shirt? Of course, maybe there was only a skull. The idea of a severed head seemed even worse than the discovery of more bones.

The wind picked up, making Dad's murmured conversation with the sheriff impossible to decipher. I shivered and Andy jumped up. "I'll get a blanket out of my truck."

Dad walked over as Andy hustled away. "Honey, you look like an icicle before the spring thaw," Dad said. "You must be freezing. Why don't you go back to the cabin? No need for you to be here."

I shook my head. "I'd like to stay. Andy's getting a blanket."

"Okay," Dad answered. "I'll head back to tell everyone what's going on."

"What is going on?" I asked. So far the action looked mostly like prep work with Deputy Lawson putting down mini-flags, measuring distances, and snapping pictures.

"The deputy's documenting the location of the bones and anything else they find in case it's a crime scene," Dad answered. "If there's a whole skeleton, they'll try to keep it intact. Transfer it to a body bag and put it on that gurney. Then they'll bag the soil around the bones so it can be sifted later and analyzed for clues about the manner of death. They'll take everything to a SLED lab in Columbia where experts can determine the skeleton's age and ethnicity."

"Will you come back after you check on Aunt Eva?"

Dad nodded. "I'll bring a thermos of hot coffee and some of those cookies Mrs. Maish dropped off from the Methodist Ladies Auxiliary."

As Dad walked away, Andy arrived with the same big, smelly Army blanket he'd spread on the tailgate for me.

Paint made a face. "Peeuuww. I'm afraid to ask how you last used this blanket. Delivering a breech calf? Wiping off Tammy's behind to give her a shot?"

Paint's ribbing made the blanket seem less godsend and more germ wrapper. But I was cold. I pictured a long hot shower in my near future.

Andy gave Paint one corner of the blanket and took the other before he plopped down beside me. In seconds, I was given the ends of the wrap, binding the three of us in a cozy, odiferous cocoon. Maybe I'd just burn these clothes. The pants already had a snag in them.

The grave diggers wasted no time. Shovels flying, they dug a wide trench around where they assumed the rest of the body might rest given the orientation of the skull. Then the coroner stepped down in the trench and used what looked like a wooden dowel to delicately prod the clay island that presumably hid a skeleton. "He's in here, boys," the coroner said. Deputy Lawson snapped more pictures.

The Webster brothers traded their shovels for small versions akin to garden trowels. They collected the dislodged soil in plastic five-gallon buckets. With surprising delicacy, they quickly unearthed ribs, then the humerus and radius bones of an arm. I recognized the parts courtesy of Anatomy 101 and the skeleton some high school buddies stole from a classroom one Halloween to deposit on our teacher's front lawn. There were bits of cloth, too. I assumed remnants of a shirt though the grime made it impossible to say.

As the grave diggers prodded the area near a finger bone, light glinted on metal.

Paint hopped off the hay bale. "Sheriff Jones, did you see that?" He pointed at a rounded bit of gold.

Using what looked like a dentist's pick, Deputy Lawson scraped dirt away from the metal. I was glad it was no longer attached to the adjacent bones.

Elbowing Lawson aside, the sheriff pulled a hanky from his pocket and polished a ruby-colored stone at the center of the ring. Apparently he didn't think the ring needed post-burial fingerprinting.

"Good grief, that looks like Dad's high school ring," Andy said. "His class was the last to graduate from Winding Creek High before they tore it down and started bussing kids around here to Central."

Andy and I leapt to our feet, joining Paint in a huddle above the sheriff and his treasure.

"What's happened? What did you find?" Dad's voice boomed as he hot-footed it from the cabin.

"A man's class ring," the sheriff answered. "Winding Creek High. Class of '79. Doubt more than twenty boys graduated that year, and I know most of them. My cousin Jed was in that class. Far as I know he's the only one who's gone missing. Looks like Eva Hooker may have more than a few questions to answer."

"My wife just put Eva to bed. Gave her a sleeping pill. Surely this can wait till tomorrow. Jed might have lost his ring. You don't even know it's his skeleton. This could all be coincidence."

Sheriff Jones studied his shoes, then stared straight into Dad's eyes. "It can wait. Won't take long to confirm this is Jed. The skull's intact, and my cousin had one of his front teeth capped after it got chipped in a football game."

My stomach dropped. Ye gods. Poor Aunt Eva. Abusive husband. Buried on her farm. She'd be a suspect for sure. And the sheriff was Jed's kin. He'd make the case a priority.

Could she be guilty? I tried to squelch the question rattling round in my brain. Aunt Eva couldn't even bear to put a crippled, old dog to sleep. Yet a niggle of doubt persisted. Maybe it was self-defense. No telling what any of us are capable of if we're pushed hard enough.

Dad took my hand. "Time to leave. I don't think we need to see or hear more."

"We may be here for hours," the sheriff said, "now that it appears to be a crime scene. I'm calling our homicide expert. This whole area will be posted off limits till we finish processing."

I trudged toward the cabin with Dad, Andy, and Paint. When we reached the porch, the vet and moonshiner bid their farewells and headed for their trucks. I stole one more glance toward the burial site. The flash on the camera bloomed and the spill of light momentarily spotlighted Sheriff Jones' face. Was he smiling?

Before I entered the cabin, Dad squeezed my hand. "I know you must be wondering. Don't. I know my sister. Eva didn't kill anyone. But Lord help her. I hope she doesn't have to prove it."

Mom was alone, stretched out on the sofa reading a book. Cashew snored softly on her lap.

"There you are." Mom sat up and Cashew woke. I picked up my dog, who squirmed in my arms, attempting to lick me to death.

"I tucked Eva into bed half an hour ago," Mom said. "Billy left a few minutes later. What's happening?"

Dad broke the news. "I'll tell Eva in the morning," he added.

"Tell me what?" My aunt appeared in the hallway. Dressed in a lace-trimmed flannel nightie, her curly hair poked every which way. She looked like a lost child. Her dog, Kai, rubbed against her leg.

"Close your mouth, Howard, or you'll catch flies. It'd take more than a sleeping pill to knock me out when they're digging up trouble in my backyard. It was Jed, wasn't it?"

Dad nodded. "They found a class ring with the bones. Class of 1979 Winding Creek High."

"Figures." Eva's smile didn't reach her eyes. "That sorry son of a gun never would wear a wedding band, but he loved his stupid class ring."

She didn't say another word, just pivoted and headed back to her bedroom. Kai padded silently behind her.

"I should stay here tonight," Dad said. "Where are you sleeping, Brie?"

"On the couch. It didn't feel right to invade Lilly's bedroom."

The minute I learned of Lilly's death I'd called Aunt Eva and asked if she wanted company. Her crusty "not necessary" answer didn't jibe with the quiver in her voice. So I told the owner of the restaurant I needed to start my two-week vacation immediately. If he'd said no, I'd have quit. I'd been job hunting in Charlotte, Raleigh, and Charleston. I loved Asheville, but, in many ways, it was a small town. I seemed to run into Jack, my ex-fiancé, everywhere I went, and the head chef had little interest in trying new dishes. Time to move on.

"Dad, why don't you both go home? I'm here if Eva needs anything."

"No, I want to stay. I'll bunk on the old Army cot Eva keeps in the barn. I have some old work clothes around somewhere unless Sis threw them out."

Mom nodded. "Should we go ahead tomorrow with the reading of the will?"

Dad shrugged. "Guess so. I'll help with the morning chores. Then we can all gather at our house. I'll let Sheriff Jones know our plans."

Mom kissed Dad's cheek. "See you in the morning, honey. Don't worry about your sister. She's one strong lady. She'll be fine."

"I know." Dad's frown didn't match his words.

SIX

My aunts had warned me they'd gone Hollywood when they penned instructions for the reading of their joint will. Actually it was the *screening* of their last will and testament—a final, double-the-trouble selfie. Lilly and Eva had been all giggly when they'd Skyped me with details a couple months ago.

Their hilarious description of how Mom reacted to their requests made me laugh until I cried. Eva and Lilly hadn't divulged the will's content, just said they had a blast playing movie producers, and hoped I'd enjoy watching the grand finale—but not too soon.

No laughing now.

I shivered and swiped at an obstinate tear. The notion of a loved one speaking to me from beyond the grave tinged my grief with a touch of the willies.

The scene inside my parents' den brought me to a standstill. Mom had pulled the drapes and lit candles. And what was that smell? Incense? If anyone pulled out a crystal ball, I was hoofing it for the hills.

I straightened my shoulders. Mom, Dad, and Eva had already gathered in front of my folks' big-screen TV. Waiting. For me.

Eva patted an empty sofa cushion at her side.

Crud. I couldn't refuse. Hard to imagine Aunt Eva's turmoil given the discovery of what was likely Jed's skeleton. It had to be added torture for her to watch a video created when she and her sister were in such good humor—such good health. Still, I'd have preferred to sit on the sidelines so I could bolt if my emotions threatened to enter sob-o-rama mode.

How would Aunt Eva manage without Aunt Lilly? They'd been

two impudent peas sharing the same pod. Same curly hair. Identical tanned and laugh-crinkled faces. Same mischievous golden brown eyes. If there was ever a time Aunt Eva needed her sister, it was now.

Mom stood and cleared her throat. "We're all here. So let's start. All supporting documents were signed, witnessed, and recorded. That satisfies the legalities. Eva and Lilly directed me as executor to show this video to surviving family should either of them die." She cleared her throat. "They also insisted on the candles and incense."

Mom nodded at her sister-in-law. "Eva, if you'd like, you can make a new will regarding the property Lilly left you."

"Can't imagine changing a thing," Aunt Eva replied. "Don't want to rack up more outrageous legal fees."

Mom refrained from harrumphing, her usual response when my aunts took good-natured potshots at her profession. Besides serving as the attorney for the City of Clemson, Iris Hooker, Esquire, also wrote wills and handled real estate closings. A decent living, but she didn't exactly belong to the Mercedes-driving, silk-suit club. I knew Mom charged my aunts exactly one dollar to handle their legal affairs.

Mom turned to Dad. "Honey, start the video."

As usual, Dad had sole custody of the TV remote. *Did Mom even know how to use it?*

The screen flickered to life. A ragtime piano played and a hand-lettered card popped into view.

ONCE UPON A TIME...

My aunts had opted for the feel of an old-timey silent film. A series of photos flashed on screen, appearing and disappearing in warp speed. The young twins frolicked with a panting yellow Labrador pup. They wobbled on high heels stolen from Grandma's closet. Then Dad joined them as a baby. The jokesters positioned their bare-bottomed younger brother to moon the camera while they mugged and pointed.

Dad choked out a chuckle, followed by a quick intake of breath. Trying not to cry.

He shook a finger at Eva. "Thought I paid you to destroy that picture."

She snickered. "Not near enough. Saving it for your book jacket when you finally publish one of your crime novels."

Another hand-lettered card filled the TV screen.

...THE TWINS GREW UP

I watched as the twins transformed into teens and then pretty young ladies. Sun glinting on mahogany hair. Big doe eyes and long lashes. Smiles that lit the screen.

"Good heavens, Brie, I'd forgotten how much you look like Eva and Lilly when they were your age," Dad said. "Same curly hair and impish grin."

"Better looking," Aunt Eva added. "But there's a resemblance."

...EVENTUALLY EVA & LILLY GOT THEIR GOATS. NO KIDDING...

The video skipped years ahead. No pictures of Jed Watson. Not even a wedding photo. The fast-forward also made me wonder for the first time why Lilly never married. In this adult section of the pictorial, the twins tended their goat herd, bottle-fed newborn kids, made and sampled cheese, and played with their guardian dogs.

I smiled despite the sad circumstances. As a kid, I'd spent many happy hours at Udderly Kidding Dairy.

Aunt Eva patted my hand and whispered, "Now comes the surprise."

The screen went black. But the soundtrack continued—a drum roll and trumpets. Eva and Lilly perched side by side on the sofa. Right where I sat now. Not a still photo but live action caught on video.

The twins glanced at each other, giggled conspiratorially, and mimed a joint theatrical gasp. "Uh-oh," they crooned in unison. "One of us has left the building...not to mention our farm."

On screen, Aunt Eva took up the narrative. I knew it was Eva, because a small tattoo—"I came first"—decorated her right inner wrist. She never tired of reminding her twin she was the older and wiser sister by five whole minutes.

"If both of us have kicked the bucket, you can stop watching. We've left everything we own to our one and only niece, Miss Brie (can-you-believe-she-won't-eat-cheese-with-that-name) Hooker."

I gasped. Before I could utter a word, Aunt Lilly cleared her throat—on screen, of course. She was dead.

Lilly nudged Eva. "My turn. If only one of us croaked, it's a bit more complicated. The surviving twin gets the farm, but wait, there's more."

She held up a poster-size photo of an old Southern mansion. "Iris, can you zoom in on this picture, please?"

An image of Summer Place filled the screen.

I'd first laid eyes on Summer Place three years ago while out for a car ride with my aunts. When we drove past the gorgeous old mansion, I immediately imagined myself as its owner. Dressed in a flouncy sundress, I'd serve sweet tea and Mint Juleps to my bed-and-breakfast guests as they savored my vegan dishes and rocked in the shade of the front verandah.

Of course, in my daydreams—which I stupidly shared with my guffawing aunts—the verandah wasn't missing half its rotting floorboards, and the mansion's fluted columns weren't yellowed with age and canted like decaying front teeth.

"Got your attention, Brie?" The on-screen Eva laughed.

A video zoom-out brought my aunty bookends back in focus. Lilly cocked her head, her impish grin unchanged from the photos taken when the twins were eight-year-old troublemakers. Half a century ago.

"Why am I holding this, Brie?" Lilly asked.

She was reading my mind.

Except that wasn't possible. The twins recorded the video before Aunt Lilly's cherry red Mustang was towed to the scrap heap. Now Lilly—well, her ashes—were scattered at the highest spot on the Udderly Kidding farm.

Goosebumps marched up my arms.

The on-screen Lilly continued. "My darling Brie, Eva and I bought this sorry, run-down mansion for you shortly after you dumped that loser of a fiancé. We planned to give it to you on your thirty-fifth birthday. 'Course, we kinda hoped to be alive to hand you the keys and toast your future B&B success."

On camera, Eva elbowed Lilly and winked. "My turn, Sis."

In the here and now, Aunt Eva patted my hand as I stared open-mouthed at the TV.

"Brie, honey, it takes both of us old bats to run Udderly Kidding Dairy," the digital Eva announced. "So, if one of us birds has fallen off the perch, we hope you can help us for a spell. Will you come live at Udderly? Help run the farm? That'll give your surviving auntie time to sell and get the *flock*—pardon the pun—out of town, or find employees to help her keep *kidding* around."

The aunts spoke in sing-song unison: "What say you, dear? Could you wait a bit longer to start your B&B?"

The on-screen Eva added, "Don't worry. We'll `still love you if you say no."

Lilly nodded her assent. "Salary? Well, our income's not dependable month-to-month, but we're profitable. You won't starve— especially if you give in and eat cheese. We understand operating a goat cheese farm isn't high on a vegan chef's priority list. Only you can decide."

Eva spoke again. "Sorry to drop this on you. Even sorrier one of us isn't here."

The image of the twins faded. A final hand-lettered card appeared.

THE END...OR MAYBE THE BEGINNING?

I blinked. What in tarnation? Me? My aunts knew I'd planned on quitting my job in Asheville. But not to move to the boonies, milk goats, and make cheese. The idea was nuts.

The image of Summer Place tugged at my resolve. How unbelievably generous of my aunts. And, if I lived here, I could tackle renovations in my spare time.

I glanced at Aunt Eva. Unshed tears pooled in her eyes. I thought about that unearthed skeleton and a sheriff who happened to be the deceased's cousin. He'd be out to nail my aunt.

Eva smiled. "Honey, don't worry. I won't press you to make a decision. When we made this will, I had no idea my dear husband's bones would surface. No point in getting you mixed up in this sordid mess."

Double crud. "No" wasn't an option. Aunt Eva needed me.

I hugged Aunt Eva. "Don't be silly. I want to stay with you."

My mind raced ahead. I needed to call my boss. Let him know I was quitting; ask if he needed me to return for a few days. If I offered to leave and forgo the two weeks' pay he owed me, I expected his answer would be, "Don't let the door hit your derriere on your way out."

I smiled. Maybe this was just the kick in the butt I needed to get out of Asheville.

I glanced over at Mom and Dad. Their frowns said they weren't overjoyed at my decision.

SEVEN

Since my stick shift skills were more than questionable in the mountains, Dad volunteered to chauffeur me to Asheville in Aunt Eva's beefy Chevy truck. I needed the loaner to haul my paltry belongings to my new Udderly Kidding home.

As I suspected, my boss had no problems saying adios if it meant saving a few pennies. Plenty of wannabe chefs applied every month for my sous chef position.

I'd been living rent-free in a swanky enclave of mini-mansions just outside Asheville's city limits. Jessica, an eccentric globe-trotting widow, was my landlady. Whenever she departed on one of her travel extravaganzas, I housesat and took care of Xena, her spoiled German shepherd. In exchange, I enjoyed a comfy, if compact, efficiency apartment above her garage. Even better, I had the run, literally, of the gated community's lush landscaped grounds and could dive into the often vacant pool whenever I wanted to swim laps. While I'd never win a triathlon, I was pretty disciplined about exercising. Maybe I'd squeeze in a few short runs before nightfall while living at Udderly. Getting up to exercise before my dawn chores seemed downright obscene.

I'd miss my Asheville digs and landlady. Our arrangement had let me end each pay period with extra bucks to put toward an eventual down payment on a B&B. When Jessica was in town, she'd served as my fearless taste-tester, willing to try any of my vegan concoctions.

Fortunately, my hasty departure wouldn't leave my benefactor or her pampered pooch in a pinch. One of my friends had already won Jessica's stamp of approval.

She had two hiring conditions: her dog had to give her lick of approval, and live-in candidates couldn't consume meat. Jessica was militant about the ethical treatment of living creatures. Since I wasn't sure if she considered milking goats an acceptable human-animal bond, I delicately sidestepped the fact I was taking off to help run a goat cheese farm.

Before starting the scenic two-hour drive from Ardon County to Asheville, we helped Aunt Eva with early (and I do mean *early*) morning chores. The drive offered my first opportunity to have Dad all to my lonesome so I could grill him about Aunt Eva and her long-forgotten husband.

For the first fifteen minutes on the road, I dillydallied, unsure how to tactfully inquire about the skeleton that publicly tumbled out of our family closet. We passed a kudzu-choked hillside. When Dad failed to make his usual crime-writer quip—"Now there's where I'd hide a body. Kudzu would blanket it in fifteen minutes."—I knew he was beyond preoccupied.

Every time I snuck a glance his way, Dad's scowl discouraged conversation. The vein twitching at the side of his temple suggested anger lurked behind his glower.

I'd almost worked up the nerve to speak when he broke the silence. "With that skeleton popping up, you're bound to hear gossip, ugly gossip. You need to understand what it was like for Eva forty years ago."

He took his gaze off the winding mountain road long enough to make eye contact. "Eva has some mean-spirited enemies. Mostly kin to Jed, country folk who were horrified when he married an outsider, and a Yankee to boot. After Jed had gone missing long enough to be declared dead, Eva inherited his farm. Given that the land had belonged to the Watson clan for five generations, some of his relatives became downright apoplectic. The fact she dared to change her last name back to Hooker didn't help."

When Dad paused for several seconds, I prodded. "I heard Eva admit she'd wished Jed dead. Why?"

Dad stole another glance at me. "The bastard beat Eva. Over a period of three years, he broke both her arms, a leg, and her jaw. Burned her once, too. Held her hand over a gas burner on their stove. You can still see the scarring on her right palm. The violence started within months of their wedding. Eva was isolated on the farm and too humiliated to admit her horrible mistake. Jed threatened to kill her if she told anyone or tried to leave."

Dad shook his head. "This all came out later. Much later. At the time, I didn't have a clue. Had I known, I swear I'd have killed the bastard myself, sent him straight to hell so his skin would feel the flames."

My throat tightened as I tried to imagine the beautiful young woman I'd seen in yesterday's video beaten by a man she'd pledged to love until death parted them. "I can't believe Eva didn't tell Lilly. Reach out to her twin. They seemed so close, I would have sworn they had mental telepathy."

"Lilly knew it was bad, but Eva refused to admit how bad. Guess she was mortified she'd let herself wind up in such a fix. She was barely nineteen, a college freshman, when Jed swept her off her feet. Lilly begged Eva to postpone marrying until she finished college, but Jed was graduating, and Eva said she couldn't bear being separated. Whenever Lilly visited, Eva always had some cockeyed explanation for her injuries. Claimed she'd been kicked by an ornery mule or tangled with some exotic piece of farm equipment."

I couldn't fathom how Eva had fallen for such a lout. "You met him, right? Jed. What was your take?"

Dad didn't speak. The past hung heavy in the car.

"All the ladies thought he was good-looking. Athletic. Only time I laid eyes on him was the day of the wedding. Spent all of what—a half-hour—talking to him, mostly about hunting and fishing. Eva seemed so happy, downright giddy. Claimed she'd never tire of Jed's honeyed Southern drawl."

"You didn't see them after the wedding?"

Dad shook his head. "They never invited family down, and Eva never made it back to Iowa. Always begged off, saying it wasn't a good time. One excuse after another. To tell the truth, I was a self-absorbed punk, thinking about football games, girls, grades, and zits. Didn't occur to me something might be wrong."

I tried to imagine Eva's happiness morphing into fear. "When did Jed disappear?"

"Eva snuck off to see a lawyer about a divorce the day after she celebrated her twenty-first birthday. The next week Jed left on a fishing trip. No one ever saw him again. There were plenty of accusations back then. His relatives screamed Eva had done him in and hid the body. Of course, there wasn't one scrap of proof. I know my sister. She's no killer. Plenty of folks thought otherwise. Still do."

Dad's shoulders slumped. "That's why your mom and I aren't keen about you living on the farm. Lots of members of the Watson clan live nearby. Your mother has brought charges against quite a few. These folks let their fists do their talking. It would be just like one of these hot heads to pay Eva a visit. Old hatreds and grudges have been simmering on Ardon County's back burner for years. That skeleton could bring the bitter stew to a rolling boil. I don't want you—or Eva—in harm's way."

The hairs on the back of my neck prickled. When I thought about Udderly Kidding, my associations were unfailingly good. Love and laughter. Sunshine and sparkling creeks. Shaggy dogs and newborn kids.

Danger? Nope.

Not unless you considered it hazardous to scarf down too many of Lilly's homemade cinnamon rolls.

"Please reconsider, Brie." Dad cut into my reverie. "Both you and Eva should move in with your mom and me. We have tons of room. What with the days getting longer, you'll have plenty of time to handle chores and still bed down at our house. You don't need to spend a single night out there in the boonies."

I shook my head. "You're dreaming, Dad. You know Eva won't leave her guardian dogs alone to deal with coyotes or trespassers. She and Aunt Lilly refused to leave the farm for more than a weekend for fear someone might decide their goats would be easy pickings on a midnight raid. Besides, Eva has a shotgun and knows how to use it. You read too many crime novels. That skeleton just rattled you. We'll be fine."

At least I hoped so. Lilly had tried to teach me to shoot. I wasn't a natural. The paper targets she hung in the gully for practice fluttered in the breeze unscathed despite an empty box of buckshot. Maybe I'd ask Eva for another lesson.

*   *   *

It took less than an hour to pack up my worldly possessions and load them in the truck. Dad and I saved my heftiest object—my stationary bike—as the last to load. Then Jessica treated Dad and me to a leisurely two-hour meal. After dessert, Dad's fidgeting signaled he was beyond ready to get going. We said our goodbyes and Jessica's German shepherd sent me off with a final volley of slobbery kisses. Xena never did grasp "Down, girl."

Dad and I didn't talk much on our return trip. As we rounded the last bend in Udderly's graveled lane, I spotted a strange vehicle in the drive. And I meant strange, even on my scale, which left plenty of room for the peculiar. The van's midnight blue paint job served as a backdrop for a galaxy of glittering stars and one super-sized harvest moon.

Dad chuckled. "The van is Mollye's newest purchase. Says it's great advertising for Starry Skies."

I smiled. "Wow. Should have guessed. Looks like the kind of ride Mollye with an 'e' would pick."

That's how my old friend, Mollye Camp, always introduced herself. "I'm Mollye with an 'e' hangin' off the hind-end of my name. Mom says six is her lucky number. The added 'e' makes me a lucky ducky."

We became fast friends at age eight when I visited my aunts over summer vacation. Mollye kept two ponies at Udderly Kidding. We rode together, camped in the meadow behind my aunts' cabin, and competed to see who could concoct the spookiest stories 'round the campfire. Not much of a competition. Mollye had a wild imagination. One reason our best adventures often ended with me occupying a chair in the corner, contemplating the wall.

"I'm glad she's here," I added. "Mollye's sure to cheer up Eva."

Dad smiled. "Your friend's 'woo-woo' store is doing a banner business. Starry Skies now sells Udderly goat soap, local crafts, and Mollye's own pottery as well as homeopathic remedies and astrological doodads. People come from all over to see her for horoscopes, astrological charts, and palm and Tarot readings."

"She's become a psychic?" My eyebrows hiked skyward. This was new. Given that I hadn't seen Mollye in a year, all bets were off.

"Not exactly. Just says we ought to keep an open mind about what we can't see or hear. She does this stuff for fun. Not out to scam anyone."

Dad yoo-hooed before we entered the cabin.

"Come on in," Eva called from her rocking chair.

Mollye sat at my aunt's feet, her legs contorted in one of those yoga poses that looked like a taffy-pull gone horribly wrong. Hunched over, Mollye cradled my aunt's open palm in her own mitt like a fragile manuscript. When she swiveled to greet us, she didn't relinquish Eva's hand.

"I'd jump up and hug you, but I've got Eva's life in my hands." She grinned. "Well, maybe just her lifeline."

I bent down and kissed Mollye's cheek. "Great to see you."

"Glad you made it back before I had to skedaddle," Mollye said.

A good thing the Starry Skies van had announced her presence and primed me for the inevitable surprise. Mollye changed her appearance as often as I traded running shoes. This time I wondered if she'd played pin-cushion with a porcupine. A tiny silver star hung from her nose ring, and, based on the variety of jingle jangles dangling from her ears, her lobes had enough holes to serve as sieves. A tattoo wrapped her forearm. What the frankfurter? First time I'd ever seen an old-fashioned quilt design stenciled on flesh. Old South meets punk rock?

A vibrant shock of purple ran down the center part in Mollye's white-blonde hair. The skunk-style streak perfectly matched her purple eye shadow.

Having called Asheville home till this very afternoon, I was accustomed to seeing people with brilliant swaths of painted hair, tattoos snaking up appendages and down cleavages, ear studs, nose rings, and personal punctures in locations that gave me the heebie-jeebies to contemplate.

But here? In Ardon County? Mollye clearly wasn't afraid to push the local envelope.

"Mollye assures me I have a long lifeline." Eva snorted. "Hope I don't spend those extra years in prison. Orange washes out my complexion. I'd look like a pumpkin topped with marshmallows.

Sheriff Jones dropped by. Informed me the skeleton's teeth matched Jed's dental records. Said the case was now officially being investigated as a homicide, and I should not make any plans to take my caboose out of Ardon County."

"Eva, I'm sorry," Dad managed. "The sheriff's off his rocker if he thinks you could have killed that skunk."

Mollye relinquished Eva's hand. "Granny agrees. She thinks Nancy Tarbox Watson murdered Jed. Says that witch has a soul uglier than a wart-encrusted toad no matter how much she tarts up her exterior."

Dad frowned. "I've never heard of this Nancy person. Who is she and why would she want to kill Jed?"

Mollye patted my aunt's hand, unwound her taffy limbs and rose gracefully to her five-foot-six height. I wasn't about to hazard a guess on poundage. Mollye'd always been husky. Never slowed her down in any department—men friends included.

"Granny says Nancy planned to marry Jed soon as he graduated college. She threw a hissy fit when he came back with a Yankee bride. The little matter of marriage vows didn't stop the hussy from flinging herself at Jed."

My old friend threw an apologetic glance Eva's way. "Rumor has it they were heating up the sheets again just before he went poof and disappeared."

Eva caught my horrified look and sighed. "This isn't breaking news. I heard her grandmother's theory years back. When Jed disappeared, I had no idea he might be doing the horizontal mambo with an old sweetheart. But the sheriff will see it as one more motive for me to have killed my husband. 'Course the opposite is true. I'd have helped Jed pack his bags if he'd agreed to split and make Nancy his new punching bag."

Mollye frowned. "I'll tell Granny to zip her lips, but surely Sheriff Jones has heard those tales. Granny claims everyone in the county knew Jed catted around." She ducked her head in Eva's direction by way of apology. "Ah, sorry, I guess everyone but you. Granny's convinced Jed had his fun, then dumped Nancy a second time. Once she figured out the relationship had no future, the bimbo decided Jed didn't deserve a future either."

My aunt snorted. "Wish I could buy that."

Eva rocked forward in her chair. "Even if this woman was madder than a wet hen, why dig a grave within sight of our farmhouse? Too risky. One heck of a sweaty job, too. Jed was a big fella. Six foot, over two hundred pounds. She'd have gotten a hernia planting him."

"What happened to Nancy?" I asked. "Does she still live around here?"

"Sure does," Mollye answered. "She's been hitched three times. Latest hubby is Eli Watson, one of Jed's cousins. Nancy's one of the owners of Hands On, that nail salon on Highway 130. She does manicures and pedicures."

I looked down at my raggedy fingernails and had a sudden urge to treat myself to a manicure. Then again, maybe not. A manicure would be a might suspicious. Nail polish and glue-on fakes were no-no's for professional chefs. Nothing like a patron spotting a blinged-up fingernail swimming in her soup. I wiggled my toes. Maybe a pedicure?

Mollye gave Eva a hug. "I'll come by Thursday to pick up more goat soap. It's one of my bestsellers. Sorry I couldn't come to Lilly's farewell. I loved her, too."

A minute later, Mollye flung her arms around me and squeezed. She'd always been a hugger, but this was the first time I worried about surviving without any transfer punctures.

"How about a girls' night out?" she asked. "Maybe movie and a pizza? I know you're vegan now. That's cool. I love veggie pizza."

"Right," I stammered, not sure what Mollye might cook up for a night out these days. I guessed the entertainment wouldn't be ghost stories and s'mores.

Dad, ever the gentleman, rose from the couch to escort Mollye to her glitzy van.

As soon as the front door closed, Eva chuckled. "You look shell-shocked. I forgot to warn you about Mollye's new look. Imagine you'll have a few more surprises living on a goat cheese farm in Ardon County. Hope one of them isn't seeing your auntie carted away in leg irons."

I knew kidding was one of Eva's ways of dealing with adversity, but jokes about jail made me shudder.

Eva turned toward me. "I wasn't surprised by my earlier drop-ins—Paint in the morning and Andy in the afternoon. They were plum disappointed you weren't here. Told each of 'em I was sure you'd love to have them show you the local sights. Gave 'em your cell phone number. I'll let you pick. Sure I kid Paint about his playboy reputation, but he's got a good heart, and it's high time Andy spent some time cuddling a two-legged companion. They're both good company and good-looking to boot. If I were your age, I might try and juggle the two of them."

Eva snickered at my panicked expression. I wasn't sure I was ready to climb aboard the dating train with one man. Two at once? No way.

EIGHT

Dad and I headed to the truck to cart my belongings inside. Eva followed, bound and determined to help schlep my worldly goods.

"I cleaned out Lilly's room," she said. "All ready for you to move in, Brie."

Dad and I stopped dead in our tracks and turned as one to face Eva. Her announcement left both of us momentarily speechless.

"Oh, Sis, you should have waited. We'd have helped you," Dad said.

I chimed in. "I didn't want you to clean out Lilly's room."

Eva harrumphed. "Stop it. I'll do much better if you all quit treating me like I've been diagnosed with a fatal illness—or maybe a mental defect. Lilly's gone. I'll grieve in my own way, thank you. I don't need to hang on to Lilly's bunny slippers to remember her."

"But I'm fine with sleeping on the couch."

"Not what Sis would want. Plenty of desperate folks will be more than pleased to wear Lilly's fuzzy slippers or her plaid parka. We finished loading Mollye's van just before you got here. She's distributing the bounty. Lilly's nicest things are headed to that new shelter for women escaping domestic abuse. Now there's a cause I'm glad to help."

Eva marched past us to the bed of the truck and plucked a shopping bag stuffed with my doodads. "Come on. What's wrong? Got a hitch in your get-along? Let's unload this truck before nightfall. Brie and I need time to squabble over the dinner menu."

I smiled and saluted. "Yes, ma'am. I'll be happy to whip up a tofu scramble for supper. That big blue cooler is full of goodies from my Asheville refrigerator."

Eva raised her hands in front of her face and made a ward-off-evil cross with her fingers. "Lordy, Lordy, protect me from tofu. Only way I can choke it down is if I top that mess with enough melted cheese and crumbled bacon."

Dad laughed. "Don't believe I'll stick around for dinner. I think I just witnessed the opening salvo in the great culinary war. You're both hardheaded. Wouldn't want to put money on a winner."

As it turned out, the night's menu was decided quite peaceably. My cooler included a container of my roasted tomato basil soup. I snarfed mine down minus the hunk of cheese Eva floated in her bowl.

After we washed the dinner dishes, I asked about the next day's chores. Eva smirked as she dried her hands on a dishtowel.

"Well, dearie, you need to set your alarm for five."

"As in a.m.?" I whined.

"Yep. Tomorrow's Wednesday, and selling cheese at the Ardon Flea Market was Lilly's gig. I figured you'd rather woman that booth than hang here and milk goats. Plus we never know when our about-to-be mama goats might need a nursemaid. But if you'd rather stay here..."

"No, thank you. You're very persuasive."

"Thought so. I'll pack three coolers with goat cheese and send you off with a thermos of coffee. We're table 117 right next to the egg lady."

"You're sure I need to get up before dawn?"

Eva chuckled. "I'm letting you sleep in. My guess is it'll be six thirty before you get set up. By then the parking lot will be half full and your double-yolker neighbor will already have sold a couple dozen hard-boiled eggs to regulars and several dozen raw eggs to early shoppers."

I knew the egg lady. First time Dad took me to Ardon's Flea Market I'd nudged him when I saw the hand-lettered sign: Fresh Double-Yolk Eggs! "What?" I'd asked. "Do her chickens live next to the nuclear power plant? How else could she glom on to so many freakish eggs?"

"Big chicken farms candle eggs—hold 'em up to a light to peek inside," Dad explained. "Since double-yolkers tend not to hatch, they sell 'em off. Twin yolks aren't common, but if you're raising thousands of chickens, the oddities add up."

Since the Udderly farm includes a flock of free-range chickens, I wondered if I'd find any double yokers when I gathered eggs.

"So what's my job at the flea market?" I asked Eva. "Please don't tell me I have to dicker. I hate that."

Dad loved haggling and went to the weekly market whenever his teaching schedule allowed. Unfortunately, he had Wednesday morning classes this semester. Otherwise I'd have sweet-talked him into pinch-hitting. Dad had so much fun bargaining he often bought...well, how to describe it? Ah, yes, junk. Mom slipped most of his "finds" into the trash within a month, and he never missed them.

Aunt Eva smiled. "It won't be as bad as you think. Just shrug if they don't want to pay what we're asking. We package our cheese in three-, five- and seven-dollar sizes. Even dollar prices make life a lot simpler. I'll pack Lilly's money belt with a wad of ones for change."

"Can I borrow your cell phone?" I asked.

"Why in the world would you want my phone?"

"I don't have a credit card app on mine. I'll get it tomorrow but not before morning."

Eva rolled her eyes. "You've been to the market. How many vendors do you suppose take credit cards? Granted we get some well-heeled retirees. They visit for entertainment as much as for deals. But they all know cash is king at the flea market."

Oh, boy. I was so looking forward to this. Not.

"It's simple. Offer cheese samples and smile. We make chump change, but we hook new customers. Encourage anyone who wolfs down a sample to take a flyer. It's got product prices, directions to Udderly, and phone and email order info. Watch out for moochers who make a breakfast out of free samples."

Eva started to offer detailed instructions on how to prepare and present cheese samples. I cut her off. "Hey, I'm a chef. I think I can handle a cheese platter for this swanky crowd."

A sudden crack of thunder shook the house and raindrops pitter-pattered on the cabin's tin roof. I grinned. The flea market sat on bottomland and, during my last visit, heavy rains had the tables floating in three feet of water. I could only hope.

Eva caught my merry expression.

"Forget it." She chuckled. "The grounds may be muddy tomorrow, but it'll be a go. Checked the weather forecast. Light showers ending before midnight. Which reminds me, it's past time to hit the hay."

Past time? Eva's grandfather clock had yet to chime nine. I couldn't remember the last time I'd gone to bed this early. Heck, at the Asheville restaurant where I work—correction, *worked*—we'd be serving dinner for two more hours and cleaning up past midnight.

I counted the hours of potential sleep between now and five a.m. and sighed. Might as well pull on PJs and try to snooze. Not likely though. I considered downing one of the antihistamines I keep for allergies to put me to sleep. Nope, I'd be groggy enough getting up at that time of day.

Eva walked over to where I curled on the couch, reading a mystery. She tucked the afghan around my shoulders and kissed my forehead. "Better get to bed, Brie. I can't tell you how much it means to have you here. I love you, honey."

My throat tightened. "Goodnight, Aunt Eva. Love you, too."

Eva chuckled. "Let's see if you feel the same at five a.m."

NINE

Ardon's Flea Market meandered over an expanse of at least three football fields. I'd visited plenty of times and knew how to find Udderly's assigned retail stall. I turned in at the third entrance. Six thirty a.m. was dark, damp, and downright chilly. Fog swirled around my sporty Prius C. I shivered. A perfect setting for one of Dad's murder mysteries.

Pools of water camouflaged the potholes that occupied half the graveled roadbed. My bouncing headlamps lit up the rutted drive like a reverse Rorschach ink blot test. The water appeared as blobs of shimmering yellow splattered across a black canvas.

Oops. One of my wheels kerplunked to the bottom of a giant muddy gully. My compact car tilted like it had downed one too many shots of Paint's moonshine. Struggling to gain traction, my captive tire flung mini mud pies in its wake.

"Sorry, car." I hated subjecting my new hybrid to a mud-wrestling contest. I'd made all of four car payments on my once-shiny red chariot and now it was becoming a country junker. I hoped my as yet unknown "salary" would let me make car payments five through sixty.

I maneuvered down a row of reserved parking spaces behind the section of warped wood tabletops set aside for "regular" food vendors. Udderly was in the "high-rent" district where the sagging tables merited an even more sagging, corrugated tin roof. For the most part, folks in this stretch sold fresh-from-the-farm produce, though some also hawked bananas, grapes, and other perishables on life support after they'd passed use-by dates. Where did they find these goodies? Did they wait in the road for these delicacies to fall off a truck?

I spotted the egg lady's dented truck and parked beside it. Three trips to the car and back and I'd muscled the cheese-filled coolers into my stall.

"How you doin'?" The high-pitched voice startled me. "Sorry to hear about Lilly. Wondered if Udderly would send anyone today. I'm Addie. Do I know you?"

I turned toward the voice. A dried apple face peeked out of the woman's oversized parka. Light cast by a space heater rigged behind her table gave the small wedge of face an eerie glow.

"Yes'm, Miss Addie," I answered. "I'm Brie Hooker, Lilly's niece."

Whew. I made it through our greeting without a startled gasp. Glad Aunt Eva had reminded me that while Miss Addie bore a striking resemblance to a witch, she was a very nice lady. "Don't worry, Brie." Eva chuckled. "The smile above that hairy mole on her chin doesn't mean she's finished off Hansel and Gretel and is sizing you up for dessert."

Addie looked puzzled. Clearly she didn't remember me.

"I helped Aunt Lilly with the booth once last year. She introduced us."

"Yes, yes," she said. "I remember. Dang calendar says spring's sprung, but it feels colder than a witch's tit on Hallow's Eve. I can spare a mug o' coffee so's you don't freeze."

"Uh, thanks, but Aunt Eva sent me off with a full thermos."

A bundle of rags shuffled down the aisle heading our way. I thought "zombie."

Addie called to him. "Hey, Jimbo. Got your eggs all ready. Think my hens are still cackling."

Official sunrise remained half an hour away when my first prospects arrived. In an hour, nibblers tore through a full pack of toothpicks as they speared free samples. I'd artfully arranged the dainty cheese cubes in a color-coded wheel. Then valiantly tried to fill in the holes as folks poached samples. After forty-five minutes, I gave in and tossed cheese on the tray. Sort of like feeding wild animals, I withdrew my hand quickly to keep all my fingers.

"Where's Lilly?"

I looked up. A red-haired spitfire had planted herself in front of the booth.

"That little scamp promised this limey she'd bring me an apricot cheeseball today," the British import continued.

She sounded quite put out. Then I saw her grin. The lady was putting me on. That didn't unglue my tongue. It never dawned on me that Lilly would have friends here who didn't know she'd passed.

My chin trembled as I fought my tears. The stranger reached across my now untidy cheese platter and squeezed my arm. "Sod it, what did I say?"

I blubbered my news and watched matching tears pool in the Brit's eyes. "I had no idea." She choked out condolences. "I'll miss Lilly. We had a good ol' time blowing smoke up each other's knickers."

During the next hour, I broke the sad news to a dozen of Lilly's regular customers. Her obit hadn't caught their eyes. Most didn't know my aunt's last name, just her teasing patter.

About eight o'clock, Paint visited my stall. I flashed him my best grin before I realized he wasn't smiling. What now?

"Hi, Brie. I dropped by Udderly after I read the morning paper. Knew Eva wouldn't look at it till evening. Wanted to prepare her in case a reporter came nosing around. Eva said you were here and asked me to warn you."

He pushed a folded *Ardon Chronicle* across the table. A two-column photo immediately snagged my attention—my smiling aunts holding some goat cheese award. The paper had superimposed a skull-and-crossbones over the picture. The headline: "Murdered Corpse Dug Up On Udderly Property."

Oh, no.

I quickly scanned the story. It did everything but flat out claim Eva'd murdered her husband and potted him in the side yard. The story insinuated Udderly's profitable business wouldn't exist if Eva's husband hadn't mysteriously disappeared allowing her to "seize" the Watson family farm. No mention of the fact the farm had been deep in debt and primed for foreclosure prior to her stewardship.

"Liverwurst and Limburger!" I spat out my curse, prompting the egg lady to look my way in alarm.

Paint looked confused. "Come again?"

"Um, I'm just riled. Mom got on my case about my language. So I switched to using processed meats and cheeses for swear words." I smiled. "Drives Aunt Eva nuts."

"You're a most interesting young lady," Paint wheezed out

between guffaws. "I'd love to hear the rest of your cheesy vocabulary."

I tried my best to glare at him even though his laughter made it hard to hide a grin. "One more snide remark, you Son of a Salami—"

He doubled over. We'd definitely gotten off track.

I glanced back at the paper and my amusement died. "How can they get away with this? They let the Watsons paint Eva as a conniving bitch. They didn't even bother to get my aunt's side of the story."

He shrugged. "The Ardon paper's a pile of uh, bologna, but they skirt just short of libel. Folks take it for school news, coupons, and obits. The only game in town."

I'd heard my father rage about Allie Gerome, the Ardon rag's publisher. Dad said the pompous idiot delighted in stirring up hatreds between noble "natives" and evil "newcomers." The natives were victims; the newcomers, vile carpetbaggers.

By ol' Allie's definition "natives" were white settlers who'd called Ardon County home for at least three generations—in other words, the Watsons. No mention of Indians, the real natives. Carpetbaggers like Aunt Eva were born elsewhere, most often in states that furnished troops for the "War of Northern Aggression," i.e. the Civil War.

"You gonna be okay?" Paint asked. "Maybe I should stay."

"I'm fine. I appreciate the heads up. I'm angry that's all."

"I'll check on you later. Long as I'm here, I'll see if I can spot any products that might sell in our store. That's how I found Udderly Kidding goat cheese, cruising the market."

I watched Paint saunter away. Could see him all the way down the aisle. His height made it easy to follow his bobbing head. He truly was head and shoulders above yahoos like Allie Gerome, people who got their jollies re-fighting the Civil War.

I took a calming breath and tried to send positive thoughts Aunt Eva's way.

TEN

Time flew. One fellow stomped off when I refused to deal on price. That's when I scribbled a note on our sign: "Our prices are as firm as Udderly's hard cheddar." Didn't hear a peep from anyone else.

Actually, ninety percent of my would-be customers weren't buttheads. They were nice, and I wished them long lives. Nonetheless I resisted warning them that Udderly cheese—no matter how tasty— could clog their arteries.

For the most part, I didn't mind the gig. I liked chatting with people—especially about food and cooking. More importantly, it gave me a break from my worries about Aunt Eva wearing prison orange. No one seemed to have read the newspaper, or if they had, they didn't comment on who might have killed Jed.

My low IQ regarding goats and cheese proved my main conversational stumbling block. Customers stumped me with the simplest questions. 'Course I didn't voice the sarcastic answers on the tip of my tongue.

"Can I eat goat cheese if I'm lactose intolerant?"

Uh, don't know, not a big concern for vegans.

"Does Udderly sell raw milk?"

Ask me about raw cashews. I can answer that one.

One whiskered old geezer asked me to list our breeds. I knew Udderly's goats came in brown, black, white, and speckled as well as in assorted shapes and sizes—sort of like bonbons in a Whitney sampler. But breeds? Not a clue.

I confessed to my idiocy, offered brochures, and promised myself I'd bone up before next week's market.

I asked the egg lady to watch my booth while I did a quick swing through the veggie section to pick up fixings for supper—fresh asparagus, oranges, cantaloupe, cabbage. I hadn't looked in Aunt Eva's pantry yet, but this was a start. I smiled to myself. I'd dazzle her with a vegan masterpiece. She'd never miss the meat or cheese. Ha.

While I flipped through my mental recipe index, I people watched. No better place for it. A young Amish woman with scrubbed cheeks and a starched white bonnet marched past me, her basket filled with overripe bananas. An old man in lavender suspenders leaned on his gnarled hickory cane as he inspected rusty hammers. One poor old lady had a hump on her back bigger than the cantaloupe she was thumping.

Then there was the subgroup of customers who embraced camouflage as a fashion statement. Whole families, from infants to geezers, dressed in various shades of camouflage. Why would anyone need a camouflaged diaper? Did they want to lose the kid in the woods?

Some of the camo guys roaming the dusty aisles carried gnarly knives, shotguns, even swords. In Ardon's booths, folks could buy almost any blade or long gun they fancied. The flea market's arms dealers could outfit a new Confederate army. And I wasn't even counting lethal farm implements like the picks, shovels, and pitchforks available for low-tech warfare.

By ten thirty, the egg lady had vanished. Time for me to pack it up, too. Most vendors left by eleven a.m. I saw no reason to be the only seller on site at noon when the flea market resembled a graveyard for warped wood.

I bent over to retrieve a cooler, my back to my stall window.

Thud.

Startled, I jumped and cracked my head on the table's underside. Then I spied a sharp blade wedged in the table less than a lasagna pan from the tip of my nose. The weapon had sliced clean through the spongy wood. My heart skittered around like drops of water in a hot frying pan.

Should I get out from under the table? What if axe-man had more weapons? Of course, the table hadn't exactly proved an effective shield.

I scooted backward and inched my head up far enough to see axe-man's face. That just made my nightmare worse. Glaring, bloodshot eyes. Greasy black hair. Flaring nostrils. A neck bigger than a bone-in ham. And, oh, yes, a menacing sneer.

"You're not Eva." His pissed off growl expressed both surprise and rage. "Who the hell are you?"

I didn't exactly decide not to answer. I was too scared to swallow, much less speak.

"Don't matter." He paused and glared at me. "I figured the bitch would be here since that car wreck turned her meddling sister into roadkill. You give Eva a message. Tell her she ain't gonna get away with murder. No way. Some fancy mouthpiece may get her off, but there's still mountain justice. Jed was kin. Watsons don't forget."

Axe-man whipped his head around to look behind him. Paint had seized his collar. "Hey, Eli, looks like you got tuckered and dropped your axe. Clumsy of you. Maybe you should apologize and leave."

Thank heaven. An ally.

I hadn't seen Paint arrive. I'd been too focused on the gargoyle who went by the name Eli.

"What the hell you doin' here, Paint? Ain't none of your business. Butt out."

Paint turned a smile on Eli that carried its own menace. "Just try me," it said.

"This lady's a friend, so it's definitely my business. Go. Now. Or I'll have to help you with that axe."

The ogre speared me with another glare. "You give my message to Eva." He turned, giving Paint's shoulder a solid thump before he stomped off. I didn't know if the axe was his or clipped from another stall, but he left it wedged in my table.

The handsome moonshiner grinned as he pried the axe from the wood. "Glad to see me? Have you been annoying customers? Did you slip vegan propaganda in with Eli's goat cheese?"

"Hey, I didn't say boo to that Eli person."

Now that axe-man had disappeared, my pulse began to saunter below stroke range. Yet being this close to the Ardon County bad boy wasn't exactly a sedative.

"Who is that guy?" I asked. "Don't know what you heard, but he threatened Eva."

"Eli's a Watson," Paint answered. "His wife, Nancy, started bad-mouthing Eva the minute your aunt set foot in Ardon County. The Watsons claim Eva killed Jed. All the men are loudmouths, but Eli's the worst hothead. Killed a guy in a bar fight. Cut him with a broken beer bottle. Got out of prison five years ago."

"Great Gouda! What if he shows up at Udderly?"

"Doubt he's eager to return to a jail cell. Imagine he just wanted to scare Eva—scare you."

"Well, he succeeded. This isn't what Eva needs. Not with everything else on her plate."

Paint nodded. "I agree, but Eva can handle herself. She'll keep her shotgun handy and listen to anything her guard dogs have to say. Those Pyrenees provide a great early warning system. 'Course, I'd be happy to drop by in the evening. My truck in the drive might give Eli pause."

"Until you leave. Your truck wouldn't be parked there all night."

His slow smile gave me a preview of his reply. "Could be. I'd be happy to spend the night, any night. Not a hardship."

There went my pulse again. Time to listen to one of my meditation audios. After going cold turkey on males, I learned that concentrating on my breathing could keep uninvited thoughts at bay. Some of the time. Okay, it worked once in a blue moon.

ELEVEN

Paint helped me load the coolers in my car.

"Thanks for coming to my rescue. How about joining Eva and me for dinner—a high-calorie thank you around seven thirty?"

Paint grinned. "Is this BYOM?" He laughed at my puzzled expression. "You know, BYOM—bring your own meat."

I rolled my eyes. "If Eva has her say, she'll add at least one carnivore-approved entrée."

"That works. See you then."

I figured Eva would enjoy Paint's company. Viewing his rogue's-gallery grin across the table wouldn't impose a hardship on me either.

Before starting my car, I had one more piece of business. I pulled out my smart phone and Googled the nail salon where Nancy Watson worked.

Paint's mention of Nancy—sworn enemy of Aunt Eva, dead Jed's one-time mistress, and gargoyle Eli's current wife—convinced me I needed a pedicure. I wanted to meet this woman. See if she seemed capable of offing Jed in a jealous frenzy or coldly conniving with some male—Eli?—to waste Jed and bury the lover who'd spurned her in a spot where Eva would get the blame.

I dialed Hands On and requested an afternoon appointment with Nancy Watson.

"What's your name, honey?"

Uh-oh. Hadn't thought this through. If I gave my real name, she'd know Eva and I were kin. No other Hookers—family members, not pros—resided in Ardon County.

"I'm, uh, Bea," I mumbled. When I was introduced, lots of folks heard "Bea" when I said "Brie." Not a huge change.

"And your last name?" she prompted.

What rhymed with Hooker? Looker, Fooker, Rooker.

The interrogator on the other end of the line cleared her throat. Come on. Think of something.

"It's Snooker," I answered with a mental grimace. "Bea Snooker."

Could I be more lame? Oh, well. My made-up name rhymed—Bea Snooker, Brie Hooker. They sounded enough alike I might turn my head if someone called out my alias.

"Your first visit to Hands On?" the appointment maker asked. "You're not one of Nancy's regulars."

"Uh, yes. First time. A friend recommended her."

"Who?"

Geez, what was with the cross-examination? I was booking a pedicure, not requesting a bank loan. My silence prompted a round of vicious gum-chewing on the other end of the line. I could hear every snap, chomp, and smack. 'Course, for all I knew, the sounds might have come from chewing tobacco.

"We give gift certificates to folks who recommend us," the overactive masticator added.

"Oh," I stammered. "I think it was...Mollye Camp." She was the only candidate I could come up with.

"Huh," came the response. "Don't rightly remember Mollye ever settin' foot in our shop. How's about three p.m.?"

"Fine." I hung up before the inquisitor could give me the third-degree about my relationship with Mollye, a girl she clearly knew. Should have guessed. Ardon included more trees than people, and Mollye wasn't exactly a shrinking violet. I'd have to give more thought to how I'd parse information at my afternoon toe gig. At least more thought than I'd given my impromptu phone call.

I texted Aunt Eva to let her know Paint had found me, and I was headed home. I yawned. Getting up at stinking five a.m. had screwed up my internal clock's wiring. Time to return to Udderly and see if my new boss would let me sneak in a nap.

I parked in front of Eva's cabin and received the usual greeting from Braden and Jim, two of the Udderly dogs who lazed near the cabin when they were off goat-guarding duty.

Tipping the scales at around one hundred pounds each, they could pass for miniature ponies. Put all five of Udderly's Great

Pyrenees in a doggie lineup and most folks couldn't tell them apart. Shaggy white coats. Shiny black-as-coal eyes and noses. Paws the size of frying pans.

Eva and Lilly had given me clues to ID the look-alikes. These two were easy-peasy. A coyote had torn off a portion of Braden's right ear, and a patch of rust-tinted fur surrounded Jim's eyes, making him look like a canine Tonto.

My aunts trained them not to jump on people. A definite no-no with a steady stream of drop-in customers and school children. However, their obedience training didn't preclude them from depositing a quart of drool on my shoes or whipsawing my shins with their hyperactive tails.

And the big lugs barked. Pitch and frequency told Eva whether new arrivals were friends, foes, or strangers placed in Braden and Jim's undecided column.

Eva walked out from behind the milking barn, wiping her hands on the coarse apron she wore over her jeans. "Did Paint find you?"

"Yes, didn't you get my text?"

Aunt Eva chuckled. "Honey, I don't text. It takes a lot less time to call someone and state your business. Even if I were inclined to text, my hands spend a lot of time in places where, well, use your imagination, if I touched a phone, you wouldn't want to drop it in your purse."

"Yuck, you're right. I texted to thank you for sending Paint. I was lucky. No reporter showed up and not a single customer mentioned that nasty story in the *Ardon Chronicle*."

"Folks probably headed to the flea market before they read the paper. Still, I didn't want you ambushed by that loathsome Allie Gerome. Would have been just like her to send a reporter to bait you until she provoked a quote to pull out of context. Just that pusillanimous polecat's style."

I laughed. Always tickled me when Eva applied her "pusillanimous polecat" label. Took me back to childhood visits with my aunts. I'd sit between them holding a big bowl of buttered popcorn as we watched DVDs of old-timey Westerns. Gabby Hayes, who appeared as a sidekick in half the shoot-'em-ups, regularly worked "pusillanimous polecat" into his descriptions of villains. Eva also loved to call me a "young whippersnapper," another of Gabby's sayings. If I'd stayed longer with my aunts, I'd have thought whippersnapper was my name.

A look at Eva's face erased my amusement. Red blotches colored her cheeks. Her narrowed eyes looked like they could shoot daggers. I hated to tell her about Eli's threat, but she needed to know. I gave a short, sterile version of the ogre's visit. Tried to mask the terror I'd felt.

"Damn him!" Eva yelled. "Hope he does come looking for trouble. South Carolina stand-your-ground laws tend to favor folks who shoot to protect their homes. Paint had it right. I'll keep my gun handy."

I heard a mini-woof. My pup, Cashew, had joined the canine chorus. Soon as I scooped her up, her energetic pink tongue tickled my chin. "Hey, didn't Aunt Eva feed you?"

Eva huffed. "I know you're trying to distract me and end my rant. And yes, I fed that furry little mop. When you're not around, Cashew's more than happy to cuddle up to me. And speaking of cuddling, Andy dropped by this morning to check on our mama goats. Now there's a man I wouldn't mind canoodling with if I were your age. I invited him to dinner. You can fix one of your veggie wonders."

I laughed. "Should be an entertaining evening. I invited Paint to dinner, too."

Eva hooted. "Interesting. They're pals, and I love 'em like sons. But I saw how both of them looked at you. Should be right entertaining."

"You have an overactive imagination." Even as I said it, I kind of hoped Eva was right. Both bad boy Paint and nice guy Andy had started me thinking it was time to lift my self-imposed male embargo. A full year had slipped by since I learned my fiancé was a cheating cad and ended our engagement.

I cleared my throat. Breathe in, breathe out. Meditate. Erase those lustful visions. Going...going...sort of gone. Meditation isn't foolproof.

"I bought some veggies at the flea market," I said. "So I have a start on a meal plan. But I promised Paint you'd add a carnivore option."

"No problem. I have a freezer full of meat—lamb, beef, chicken— everything but goat and pig. I'm a sentimental old fool, can't eat animals I've called by name. Good thing I never name my hens. 'Course

I'd never cook Riley Roo, my cock-of-the-walk rooster.

"You must be starving," she added. "Let's go inside, grab some lunch. When I couldn't sleep last night, I got up and listed all the chores. I know you'd rather be broiling mushrooms or turnin' radishes into frou-frou flowers—whatever you vegan chefs get up to. So I figured least I could do is give you a say in how you spend your days—and nights." She grinned. "The vet and the moonshiner could definitely make your nights more interesting."

I rolled my eyes. My aunt had zeroed in on my love life as a subject ripe for ribbing. "Did you forget about my slimy ex-fiancé? I'm doing just fine. I don't need to be half of a couple. I'm not on some man hunt."

"Pish, posh," Eva waved her hand like she was shooing away a pesky fly. "Doesn't mean you can't have fun. I'm the last person to push marriage. But you got rid of the jerk a year ago. You're only young once."

She helped me carry in my groceries. I heated up leftover tomato basil soup while my aunt grilled a big fat cheese sandwich. Then, sitting side by side in the kitchen alcove, we went over the lengthy duty roster she'd compiled. I was delighted to see Eva's part-time employees—Clemson Ag students—were first at bat on some of the yuckier jobs, like cleaning poop out of the milking barn.

"Aunt Eva, don't worry about me. I've spent enough time here that I have half an idea how much work it takes to run Udderly. I don't mind most chores. Just not sure how good I'd be at some of them. Chatting with customers this morning made me realize I'm a dimwit about goat breeds and dairy production. But I'm a fast learner."

Eva patted my hand. "I know you are, dear."

The familiar sound of wheels crunching gravel prompted both of us to glance out the window. Jim and Braden barked a warning chorus. As soon as I spotted an Ardon County Sheriff's cruiser, I knew why. This company wasn't welcome. We pushed aside our unfinished lunches and stood as Sheriff Jones and a deputy sidekick exited their vehicle and headed for the cabin. Eva opened the door before the sheriff could knock. I stood right behind her.

Cashew scampered to my side. Normally she played the vamp, begging any newcomer to pet her. Sensing the tension, she snarled. I picked her up and held her tight so she couldn't nip one of the officers.

"Miss Hooker, we have a search warrant," Sheriff Jones said. "It covers all buildings on your property. Several officers will help with the search. You and the girl may remain on the premises, if you don't interfere. But you'll stay where I tell you."

Eva laughed. "Those bones you dug up say Jed's been dead for decades. You think I killed him and kept souvenirs for forty years? I'm not daft. But, hey, search away."

TWELVE

Eva bowed the sheriff and deputy inside—a mocking gesture. I looked out the window and saw two more cruisers pull in. What? This merited a SWAT team?

Outside the canine chorus had reached full pitch. "I'm going out to calm the dogs. Stop me and one of your deputies is likely to have canine teeth marks on his rump."

The sheriff grunted but made no move to stop her.

"Can I put my dog on the screened porch so she won't get under foot?" I asked. The deputy who'd come inside with Jones nodded, and I carried a squirming Cashew to the back and shut her in. Her whine said she wasn't pleased. I scooted to a corner of the porch, pulled my cell phone out of my pocket, and hit speed dial for Mom, our in-family legal counsel.

"Hell's bells," Mom swore. "Read that warrant and see exactly what it says, pay attention to the search limits. Tell Eva to cooperate. I'm on my way, but it'll be half an hour before I can get there."

I walked outside to find Eva and share Mom's instructions. She was kneeling, stroking the head of a large shaggy white dog. The warrant, clutched in her free hand, had been crushed into a ball.

I asked to see it, smoothed the wrinkled paper, and scanned the legalese. The search listed guns, property deeds, diaries, and any papers related to Eva's marriage and Jed Watson's death.

Guns? Did that mean Jed was shot?

I sighed. "At least the warrant doesn't mention computers."

"Oh, what a blessing." Eva's sarcasm was easy to understand.

My aunt herded me back inside. Then she yanked her jacket from a peg by the door. "Stay in the cabin. I need to watch those bozos search the milking barn and dairy. Can't let them contaminate the milk."

The front door slammed behind her as she speed-walked toward the milking barn. Deputies from both cruisers were entering there, apparently an assigned starting point. We referred to the structure as the milking barn, though there were actually two buildings under one roof—the milking barn and a modern dairy processing plant filled with stainless steel vats and gizmos I hadn't a clue how to operate.

When I turned from the front window, Sheriff Jones and the unnamed deputy were no longer in the cabin's main living area. I found them looking through drawers in Lilly's—now my—bedroom. If I hadn't felt so angry watching them finger my silk panties, I might have laughed. Their hottest find would be a stash of jalapeno pistachios—a gift from a Texas friend I didn't plan to share.

I leaned against the doorjamb. The sheriff sensed my presence and turned. He paused in his maul-the-undies routine and shook his head like a water-logged spaniel. Guess he finally deduced my aunt wasn't likely to wear patterned tights or bikini briefs.

"This your room?" he asked.

I nodded.

He turned toward his deputy helper, who gave me a goofy smile. "Let's move on," the chief barked.

They traipsed across the hall to Eva's bedroom, and I assumed a lookout post in the doorway. Sheriff Jones' face broke into a gleeful grin as he sighted Eva's shotgun leaning against the wall by her desk. "Tag it and take it to the cruiser," Jones ordered his deputy. "I'll start on the desk."

He pulled out the desk's middle drawer and dumped it on Eva's hand-quilted spread. Ink pens and pencils, grimy pennies and nickels, scissors, and tattered business cards spilled onto the bed.

"What are you doing?" I sputtered. "You're ruining Eva's quilt. Any fool can see that's a junk drawer. No documents."

The sheriff pulled a scrap of paper free of the drawer debris and waved it at me. "No, missy, you're wrong. This is a document."

I wanted to scream. The scrap was probably a note to self, something as incriminating as "buy cumin."

Inspiration struck. I pulled out my cell phone. "Go right ahead with your search, Sheriff. I'll just snap photos and maybe a video or two. You won't mind me posting them on Facebook and YouTube to show how conscientious you are?"

The sheriff's eyes narrowed and his nostrils flared. He lunged toward me, making a grab for my cell. I jumped clear and snapped another photo. "I read the warrant. Nothing about cell phones. You have no right to take this."

"You little..." He stopped, took a step back, and straightened his shoulders. "You're a cheeky one. Interfere with our legal search and I'll haul you in for obstruction." His black eyes glittered, apparently thrilled with the idea of me behind bars.

I was less thrilled.

I shrugged, trying for nonchalance even as my heart pumped blood so fast I could hear it whooshing through my veins.

"I'm just taking pictures. That's not interfering. Go ahead with your *legal* search."

I mentally urged Mom to step on it. She'd speak softly, almost sweetly. But she'd know exactly what to say to make the sheriff's nether regions pucker. Pucker-producing wordplay must be a mandatory course in law school. Mom sure had mastered it—a definite plus for a size-two petite.

Deputy Goofy grinned at me as he returned from his shotgun confiscation run. "Howdy, again, ma'am. Sorry for the inconvenience."

This fellow reminded me of an eager puppy. Big feet. Soulful eyes. Just missing the lolling tongue and wagging tail. He looked harmless and definitely lacked the sheriff's animosity.

"Hey, Sheriff, I fetched those big bags you wanted," he said.

"Well, bring 'em here, Danny," Jones snarled.

I snapped more photos in an attempt to document everything they carted off. At least they didn't dump anything else on Eva's quilt.

The officers weren't wearing gloves. Apparently fingerprints weren't a consideration. The sheriff grabbed one of Eva's photo albums and shoved it in a bag.

"Hey," I objected. "Those are pictures, not documents."

The sheriff's lips lifted back in a parody of a smile. "I know who you are. Your mother can file her objection later. I'm betting there's writing on the back of those photos."

Sheriff Jones and Danny moved on to the kitchen. I followed.

"Take a look at the top of those cupboards," Jones ordered. "Maybe she hid a diary up there."

"Sorry, ma'am. I'll try not to dirty your counters," Danny said as he shucked his muddy boots before clambering up. A thoughtful gesture though I doubted his dingy socks were much less germ proof than his size thirteen clodhoppers. The deputy still couldn't see over the decorative rail atop the cabinets, so he waved his hand across the space, sending more than a few dust bunnies into freefall.

I heard the front door open and looked down the hall. Mom. She had an arm around my aunt's waist. When they walked past Eva's bedroom, my aunt gasped. "Damn them. My grandmother made that quilt."

I hurried to greet them and gave each a fast hug. I proudly waved my cell phone. "I took pictures. Documented everything they took from your room." The pained look on my aunt's face doused my prideful glee. "Eva, I'm really sorry. They took a lot of papers, even snatched your photo albums."

My aunt's lips twisted and her jaw jutted forward. A clear sign she was spoiling for a fight. I wouldn't have been shocked to see sparks leap from her forehead.

Mom clamped a hand on Eva's forearm and squeezed. "Take a deep breath. Don't say a word. I have this under control. As your lawyer, I have the right to see everything they've taken once it's catalogued. I'll force them to return anything not covered by the warrant."

Eva glared at the men rattling pots and pans in her kitchen cupboards. "Nobody would be here if Jed and Sheriff Jones weren't kin," she muttered. "This is ridiculous."

The cabin's front door opened, ushering in a cold gust of wind. I shivered.

A grinning deputy held a rifle above his head like a triumphant rebel. "Hey, Sheriff, looky what we found in the horse barn. I poked around the loft and spotted this old blaster taped to the backside of a beam. Hidden real good."

"Good job, West." Sheriff Jones smiled broadly enough to show his back molars.

"Now why d'ya suppose somebody'd hide a gun there?" Jones

asked as he stopped beside my aunt. "Want to answer that question, ma'am?"

Aunt Eva's chest heaved. "That's Jed's rifle. I can see his initials on the stock. Jed took it when he left. His killer must've hid it up there." Her hands curled into tight white fists. I feared she'd either sock the sheriff in the jaw or spit on him. Mom stepped between the combatants.

"If you're finished, please leave," Mom said. "Now. I'm Iris Hooker, Eva Hooker's lawyer, and I expect to see everything you've taken from this farm catalogued by tomorrow."

Sheriff Jones worked his jaw as he glared at Mom. The ultimate smirk said he welcomed her challenge.

He tipped his hat. "Ladies, I plan to see a lot more of you. Have a good day, now. I know I will."

The cruisers fishtailed in the gravel and headed down the drive.

"I'm going to go visit the Ardon County Solicitor," Mom said. "Make sure he sees to it that Sheriff Jones doesn't dillydally in compiling a list of what he took."

She hugged Eva and me, then hurried outside to her Honda. As soon as she left, Eva walked over to the cedar plank table that held the remnants of our lunch. The cheese in her sandwich had congealed into a gelatinous mass. Bloated crackers clogged the bottom of my soup bowl. Didn't matter. We'd both lost our appetites.

Eva picked up her plate and headed to the kitchen sink. I followed. We scraped our leftovers into a slop bucket for Tammy, our spoiled potbellied pig.

"Want me to call Paint and Andy?" I asked. "Cancel dinner tonight?"

"Not on your life," Eva barked. "There was a time I let a bully make my life miserable. Never again. I won't cower. Won't hide. Won't change my life. I'm not afraid of Sheriff Jones or Eli Watson." She straightened. "You've had enough drama for one day. Take the afternoon off. I'd just as soon be alone. Traipse up the hill to where I scattered Lilly's ashes. Have a chat with Sis. Don't worry. I'll be fine by dinner."

"Any special requests for supper?"

"I'll thaw steaks for us meat eaters. You figure out the rest."

I smiled. "Will do. I'll be home by five. Plenty of time to whip up my dinner contributions."

I didn't mention my afternoon outing included a visit to a murder suspect, one I presumed would be armed with commercial-grade scissors and a stainless steel nail file. Too bad you had to take off your shoes to have a pedicure. I don't run as fast barefoot.

THIRTEEN

Hands On was plunked smack dab in the middle of a down-and-out strip mall. Potholes dotted the parking lot. Discount Freddie's occupied the building at one end, while Harry's Hot Dogs held down the opposite corner. The small shops on either side of Hands On were vacant.

Yet someone had paid more than a few pennies to draw attention to the Hands On storefront. A six-foot carved hand guarded the entrance. The carving's painted nails showcased a variety of neon shades and add-on bling—initials, interlocking hearts, even a smoking gun on a thumbnail. Why wasn't I surprised?

I took a deep breath, silently apologized to my virgin toes, and walked inside.

"Hiya." I recognized the voice. Same woman who'd quizzed me over the phone. Her dirty blonde, bleached hair looked like someone'd dumped a basket of hay on her head. The rat's nest was desert dry and ended in a cascade of split ends. Gooey, blood-red lips punctuated a puffy face. Not exactly a winning recommendation for beauty treatments.

"You Bea?" she asked.

"Um, yes. Here for my pedicure." I glanced at the nameplate parked on her desk. "You're Diana?"

"Yep," she said. "Nancy will be with you in a sec. Have a seat."

She waved me toward a loveseat that once upon a time might have been daisy yellow. Grime gave it a mustard patina. The phone rang. She answered and laughed. A pal. She turned sideways and put up a hand so I couldn't eavesdrop. Thank you, Lord, for small favors.

Would she notice I chose not to sit? I studied the mix of licenses and awards lining the entryway. Nancy Watson had earned two attagirl plaques from nail product manufacturers.

I leaned in to check the dates when a throat clearing told me I wasn't alone.

The woman who'd crept up behind me pasted on a smile.

"I'm Nancy Watson," she said. "You here for a pedicure?"

She was shorter than me. Maybe five-three if you included her teased blonde 'do.

"Brittle" was the first word her appearance brought to mind. The skinny broad was flirting with sixty, but she'd had work done. Evident in her taut face and perky headlamps. The skin on her face stretched drum tight, forcing her eyebrows to mosey up her forehead. I wondered if her plastic surgeon had over-inflated her boobies. Helium? Ye gods, they almost pointed at her chin.

I gathered my wits and stuck out my un-manicured paw for a handshake. "Hi, I'm Bea. Here for that pedicure."

Her red-tipped claw grazed my hand, not quite a handshake. Nancy's attempt at a smile looked painful. I hoped her skin wouldn't split like an overripe tomato. Hard to believe this woman and my aunt had once loved the same man. Even though it was the distant past, I couldn't imagine two females being more different.

"Follow me," she said.

We walked down a darkened corridor. Though a pedicure novice, I was a big fan of massages, so I was no stranger to salon ambiance. The diffused lighting and the nature soundtrack of tinkling water were on purpose, not the result of unpaid electric bills and leaky plumbing. How could tinkling water make anyone relax? It made me look for the nearest bathroom.

Nancy waved me toward a massive recliner on a raised platform. She plunked her scrawny self on one of those wheeled stools doctors use to play bumper cars with furniture while your bare ass hangs out of a paper gown. Then she scowled at my tennies and crew socks.

Her frown looked a lot more natural than her smile. "You can't put those shoes and socks back on. Until the polish hardens, the weave in them socks transfers. I won't guarantee nothin' if you put socks on."

Oh, chicken livers, I'd forgotten to bring flip flops. Mollye'd clued me in about footwear when I told her she'd "referred" me. After I admitted I'd never had a pedicure, she heehawed and gave me a Cliff

Notes version of tootsie protocol.

"Sorry. I meant to bring flip flops. I forgot."

"We keep throwaways for people who forget." Nancy's tone indicated my IQ didn't rise to double digits.

She ordered me to take off my shoes as she ran the water for the foot basin and added a green powder. Once I peeled off my socks, she stared at my naked feet with obvious disdain. "When was your last pedicure?"

Like forever. "Um, I've been busy."

"Those callouses are nasty. You spend a lot of time on your feet?"

"Afraid so. I'm a chef." Careful. Don't volunteer too much info. Next she'll want to know where you work.

My worries proved for naught. Nancy wasn't into chitchat unless it pertained to pricey extras.

"It'll be another twenty dollars for a foot scrub. You need it."

I nodded. "Fine." I wanted to offer Nancy and her hubby a free mouth scrub.

Nancy seized my left foot and plunked it in a pool of swirling hot water. At least my teeth wouldn't chatter while she did her wheelies.

The floozy made no attempt to talk to me. The hot water felt kind of good, though my dry right foot was feeling a might neglected. Better yet, I'd discovered the recliner had massage functions. Might as well vibrate, give her a challenge. Let's see her paint my toes while my little wigglies bounced around.

I relaxed more than seemed prudent in the enemy camp. Nancy practically woke me when she yanked my left foot out of the bath, pushed righty into the water, and began pummeling my shriveled left foot.

Strong hands. Hmmm. Given the sheriff's glee at finding guns at Udderly, I figured a bullet ended Jed's life. No doubt Nancy could shoot a gun. According to one news report, a Chihuahua had managed to fire one.

The real question: could Nancy dig a grave and wrestle a two-hundred-plus-pound male into the ground without help? Stringy muscles stood out on the woman's forearms. So, perhaps, given enough time she could. But time would have to be at a premium if you were planting a corpse within sight of a farmhouse. Even if she knew no one was home, she'd have to worry someone might return at any moment.

Nancy retrieved my wrinkled right foot from its baptism and started scrubbing both feet with some sort of pumice. It felt like the stone would go right through to bone. I bit my lip to divert the pain from foot to mouth. I wanted to sing hallelujah when she stopped. My giggles surprised me as much as they did Nancy. Whatever she was up to tickled.

Nancy looked at me like I'd farted in church. "You ticklish?"

"Afraid so."

She sighed and squeezed my left instep as if she was pulping a ripe orange. Punishment? I flinched. No more giggles.

"Sorry," she said in a sing-song I-have-to-say-this-but-I'm-not-a-bit-sorry tone. There went Nancy's tip.

When Miss Personality switched from pumicing to shaping my nails, I asked, "Worked here long?" A friendly, open-ended question.

"Four years."

"I'm new to the area. Did you grow up in Ardon County? Do you like it?"

She shrugged. "Lived here my whole life. Guess it's all right."

After her umpteenth curt, mumbled answer, I surrendered. She had no interest in anything except my feet and my wallet. While I felt grateful she wasn't as nosy as the woman at the front desk, I was frustrated. Not sure what I'd hoped to find out, but something beyond her willingness to invest in plastic body parts.

"What color you want?" She nodded at a display of polish bottles.

"That one." I pointed. "The pale pink."

Her look said, "You wuss. Why bother?"

She slid the promised foam throwaways on my feet. The pink "foam" wasn't exactly cushy, a might thicker than a human hair. Next she stuck neon green plastic dividers between my toes. My feet looked like they'd sprouted poisonous mini-mushrooms.

Nancy opened the polish. My pedicure was fast coming to an end. My questions had led nowhere. Wasn't there any topic that would loosen her tongue? Everybody likes food, right?

"What's your favorite restaurant?" I asked.

"Nothing fancier than meat-and-threes 'round these parts."

I already knew "meat-and-threes" referred to diners that offer a meat du jour—meatloaf, pork chops, fried chicken parts—plus three sides. Invariably the sides included spuds in several guises, cauliflower, and other vegetables that might have been healthy if they weren't awash in bacon grease.

Had to admit it. This visit was an intelligence-gathering bust. Time to take a chance. "Say, I heard there was a little excitement in Ardon this weekend. Didn't someone dig up an old skeleton?"

Nancy's brush slid right off my nail and painted a pink stripe across my big toe. Her eyes narrowed. "Why're you interested?"

"Just making conversation. Saw an article in the paper. Sounded like a good murder mystery."

She glared at me. "No mystery. That Hooker hussy shot her husband and buried him where she could keep an eye on the grave. The bitch is a murderer and a thief."

I bit the side of my mouth. *Keep cool.* After all, I'd baited her. This was what I'd wanted.

"A thief?" I asked. "What did she steal?"

"A farm that shoulda stayed in the Watson family. Then there was Jed's share of his granddaddy's timberland up in the mountains. After he was gone and couldn't say different, they claimed Jed sold it for a dollar right afore he disappeared. He told me he'd never sell land to that carpetbagger Kaiser. He may have pulled the wool over most folks' eyes, but not Jed's. The hussy must have forged Jed's signature and collected money from Kaiser under the table."

Hmmm. Who in Hades is Kaiser? Keep her talking. "Sounds like you know a lot about this Jed Watson. Was he kin?"

"By marriage."

She sighed; her eyes had a glazed faraway look. "Jed and I were engaged once. He was a real catch. College boy. Owned his own farm. Don't know how that Yankee cow seduced him."

I dug my nails into my palms to keep from slapping her. Nancy'd retreated into silence—a surly, put-upon silence.

"You say you're kin by marriage?" I prodded.

"Yeah. My husband, Eli, is Jed's cousin. Eli's all het up about the murder, says he'll make sure the Hooker broad pays this time."

"You think a jury will find her guilty?"

She shrugged. "Don't matter," she mumbled. "She'll pay." Nancy stood and commanded me to do the same. "The dryer's in the room across the hall."

I tried to walk with dignity. Wasn't going to happen. I squeezed my toes together in an attempt to keep the throwaways from sliding off. The flimsy soles had a mind of their own. When the front edge of the left floppy curled under, I almost head-butted the wall. Time to quit trying for poise. A duck could waddle with more class.

When I finally sat at the dryer station, she flipped a switch and air blew across my feet.

"I'll be back in a few," she said.

Mollye'd warned me about toenail drying time, so I'd brought my Kindle. I opened a recent download. When I reached the end of the second page, I had no idea what I'd read. My eyes roved over the words; my brain had other ideas. I gave in and let my mind churn while I stared into space.

Nancy reappeared, shut off the dryer, and led me to the front desk. I followed at my fastest duck waddle. A large sign on the desk claimed a twenty percent tip was customary. Nancy stayed glued to my side as I fumbled with my purse. A form of tip intimidation? It had less chance of working than an ice cube's chance in the Carolina sun. I opened my wallet, careful to keep my thumb over my driver's license.

"That'll be thirty-five dollars," Diana twittered. I fished out two twenties, well aware that Nancy Watson didn't expect me to ask for change.

The receptionist grabbed my money. "It's Bea Snooker, right? Should we add you to our email list? That way we can send you coupons."

Nancy Watson snagged my arm above the elbow and squeezed. "Snooker?" Her eyes narrowed. "Never heard that name before. Rhymes with Hooker."

Before I could blink, she snatched the wallet from my hand and stared at my driver's license. "You're a Hooker," she spat. "Don't know why I didn't see it. You look like that murdering witch did years back. You're kin, aren't you? Bet she sent you."

I grabbed my wallet, shoved it in my purse, and smiled at the front desk lackey who still held my twenties. "You owe me five dollars change."

Straw blonde's mouth opened in an imitation of a hooked bass. No sound came out.

I heard chatter. Another Hands On manicurist was escorting a client to the front door. Diana quickly threw five ones in my direction, probably hoping to avoid a scene. About the same odds of that happening as Eva taking a second helping of tofu.

"Think you're real cute, don't you?" Nancy hissed. "Waltzing in here. Pretending to be someone you aren't. Well, we'll see who has the last laugh."

Nancy trailed me outside, running through her entire vocabulary of curses. Wasn't like I could make a rapid escape with my toes divided by green mushrooms and foam floppies determined to veer off in odd directions. Straight ahead wasn't one of them. My slower-than-a-snail pace offered her the opportunity to insult my mother, both of my aunts, my intelligence, my virtue, and my dog.

It was all I could do to keep my mouth clamped shut. I was dying to let loose with a few curdling cheese curses but figured they'd go right through the holes in her Swiss cheese brain.

My mission hadn't quite gone as planned.

I gracelessly flopped into my car, locked my doors, and buckled my seatbelt before I dared to look at Nancy again. She leaned in, her nose pressed against the driver's side window. Her glare had the same hateful intensity as her axe-wielding hubby had when he rounded on me that morning. While Nancy lacked Eli's size, she shared his volatile disposition.

"Don't you dare come back here, bitch."

I put the car in reverse, smiled, and gave a jaunty wave as I backed up. Then I hauled butt like a Formula One racer.

FOURTEEN

I parked in front of my new log home and waved at Eva, who seemed to be taking out her frustration by beating the front porch with a stiff broom. She stopped when she spotted me with an armload of groceries.

"Need help?" She smiled.

"No, thanks, got it."

Had I not known better, her smile would have told me the broom therapy was working and everything was hunky-dory.

Eva checked her watch. "Better hustle. Not a lot of time before two hungry gents arrive on our doorstep. What are you cooking?"

Since Eva played it cool with no mention of the sheriff or search warrants, I did the same and rattled off my proposed menu. "Stuffed portabella mushrooms, asparagus-orange salad, spiced quinoa, and pumpkin brownies with coconut whipped cream. I had no time to bake bread, so I cheated. Bought a rosemary olive oil loaf at Dee's Bakery. I'll whip up pumpkin brownies first and get them in the oven."

En route to the kitchen, I peeked in Eva's bedroom. Neat and tidy. No sign of the sheriff's frenzied dump-every-drawer search. A frilly comforter I'd never seen covered my aunt's bed. Not her taste. And it didn't exactly coordinate with the rifle resting against her chest of drawers. Where had the gun and the box of shells on her pillow come from? Should I ask?

Later. If she didn't mention it first.

"I'll leave the kitchen to you," Aunt Eva said. "I set the table and straightened the cabin a bit. Now I have some dairy chores to finish. Yell if you can't find something. I'll be in the milking barn."

I hummed as I started cooking. I loved everything about my profession. The road from banker to chef wasn't exactly straight, but the rewards were awesome. I loved the colors and aromas. The textures and tastes. The chance to experiment. The immediate gratification when a perfectly browned entrée popped out of the oven.

Becoming a chef wasn't a lifelong dream. When I graduated high school, I planned to follow in Mom's footsteps, become a lawyer. Then I interned freshman summer with one of Mom's attorney friends. Ugh. Research in musty county court offices proved mind-numbing. Searches of online databases involved less sneezing but equal tedium. As a lawyer, I figured I'd spend more time pushing paper than interacting with people, especially people I actually liked. So I switched to a business major and wound up at a bank, doubling-down on ugh.

As a chef, I had a smidgeon more control. I wasn't forced to consort with dumb or vicious criminals, arrogant judges, or greedy developers.

Thinking about my stint as a legal intern and my years as a banker inspired me. I *did* know how to research, and I didn't mind tackling a project when I had a clear-cut mission, one that meant something to me. With all this talk of Eva "stealing" Watson land, I wanted facts.

Though it might have zip legal bearing, it would be nice to prove her ingenuity and hard work were the sole reasons for Udderly's profits. I bet I could prove Dad's contention that the farm had been next to bankrupt when she inherited it. It would help erase one murder motive. Tomorrow I'd search deeds and tax records at the Ardon County courthouse.

Mom was on my mind when she phoned. With the help of the County Solicitor, the sheriff had been forced to return Eva's address book and photo albums after copying items "of interest."

"He was fishing," Mom said. "I'm surprised the judge gave him so much latitude with the search warrant. Tell Eva I'll bring the returned items back tonight. Why don't your dad and I join you two for dinner? I can pick up a couple of pizzas, one vegan, of course."

"Uh, sorry but Andy and Paint are coming to dinner at seven thirty," I stammered. "You're welcome to join us. I'm sure we have enough food."

Mom chuckled. "No. We'll pass. Though I wouldn't mind seeing those young men compete to impress you. Should make for lively dinner conversation. How did you wind up with the two of them as dinner companions?"

I explained the overlapping invitations—me asking Paint, Eva inviting Andy. I didn't say why Paint visited my flea market booth. I also skipped any mention of my encounter with Nancy Watson and the appearance of a new gun in Eva's boudoir. No point compounding my parents' worries. They'd just insist once more that we pack up and move in with them. Pointless. Eva wouldn't budge.

"I'll be by for breakfast," Mom said. "Unless Eva tells me she needs something the sheriff carted off sooner."

Good. A chance to pick Mom's brain about my research project. She wouldn't object to a paper chase.

Paint arrived first with two bottles of wine, one Chardonnay, one Zinfandel. "Didn't know the menu so I brought white and red," he said. "Of course, my moonshine goes with everything, but I figured we'd save it for dessert."

Andy showed up five minutes later with his own dual wine supply.

"Guess I'd better find a wine opener." Eva chuckled. "Don't mean to insult either of you fine gentlemen, but this could be a spirited evening if we down all four bottles—one a piece."

My aunt checked on the charcoal grill out back and reported the coals were perfect. "I'll start the steaks. No point dillydallying. I'm starved. What's your pleasure boys—rare, medium rare, or ruined?"

Paint and Andy answered "rare" in unison. Their true preferences or my aunt's not-so-subtle nudge? Who knew?

When Eva exited to mind the steaks, I shooed our guests outdoors to keep her company. She greeted them with one of her favorite jokes.

"To a dedicated carnivore like me, there's nothing like the smell of meat sizzling on a grill," she began. "Always wonder if Brie's stomach starts to rumble whenever I mow the lawn."

Cheeses. I shook my head and closed the door, glad to have the small kitchen to myself as I plated my contributions and carried them to the table.

The dinner chatter started off light and teasing. Paint talked about the bearded dude he'd hired to play a moonshiner in a series of TV commercials. When the guy showed up for his audition in dirty bib overalls with what looked like sprigs of moss stuck in his whiskers,

Paint was sold.

Andy entertained with his tales of daring-do, diagnosing an ailing pet python—his first serpent patient. "Give me a goat or pig any day." He laughed. "It's hard to feel warm and fuzzy about reptiles."

No one mentioned skeletons, the sheriff, search warrants, or Eli Watson's threats. A perfect escapist evening until Andy commented on my car's early afternoon whereabouts.

"Brie, I saw your Prius parked in front of Hands On this afternoon."

"My Prius?" A stupid question, but I was stalling.

"Sure, nobody could miss your 'MeChef' license plate. You didn't run into Nancy Watson, did you? She works there."

Eva dropped her knife mid-slice. It clattered on her plate. She gave me her evil stink eye. "Do tell, Brie. What were you doing at Hands On? I've never seen you with a manicure, and I don't see one now. You knew that witch worked there. Mollye Camp told you."

Uh-oh. Caught pink toe-nailed. I shrugged. "No biggie. Got a pedicure. Very relaxing." Until Nancy figured out I was a Hooker.

Aunt Eva wasn't about to end her beady-eyed interrogation. "Did you speak with Nancy?"

"Uh, yes. She did my pedicure."

"And you just chatted about the Kardashian girls and traded recipes for cheese grits, right?" Eva sniped.

"If you must know, it was Lady Gaga and Pit Bull."

"Come on, give, girl. What happened?"

I sent a pleading look toward our male dining companions, hoping they might run interference. The cowards left me on my own.

"My toenails really needed—"

"Don't even."

"Nothing worth mentioning. I wanted a firsthand look at the woman. Wanted to see if she seemed capable of killing and burying a two-hundred-pound man all by her lonesome."

"And your conclusion?" Eva prodded.

"She has a hot temper and impressive, flinty strength for her size. I know Jed was murdered when she was decades younger, but she'd still have needed help putting him in the ground. She's no dimwit. On her own, it would have taken her hours to bury his corpse. Even at night, playing lone gravedigger would have been a risky proposition with your cabin so close."

"You're making a bad assumption," Eva said. "What if the cabin was empty, no one home? As soon as Jed took off on what would be his last fishing expedition, I hightailed it. Just wanted to get the hell away."

"Where'd you go?"

"Jed drove off in his truck, but I had my old Fairlane. I rounded up our hound dog, Butch. Back then we grew cotton, so I didn't have to worry about leaving any other animals. Didn't know when I'd come back—if I'd come back."

"How long were you gone?" Paint asked.

Eva closed her eyes and shook her head. "I didn't have more than a dollar or two. Stopped at a campground and slept in my car. Wasn't eager for anyone to see me, what with a black eye and a swollen jaw. I was only gone the one night and didn't speak to a soul. I was preoccupied, wondering the best way to go about divorcing Jed's sorry butt."

"Dang," I said. "That could have been an alibi."

She shrugged. "No one knows when Jed died, so there's no such thing as an alibi. He could have been killed the day he went fishing. Or the next day or a month later."

"Guess you're right," I agreed reluctantly. "It's not like testing decades' old bones can tell anyone precisely when they were buried."

Eva sighed. "We don't even know where he died. Maybe he tussled with his killer on the farm. Or maybe he was murdered on the river and his killer carted his body back here."

Since the topic of Jed's murder had been broached, I filled Paint and Andy in on the sheriff's search of Udderly property.

"They took your shotgun, Eva?" Andy asked, alarm evident in his voice. "What if Mark decides to visit tonight?"

My pulse skyrocketed. "Mark?" Alarm made my voice go up an octave.

Eva laughed.

Then I remembered. "Oh, right, Mark's that wily old coyote."

My aunt nodded. "Yep. He haunts the creek along the edge of our property. Lilly named the critter Mark after the umpteenth time she heard me swear, 'Mark my words, that coyote's dead.' In the past two years, he's cost us four goats and one beautiful guard dog."

We were seated boy-girl at the small dining table. Eva patted Andy's hand. "Don't you worry. Miss Brie wasn't the only one to go on an afternoon walkabout. I stopped by a pawnshop. Got me a new—well, new to me—rifle, Ranch, Mini-14, stainless steel with a wooden stock, two twenty-round magazines and a fifty-round box of .223 shells. I can deliver twenty rounds as fast as I can pull the trigger. I'm ready for Mark or any two-legged critter that comes prowling 'round here."

"Sure you don't want me to spend the night?" Paint asked. "Be glad to sleep on the couch. I doubt Eli will bother you, but seeing my truck here would give him pause."

"What?" Andy exclaimed. "Did Eli Watson threaten you?"

I gave a short replay of my flea market adventures.

Andy shook his head. "That is one sorry specimen. Eli keeps a pit bull chained in his yard. Dog's hooked with a logging chain. Sheet of plywood for shelter. No water half the time. Keeps just enough weight on the animal to keep the Humane Society off his case. Not a blade of grass left from that poor animal's frustrated prowling. Damn, I wish South Carolina would make it illegal to chain dogs, but I don't have a lot of hope."

Since we were well into the murder topic, I figured I might as well do some fishing of my own.

"You two grew up here." I looked at Andy, then turned to Paint. "That gives you both a leg up on knowing Ardon County bad seeds—male and female. Who would you nominate as Jed's killer?"

Eva smiled. "Feel free to name anyone but me, boys."

Andy glanced at Paint, who nodded. "Sure, we've talked about it. Asked our dads what they thought. Consensus is the killer was either some pissed-off Watson kin, one of the buddies Jed boozed, gambled and whored with, or a jilted hussy he made promises to with no intention of keeping a one of them." He stopped, bit his lip, and looked down. "Pardon me, Eva."

"No pardon needed, Andy. I found out what Jed did, who he really was, a few months after I married him. A few months too late."

"Any hussies—besides Nancy—would have the same problems with body disposal," I said. "Who were Jed's boozing buddies?"

"Dad only remembers two of them," Paint said. "One is Bubba Deacon. He's serving a thirty-year stretch in Broad River prison for felony murder. Store clerk got killed in the shoot-out. Then there's Aaron West. He's a deputy, probably tagged along with Sheriff Jones when he searched your place today. Skinny, balding, crooked teeth. See him?"

I was about to answer when flashes of blue light painted the window beside our table. Crap. Had to be the sheriff or his flunkies. Why was he back?

Eva left the table and opened the front door before Sheriff Jones finished stomping up the stairs. The scrawny guy standing behind him fit Paint's description of Deputy West, though he hadn't mentioned how scary those crooked yellow teeth looked when the man bit his lip.

Paint, Andy, and I took up positions flanking my aunt. We weren't about to let the lawmen bully her.

Sheriff Jones pushed in. "I need to speak to Brie Hooker."

Huh? I swallowed. What could the sheriff want with me? That third glass of wine—one beyond my usual limit—suddenly felt warm and accusing in my stomach. I felt a tad tipsy and light-headed.

"Come in," Eva said. "State your business and let's get this over with."

The sheriff stared at me. "You're Brie Hooker, right? You need to answer some questions. Where were you this afternoon?"

"Why is it any of your business?" Andy jumped in.

"She doesn't have to answer," Paint added. "You know, the right to remain silent and all."

I appreciated the moral support, but I had nothing to hide. My guess was Nancy Watson had concocted some phony baloney story that I'd threatened her. Might as well answer his stupid questions and get the jerk out of Eva's hair.

I took a deep breath and straightened my shoulders. "I had an uneventful afternoon, Sheriff. I left Udderly about two thirty and drove to the Hands On salon for a pedicure. A three o'clock appointment. Afterward, I shopped for groceries at Publix in Clemson and stopped at Dee's Bakery for a loaf of bread. I arrived back on the farm about six."

"The Hands On receptionist says you gave a fake name. Pretended to be someone else. Why?"

Spam in a Can. "No harm, no foul. Just didn't want to stir up unnecessary trouble. I'd heard Nancy wasn't on the best of terms with Eva, and I saw no reason to announce I was kin."

"But she found out, didn't she? You had a heated argument with Nancy Watson outside Hands On."

I shrugged. "Not exactly an argument. Mrs. Watson did all the yelling. I just listened. Why?"

I hazarded a glance at the deputy, wondering if his expression would give me any clues. Deputy Snaggletooth was staring at my boobs.

"Nancy Watson is dead. Poisoned by the look of it. Autopsy will give us a definite answer. I hear tell your father, Howard Hooker, keeps some fancy garden on this farm, one filled with poisonous plants. Is that true?"

My mouth gaped open like a steamed clam. I couldn't quite get enough oxygen. Mom's words of wisdom swirled through my brain— "only idiots talk to police without a lawyer and help dig their own graves." I felt the shovel in my hands.

I'd shut my trap. Not another word.

Eva stepped between Sheriff Jones and me. Ramrod straight, she looked ready to sock him. "Sheriff, my niece has nothing to do with whatever happened to that trash. Sounds like you're leaping to mighty stupid conclusions. The floozy probably overdosed. Wouldn't doubt she did drugs. You should leave. Now. Any more questions, contact our lawyer, Iris Hooker."

Thank you, Aunt Eva—though it might have been better if she hadn't called the deceased a floozy and the sheriff stupid. Too bad I couldn't manage to suck in enough air to tell off Jones myself.

The sheriff's smile chilled me. "We'll be in touch with Miss Hooker's lawyer," he drawled. His eyes narrowed as he attempted to stare down my aunt. "I was about to ask your whereabouts this afternoon. But I have the feeling you won't answer. You'll hide behind your mouthpiece, too. Believe me, you'll both answer eventually. Answer for everything."

Deputy West trailed the sheriff. He glanced back over his shoulder long enough for his creepy gaze to rove over my body. His lips curled back imprinting the sorry image of his crisscrossed choppers on my brain. Eva slammed the door. Relief.

My aunt sank into the nearest chair. "Aren't you boys glad you stayed for the floor show? Normally, we charge extra for the entertainment, and it doesn't start until after dessert's served. You made dessert, right, Brie?" Trembling hands betrayed her brave words.

If Aunt Eva could pretend she was fearless, so could I. "Pumpkin brownies coming up," I said. "Who wants coffee?"

As if any of us would need caffeine to stay awake tonight.

Who killed Nancy Watson? And why?

Tomorrow I'd quiz Eva, try to find out more about Jed's possible enemies.

FIFTEEN

I woke up strangling my pillow, my sheets wound around my legs tighter than a mummy's shroud. A bad night tossing and turning. My room was blacker than dark chocolate. Could it really be morning? The alarm's insistent buzz said it didn't matter. I had to get out of bed.

A long day ahead, and Eva needed help.

A stiff wind rattled the cabin's windows. A strong incentive to slip on jeans, wool socks, a heavy sweater, and a down jacket. It might be spring, but it would be hours before any of the farm's breathing occupants saw forty degrees.

I peeked in Eva's bedroom. Empty. Already up and at 'em. Did she ever sleep in? Foregoing a much needed mug of coffee, I forced myself to hustle to the milking barn where Orville and Frank, the Clemson Ag part-timers, greeted me.

Frank grinned. "Your aunt's playing midwife at the horse barn."

The horse barn sat catty-corner to the milking barn and housed Eva's horse and Lilly's mule. Unfortunately, Mollye's Shetland ponies had long since gone to their ultimate green pastures, and my aunts had quit boarding horses as their goat herd grew. That meant the two remaining equines often had a Noah's ark collection of roommates in need of temporary housing. Newborn critters and their mamas got first shot at the barn condo. Pushing hard on the warped barn door, I almost toppled when it gave way.

Eva knelt beside a bleating black nanny.

"How many?" I asked.

"Two." Eva's grin stretched ear to ear. "Come meet them."

One kid was already swaddled in a colorful wrapper Eva'd knit last winter. Her creations were unique. Her motto: "Goats don't care if the colors clash."

Baby number two was still wet; the afterbirth glop washed away. Eva was warming the newborn with a hair dryer to get its blood circulating.

Watching the kids' first attempts to stand on toothpick legs made me giggle. But assisting with the messier aspects of birth—yuck. Too bad babies weren't actually delivered by storks.

If I ever had babes of my own, I planned to be in a hospital, suitably drugged, with a masked-and-gloved stranger standing by for cleanup. I'm not big on pain and have a weak stomach. Maybe I'd never have kids. Hey, I hadn't even found a candidate for Daddy.

I knelt beside Eva. "They're sweet, perfect. What can I do?"

"Not much left to do here." Focused entirely on the baby, Eva barely spared me a glance. "Go see if Orville and Frank need help with any chores."

Their jobs on Udderly's crack-of-dawn milking shift included cleaning the goats' undersides, monitoring the automated milking machines, and sterilizing equipment. Udderly's Border collies herded the does in batches for milking. As I approached, two collies darted in and out of the scattered goats, encouraging dawdling does to head to milking stalls.

Dawn had painted the thin scattering of clouds in brilliant pinks and oranges. It looked like the beginning of a clear, beautiful day—well, except for the fact that I was now a murder suspect. No matter how lovely the weather, I wondered if a tornado loomed just over the mountain peaks. Couldn't shake my sense of dread.

Frank looked up as I approached. "How's our new mama?"

"Just fine. Two healthy babes. Would you or Orville like some help?"

"I'm fine. How about helping Orville with his egg treasure hunt?"

"Will do." I smiled though I'd have preferred a toasty warm, indoor assignment.

Our free-range feathered menagerie included a pair of peacocks, a few Muscovy ducks, a rooster, and a flock of egg-laying hens. The females were far more devious than the Easter Bunny in hiding eggs. The irony of wandering through hoar frost foraging for eggs I wouldn't eat wasn't lost on this vegan.

An hour later, I held a mug of hot coffee against my frozen cheek.

Once feeling returned to my face—my nether cheeks were on their own—I started whipping up a batch of egg-free banana and coconut cream batter for French toast. The bread sizzled in coconut oil while I crisped bacon in a separate pan for the meat eaters. Everyone but me.

Gravel skittering in the drive announced my folks' arrival. I'd phoned them last night, describing Sheriff Jones' accusations and threats. Dad was apoplectic that anyone could consider his only daughter a murder suspect. I'd rarely heard him cuss before. He put words together with great creativity. Mom, who couldn't abide foul language, didn't even scold him. Maybe I should share some of my cheesy options with Dad. I had the feeling there'd be plenty more occasions to cuss in the days ahead.

Mom barreled into the cabin without knocking. Her embrace squeezed the breath out of me. Then Dad tagged in with a crushing papa bear hug.

"Oh, Honey, I can't believe that dipwad sheriff questioned you like a common criminal," Dad began.

Mom nodded. "I might have given Sheriff Jones a pass for doing his job, if he hadn't said you and Eva would answer for your sins. He has an agenda, and finding the truth isn't on it. But, Brie, you didn't help matters, traipsing off to Hands On and pretending you were someone else. What were you thinking?"

The expected rebuke still stung. "Yep, in hindsight that appears lame. Of course, I never expected Nancy to drop dead."

Eva joined the group and shared in a round of hugs before breaking free. "Let's eat, I'm starved. We can talk over breakfast."

Turned out, Mom had practically worn out her speed dial calling in favors. One of the EMS responders she knew gave her a blow-by-blow of the futile efforts to revive Nancy Watson.

"They got to Hands On about four fifteen," Mom said, "responding to a call from a receptionist who claimed Watson was foaming at the mouth when she staggered to the front desk and collapsed. Even though EMS got there in under five minutes, CPR was a no go. She was already dead."

My hand flew to my mouth. "Holy Swiss cheese. No wonder the sheriff came calling. At four o'clock, Nancy was screaming at me in front of the store. If I didn't know better, I'd suspect me."

Though Mom had tapped another source to get the eventual lowdown on the autopsy, she had no clout with the Ardon County Sheriff's Department. Her inability to sniff out details of the homicide investigation frustrated her.

"Poisoning seems to be the likely cause of death," she said.

Dad's headshake said he disagreed. "Even the fastest acting poisons—at least ones folks in Ardon County might lay hands on—take a lot longer than thirty minutes to kill someone. It would take hours, more likely days, before any of the poisonous plants I grow could kill off a healthy adult."

"Well, thank heaven for that," Mom said. "Once the contents of Nancy's stomach are analyzed, it should put an end to this nonsense about Brie poisoning Nancy with goodies from your garden. I'll bet the woman ingested one of those new synthetic drugs. Lots of options. The EMS guys bagged what looked like brownie crumbs in the break room. The drug might have been baked into a treat."

"Wouldn't that still make Brie a suspect?" Dad asked.

"What?" My mouth dropped open. "You think being a chef makes me a suspect? Even ten-year-olds can bake brownies."

"No, Honey," Mom answered. "You're a suspect because you were the next to last person to see Nancy alive, and you could have brought in a drug-laced treat."

I rolled my eyes. "Like that woman would have scarfed down anything I brought her."

Dad's fingers drummed the tabletop. "You lied about your name. The sheriff can argue Nancy ate your treat because she didn't know you were a Hooker. He'll probably claim you can access designer drugs through your Asheville pals. In these parts, Asheville's practically synonymous with Sodom and Gomorrah."

"So when can I expect my arrest?"

"Don't worry." Mom's tone sounded like she was trying to talk a potential suicide down from a ledge. "There's no actual evidence and no motive. Why would you kill Nancy Watson?"

Eva jumped in. "It's about time someone asked that. Who would want to kill Nancy Watson? She's a nobody. The sheriff will probably put the floozy on my enemies' list for sleeping with my husband. Really? If I'd wanted revenge, she'd have been planted six feet under decades ago."

Dad tapped his spoon against his coffee cup. He appeared deep in thought. "There must be some tie between the discovery of Jed's skeleton and Nancy's murder. The timing can't be coincidental."

"I agree," Eva said. "Maybe Nancy knew who really killed Jed, and the murderer thought she'd rat him out. Or she killed Jed and her accomplice figured she'd squeal. Same motive."

"I like it," Dad said.

I sighed. "Wish I shared your enthusiasm since it drops me from the suspect list. But unless Nancy was one heck of an actress, she truly believed Eva killed Jed."

"No point speculating until we get the toxicology results." Mom shrugged and turned toward Eva. "I brought back your photo album. Sheriff Jones copied a lot of old pictures, especially ones with names or notes on the back. He didn't put the photos back in the albums. You might sort through and see if you can figure out why he'd be interested in a bunch of old photos."

We'd progressed from Nancy's death to the sheriff's efforts to nail Aunt Eva for Jed's murder. Seemed a good time to ask Eva some questions and share my research plans. I figured not even my overprotective mom could see any harm in my digging through Ardon County deeds, tax, and court records.

"Eva, what did you think when Jed disappeared? Did you believe he was dead?" I asked.

My aunt tilted her head back. Her eyes closed. "After about a week I knew he was dead. It was more than a feeling."

She massaged her forehead, then opened her eyes. "I searched his things and found a strong box. Used bolt cutters to open it. Four hundred dollars inside—most likely poker winnings he hadn't had time to lose again. Jed would never have abandoned so much cash voluntarily."

"Did you suspect murder?" I was curious.

Eva shrugged. "I thought it possible. I knew he kept unsavory company, but I never met any of his gambling buddies. Jed thought his wife's duty was to cook, clean, serve as a punching bag, and never, ever question him."

Dad frowned. "I always wondered. Given you'd been so miserable here, why didn't you just come home to Iowa? Why stay?"

Eva slowly shook her head. "I used that four hundred dollars to pay back taxes and get the farm out of foreclosure. I always loved this land. It's beautiful, peaceful. I'd made a few women friends—Mollye's mom for one. They suggested I could board horses and raise goats to make ends meet. When Lilly arrived to help, a happier future seemed possible." A few tears meandered down Eva's cheeks. She briskly swatted them away. "Enough talk about the past."

"Okay," I agreed. "But I plan to spend some time at the courthouse, see what information I can dig up. As a former banker, I know old records sometimes spill forgotten secrets."

"Try to avoid lying about who you are, Brie," Mom chastised. "That will always get you in trouble."

"Lesson learned the hard way. If asked, I will promptly identify myself as Brie Hooker, overall nice person, non-killer, and amateur snoop."

SIXTEEN

I was clearing the breakfast dishes when Mollye phoned with a lunch invitation. Faster than speeding Facebook, the small town grapevine had alerted her that Nancy Watson's death coincided with my rash visit to Hands On. Heck, she probably knew what I'd worn and how much change I'd had in my pocket.

"I want to hear all the details, girlfriend," Mollye chirped.

I'd willingly dish about my pink toenails and Nancy's angry outburst in exchange for Mollye's insider intel. Surely she'd have the hometown down-and-dirty on scandals present and past.

"Can we meet at one?" I figured my aunt's plans for our morning would keep me busy past noon.

"Works for me. How about Abby's Diner just down the block from the courthouse?"

"Excellent." That fit my plans perfectly.

After I hung up, I struggled to turn my thoughts away from dead bodies and impending incarceration to concentrate on Udderly revenue and expenses. Aunt Eva loathed pencil-pushing endeavors. The computer age expanded her hatred to all things electronic. She'd rather muck stalls or coax a mule into taking a pill the size of Nebraska than sit in front of a computer monitor. Since I had an MBA and banking experience, she jumped at the chance to put me in charge of anything related to computers, accounting, and banking—tasks that were once Lilly's exclusive domains.

I soon discovered the breadth of Lilly's responsibilities. She filled online orders, maintained Udderly's website, and registered newborn goats with breeder organizations. Who knew the hairy little kids had birth certificates as well as ear or tail tattoos for lifetime positive IDs? Next thing you know some well-meaning politician will decide we should tattoo human kiddos, too.

Eva plopped down beside me and spieled off a list of wholesale accounts longer than my ingredient list for vegetarian paella. A four-hundred goat herd spawned a ton of paperwork. Looked like I'd be spending hours superglued to the computer. Realizing those hours wouldn't be spent cleaning goat udders was a definite mood lifter.

I was no animal whisperer. On prior Udderly visits, I'd learned goats, ponies, dogs, chickens, pigs, and the rest of the barnyard menagerie were less likely than humans to do what I asked. Sometimes they even punctuated their refusals with head butts, kicks, drool, and snorts. Bottom line: my new duties felt like a major promotion.

At noon, Eva closed a large wholesale order book and massaged the back of her neck, "I've had all I can take for one day."

"Agreed. My eyes are crossing."

I helped corral the papers scattered across the table and logged off my laptop, which now served as a repository for QuickBooks and Udderly's accounting files.

"I'm glad you're tackling this." The dismissive sweep of Eva's hand included every scrap of paper on the table. "Bores me to tears. Computers hate me. With me at the keyboard, what Sis called 'The Blue Screen of Death' had more lives than a barnyard cat."

I smiled. "No problem. Lilly backed up to the hard drive and the cloud. I'll do the same. The Udderly website is really clever. Did Lilly design it?"

Eva's eyes glistened. "Yes. It was her baby." These days as she wrestled with grief, her tears always seemed to lurk, waiting for another trigger.

"I want to leave all the photos of Lilly on the web," she added. "I love that video of her playing with last year's batch of kids."

"No problem. Lilly did a fantastic job," I agreed. "Anything you need from town?"

My aunt shook her head. "I'm heading to town, too. Since we're both bound for the big city, let's stop by First Bank of Ardon and get you listed on Udderly's bank accounts. Should only take a minute or two."

*   *   *

Eva and I parked side by side in Ardon's town square. The county courthouse sat on an expansive green boxed in by four busy commercial streets. Buildings included Ardon's mainstay banks, a sprinkling of retail shops, an eclectic mix of restaurants, the offices of long-standing societies like the Daughters of the Confederacy and the Masonic Lodge, plus the offices of lawyers eager to be within walking distance of a revenue source.

Eva ushered me inside Udderly's bank and led me toward a windowed corner with "Office of the President" etched on the open door's glass panel. Inside I spotted a roly-poly bald guy hunched over an old-timey mahogany desk. I presumed baldy was the bank president. The secretary's desk guarding his office sat empty, leaving him easy prey for unhappy depositors.

Eva rapped on the doorframe. "Hello, Victor. Have a minute?"

He peered over half glasses parked on the end of an oily nose. His rheumy eyes looked almost colorless. He blinked rapidly as Eva marched in. I followed in her determined wake.

"What can I do for you, Miss Hooker?"

The way he said "Miss Hooker" sounded just shy of hostile. My aunt introduced me, punctuating his full name, Victor Caldwell. At least he wasn't a Watson, unless he was related to the enemy camp by marriage. Half the county's population seemed to be.

"I want to add my niece's name to Udderly's corporate accounts and give her full authority without a counter signature," Eva said.

Victor pushed up his glasses and licked his lips. His expression reminded me of someone caught farting in an elevator. Why did he look so guilty?

"Something wrong?" Eva asked.

Two open files sat on his leather-bound ink blotter. When I glanced at them, he quickly snapped both closed and shoved one under the other. Despite his shell game, I read the tab on the bottom file— "Burks Holdings"—before he hid it. His pudgy fingers scampered to cover the top file's tab, but he wasn't quick enough. A neatly typed label announced the thick bundle of papers belonged to Udderly Kidding Dairy.

Why was Udderly's file open on his desk?

"Well, aren't you efficient?" Eva asked. "I see you already have our corporate folder on your desk. Were you expecting us?"

Apparently she shared my suspicion that the file's appearance wasn't coincidence. Eva hadn't told Victor we were coming.

The banker's lips twitched. "Uh, no, well, uh, I had an inquiry about your account."

"Do tell." My aunt's tone could form frost on a mug of hot tea. "Do you routinely give out our banking information without our authorization?"

"Certainly not," Victor huffed. "But we cooperate with the authorities."

"Let me guess," Eva continued, "Sheriff Jones wanted copies of all our banking records?"

Victor straightened. "I don't believe I should answer."

"Well, I don't believe Udderly Kidding Dairy should bank here," she replied.

Victor sputtered. "We're only following standard practices."

"Of course, you are." Eva's volume hitched up a notch. "Which makes me wonder if your standard practices are legal."

A middle-aged frump in a boxy suit rapped her knuckles on the doorframe. Her eyes were wide, her lips puckered in a disapproving moue. Had to be Victor's pit bull secretary. I wondered if the lady was huffy because Eva's loud complaint had aroused the curiosity of several customers in the teller lines.

"Can I be of help?" the frump asked.

"You betcha." Eva turned her back on Victor. "Please provide us with the necessary documents to give my niece full access to our corporate accounts. I'd also like whatever paperwork we need to close all our accounts in the near future."

Though the secretary's eyebrows shot up, she simply nodded. "This way, please. I can print what you need at my desk."

The banker stood but remained mute. Neither he nor Eva muttered a goodbye.

Ten minutes later I'd put my John Hancock on five multi-page documents. As a former banker, I knew the gist of the cover-your-ass wording, so I didn't need to read the small font boilerplate. We left the bank with copies of the forms and the raft of paperwork required to close or transfer our accounts. Eva didn't speak until we reached the sidewalk.

"I wanted to deck that pompous windbag," she grumbled. "Never trusted him. Every time I phoned, I could tell I was on speakerphone. What kind of idiot banker is too lazy to lift a phone to his ear so people won't overhear his client's business? Think I'll sic your mother on him. Bet he gave the sheriff our banking records without any court order."

"You're right, and I agree about moving the banking business. But could we wait to switch banks until I figure out how Lilly set up the accounts? I don't want to create any problems with direct deposits or automatic payments."

Eva sighed. "Good thinking. Another reason I'm lucky you're handling the finances. I'm just angry. My whole life suddenly seems to be everyone else's affair."

"Did you notice that other file on Victor's desk?" I asked. "He had the Udderly file and another one sitting next to it like he was doing some sort of comparison. Do you do business with Burks Holdings?"

"Burks Holdings? Ha. Not hardly. That's the company developing Sunrise Ridge, a hoity-toity mountain resort. Cheapest homes start at a million. Heard a real estate agent say the last Sunrise house sold for ten mil. A lot of locals aren't thrilled with the development, but I'll hold my nose if they want to place an order for a few thousand dollars' worth of goat cheese."

I shrugged. "Maybe it was a coincidence Victor had both folders out. But it sure looked like his beady little eyes were darting back and forth between the two when we walked in. If I have time this afternoon, I'll look up Burks Holdings. If it's an LLC or a C corporation, it has to be registered."

"Glad you know how to dig out information." Eva hugged me. "But don't spend all your time inhaling dust mites in the courthouse basement. Have some fun with Mollye. I'll see you back at the farm."

My aunt climbed into her truck and waved goodbye.

I couldn't wait to hear Mom's take on the sheriff snooping into Udderly's bank records. Were legal niceties like court orders overlooked in tiny burgs with pretty town squares?

SEVENTEEN

I spotted Mollye's purple-streaked hair the minute I entered the diner. To make sure I saw her, she waved her arms like she was guiding a jumbo airliner to its gate. The bracelets circling her pudgy arms jangled like muted cymbals. Her jolly welcome made me grin.

"Hey, girlfriend," Mollye greeted as I slid into a seat across from her. "Hope you can find something you like on the menu."

"No problem. I've been here with Aunt Eva. The vegetarian hoagie is great, and it's served on ciabatta bread, a vegan favorite. I just ask them to hold the cheese."

Mollye shook her head. "Don't know how you do it. I could probably give up meat with the help of a good twelve-step program, but cheese and ice cream? Never."

I had to laugh. "I only needed eleven steps. Luckily, I've found tasty substitutes like cashew and almond blends that work in almost any recipe calling for cheese."

A waitress decked out in retro white-apron attire came to take our order.

"Hi, Madge." Mollye smiled. "Did your mom like that pottery bowl you bought for her birthday?"

"Sure did," the waitress answered.

"Madge, this is my friend Brie. Just moved here. I'll let her order first." Mollye chuckled. "She's vegan, and just thinking about going cheese-less made me crave something loaded with it. I need to consider my options."

I ordered my veggie delight. Mollye opted for a burger topped with melted pimento cheese.

As soon as Madge bustled away, my friend leaned across the table. "So give. What the heck happened at Hands On?"

Was Mollye trying to whisper? She managed to lower the pitch, but even dialed-down, her booming voice caused folks two tables away to jerk their heads in our direction like startled deer.

"Did that twit Diana at the front desk ask how come I recommended Hands On?" Mollye asked. "My *endorsement* must have surprised the heck out of them. Mom and Nancy are long-time foes. Not a chance I'd give Hands On any of my hard-earned nickels."

I assured Mollye her referral never came up.

"What *did* happen?" she prodded.

As I gave a blow-by-blow of Nancy's useless answers, I suddenly recalled the deceased's comment about Jed signing away his rights to timberland and asked Mollye if she knew anything about it.

Her eyebrows scrunched. "Hmm, I do seem to recall something about old man Watson, Jed's granddaddy, owning timberland. I'll ask Mom what she remembers." She paused. "So tell me about the screaming match. The most popular version is a full-blown cat fight with bite marks and snatched hair."

"Ye gods, not even close. True, there was a bit of screaming, but Nancy performed solo. I just gave a queenly wave as I backed out of the parking lot." I raised my hand to demonstrate my most regal wave.

"Ooh, that must have pissed her off good." Mollye giggled.

"Sounds like you two are having fun." Madge plopped down our orders. "Want to share the joke?"

My laughter died as I realized I was being a jerkwad, laughing at the expense of someone now on ice in the county morgue.

"You kinda had to be there," Mollye answered.

Once Madge took off, our conversation took a backseat to chowing down until Andy walked in and spotted us.

"Hey, can I join you?" he asked.

"Sure thing, handsome." Mollye scooted to the far side of the booth and patted the empty space beside her. As soon as the lanky veterinarian slid in, she leaned over and sniffed his jacket. "Peeuww. Maybe I should'a said no. You kinda smell like a barnyard."

Andy grinned. "Yeah, I think my ex-wife listed cruelty to her olfactory senses as one of her many reasons for divorcing me."

Ex-wife? Breaking news. Would have to ask Mollye for the lowdown.

"Well, it's about time you started dating again," Mollye said. "What's it been—a year?"

Andy laughed. "You offering to fix me up? About the only time I meet young ladies is when I'm neutering their pets or sending them to doggie heaven. Not the best time to ask for a date. My truck smells like wet dog. There's so much animal hair stuck to the seats they look like they have fur covers. What woman in her right mind wants to ride to dinner in that?"

"Me, me." Mollye bounced up and down and waved her arms. "Oh, don't get that petrified look. I'm kidding. You're not my type. Too sweet. But you might have a shot at Brie here."

I felt the flush climb my neck and head straight to my cheeks. Did everyone think I needed to be set up?

"How about it?" Andy coaxed. "We both need to eat. And who wants to go to a restaurant alone? Since you're vegan, I went online to see if there were any places around here that served vegetarian meals. To my surprise, I found one that even claims to be vegan friendly."

"Good to know." Andy really was a sweetheart.

"Do you like Indian cuisine? A restaurant called Swad serves vegetarian and vegan dishes. Online reviews say the place isn't fancy, but the food's great. Can I take you there?"

"You were suckered," I said. "Don't let Mollye bully you into taking me to dinner."

"Believe me, Mollye, bless her devious heart, has no powers of persuasion over me. Join me for supper. I'd hate to think I wasted all that research. I even promise to vacuum my truck."

Mollye chuckled. "Andy's definitely smitten. Don't think that truck's ever been cleaned on the inside."

"Cut it out, Mollye." I met Andy's gaze. Yep, he was talking friends, but I thought I detected a hint of interest in something more. Still, as Andy pointed out, we both needed to eat, and it would be kinda nice to spend an evening with a considerate male.

I smiled at Andy. "I'd love to have dinner with you. But things are a bit," I paused to search for the right word, "unsettled at the moment. You might need to bail me out of jail first."

His grin faltered. "Don't worry. Sheriff Jones is just hassling you because you're Eva's niece. Nobody thinks you killed Nancy. This will blow over. Fast. If I had to nominate a murderer, I'd put my money on Eli, Nancy's husband. They had plenty of public knockdown drag-out screaming matches."

I shook my head. "The leading theory has Nancy eating a brownie laced with ingredients you can't find in Publix. Eli hardly seems the baking type."

Andy shrugged. "True. That man's more likely to brain someone with a two-by-four than whip up a batch of poisoned baked goods, but he knows people. Hangs out at that Hog Heaven biker bar. All kinds of drug deals go down there."

Mollye put the back of her hand to her forehead like a swooning Southern belle. "Why Andy, I'm shocked. An innocent like you knowing about Hog Heaven."

Andy laughed. "I'm not that innocent. Hey, I'm a divorcé; I know stuff. But you're right. I don't hang at Hog Heaven. Unfortunately, I treat dogs that get into their owners' stashes. Not pretty." He turned his attention to me. "Brie, it's been a long time since I had a chance to take a pretty lady out to supper. Not about to give up when I hear a maybe. It'll take about an hour to get to Greenville. How about I pick you up at five thirty tomorrow? If old Sheriff Jones carts you away in handcuffs, make me your one call. I'll bail you out, and we can leave from jail."

I laughed. "It's a deal."

How could I say no to that grin and those twinkling green eyes? Andy was a charmer, and by all accounts, a good guy. Wonder what happened to his marriage.

Madge stopped by the table. "Here's your takeout, Andy."

"Are you a mind reader or what?" Mollye asked. "Never heard Andy place an order."

The waitress scrunched her face and closed her eyes in mock concentration. "I'm seeing tuna on rye, chips, and sweet tea." She opened her eyes. "Wait. That's the same as yesterday, the day before, and last week. Same takeout every day."

"I appreciate a man who finds something he likes and sticks with it," Mollye said.

Andy's emerald eyes focused on me. "I know what I like, and I'm faithful to my favorites, tuna included."

Had someone bumped up the heat in the restaurant?

"Gotta go," Andy said. "A horse named Kicka is waiting for me. Her owner watched a lot of *My Friend Flicka* reruns, but decided the feisty mare's name should warn folks to stay clear of her backside. See you tomorrow night, Brie."

As soon as he was out the door, Mollye winked at me. "You lucky devil. I wouldn't mind a few fur balls sticking to my behind if it meant I got to cuddle with that hunk."

"Hey, I thought you said Andy wasn't your type."

Mollye shrugged. "Not long term. But he'd do for a night. Or two. Well, maybe a week or three. Imagine he's seen randy studs mount plenty of mares. Bet there's real animal passion simmering beneath that sweet-tea exterior. Hoo-ha."

I laughed. Couldn't help it. Mollye had a gift for taking my mind off murder. At least for a time.

"What's the story on Andy's divorce?"

Mollye rolled her eyes. "Andy met the witch online. He wanted to settle down, have kids. But starting a veterinarian practice kept him too busy to even date. The woman proved a terrific pen pal. Said all the right things. Too bad she thought anyone with 'Dr.' in front of his name meant his wife would lead a life of leisure, shopping her only duty. The reality of Ardon County, sharing a home with sick animals and dog hair everywhere, wasn't what she had in mind. I say good riddance, but the experience has made Andy gun shy."

After we paid our bills and stepped outside, Mollye leaned in to whisper in my ear. "I'll see if I can coax some information out of Danny McCoy. He's a deputy, but he's a sweetie. Not a mean bone in his body."

"I think I met him," I said. "Reminded me of a puppy. Big feet."

Mollye chuckled. "Yeah, and at least in Danny's case what they say about big feet is true. And like a puppy, he likes to lick everything." My friend's eyebrows bounced up and down as if they were doing an Irish jig.

I smiled as she waved goodbye and hurried off to her woo-woo store, which I promised to visit soon. Maybe Mollye could get us a little insider info from the Sheriff's Office courtesy of Deputy Licks.

I headed to the courthouse. After two hours, I'd accumulated twenty dollars' worth of prints of old microfilmed documents. Wasn't sure I'd copied anything of value, but I planned to sift for treasure. My homework included deeds, foreclosures, land sales, and transfers, Burks Holdings' incorporation documents, and old newspaper accounts of Jed's disappearance.

As I exited the courthouse, Deputy Aaron West brushed past. "Mornin', ma'am." His breath reeked of onions. Must be hell flossing between those teeth.

"Whatcha doin' here?" The saggy skin on his forehead bunched as he frowned.

I paused long enough to meet his gaze, wanting to make it clear none of the sheriff's minions intimidated me. I kept walking, didn't answer. Would he turn? Follow me to my car? My heart rate be-bopped up a notch. Did I hear footsteps?

I didn't glance back until I reached my car door. The deputy was nowhere in sight. I didn't realize I'd been holding my breath until the air whooshed out of my lungs in a relieved huff.

A leather-clad biker rumbled past, swerving so close the heat from his Harley threatened to raise welts on my legs. Someone else hoping to frighten me?

I caught myself before giving the biker a middle-digit salute. My disastrous visit to Hands On had temporarily cured me of spontaneous gestures.

After opening the driver's side door and tossing my pile of papers onto the passenger seat, I started the engine. In the distance, Harley Leather-Britches' tires squealed as he zoomed away from the town square.

Was this a sign? Were the answers I needed in the documents I'd collected, or could they be waiting for me at a biker bar?

EIGHTEEN

I took a detour on my way home for a short visit to Summer Place. I pulled into the driveway and stared at the lovely, yet admittedly forlorn-looking, mansion. Neglect had dappled her once snowy-white columns with mold. But despite the need for substantial repairs, I knew she had good bones. Dad told me he and Billy accompanied my twin aunts to inspect Summer Place before they bought her. Other potential buyers planned to raze the mansion and erect student condos on the site—a valuable one since the land was unrestricted and sat near Clemson and the Pickens County line. The sentimental seller let my aunts buy at a reduced price because they promised to save the historic beauty.

When would I have the time and energy to keep their promise? Summer Place's good bones would have to wait until we buried the ugly past dug up with Jed's skeleton.

I started the car, backed down the drive, and headed to the highway. In a matter of minutes, Magic Moonshine's pampered zoo came into view. A fenced area adjacent to the building had a jumble of colored cubes randomly stacked at its center. A goat's Jungle Gym. Near the building, a sloped ramp let the hyperactive goats scamper to the roof's feed troughs. Paint said the gimmick worked. If Pops was driving down the highway, he'd slow the minute Ma exclaimed, "Honey, do you see what I see? Danged if there aren't goats on that roof."

I'd asked Paint, "Why goats?"

"I like 'em," he'd answered. "They're curious, independent, friendly. Plus they fit the hillbilly image that's part of my outlaw moonshine brand."

Goats were one of the bonds that cemented Paint's friendship with my aunts.

Lowering my gaze, I spotted a crusty old dude in overalls. He stood roadside waving at passing cars and hoisting a jug of moonshine every few seconds for a pretend swig—at least I assumed the swig was for show. Another effective gimmick. I'd certainly ease my foot off the gas pedal to take a closer look. Stopping to visit was a logical next step.

Paint had described his roadside salesman perfectly. The wooly bearded gent looked like he'd just sauntered out of the backwoods with a shotgun over his shoulder.

I looked past the huckster. Two vehicles were parked by the door—Paint's truck and a Harley. The same bike that practically singed my legs in Ardon?

Since Paint was minding the store, I had no qualms about dropping in. Maybe I'd even give a piece of my mind to one of the idiots determined to annoy me.

A bell tinkled when I entered the store. Center stage was reserved for a shiny three-piece copper moonshine still. At Aunt Eva's dinner table, Paint admitted the contraption no longer worked, but he'd kept it for theater. It had belonged to his granddaddy—the only true moonshiner in his family. Paint portrayed himself as a third generation bad boy, part of Magic Moonshine's mystique. No mention that his dad was a high school principal or that Paint had earned an MBA from Clemson University.

"Well, hello there, sweet thing." The biker's smoke roughened voice startled me. His beefy, leather-encased bod was bellied up to the counter. He was indeed the idiot who'd nearly sideswiped me.

"She's not your sweet thing, George." Paint's tone underscored his hands-off message. "This lady's my friend."

Paint had entered from a side room, a jar of moonshine in hand. He put the jar on the counter that doubled as a tasting bar.

George dipped his head and mumbled what I assumed was either a polite hello or an apology. Paint's appraising and proprietary look flustered me as much as it had George.

"Hi, Brie. Did you drop by to try more flavors or can I hope you just wanted to see me?"

"Thought I ought to visit your store." I tried to sound nonchalant, though my racing pulse paid no mind to my brain. "Your moonshine barbecue sauces sound interesting. I think I'll try basting portabella mushrooms with the peach-flavored one."

"Dang. I'm disappointed you aren't here to keep me company. But I never turn down a sale—especially when it gives me a chance to spend time with someone a lot better looking than George here."

Paint turned toward his leather-encased customer. "You've sampled all the choices. You gonna buy a jar?"

"Later, man. I'll be back." The biker didn't even glance my way as he clomped out of the store.

Once he was gone, I smiled at Paint. "I do want to buy one of your sauces. But seeing that guy's bike parked outside gave me an added incentive to stop."

Paint's eyebrows lifted. "You into bikers and leather? I might have an old leather jacket somewhere. If not, I'll buy one—and a Harley—if that's what it takes."

His grin was infectious. The deep dimples hard to resist.

"Nope, I have no desire to become a biker babe. But at lunch Andy mentioned Eli Watson hangs out at Hog Heaven, a bar where drug deals go down. It looks as if Nancy could have died from a designer drug, and Andy seemed to think Hog Heaven could be the drug source."

"You met Andy for lunch?" Paint asked. "I'm crushed. Looks like my buddy and I share another interest, and he beat me out of the starting gate."

"Actually, I was having lunch with Mollye at Abby's Diner. Andy just dropped in to pick up some takeout."

Hmm. Now why did I feel compelled to tell Paint my meeting with Andy was happenstance? Especially since I'd accepted Andy's dinner invitation. Dang, my brain was flashing signs—trouble, trouble, trouble. Other body parts were sending a somewhat different message.

"Whew," Paint said. "Knowing how Andy's aw-shucks-nice-guy routine can charm the ladies, I feared I was already behind the curve. I'll tell you a secret. Andy and I have been buddies forever. He's not *that* nice. We've had us some adventures." His eyebrows wiggled up and down.

I shook my head. "You're impossible."

Unfortunately, his report on Andy's adventurous side only

increased my interest in the gentle pig-whisperer vet.

"No, I'm quite possible," Paint said. "But let's go back to the biker bar. Do you want to see the place? Bet Andy didn't volunteer to take you there. Hog Heaven's owner buys cases of my moonshine every week. Not the namby-pamby flavors. Those wouldn't cut it with that macho crowd. They're into the straight white lightning that fits the badass image. I'm due to make a delivery. What say you come with me tonight?"

Should I? Lord, help me. A week ago, I'd never have considered strolling into a biker bar arm-in-arm with a moonshiner. Eva'd cautioned me about Paint's love 'em and leave 'em tendencies. Told me to put him in the same category as an exceptional chocolate mousse. Excellent for instant gratification, but known to have a relatively short shelf life.

"Great, what time?" My mouth answered before my brain could object.

"I'm meeting a wholesale distributor for dinner, so it'll probably be eight o'clock before I can pick you up. Will that work?"

"Sure. See you then."

I'd turned to leave when Paint walked out from behind the counter. "Not so fast." He sauntered over, stopping mere inches away. He lowered his head, bringing his mocha eyes and those seductive black lashes even with my gaze. His warm breath grazed my cheek. Good googamooga, was he going to kiss me? His arm snaked around me. A second later he handed me the Mason jar he retrieved from the shelf behind me. I looked at the label. Moonshine barbecue sauce, peach-flavored.

"On the house."

"Thanks."

Might I have preferred the kiss?

Apparently I was over my broken engagement. I simply needed to heed Mom's frequent admonition—"don't jump from the frying pan into the fire." There was definite sizzle in Paint's direction. But who would get burned? I wasn't exactly a babe in the woods.

Why shouldn't I enjoy a couple of evenings out with entertaining male companions?

NINETEEN

Eva and I ate as soon as we finished the evening chores. She tried to tempt me with chicken parmesan, one of my favorite dishes from childhood. My aunt had no more success seducing me than I had waving a stuffed portabella mushroom under her nose.

"No trade," she huffed. "I have zero interest in eating an oversized pile of fungus. There's such a thing as too healthy. Don't think I didn't see that printout you put on my pillow. Some study about Chinese rice eaters living to a ripe old age. If they'd had a choice, bet they'd have swapped a couple years in their nineties for a juicy filet mignon."

I sighed. Looked like I'd be cooking for one for a long time, and I expected a retaliatory refrigerator note come morning.

"Uh, Eva, I'm planning to go out for a drink with Paint tonight. He's coming by about eight. Do you mind my leaving you alone for a couple of hours?"

Eva snorted. "Don't go acting like your parents. I'm not afraid to be alone. I invited you to live here. Never planned to take you prisoner." She winked. "Kick up your heels a little, kiddo. You're only young once, and Paint's one fine specimen. Stay out all night if you want."

I rolled my eyes. "Give me a break. We're going out for a drink, not heading to the nearest No Tell Hotel."

She laughed. "Hey, I'm not your momma. You're old enough and smart enough to know all about safe sex. It's one foolproof stress reducer. In fact, I think I'll ask Billy over tonight now that I know I have the house to myself. How about a pact? Paint's picking you up at eight, right? Don't come home before eleven."

"Can't promise that, but I'll tiptoe in. Won't knock on your bedroom door if I come home sooner."

I hadn't mentioned our Hog Heaven destination. I doubted I'd want to spend three hours in a place I assumed would live up to the hog part of its name.

"We have a couple hours before Paint arrives," I said. "Want to help me sort through those papers I copied at the courthouse?"

"Sure, though I'm not clear about what smoking gun you hope to find."

We sat at the dining nook, papers spread across the table. My aunt started scanning the documents related to her farm, and I picked up the incorporation papers for Burks Holdings, LLC.

"Whoa, what have we here?" I'd come across a list of the original LLC partners.

Eva looked up. "What did you find?"

"Guess who owns a piece of Burks Holdings?"

"We only have an hour until you need to get 'purty' for Paint. Let's not waste time on guessing games."

"Ray Burks owns forty percent of the LLC. Not a huge surprise, though I'd have thought he'd keep at least fifty-one percent for control. But I about swallowed my tongue when I saw the other three partners. Each owns twenty percent of the company."

"So give already. Who are they?"

"Victor Caldwell, your favorite banker, Sheriff Robbie Jones, and Deputy Aaron West."

"You're shitting me." My aunt's language became a mite saltier when my mom wasn't around.

"No. I'm not."

Eva shook her head. "Victor's not a shocker. He comes from money. That bank's been in his family for decades, and his folks bought up lots of land when it was cheap. So Burks would have put him at the top of any list of potential Ardon investors. But Jones and West? The Sheriff's Department isn't known for lucrative pay. Neither man is poverty-stricken, but I can't imagine either of them scraping together enough coin to help finance a fancy resort."

"Interesting. Wonder if Paint or Andy might have an explanation?"

Eva grinned. "Be sure to work in those questions between smooches." She laughed at my expression. "Just teasing. Better get used to it. That's one of the things I miss most. Lilly could give pretty good. We had us some fine sparring matches at least once a day."

"I'll remember that. Now I'm going to try to get 'purty' since you seem to think I need help in that department."

"Never said that, Brie. You're about the prettiest young woman I know."

I laughed. "You're only saying that 'cause Dad claims I look just like you did at my age."

"Well, there you have it. You're not pretty, you're gorgeous."

"Wow," Paint said when I answered the door. "Not sure I should take you to Hog—"

Before he could say more, I placed my fingers on his lips. "Eva doesn't know where we're going," I mouthed.

He grasped my hand and, one by one, kissed the fingers I'd pressed against his lips—his moist, soft, warm lips. "I can keep secrets," he whispered, "for a price." His gaze started at my feet and slowly climbed to my red sweater. "Love those boots." He raised his voice a notch above normal so Aunt Eva would hear. "And red is my favorite color."

My pulse climbed right along with his no-holds-barred appraisal. If he liked my red sweater, bet he'd go bat shit over my bra. Where did that come from? I had no plans for Paint to get a peek at my bra. Of course, my cheeks, undoubtedly flaming, were now his favorite shade.

I engaged in a little appraising of my own as he brushed a shock of shiny hair back from his forehead. My fingers itched to do it for him and find out if it felt as silky as it looked. His nearly black eyes shone like onyx. Crinkly laugh lines framed his eyes, hinting at lusty mischief. Was it getting hot in the cabin or what?

The unmistakable clippity-clip of tiny nails on pine floorboards broke the spell as my pup scrambled over to greet him. Paint laughed as Cashew bounced around his legs in excited circles. He scooped her up and grinned as Cashew's tongue painted the air. She was trying her darndest to lick him to death.

She liked him. Good sign. Not that it would have stopped me if she didn't, but a rebuff might have slowed me down. Another glance at those eyes crowded out all consideration of my pup's lickable rating scale.

"Evening, Eva," Paint said as my aunt joined us. "How are you doing?"

"Almost ready," she teased. "Brie told you I'm coming along to chaperone, didn't she?"

"Great," Paint answered. "A beautiful woman on each arm. I'll be the envy of every guy in the joint."

Eva punched his arm. "You're no fun. Can't get your goat no matter how hard I try." She made a shooing motion. "Go on, you two. I have my own entertainment plans for the evening. Billy will be here in a few minutes." She wagged a warning finger. "Don't bring Brie home too soon."

"Eva!"

Paint and my aunt chuckled as he put my squirming puppy back on the ground.

"Glad to see I can still get someone's goat," she said.

Hog Heaven was everything I expected. The parking lot was chock-a-block with motorcycles of every vintage, shape, and horsepower. Although mostly Harleys, a few rice rockets held their own. Yet with all the bikes, Paint's truck was no outlier. There were at least a dozen behemoths. All, including Paint's, sported gun racks. Paint's bright red truck was distinguished by the oversized decals pasted on the doors. The signs featured a buxom babe hoisting pints of white lightning, Magic Moonshine emblazoned across her boobs. First place males would focus.

"Promise it'll only take a minute for me to run my delivery around back," Paint said. "Wait for me."

"Yep. I'll be right here." Like I'd saunter into Hog Heaven by my lonesome.

Paint was as good as his word. Couldn't have been more than three minutes before he was back to open my door.

As soon as we walked inside, my eyes began to water. The bar's designated smoking area was a joke. The indoor smog would seriously test my mascara's waterproof claims. No need to waste money on a cigarette or reefer of my own, all I had to do was inhale.

Though the light was murky, it was easy to tell females were a minority. I guessed the gender mix at seventy-thirty. I was happy to have Paint's nicely muscled arm possessively draped around my shoulders. Four big bruisers left a booth and Paint led me toward it. The table held two empty pitchers, foam still clinging to the rims, four mugs, peanut shells, and shredded napkins. The overflowing ashtray had to have at least twenty butts.

"You hold our seats," Paint said. "I'll order drinks and ask Cindy to clean the table. Can you handle my moonshine? Bad advertising if a moonshiner doesn't drink his own product."

"From what you told me about Hog Heaven, my choice of flavor is white lightning or white lightning. Guess I can handle one. Don't count on me to down more than two glasses. You'd have to carry me out."

"I may stop you at one. I'm obliged to be a complete gentleman with tipsy ladies." His eyebrows hiked up. "Sober ones? Well, I'm sure Eva warned you about us moonshiners."

I enjoyed the view as Paint sauntered away.

"I'll rack 'em this time. Lady Luck ain't gonna help you again." The slurred voice coming from the pool table nearest our booth sounded familiar. All I could see was the stocky speaker's boots, legs, and flat, wide butt. His jeans looked dirty enough to live on without any underlying fabric. Red mud caked his scuffed boots.

A waitress walked close enough to casually hip-check my date just before he slid into his seat. She gave me a nanosecond's attention and a curt nod as she transferred the dirty glasses and pitchers to a nearby stand and swiped our table with a damp cloth. The babe kept her eyes fastened on Paint. Once she sashayed off, he slid along the bench.

As Paint's thigh cozied up next to mine, the skunked pool player straightened and turned.

Holy Havarti! No wonder the voice sounded familiar.

I clamped onto Paint's arm. "We need to leave," I whispered.

"What? We just got here. Thought you wanted to case the joint. See if we could talk to some folks here who know Eli."

"Not anymore. Look who's playing pool. The grieving husband. If he sees me, Eli may go postal. He swung an axe at me before we'd even met. Now the sheriff's probably convinced him I murdered his wife."

Paint stared at Eli and squeezed my hand. "Don't worry. The owner of Hog Heaven's my friend. So's his bouncer. I have a lot more clout than Eli. If it gets ugly, they'll chuck him out."

Scenes of bar fights danced through my head. Broken beer bottles. Flying fists. Bloody mouths. Cool it, I told myself. This is real life, and Paint knows the turf.

I watched Eli laugh, then take a big swig of beer. His wife was in the morgue, slit stem to stern for an autopsy, and he was boozing it up, shooting pool, laughing. Maybe he really was the killer. A happy one at that.

"You look scared to death," Paint said. "Hope nobody thinks I'm the cause. Take a sip of moonshine. It'll take the edge off. I won't let anything happen to you."

I thought Jack, my ex, had cured me of interest in Alpha males. Yet Paint's promised protection warmed me down deep where I didn't need warming. I took a big gulp of moonshine for courage. Remembered too late his recommendation to keep my danged mouth closed. I sputtered and coughed as oxygen ignited the fiery liquid sliding down my gullet. Paint patted my back.

My hacking carried over the barroom clatter. A dozen heads turned our way. Eli's included.

His eyes narrowed into a vexed squint. He shook his head like a dog who'd stuck his nose in a patch of pepper. His expression said he couldn't quite believe his eyes. It also suggested three sheets to the wind wouldn't quite capture his condition. Eli sober wasn't pretty. But Eli soused?

He lumbered our way, a sturdy pool cue in hand. Paint stood.

Spam in a can. What now?

"What's that murderin' bitch doin' here?" Eli snarled.

Ninety percent of the bar's leather-clad cronies stared at us. A circle began to form.

"Think it's time for you to leave, Eli." Paint raised his hands in the universal stop signal. "Know you just lost your wife, and you tipped back a few to ease the pain. But this lady here has nothing to do with you or your loss. Leave it alone. Go home."

"The hell I will." Eli swung the pool cue with all his might.

Paint ducked, waited for the stick to pass, then shot up to steal the weapon from the surprised drunk's hands. He jabbed the butt end deep into Eli's flabby stomach. Paint now had full custody of the pool cue. The drunk yelped and sank to the floor. Looking almost bored, my date tossed the pool cue away as Eli writhed in pain.

"You summabitch," Eli moaned. "I'll get you and that bitch."

Paint turned toward the man who'd been shooting pool with Eli. "Can you take him home, Aaron?"

Aaron? I hadn't paid Eli's drinking buddy any attention. None other than Aaron West, the deputy sheriff who'd been all too happy to show off the gun he'd found in Eva's barn. The same deputy who owned twenty percent of Burks Holdings.

"I think I'm gonna puke." Eli's hoarse declaration prompted retreats by most of the looky-loos who'd been hoping to see two dudes duke it out.

"Let's make sure you do it outside." Paint grabbed Eli's right arm and Aaron took the left. They yanked, and Eli lurched to his feet. Before they could perp-walk him to the nearest exit, the drunk tried to spit on me. The slobber just dribbled down his chin.

Alone in our booth, I tried not to squirm, knowing I'd become an unwanted center of attention. Come on, Paint, hurry. The two minutes he was gone seemed like hours.

"Aaron's taking Eli home," Paint said. "He won't be bothering anyone tonight." He looked at my empty glass. Everyone in the bar seemed to be watching, waiting for Act Two. Having downed one moonshine for liquid courage, I felt a tad light-headed and less than eager to hoist another one or stay long enough to merit an increase in Cindy's tip jar. Get me outta here.

"You ready to leave?" Paint must have read my mind. "Why don't we go to my place for a night cap? Eva will skin me if I bring you home this early."

My reason for visiting Hog Heaven—chatting with some of Eli's friends—was long gone. "Let's go."

My brain cartwheeled. Paint's place? I was pushing my luck—and willpower—heading to his lair. Being alone with him. My red bra would definitely be to his liking. But he wasn't going to see it.

Note to self: red is the color for stop signs.

TWENTY

I wondered if Paint was sorry he'd suggested we leave Hog Heaven. Nerves had turned me into a chatterbox. Bet he'd love to find an off switch.

"Aaron and Eli are buddies?" I asked.

"Not really. But Hog Heaven's where they both like to drink and shoot pool. Aaron comes when he's off-duty. He pretends it's part of his lawman routine, keeping an eye on what's going down. If that's true, he does a piss-poor job."

"Could Eli have bought drugs there? Something he might have used to kill his wife?"

"It's possible. Jimmy, the owner, turns a blind eye when his customers smoke marijuana, but he doesn't tolerate drug deals inside Hog Heaven. The empty lot next door is a different matter. Deputy Aaron knows what goes on there, too. Just ignores it."

"Eli looked like he was a happy camper tonight. Not exactly grief stricken."

"I don't know about that." Paint shrugged. "People handle loss differently. Eli and Nancy had some nasty public fights, but I've also seen them all lovey-dovey the next day. I can't imagine the man killing her with drugs. Too premeditated. Knife her, shoot her, wring her neck? Yes, Eli might do any one of those in a fit of rage. What I can't see is him getting mad, then buying drugs and biding his time to get even."

The more I thought about it, Paint's analysis had the ring of truth. The murder method didn't jibe with what I knew of Eli's character. But if Nancy's husband didn't do her in, who did?

Back to square one. Who wanted Nancy Watson dead? Were there any suspects beyond Aunt Eva and yours truly?

Paint turned down a rutted dirt road. "We're almost there."

There, where? We hadn't seen a streetlight in miles. Squinting, I could just make out a falling down shack. Paint's home? I'd expected rustic, but I figured there'd be an actual roof.

We drove past the shack. A minute later, a log cabin came into view.

Paint laughed. "I heard that sigh of relief. You thought that shack was mine, didn't you?"

"No, of course not," I lied.

An eerie howl raised goosebumps up and down my arms.

"That's Lunar welcoming us home," Paint said. "A farmer found him huddled against his dead mother and took him to the animal shelter. They called me, since they knew my folks had raised an orphaned wolf."

"Your pet is a wolf?" I swallowed.

"Yep. Don't worry. He's a ladies' man. Doesn't cotton to my male friends, but he's a complete gentleman around the ladies."

What was I getting into? Alone with not one wolf, but two.

"Just let Lunar sniff your hand when we get out."

Paint punched some gizmo on his key chain and a spotlight came on, bathing his cabin's front yard in amber light. The first thing I saw was a wheelbarrow filled with colorful pansies. Then I spotted Lunar. Sleek grey fur, piercing blue eyes. Beautiful. Scary as hell.

Paint walked around the truck and opened my passenger door. Lunar padded over to meet me. I held out my hand. He sniffed, then crept away. Tacit approval? Little Red Riding Hood had survived one wolf. A quick glance at Paint made me wonder if I'd make it past number two.

The cabin interior was sparsely furnished, but spotless and cozy. The main living space included a couch and recliner next to a potbellied stove. The open floor plan also included a one-butt kitchen with a pine table and two chairs in an adjacent nook. Two partially opened doors provided a glimpse of the rest of the cabin. One door led to a bedroom. The other to a bathroom.

The décor was almost Cracker Barrel country. Colorful quilts and slipcovers. A needlepoint sampler was mounted on the wall beside an antique rifle.

Paint grinned as I scoped out the place. "I confess. I built the cabin, but Mom decorated. I like it though. It's homey."

I nodded. "It's great. Very comfortable, cozy."

He smiled. "Sit, and I'll get us the nightcap I promised."

The couch proved as comfortable as it looked. Paint handed me another small glass of moonshine. "Remember, now, keep your mouth closed when you sip."

He sat beside me, slid an arm around my shoulders, and pulled me closer. I took a sip, followed instructions, and didn't sputter. Nonetheless, I felt the fire. This time it wasn't an inferno. More like banked, glowing embers. The warmth ambled from my lips to my stomach to my toes, but seemed to concentrate right where Paint's fingers stroked my arm. Once again my little voice warned, "Trouble. Trouble. Trouble." My body replied, "Oh, shut up."

We talked about this and that as we sipped our respective brews. Though I was a virtual stranger in Ardon County, I felt I could trust Mollye, Andy, and Paint. I'd known Mollye forever, and Eva bragged that Andy and Paint were like sons to her. I had no qualms about telling Paint what I'd found researching Burks Holdings' partnership roster.

His mouth dropped open. "Really? Victor Caldwell's a no brainer, but Sheriff Robbie Jones and Deputy Aaron West?"

His reaction matched my aunt's.

"I don't know where Robbie or Aaron would have found money to invest—unless..." Paint frowned as he paused. "Guess it could be we'll-look-the-other-way drug money. As often as Aaron hangs at Hog Heaven, he has to know about the vacant lot deals. If he and the sheriff are raking in payoffs, maybe they're using Burks Holdings to launder the money. They give Burks cash under the table, and he pays them back in eventual profits."

He tilted his head back and closed his eyes. "I can only think of one other reason Burks would welcome those two into the fold. Blackmail. Maybe he got caught doing something illegal—bigtime illegal—and Jones and West agreed to cover it up for a piece of the action."

Something illegal like murder? My brain jumped to Nancy Watson's death. Unfortunately, the evil quartet—developer, banker, sheriff, and deputy—had formed long before Nancy died. I couldn't figure any way to tie her murder to a blackmail scheme.

I'd have to give Paint's theory more thought. Later. Much later. Thinking didn't seem to be among my top skills at the moment. Mostly I was feeling. Warm and tingly. I almost wished Paint would be more like the wolf I'd imagined. The one that scared me. The one I had fantasies of taming.

He drove me home. The porch light was on, and Billy's truck sat in the drive. Not a single light on inside the cabin. Paint walked me to the door.

He stuck out his hand. A handshake, really?

He grinned. "First date I always like to prove I can be a gentleman."

I grasped his hand and pulled him toward me. Then I leaned in, trapping him against the porch railing. True, I was more than a smidgeon tipsy.

"And on first dates I like to prove kissing is one of my talents."

The kiss took my body from pleasantly tingling to sizzling. The heat of his white lightning sent blazing signals to all parts of my body. Brain excepted. Yowzer. I hadn't intended for our tongues to become that well acquainted.

Paint was practically panting when the kiss ended. "You proved your point," he said. "Kissing is one of your exceptional talents. And, if I don't leave now, my first-date protocol will go down in flames. A man only has so much willpower." He kissed my forehead and turned. "Goodnight, Brie. I'll call you. Can't wait to see what you want to prove on a second date."

Uh oh. Hadn't thought that one through.

TWENTY-ONE

Would leaving a warm bed before dawn ever get easier? Doubtful if I kept staying out past midnight. Shuffling toward the bathroom, I noticed Eva's bedroom door sat open, the bed neatly made. I glanced out the front window. Billy's truck was gone. At least I didn't need to cross my legs waiting to pee.

Outside, Eva's cheerful whistle helped me locate her. She was once again tending to newborns.

"You sound happy," I observed.

"You betcha," Eva answered. "Told you. Sex is a great stress reliever. So why aren't you whistling, Brie?"

I looked heavenward. "Paint was a perfect gentleman. We had a couple drinks, talked, and he brought me home. Period."

"Oh, no, you're ruining my image of the boy. Maybe I need to have a chat with him."

Eva was kidding, right? Just in case, I added, "Don't you dare."

My imagination always stalled, imposing a don't-go-there barrier to any thoughts of my parents engaged in boudoir activities. Yet my brain accepted that my sixty-two-year-old aunt wasn't a celibate creature. Nonetheless, I had no desire for details.

Eva smiled. "You did miss one call last night. Your folks are coming to breakfast. Getting to be regular freeloaders. Maybe we ought to wean 'em, just give 'em bread and water."

"What's up? It's a long drive for a cup of coffee."

"Your mom got a heads-up on the toxicology findings and wants to fill you in before the sheriff interrogates you. Iris told Jones you'd voluntarily come to the Sheriff's office at ten o'clock. Of course, she'll be with you."

"Just how I wanted to spend my morning. When are Mom and

Dad due?"

"Seven. Both have early morning appointments. After you feed the animals and gather eggs, throw together some breakfast, will ya? There's enough bacon in the fridge for the three of us. You're on your own for protein. Black bean mush? A soy sundae?"

"Funny." I made a face.

By five after seven we were seated at the breakfast table. Even Eva asked for seconds of my whole wheat blueberry pancakes. In deference to our digestion, Mom skipped over the gruesome autopsy slicing and dicing details and skipped straight ahead to toxicology.

"A fatal dose of a designer drug did Nancy in. They analyzed her stomach contents and the crumbs left in the break room. Definitely the tainted brownie."

"How could the killer be sure Nancy would eat the brownie?" I asked. "Or didn't he care if someone else died?"

"Working theory is there was a single brownie square, a personal treat. Since the woman wasn't known to be the sharing type, the killer wasn't putting other lives at risk. The Hands On receptionist gave the sheriff a complete list of employees and all the clients they saw that day. Jones claims everyone will be brought in for routine questioning."

"Right. I'm sure his questions for me will be 'routine.'"

Mom patted my hand. "Don't worry, honey. I'll be there. I won't let him bully you."

I debated mentioning my visit to Hog Heaven and the inebriated Eli Watson's seeming lack of grief. In the end, I zipped my lips. Mom would be upset that I'd gone to a biker bar, but not quite apoplectic. Dad would have a cow. Eva would understand, maybe. I'd tell her later.

Dad looked so depressed I decided to change the subject.

"I weeded your garden, Dad. It's looking great. The perennials are starting to sprout. Looks like you'll have a good crop."

"Thanks, honey. One of the researchers emailed, said she had promising results from last season's extracts. Wants even more plants this year."

Dad's unusual garden supplied a potpourri of poisonous plants to researchers at the Medical University of South Carolina. Dad's horticultural classes included the study of deadly flora, and he was quick to remind folks the most effective chemotherapy drugs wouldn't exist without the poisonous caster bean.

"Don't forget to weed Lilly's herb garden," Eva said. "We need her herbs for our next batch of specialty cheese blends."

I smiled. "Already took the hoe to that patch. Don't worry. I won't mix Dad's plants with ours."

At nine thirty sharp, I left the cabin to head to the Sheriff's Department, which was located beside the county jail on the outskirts of Ardon. I figured the drive would take fifteen minutes max, but I didn't want to chance being late given that a thick white spring fog had unexpectedly rolled in. If I failed to show on time, Mom might lock me behind bars herself.

Droplets from the mist collected on my hair as I walked to my Prius. The windshield wipers let me see the car hood—sort of. The road appeared as little more than a hint. I played with the headlight settings. The glare of high beams would make it even harder to see. But I wanted other drivers to spot me before they rearranged my bumper. Unable to determine the edges of the gravel drive, I inched forward in the center of the lane.

Once I hit paved road, I bumped my speed up a notch. Not too fast. I knew gullies bracketed the road, even if they were invisible in the cotton-wrapped scene. The fog not only tricked my eyes, it deadened all sound. The eerie quiet took me back to my childhood and our Iowa yard under a four-foot blanket of snow. Dad held my mittened hand as we ventured into a pristine land. The moonlit drifts looked like sparkling snow cones before they poured on the cherry syrup.

Sound. Loud. So much for silence and pleasant memories.

The noise grew louder. An engine, a big one. Oncoming traffic? I squinted, peering into the opposite lane. Nothing. I looked in the rearview mirror. No headlights. Where was the fool?

The engine growled louder. Suddenly a dark, hulking shape broke through the swirling mist. Right on my tail. I hit my emergency flashers, fumbled for my horn.

Wham! My body whipsawed as metal screeched. My teeth

snapped together so hard I feared they'd crack. A gunshot? Loud, near. I blinked. I'd gone blind. A different blind than fog. I punched at the inflated airbag, sneezed as white dust flurries swirled like snowflakes.

My car lurched sideways. Oh, no. The ravine. My brain froze. My foot doubled down on the brake pedal. The car tilted another twenty degrees. My chest hurt. A heart attack?

Breathe. You'll be fine. Take another breath.

Wham! God in heaven, had the idiot backed up to ram me again? My poor little car shimmied like a leaf in a stiff wind. My stomach dropped in sync with the car's front wheels. My sporty Prius bounced and slid down, down, down. The car shuddered to a stop. Must have reached the base of the ravine. Dad's jokes about hiding dead bodies in kudzu-choked gullies popped unbidden to mind.

Was someone trying to kill me?

I'd no sooner formed the thought than it took root. Eli had a monster truck, and he'd had murder in his eyes last night.

Mired in off-road mud, I was out of range for more ramming. But a raving maniac wouldn't need to leave the pavement to shoot me. I realized the exploding airbag made the "gunshot" I'd heard. Didn't mean the attacker's truck lacked a gun rack—practically a mandate in Ardon County.

Should I get out of the car? Or was I safer inside?

The snarl of the big engine receded. Or maybe I was losing consciousness. I held my breath. Silence. No sounds of traffic, no birds, no sirens announcing help coming to the rescue.

Thank heaven for cell phones. I fumbled for my purse. Eureka, a signal. No way was I calling 911. That would only bring the sarcastic sheriff or his snaggle-toothed deputy. I fished in my purse for my billfold and pulled out my AAA card. I silently thanked Dad for insisting I keep my membership. I called for a tow.

My second call was the first number on my speed dial. Mom. Should I tell her I'd been attacked? No, she'd take the news better if she could see with her own eyes that I was still in one piece.

"Mom, I had a little car accident. I'm fine, but I can't drive my car."

"What? A little accident? Are you hurt?"

"I'm okay, but there's no way I can get to the sheriff's office for our ten o'clock. AAA is en route to tow my car. Can you pick me up? I'm about two miles north of Udderly on the highway."

"Of course I'll come get you. You sure you're all right, honey?"

"I'm sure. Just tell the sheriff we'll be late so he won't think of another trumped-up charge to add to my rap sheet."

The fog was so thick I couldn't see what waited for me outside my door. I opened it slowly and climbed out. My feet sank into gooey mud. The roadbed sat six feet up a steep embankment. The tow truck would have fun pulling my car out of this ditch.

I grabbed a handful of bramble to haul myself up to the pavement. The damp fog swirled around me. Goose liver. I'd be invisible to anyone driving down the road. One little swerve and I'd be roadkill. Or the jackass who rammed me might return. I shivered.

No. If he'd wanted to finish the job, he wouldn't have driven away. He knew exactly where to find me, a sitting duck.

I took inventory. My hands were bloody, torn on the thorny "mile-a-minute" vines I'd grabbed to hoist my butt out of the ditch. My head throbbed. My aching body listed to port, and my knees refused to cooperate with the orders I sent. That danged airbag had whacked me but good.

My wardrobe was a disaster, too. Red clay caked my boots. I'd worn my best innocent-preppie, I'm-not-a-killer outfit for the interrogation. My skirt and jacket were torn, muddy, and sported a few blood spatters for good measure. Great.

Would the sheriff believe someone had deliberately hit me, not once, but twice? He'd probably think I'd been taking some of those designer drugs he thought I used. Was it even worth sharing my suspicion that Eli might have been the fiend driving that truck? If the sheriff had a choice of thinking ill of a Watson or a Hooker, I knew where his sympathies would lie.

We arrived at the sheriff's office almost two hours late for my "interview." Mom insisted on taking me to an urgent care clinic to be checked out first. The doc pronounced my bones intact. Said I was banged up but fit for interrogation. Mom thought I should be home in bed. At a minimum, she wanted me to change out of my tattered, dirty clothes before presenting myself at the sheriff's office.

I disagreed. I wanted the "interview" finished, and I figured the sheriff had seen people dressed a lot worse. I did use a few of the wet towelettes Mom kept in her car to wipe mud off visible skin surfaces.

Once the interview began, Mom's displeasure shifted from daughter to sheriff as he asked the same questions over and over like a stuck record. I snuck a look at my watch to see how long he'd been grilling me. Fifteen minutes? I tapped my watch to make sure it was working. It felt like hours had passed.

No matter how Jones rephrased his questions, my answers never changed. No, I do not do drugs, nor do I know how to buy them. No, I was never in the Hands On breakroom. Other than Nancy, I saw only three people at the salon—the receptionist, an auburn-haired manicurist, and the senior citizen customer she escorted to the front desk.

When the sheriff paused to scribble something on his notepad, Mom sat up a tad straighter and lifted her shoulders. The lady barrister was about to take the floor.

"Sheriff Jones, you've been asking all the questions. You seem to have no interest in finding out who ran my daughter off the road. Are you going to investigate? The auto club will confirm the dents on the car's mangled bumper are new. I hope you plan to take paint samples and try to match them. This Eli Watson person threatened my sister-in-law and my daughter. You should pay him a visit. Ask him a question or two."

The sheriff slowly raised his eyes. His lips twitched like the proverbial canary-eating cat. "Yes, I plan to pay a condolence visit to Eli today. He just claimed his wife's body yesterday and arranged delivery to the funeral home. I doubt he had time to lay in wait for your daughter—even though turnabout might have been fair play. Last night Miss Hooker followed the man to a biker bar and taunted him, just like she did his dead wife. Only last night your innocent little darling brought her boyfriend along to beat up on Eli Watson."

"What?" My mother and I yelped in unison.

Unfortunately, I knew how Paint's and my visit to Hog Heaven and the ensuing altercation could be spun into a story one-hundred-and-eighty degrees opposite from the truth.

As I fumbled through my rebuttal to the lawman's accusation, I imagined I could see smoke swirling out of Mom's ears. She'd be furious I hadn't told her the whole story before Sheriff Jones sprung his trap. Mom said clients who failed to come clean with their attorneys were the bane of her existence. Daughters who kept secrets had to be the bottom of the barrel.

TWENTY-TWO

I could almost feel sparks shooting off the force field crackling around Mom's rigid body. Maybe I shouldn't follow this close as she power-walked toward her car. Mom might stand five-two, but her wrath was like a black hole that could suck you in and compact you—mind, body, soul—to the size of a pin. I was in line for her full fury as soon as we reached her BMW. Well, she might wait a second to roll up the windows and crank the engine. Wouldn't want outsiders to hear. Our family business—and her tirade—would be private.

"Brie, what in Hades were you thinking, going to a biker bar? I've shared enough stories from court about what can happen in places like that. And you knew this Eli, a man who'd threatened you, frequented that place. I'm going to give Paint a piece of my mind. He had no business taking you there."

"Come on, Mom, we went to Hog Heaven to chat up Eli Watson's friends. We had no idea he'd actually be there. In what universe does a grieving husband go out to drink and shoot pool when his wife is in the morgue?"

"Actually, it happens plenty. People drink to forget. They go where they feel comfortable. You and Paint should never have—"

"Leave Paint out of this," I interrupted. "He did me a favor. I wanted to go. Hog Heaven is one of his customers. He's friends with the owner and bouncer. He knew I'd be in no danger."

"Oh, and he stops bullets, too?" Mom sucked in a deep breath. "Tell me again what you thought you'd accomplish sashaying into Hog Heaven?"

I slumped in my seat. Nothing I said would change Mom's mind. "I thought we might talk to some of Eli's drinking buddies, find out if he bought drugs or ever hinted about wanting an easy out of his marriage. I hoped we'd find a lead and get the sheriff to look at someone besides Eva and me as potential killers. Eli's capable of murder. I know it. Far as I'm concerned, he's at the top of the list as his wife's killer."

Mom sighed. Her anger was winding down. "Well, that sure backfired. Now the sheriff thinks you're the off-kilter bully. Brie, your dad and I are worried sick. I know you're an adult and need to make your own decisions, but please reconsider. Move in with us until some of this craziness resolves itself. You can help Eva during daylight hours."

She looked at me, eyes pleading. I felt bad. The situation was costing her, but I couldn't abandon Aunt Eva. And I wasn't convinced I was truly in danger. Whoever rear-ended my Prius was interested in scaring not killing. He had to figure he'd accomplished that goal.

Aunt Eva walked onto the porch the minute we stopped in front of her cabin. She froze when she saw me. "Did you duke it out with a prickly cactus and lose? What the heck happened to you, Brie?"

I gave a synopsis of my roadside adventure, ending with my belief that Eli Watson was behind the wheel of the kamikaze truck.

Eva shook her head. "You haven't been listening to the radio. The news is all about Eli Watson."

Mom's head shot up. "Did the sheriff take him into custody for running Brie off the road? Did he admit it?"

"Hardly. Eli's dead. Hanged himself. A friend he'd been drinking with the night before found him early afternoon. He'd been strung up for hours."

My skin felt icy. What in blazes? Eli didn't seem the suicidal type—not unless he could take someone with him.

Then it hit me. If he'd been dead for hours, he couldn't have been the one ramming my Prius this morning. Could I have made another enemy? Someone else who held a grudge and felt justified turning a vehicle into a battering ram?

We hurried inside. Eva had set out a nice lunch, and she hadn't even attached a Post-it note to my leftover moatloaf. Didn't matter. I'd lost my appetite. It looked as if the feeling was shared. Still, we all took seats at the small table, the best place for conversation.

Mom pushed her plate away and stabbed at the numbers on her

phone. "I'm calling my EMS friend. Try to get some details about Eli's death."

Eva and I sat quietly, waiting for Mom to end her call's one-sided conversation. Mostly Mom listened. After a minute or two, Eva went to the kitchen and returned with mugs of hot tea. My fingers gratefully closed around the warm mug. I held it to my cheek.

"Thanks," I mouthed. Eva nodded.

Mom thanked her friend and put her cell phone on the table. Her frown and knitted eyebrows suggested grim news.

"A buddy found the body about noon and called EMS. The friend said he dropped by to check on Eli since he'd been in bad shape when he left Hog Heaven. Claims he found Eli hanging from a beam, a chair kicked over nearby."

"Did they find a note?" Eva asked.

"Yes. Eli admitted to killing his wife. Couldn't live with the guilt. Said he bought the lethal drug, baked it into a brownie, and packed it in Nancy's lunch. Told her a cousin was testing a new recipe."

Eva shook her head so violently she looked possessed. "No way, Jose. I've known Eli Watson forty years. He's not that organized. And he'd never spend money buying drugs when he had bullets to spare. But what sticks in my craw is the note's suggestion that a guilty conscience prompted him to commit suicide. That's total bullshit."

I glanced at Mom. She looked pensive. "It'll be treated as a suspicious death," she said. "There'll be an autopsy. If the note's handwritten, they'll compare it with other samples of Eli's handwriting and check fingerprints."

Eva snorted. "That may be tough. Doubt the man ever picked up a pencil after high school. Guess I shouldn't badmouth the dead, but those Watsons have been enemies a long, long time."

Mom suddenly looked over at me. "My God, if Eli was dead hours before they found his body, he couldn't have driven the truck that rear-ended you. If it wasn't Eli, who was it?" Her eyes pleaded as she looked from me to my aunt. "Brie's not safe. Eva, maybe you can talk her into living with us for the time being."

"Eva, Mom, listen. Whoever drove that truck didn't try to attack me on the farm, and he didn't wait for nightfall. I'm as safe at Udderly as anywhere else. The real question is—who did I make this mad?"

Mom nodded. "Yes, that's the question. And you're right. Maybe you're not safe anywhere in Ardon County. You should go back to Asheville."

"Not happening. I quit my job. Someone else has moved into my apartment. And Eva needs me. We just have to get to the bottom of this. Maybe that truck incident doesn't have a thing to do with Eva, the Watsons, or Udderly Kidding Dairy. Maybe it was just good old-fashioned road rage."

Too bad I couldn't convince myself.

TWENTY-THREE

After Mom left for a plea bargain hearing, I helped Eva with chores until she shooed me inside to check internet orders and work on Udderly's books. Cashew welcomed me like I'd been freed from a year in the hoosegow. A frantic lick for every second away. Nice to know someone loved me unconditionally. I gave her a hug and a well-deserved doggie treat. Cashew thought I was brilliant.

Back to reality. I needed to understand Lilly's accounting system before we switched banks. My digital exploration quickly convinced me my aunt's accounts were straight forward. I wouldn't screw up if I just followed her lead.

While the accounting system revealed no surprises, the numbers did. Udderly processed one boatload of long-distance internet orders. I downloaded a sizeable rush order from a Napa Valley winery for Udderly's soft cheeses. The vintner's note said he learned of Udderly when one of its specialty cheeses won an international award. Impressive.

I printed the rush order for the winery's upcoming soiree plus half a dozen less urgent orders. Then I went searching for Eva. She was humming away as she performed her cheese magic in the dairy enclave. The woman's optimism was impressive. Or else she was a fatalist. Que sera, sera. Enjoy it while you can.

"Need some help filling these orders?" I asked.

Eva glanced at her heavy-duty steel watch. "Too late for FedEx today. We'll put the orders together tomorrow. I'll schedule a pickup for the morning."

"Isn't Andy supposed to be here in an hour?" she asked. "Go on. Get ready. You're not headed anywhere dangerous tonight, are you? Snake-handling at the church in the woods? Busting up a cockfight ring? Your father will shoot me if you have another exciting evening."

"We're going to an Indian restaurant in Greenville that caters to vegetarians. The most excitement may be pleas for pitchers of water if the food's too spicy."

"Don't assume your entrée is the only spicy option." Eva winked. "That gold digger who divorced Andy was nuts. He's a very nice fellow. But nice doesn't equate to bland."

The cell phone in my pocket vibrated. Good, an excuse to avoid answering my aunt, who was way too enthusiastic about meddling in my love life—or lack thereof. I looked at the caller ID. Speak of the devilish angel.

"Hi, Andy."

Eva tilted her head. She studied my expression as I listened to Andy's rushed words. I put my phone back in my pocket.

"Looks like I have an extra half hour to get ready. Andy will be a little late. Deputy West called him to the Watson farm to pick up that pit bull Eli kept chained in his yard. With both Nancy and Eli gone, the deputy asked Andy to put the dog down. Said the county would pay."

Eva frowned. She couldn't bear to have animals mistreated.

"That's a danged shame. That pit bull's little more than a puppy. No chance for a real life. His bad luck that no-goodnicks bought him." She sighed. "Guess if Andy puts him down at least he won't suffer anymore."

I shook my head. "I didn't finish. Andy will be late because he's taking the dog to his clinic. Wants to feed him and get him comfy. He's going to contact a rescue group for abused pets. Hopes to find the Watson dog a foster home. Since Andy's already calling the pit bull by name—Jethro—my hunch is our soft-hearted vet will wind up being Jethro's foster dad."

The guardian dogs announced Andy's arrival. Their excited, happy greetings said they welcomed a friend.

Eva grinned. "That danged vet spoils my dogs. Always brings them treats."

I opened the front door before Andy reached the cabin stairs. Wow, handsome didn't do him justice. His bronzed skin came courtesy of his job, not a tanning booth. It set off a smile any toothpaste advertiser would envy. Streaky blond curls kissed his forehead.

Tonight he wore crisply pressed tan chinos. The collar of a starched white shirt peeked out of the neck of a Kelly-green V-neck sweater.

"Get Jethro settled?" I asked.

"Sure did. He's really a sweet dog. Should be fine tonight. Hope I can find him a new home tomorrow."

Cashew, the shameless flirt, was dancing around Andy's legs. He laughed, picked her up, and gave her one of the treats that seemed to fill his pockets.

"Want to come in for a drink?"

He shook his head. "No, I'll just say howdy to Eva before we leave. We need to get on the road if we want to get to Greenville before the restaurant quits serving. I warned you. Swad isn't fancy. It's a family restaurant adjacent to a grocery store. One reviewer said it was like dining in someone's living room. The owner's a lifelong vegetarian."

"Sounds wonderful. Just what I need after my day."

Andy put Cashew down and looked up at me. Brows knitted, head cocked to the side. No wonder he looked puzzled. Andy had no clue I'd been run off the road or interrogated by a smirking Sheriff Jones. The odds were also good he was unaware that I'd stepped out with Paint last night. Hmm. I couldn't very well catch him up on my run-in with the late Mr. Watson without mentioning I'd spent the evening with his very-much-alive best friend.

Maybe his response would help me figure out if spending time with both men was a problem. I shook my head. *Get over yourself. You're not on some pick-a-bachelor TV show, and Andy more or less said he was simply looking for a dinner companion.*

Andy greeted Eva with a kiss on the cheek. He promised to bring me home safe and sound and said he'd drop by late tomorrow to give the newborns a once-over.

As I climbed inside his truck, I noticed my passenger seat sported nary a fur ball. "Wow, I am getting the royal treatment. You vacuumed."

Andy laughed. "I keep my promises. Especially to pretty ladies."

No question. Andy and Paint had very different personalities. But it was easy to see why they were fast friends. How could anyone help but like both men? I couldn't.

As we drove to Greenville, I asked Andy for a full report on his visit to Eli Watson's farm.

"By the time I arrived, Eli's body was gone," he began. "And Sheriff Jones, Deputy West, and the County Solicitor were huddled in the living room. When I went inside to look for Jethro's dog food, I walked in on a heated argument."

"The DA was there—at a suicide? That's a surprise."

From what Mom told me, solicitors, South Carolina's version of district attorneys, didn't usually visit suicide scenes.

"Imagine Nancy's death and Eli's confession obliged the solicitor to make a cameo appearance," Andy answered. "He sure wasn't happy."

"Was he mad at the sheriff?" Anyone who took issue with Sheriff Jones was A-OK in my book.

"The solicitor wasn't happy that Eli's body was cut down before the scene was photographed. He also chastised the sheriff for not putting on gloves when he pulled Eli's suicide note out of the computer printer tray."

"Computer? I assumed the note would be handwritten."

"No. Printed and not even signed."

"Wow, I can't blame the solicitor for getting on West's case. Don't Ardon officers watch *NCIS* or *Criminal Minds*? Dad would immediately suspect the sheriff and deputy of trying to contaminate the crime scene."

"Your dad? I knew your mother was an attorney, but what's your father's tie to law enforcement?"

I laughed. "Strictly fictional. Dad may teach horticulture, but he loves murder mysteries. He's convinced he'll write a best-seller someday. Spends a lot of time researching police procedures. He takes a week of vacation every year to attend the Writers' Police Academy. Sounds like so much fun I plan to go with him one summer."

Andy bit his lip. "The fellow who found Eli said he cut him down because he couldn't stand to see a friend strung up like an oversized piñata. Maybe. But something was off. The sheriff claimed he had no idea that paper in the printer had anything to do with Eli's suicide. I didn't buy Jones' excuse. Don't think the solicitor did either.

"But that's not the main reason I'm suspicious. I'm convinced someone else typed that suicide note. Eli was a 'prepper'—do you know what that means?"

I shook my head. I'd heard the term but couldn't place it.

"Preppers believe civilization is going to implode—soon—and they plan to be the only ones prepared to live through the end times. The ultimate survivors. Eli was rabid about computers. Said technology was destroying our society, turning children into zombies. I heard his rave firsthand when he brought Jethro in for shots. He was furious Nancy'd bought a computer. Said he'd never touch the thing. Hard to imagine him choosing to type his last words on a computer."

Yes, I was right to doubt suicide. It was totally out of character. Now murder felt like a certainty. Someone had killed Eli.

Only one fact remained indisputable—a dead Eli couldn't have run me off the road. The EMS crew—folks Mom trusted—confirmed he died long before a monster truck played bumper cars with my little Prius. Who was it?

Swad, the restaurant, charmed me, as did my dinner companion. Andy put himself entirely in my hands, suggesting I order for both of us since he knew zip about Indian food. He promised to try anything. I hoped he wouldn't be disappointed. With all the questions I'd asked on our ride, Andy must have felt like he'd been locked in an interrogation room.

The pressure to select foods Andy might like vanished when my date told Swad's owner I was a vegan chef. We instantly became visiting royalty.

"Some of our vegetarian dishes include dairy, but we have lots of vegan choices," he said.

When the man hurried to the back of the cozy establishment for our hot tea, a woman wearing an apron emerged from the kitchen to chat us up.

"We've been here over twenty years," she said proudly, her English only slightly accented and easy to understand. "We want to prepare a sampling of vegan dishes for you."

When I raved about one sample, Andy took a big bite before I could warn him it merited a nine on my hot pepper-meter. Two large glasses of water later Andy's cheeks began to lose their fire-engine tint, and I could no longer count the beads of sweat on his forehead.

Andy laughed it off. A good sport. As I learned more about him, I understood why. He was the oldest of six kids. With five little sisters, he had a big leg up on understanding women, though it hadn't made him immune to his ex-wife's wiles. His family owned a farm and had the usual assortment of animals. He laughed when he admitted he sometimes hid out with the critters to escape his siblings for an hour or two of peace.

Our dinner conversation was light and easy. He was a good listener. I told him about my visit to Hog Heaven. Said Paint volunteered to escort me when I told him I'd love to do a little snooping. Andy took my outing with his friend in stride. No hint of jealousy. Of course, I didn't mention the end of the evening's make-my-toes-curl kiss.

After dinner, we drove to Greenville's trendy West End and strolled across the artsy suspension bridge that spanned the Reedy River. Though it was a tad cool, lots of couples were out, spooning on benches, smooching by the river. Friday was definitely date night. We paused in the middle of the footbridge to enjoy the Reedy River's spotlighted falls. Not Niagara, but pretty. The couple nearest us wasn't sightseeing. They were engaged in an enthusiastic lip lock.

"Guess tonight seems a little tame." Andy's arm snaked around my waist and pulled me closer. "If I'm going to compete with Paint, I'll need to figure out more exciting destinations."

"Tame feels wonderful," I answered. "This is exactly what I needed. Can't remember the last time I felt so relaxed."

Andy reeled me into his arms and settled a gentle kiss on my lips. His fingers slid through my curls. "I'm out of dating practice. But I wanted to do something to make those little worry lines between your eyebrows take a vacation."

Tasting like the spices we'd shared, the unexpected kiss made me feel warm and tingly all over. Aunt Eva was right. Nice didn't mean bland. Intuition told me Andy Green would be one incredible, caring lover.

What the heck was I going to do? I really, really liked Paint, and I really, really liked Andy. Never in my life had I dated two men at once. It felt wicked and sneaky, even if both men knew what I was doing. My Girl Scout upbringing was killing me—and my potential love life.

TWENTY-FOUR

The winking green digits on my clock confirmed the time: 5:37 a.m. I felt groggy, but, surprisingly, not grumpy. Maybe Eva was right. A little lovin'—even just a sweet kiss—was a definite mood booster. I threw on the clothes I'd laid out when I got home and hummed as I walked to the dairy.

"Morning," I greeted Eva.

"You're chipper this morning. So, who's it going to be—Andy or Paint? Or are you thinking ménage à trois?" Eva tilted her head back, and I think the correct term is "guffawed."

I rolled my eyes.

"Nope, can't see those boys sharing, even though they are best friends." My aunt was a champ at yanking my chain.

"I'm sure there's no scarcity of women who'd love a shot at Andy or Paint. Neither one would be devastated if I disappeared tomorrow."

"Don't kid yourself. They're both smitten. I can tell."

I had no desire to discuss my love life with Eva. Especially since I wasn't sure what I'd do if either man asked for a second date. I only felt certain about one thing. I wanted to keep Andy and Paint as friends.

Well, I knew one more thing. I was over Jack and ready to open a new chapter. I'd stayed with my cheating fiancé much longer than I should have. From the get-go, there'd been plenty of clues about his true character. I ignored them. Why? Did I mention Jack was a charming, sexy hunk? I'd taken a relationship sabbatical partially in hopes of curing my susceptibility to handsome—but deceptive—male packaging.

And it had. Granted, Paint's and Andy's exteriors were exceptionally fine. Yet I felt confident their good looks wouldn't stop me from noticing major character flaws—if they had any. So far so good. Too good.

Time to change the subject. "When is FedEx coming, and what can I do to help get the orders ready?"

Eva gave me my cheese-packing instructions, and then switched the radio to an old timey rock-and-roll station. She sang along as we worked. Eva knew all the lyrics, and she had a great singing voice. Deep, throaty. Her periodic gyrations—I assumed they were meant to be dance moves—were less impressive.

The music proved another mood lifter. I almost forgot someone out there with a monster truck had no qualms about forcing me to play demolition derby. Or that the sheriff wanted to seat my aunt—and, yes, me too—in state-provided electric chairs.

We packed the cheese in special Styrofoam shipping containers with little freezer bricks to keep the contents cold a minimum of forty-eight hours. Plenty of time for FedEx delivery.

"Glad we're done. I need to round up my show goats," Eva said. "We have students arriving at ten. They're enrolled in Tri Tech's program for veterinary assistants. Andy arranged the visit. Wonder if he'll sit in?"

"No, he told me he couldn't make it. Has to spend the morning at Gage's horse farm."

My father arrived just ahead of two van loads of vet assistant students.

"Dad, I didn't expect to see you until afternoon."

"Figured I might as well come over early. Your mother left for Columbia at six this morning for her law conference. She considered canceling, what with all the goings-on at Udderly, but she's a presenter. Not politic to cancel last minute, especially with a bunch of lawyers in the audience. They'd probably sue her for breach of contract."

"So you're going to spend the day with us?"

"Yep, and the night. Your mom won't be back until tomorrow afternoon. Since you refuse to come home, I'll bunk on Eva's couch. I know, I know. You two ladies don't think it's necessary, but it'll make me feel better."

I gave Dad another hug. "It's fine by me. Gotta run though. I want to hear Eva's spicl on goat breeds. I felt so dumb selling goat cheese and not knowing how to answer questions about Udderly's herd."

Dad nodded. "Eva makes learning fun. She'd be great in a classroom. Too bad she can't stand to spend more than thirty minutes indoors if the sun's shining. I'll join you soon as I stash my overnight bag."

I slid into an empty spot on the back bench. After Eva and Lilly started doing presentations for 4-H, scouting, and school groups, they set up an outdoor theater with rough-hewn benches clustered in a "V" around a huge oak stump. Eva was now perched on the stump, petting Kai, and telling all about the breed represented by Udderly's super-spoiled pet goat.

The Clemson part-timers, Orville and Frank, served as stagehands. As soon as Eva finished describing one breed, Frank led the model goat over to the benches so students could pet its coat and take a closer look at its distinctive features. Meanwhile, Orville ushered in the show goat for the next breed.

Halfway through the hands-on lecture, Dad settled beside me. "Learning anything?"

"Lots. I knew Udderly goats came in assorted sizes and colors, but I had no idea where the various breeds originated or anything about their history."

By the time Eva invited the group to the dairy barn, I'd learned Udderly kept five distinct breeds—Nigerian Dwarf, Pyrenean, Alpine, Anglo-Nubian, and La Mancha.

While the students toured the dairy, Dad and I set out cheese samples in the outdoor picnic area. As he unloaded a tray of crackers, plates, and napkins, he stopped and stared toward the spot where Tammy the potbellied pig had dug up Jed's skeleton. Worry lines crisscrossed his forehead. I felt awful that my stay at Udderly was adding to his grief for Lilly.

But I knew he'd make the same choice. I made a commitment to my aunt, and I'd honor it. Surely all the craziness would end soon. No matter how hard the sheriff tried, he couldn't railroad Aunt Eva. Mom would never let him frame her for Jed's murder. This was one time Eva wouldn't give Mom a hard time about her profession.

*   *   *

At lunch, Eva informed Dad and me that Frank and Orville were scheduled to work all day, and Shirley, a retired schoolteacher, would take her usual Saturday shift in the retail cabin. "Translation: I don't need you two. Find another way to amuse yourselves this afternoon. And Howard, you're welcome to sleep on the couch tonight, but I already made arrangements for a man on the premises. Billy will be spending the night."

Dad chewed his lip. He wasn't a prude, but the idea of his sister sleeping with a man she wasn't married to triggered a blush. "I'd still like to stay if that's okay."

"Fine. Guess everything's settled." A slight smile played on Eva's lips. I sensed she liked to prod her little brother occasionally just to watch him wriggle.

Seemed like a good time to jump in with my project. "Dad, will you help me go through the documents I copied at the courthouse?"

He'd barely gotten "sure" out of his mouth before I plunked a pile of papers in front of him. I put a second stack by my chair, while the floor received a pile of rejects Eva and I determined shed no light on Jed's mysterious disappearance and murder.

Dad tapped his pencil on the table as he eyed his homework. "Maybe we should treat this like we're plotting a murder mystery. You read through all the old newspaper stories, right? What did they report about Jed's disappearance? When? Where did they search for him? How long before they began to suspect foul play?"

I organized my thoughts. "Jed took off midday on a Friday. Within the hour, Eva packed up her dog and made her own getaway. She stayed out overnight, slept in her car, and returned Saturday afternoon. It was Monday night before she called any of Jed's friends or family to ask if they'd seen him or knew where he might be. She didn't report him missing until Wednesday."

"Did anyone find that strange?" Dad's eyebrows practically shook hands in the center of his forehead as he processed the data. "When did folks start searching for Jed?"

"The newspaper first reported him missing on Friday, exactly one week after he left. No one really worried or started looking for Jed in earnest until then," I answered. "Even his relatives shrugged off a week-long disappearance. Watson males often went on extended benders. Jed's buddies checked out his favorite fishing spots. Imagine they also visited red-light districts and gambling joints. Of course the newspaper makes no mention of that part of the search."

Dad tapped his pencil a little faster. "So no one actually poked around Udderly that first week. If Jed was killed and buried the day he disappeared, I wonder why someone didn't notice the freshly turned dirt and investigate."

I shook my head. "Jed's truck was gone. Probably didn't occur to Eva or anyone else that he might still be on the farm—dead or alive. His truck was never found. I looked at weather reports for that week. A ton of rain. The area where he was buried wasn't developed back then, and mud would have made it hard to spot any sign of a grave."

Dad nodded. "I'm leaning toward Jed being murdered the day he supposedly left to go fishing. But if we rule out Eva as the killer—and she's the heroine in my book—why would someone bury Jed on his own farm? To frame Eva? If not, what's the motive?"

I thought about Eva and Jed's troubled marriage, his physical abuse, and how things might have turned out for my aunt if he'd discovered her plan to divorce him. Usually fleeing wives were the ones who ended up with toe tags, not their bullying husbands.

"Dad, what if the killer planned to stage a murder-suicide? Make it look like Jed killed Eva because she had the gall to leave him, then regretted it, and took his own life? Or the flip, make it appear that Eva killed Jed and committed suicide. Either would have played in Ardon County four decades ago. Who'd question a murder-suicide if the bodies of a quarreling husband and wife were found together?"

Dad nodded. "If I buy your theory, what went wrong?"

I thought I knew.

"Eva wasn't here. Her car was gone. So was her dog. Night fell and she didn't return. The killer couldn't know if Eva ever planned to come back. Plus she might well have an airtight alibi if she did. If the killer couldn't finagle a murder-suicide, what was the next best thing?"

Dad smiled. "Maybe you should be the mystery writer. I like it. You're thinking he scrapped his original plan and buried Jed. Didn't want to tool around the countryside with a corpse riding shotgun.

When the body was eventually found, Eva would remain the prime suspect. If enough time passed, time of death would be uncertain and any alibi irrelevant. Unfortunately, the murdering SOB was right."

"Too bad we don't have a motive or a single candidate for the killer," I added. "When Mom's wearing her prosecutor's hat, she complains about the defense confusing the jury by parading a dozen potential suspects in front of them. We've yet to come up with anyone besides Eva who had a motive to murder Jed."

"Guess we should ask the old question: who profits?" Dad rifled through his stack of papers. "Let's read some more. Maybe the answer's buried in here. The body's been hidden for decades. The motive's been buried just as long."

Less than an hour later, I found a possibility.

"Dad, listen to this. Nancy was right about something. The day before Jed went missing he supposedly signed over his rights to a piece of property. Says here he did it in consideration of one dollar and some shares of this Kaiser guy's gold mine. According to Nancy, Jed knew Kaiser was a crook. That makes this sale mighty suspicious. Let's search for property transfers related to the parcel Jed sold."

We sifted through the property-related documents I'd copied—deeds, title transfers, liens, quit claims. In no time we'd pieced together part of the sales history for a large tract of mountain timberland. Eons ago it belonged to Jed's grandfather, Benjamin Watson. His two sons inherited. One son was Jed's father, the other was Willard Watson, whose only surviving child, Abigail, married Sheriff Robbie Jones.

"So when the sheriff said Jed was his cousin, he meant by marriage?" I wondered aloud.

"Yes." The affirmative came from the doorway. Paint smiled at me and nodded at Dad. "Hey, Howard. Good to see you. Looks like you transplants could use a little help with local genealogy."

"Definitely," I answered. "Have a seat. Do you know anything about some timberland Benjamin Watson, Jed's granddaddy, bought in the 1950s?"

Paint walked over and took my hand. "Seek and you shall find." He pulled me to my feet and led me toward an antique map mounted on the cabin wall. Dad walked over to join us in front of the drawing.

While not drawn to scale, the key mountains and passes carried the same labels today as they did when the map was created in the late 1800s. Only a few spellings had changed.

"That parcel is right about here." Paint's finger stabbed at a patch of green not far from a mountain peak.

"Isn't that near Sunrise Ridge?" Dad asked.

Paint laughed. "You get the prize. It *is* Sunrise Ridge, the same fancy resort that counts our very own sheriff, deputy, and local banker as investors."

"Wait a minute," I muttered. "We just learned the sheriff's wife, Abigail Watson-Jones, and Jed Watson sold that land to a Blue Ridge Consortium for a dollar each."

"That's the story," Paint agreed. "A dollar *plus* several thousand shares of Blue Ridge. Only the consortium was a big scam that fleeced lots of folks in these parts. My grandparents included."

"Would you two like to see Sunrise Ridge?" Paint asked. "It's a ritzy gated community. My cousin works security part-time on weekends. I can call. If he's working, he'll wave us through. If not, maybe he can call in a pass at the gate. It's a nice drive, not even an hour away." Paint's smile was a tease. "I promise to tell you all about the Blue Ridge Consortium swindle on the ride. How about it?"

I looked at my father, and he nodded.

"It's a deal," I said.

"Sounds like a humdinger of a story," Dad added.

Paint had certainly whetted my appetite. Had Jed really sold property rights to someone he'd pegged as a swindler? How had Sheriff Jones and Deputy West managed to climb into bed with Sunrise's developer?

Paint's version promised to be fascinating.

TWENTY-FIVE

Dad drove. His hybrid SUV, a black Toyota Highlander, was a lot roomier for our detective trio and less of a gas guzzler than Paint's truck. Plus we didn't want our visit to Sunrise Ridge to attract attention. Dad's ride was less conspicuous especially given Paint's Magic Moonshine signage.

I claimed the backseat, noting I needed less legroom than Paint. And Dad, who refused to admit to a slight hearing loss, would be better off sitting beside our local history docent.

Paint started talking as soon as Dad exited the Udderly Kidding driveway. "The other night I asked Dad what he remembered about Jed. He brought up all the hoopla about Kaiser's gold mine scam."

According to Paint's colorful synopsis, the glib, fast-talking Claude Kaiser introduced himself as a geologist/prospector upon his arrival in the county. The man claimed he'd discovered a rich gold deposit in the mountains. He showed off a big chunk of gold and said he just needed investors to finance the mining operation.

"The fraudster hooked investors left and right, had 'em lining up to plunk down money for shares in the mine," Paint said.

"So Kaiser was a complete scam artist?" I asked.

Paint grinned. "Yep. A Yankee, of course. He snuck out of town with all the cash before the bubble burst. Disappeared about the same time as Jed. Nobody ever saw hide nor hair of him—or their money—again."

I shivered. Disappeared, huh? Could there be another skeleton buried on Udderly?

"How does the Watson timberland fit in?" I asked.

"Ah, you Yankees don't appreciate Southern storytelling; always want to cut to the chase. I'm getting there. Relax. The sheriff's wife,

Abigail, convinced her husband it was the chance of a lifetime, but—as my granny would say—the couple didn't have a pot to pee in. That's when Kaiser offered to take the Watson timberland in lieu of cash. Problem was Abigail and her hubby couldn't transfer the title to Kaiser without Jed agreeing to it. And my dad recalls that Jed balked."

"Whoa." I interrupted. "Jed also told Nancy the gold mine was bogus. Did the sheriff try to force his brother-in-law to sign over his rights?" I couldn't keep the excitement out of my voice.

"Excellent question." Paint swiveled in his seat and grinned at me. "Won't try to sell you any bridges."

"Come on; let's hear the rest of it. Don't be a tease." Paint's land scam history lesson seemed to promise a boatload of murder motives.

"Who knows if Jed actually signed," he continued. "Once he disappeared, no one questioned his signature."

Dad looked in the rearview mirror and caught my eye. "Victor's name was on that deed transfer as a witness. The banker's signature would have kept Sis from questioning the sale. She already had the Watson clan accusing her of foul play. An added fight with Jed's cousin, Abigail, and her sheriff husband would have made matters worse. Besides, I don't imagine folks thought that land was worth much back then. Few roads. Remote. Plenty of timber closer and easier to harvest. Who'd have dreamed it would become a retreat for multimillionaires a few decades later?"

I nodded. "I wonder if Aunt Eva even knew Jed had a half-interest in that timberland. I doubt he was the type to tell his wife anything he considered his business."

"You have him pegged," Dad replied.

"At least we have some possible motives," I said. "Maybe Abigail and the sheriff killed Jed and paid Victor to lie and say he witnessed Jed's signature."

Paint laughed. "What a devious mind. I like it. Trouble is I don't see any link between Jed's murder decades ago and Nancy Watson's murder in the here and now."

He had me there. I hadn't a clue.

"We need to add Eli Watson to the murder list." I explained all the reasons I doubted he committed suicide. Paint and Dad nodded their agreement.

For a few minutes, we all sat quietly. In my case, my brain wasn't quiet. It was scrambling to find some way to fit all the puzzle pieces together.

We passed a mountain stream that had overflowed its banks to create an impromptu waterfall near the road. Miniature rainbows winked from the wet rocks surrounding the gurgling water. I buzzed down my window and sucked in a lungful of pine-scented air, hoping it would clear my mind.

"Beautiful," I said. "This is such a pretty drive."

"Doesn't take long to get into high country," Dad commented.

"That's what I love about Ardon County," Paint said. "We cozy right up to the mountains. Best place in the world to hunt and fish."

"What do you hunt?" Dad asked.

"Deer mostly, occasionally bear. I like the bow and arrow season best, though I have better luck with my .30-06. I like to fly fish, too. Know some great trout streams. Want to join me sometime?"

"Love to," Dad answered. "Haven't had my .22 out in ages. The deer won't be in much danger. Doubt I'd have any better luck fly fishing. Not how I used to pull catfish out of the river. But it would be fun to try."

Dad's response surprised me. I knew he'd gone pheasant and rabbit hunting when he was growing up in Iowa. Just didn't realize he still owned a gun or had any inclination to use one.

Paint twisted in his seat to draw me into the conversation. "Hey, you're invited, too. Don't want you to think I'm sexist. Have no problem with gun-toting ladies, unless they're mad at me."

I laughed. "Eva's giving me shooting lessons, so you'd better be nice."

Dad's head whipped around. "Eva's teaching you to shoot? Why?"

"Coyotes, Dad. Relax. I'm not chomping at the bit to get a concealed carry permit. I plan to restrict my mountain hunting to wild mushrooms and berries."

A horn blasted, and I looked behind us. A beat-up truck flying a large Confederate flag was practically kissing our bumper.

"Idiot," Dad muttered as he swung into one of the twisting road's scenic pull-offs to let the redneck shoot by.

"Plenty of idiots to go around," Paint said.

Five minutes later Dad pulled up to a guard hut. It looked like an overgrown Barbie dollhouse and sat a few feet ahead of scrolled wrought-iron gates. A uniformed guard stepped out of the playhouse as Dad rolled down his window. Paint leaned across the front seat to put his mug in view.

"Hi, Cuz," Paint said. "Gonna let the riffraff through?"

The moonshiner's cousin, a fresh-faced, innocent-looking representative of the Paynter gene pool, chuckled. "I see one riffraff and two potential buyers. Put this visitor card on your dashboard and don't get in any trouble. No speeding, no spitting, no bare butts pressed against windows. The Tisnomi folks from Japan are visiting today. Hope they'll be my new employers, so be on your best behavior."

"Got it," Paint said. "Thanks."

With our visitor permit properly displayed, we rolled through the slowly opening iron gates. Dad nodded at the posted speed limit—twenty-five miles per hour. "Not sure I can coast that slowly on the downhills. Looks like there are some pretty steep grades."

Indeed. We'd entered the development at a high point near the peak of the mountain. The mountain vistas, speckled with impressive mansions, were spectacular. But the roads crisscrossing Sunrise Ridge rose and fell like the framework of some giant roller coaster. The next sharp turn put us beside a sparkling lake.

"Hope your brakes work," I mumbled. "What do these folks do in winter if there's an ice storm and someone has an emergency? It would take an ambulance forever to skate its way up here."

"Sunrise has its own helicopter and helipad," Paint answered. "That's how the rich folks arrive. Helicopter picks 'em up at the Greenville airport. They leave a spare SUV or two here plus a golf cart to tool around the neighborhood. Their lackeys stock the houses in advance with whatever they want. Quite the pampered life."

"Wonder if there are any vegans looking for a live-in chef?"

Dad laughed. "You'd go nuts. Bet there aren't many people under fifty."

"Yeah, but it is beautiful."

My opinion didn't change as we slalomed up and down the hills. There weren't a lot of houses, but the ones that had been built were stone-and-glass masterworks. Each home commanded its own acre or two of manicured grounds. Yet, after twenty minutes of driving, the custom mansions began to look sterile and cookie cutter despite the variety of quarried stone and the addition or subtraction of add-on towers and porches to change the profiles.

"Maybe it's just me, but this looks like a movie set. I'm beginning to wonder what's behind the facades."

"The landscaping screams Stepford Wives," Dad said, adding his horticultural critique. "It's as if each owner's given a list of plants they can install. Did someone tell these folks 'natural' and 'nature' were dirty words? I haven't seen a single native plant. For that matter, it's a gorgeous day, and I haven't seen a single homeowner puttering in a yard. Just hired help."

"Right on the money on all counts." Paint smiled. "The Sunrise covenants not only specify what you can plant but call out sizes. Every landscape plan has to be approved by committee. Me, I want to decide what I want on my land—trees, plants, chickens, dogs—"

"And a wolf, right?" I chuckled, then noticed Dad's puzzled look in the rearview mirror.

"Brie's talking about my pet wolf, Lunar. Adopted him as an orphaned pup."

The road we'd been following dead-ended at another elaborate gate. It barred the entrance to the dirt lane that lay beyond. A sign read: Sunrise Ridge Phase III. A limo sat just inside the gate where a gaggle of short, raven-haired gentlemen in business suits were studying what looked like a large plat map.

"Got to be the Tisnomi folks," Paint said.

"No doubt," Dad added. "The Sunrise Ridge investors must be relieved they finally settled the conservation lawsuit blocking development. Wonder how Sunrise promised to protect the fragile hillside. The lawsuit claimed erosion would contaminate a creek and pollute public land downstream."

"Even with the settlement, the scuttlebutt predicts the current owners will be forced to file for bankruptcy if this sale falls through," Paint added. "That Taj Mahal clubhouse, the riding stables, the fitness center, swimming complex—all were cost-justified using optimistic arithmetic that assumed a quick sale of all lots in Phases I, II, and III. The environmental lawsuit stalled Phase III for a decade and cut off

Sunrise Ridge's main revenue stream. The project's been bleeding greenbacks ever since, trying to keep up the spiffy amenities with too few owners to fork over monthly dues."

"Ouch," I said. "No wonder they want this Tisnomi sale."

Dad turned the SUV around and we headed down the mountain. Sunrise Ridge offered nifty views. But...would I really want to live in a house with six bathrooms I had to clean? And covenants that dictated what posies I could plant? Wonder if they'd even let me grow my own veggies? Aunt Eva's log cabin was looking mighty attractive—even if the yard art snorted and barked and the doggie deposits were plentiful.

We were halfway home when an Ardon County Sheriff's cruiser zipped by, headed up the mountain. I spotted Sheriff Jones at the wheel with fellow investor Deputy West riding shotgun. Were they checking on their investment? Taking a course in Japanese?

Of course, Sunrise Ridge did reside in Ardon County. They could be answering a complaint. Maybe an owner reported some riffraff had snuck inside the gates on a sunny Saturday afternoon.

Did the lawmen notice said riffraff as they whizzed by in the opposite direction?

TWENTY-SIX

It was after four o'clock when Dad pulled into the parking apron at the end of Udderly's drive. Judging by the number of cars parked catawampus in the crowded space, Eva was having a terrific sales day. I scanned the lot for hearses, ambulances, and cop cars. Automatic reflex. Kind of depressing it had come to that. Still, I was thrilled all vehicles looked like they'd be suitable rides for soccer moms.

Dad turned to Paint as we exited the SUV. "Want to join us for supper? I'm an uninvited guest, so I figured I'd spring for dinner—either takeout or a restaurant."

"Believe me, wish I could." Paint cast a lingering glance my way. "But Saturday evenings are mighty busy at Magic Moonshine, and I'm short-staffed. I have just enough time to pick up some fried chicken—sorry Brie—and head to work. Won't get off until I close 'er up at nine."

"Gee, what a shame," a male voice interjected.

Paint jumped. "Andy, what'ya doing here? Didn't see your truck."

"Working, what d'ya think?" the lanky vet replied. "Checking on new kids. Quite a crop this week. Pulled behind the barn to leave room for customers."

"Oh." Paint flicked another glance my way. His eyes narrowed as he nodded at Andy. "Well, as I said, got to run. See y'all soon. Don't do anything I wouldn't do."

Andy laughed. "You're kind of leaving the door wide open."

Sometimes Dad could be pretty slow to pick up on undercurrents, but his grin said he realized two bulls were pawing the ground to impress his little heifer. I felt flustered and flattered.

Andy waited until Paint climbed in his truck to tell us Eva had invited him to dinner. "She mentioned burgers—guess the black bean variety for you, Brie. Billy's bringing dessert—an apple crisp he promises is one hundred percent vegan. Now there's a man who knows how to cook. Me, I'm useless in the kitchen."

"Maybe Brie can give you lessons." Dad's twinkling eyes said he was enjoying himself.

"Sounds great. I'll be back soon as I shower and change clothes. Essential if I want anyone to sit by me."

The burgers were good. Well, my black bean version was scrumptious. Cooking on a grill made everything taste better. I assembled veggie shish kebabs to go with the burgers.

Billy's whiskered face sported a big grin as he served his apple crisp. "Eva told me you might not eat it if I used butter. Broke my heart to tinker with my ma's fail-safe recipe, but it looks like that coconut oil didn't hurt it none."

"I'm having mine a la mode," Eva said. "Who else wants ice cream? This pandering to vegans can only go so far."

I arched my eyebrows. "Like you ever 'pander' to me. Sure you don't want melted cheese on your crisp?"

Eva laughed. "Nah, ice cream will suffice."

One bite and we all certified the crisp as delicious. Of course, mine was the only pure vote since it wasn't contaminated with dairy.

After clearing the table, we broke out the cards for a game of hearts. Aunt Eva and Dad were demons at the game. Billy, Andy, and I competed fiercely for last place.

We were on a third game when the barking began. One of the Great Pyrenees raising a ruckus.

"Coyotes?" Billy suggested. "Old Mark seems to know whenever tasty little kids arrive. He might have brought along a girlfriend. The old coot has a knack for recruiting a coyote honey to help distract the dogs."

Aunt Eva jumped up. "Let's go. I'll grab my shotgun."

"My gun's in the truck," Andy and Billy said in perfect unison.

Both men hustled toward the door. "Can't let that coyote harm another of your dogs," Andy added. "Love those big shaggy mutts."

Dad and I stood, ready to keep the gun-toters company. The coyotes only posed a danger for goats and dogs. They didn't tangle with humans, at least according to Aunt Eva's past lectures on the varmints. And, even though I trusted her completely, I confirmed her facts with a Google search.

Coyotes are smart, secretive, and adaptable. No wonder the cartoon version's named "Wile E." Their numbers and range keep growing. Humans rarely see them. When they do come in contact with people, they run. Eva claims they're good for forty-mile-an-hour sprints. Not much danger of humans catching them. Unlike wolves, they typically hunt alone or in pairs. Only form packs when food is in short supply.

Eva spotted Dad and me waiting for her by the door. "Keep your butts behind our guns. I'm already accused of killing my husband. Don't want to add notches for any kin I actually like."

Eva and Dad grabbed two flashlights stored on the windowsill. Without my own light, I was determined to stay on Dad's heels to avoid breaking an ankle.

The barking continued at full throttle as Billy and Andy, both toting rifles, caught up with us in the front yard. Eva and Dad led us toward the commotion. A shot rang out, followed by a horrible yelp.

What the Feta? None of our shooters had pulled a trigger.

"Damn!" Eva yelled. "Someone shot one of my dogs."

She ran and we stumbled after her at breakneck speed. A broken ankle had become the last thing on my mind. A tiny niggle in the back of my brain argued, "You're running in the dark. Toward gunfire. Are you nuts?"

I didn't listen. One of Eva's Great Pyrenees was in pain.

As we crested a hill, headlights flared on the dirt road running parallel to Udderly's northern boundary. An engine growled and the lights vanished. Total silence, except for a dog's whimper.

Andy was the first to reach the Great Pyrenees, who lay on her side whining. Eva positioned a flashlight so the veterinarian could see to probe a patch of bloody fur on the dog's chest.

"The bullet grazed her, didn't enter," he said. "She'll be fine. She's just in shock."

"Thank heaven," Eva murmured, stroking Socks' furry head. "Billy, will you go back and get the ATV? Socks weighs over one hundred pounds—awful heavy and awkward to carry. Besides jostling might hurt her more. I want to stay with my girl."

"I'll be right back." Billy took off at a fast trot.

"Someone was messing around on your property," Dad said. "They shot your dog. We should call the sheriff."

Eva snorted. "Normal times, I might agree. Not now. Ol' Sheriff Jones wouldn't walk across the street to figure out which of his damn relatives is taking potshots. Unless he wanted to buy the shooter dinner. I refuse to invite that man on my property for any reason. Let's just take care of Socks."

I shivered. Hadn't thought of putting on a jacket when we ran out of the cabin. A chilly wind made it feel like we'd rolled the calendar back to February. As we waited for Billy, Eva murmured soothingly to her injured dog.

When Socks tried to lever herself up, Eva gently pushed her back down. "Just a few more minutes, girl. We'll take you to the house. Andy'll fix you right up. You'll sleep inside with me tonight."

I was spitting mad. Who did this? I was pretty sure it wasn't poachers. But why did they have to shoot Socks?

I stamped my feet to rev up my circulation and fight off the cold. The moon was nearly full, and my night vision was steadily improving. As my gaze raked the area, I spotted boot prints and followed the tracks. I'd only gone a few yards when I almost fell in a hole that was maybe four feet deep and a couple feet across. A mounded pile of fresh dirt and the dig's squarish edges shouted animals weren't to blame. I squatted and squinted, trying to see anything besides dirt in the pit. Moonlight glittered on a narrow strip of white.

"Andy, Dad, could one of you bring a flashlight over?" I asked.

Both walked over and probed the hole with their beams.

"Good God, is that a bone?" Dad muttered. "Another damn skeleton?"

"What the hell?" Eva exclaimed. "Are you telling me somebody was burying another body? Are they trying to turn my farm into a damn cemetery?"

Billy pulled up in the ATV just in time to hear Eva cursing. "Was Socks digging up some animal carcass?" he asked.

"No." Andy lay on his stomach and reached down to extract a long, thin bone. "Looks like a tibia—the larger of the leg bones below the kneecap."

"As in human kneecap?" I asked.

"'Fraid so," he answered.

"Hell's bells," Aunt Eva said. "Put that back where you found it. Daylight's soon enough to scout for more bones. Right now, it's time to get Socks fixed up. And for me to fix one tall bourbon. Maybe two."

Back at the cabin, Andy cut away a patch of Socks' fur, cleaned the wound, applied some sort of medical goo and a bandage. Then we all had a stiff drink.

Dad turned to Andy. "You really think we have another human skeleton out there?"

Andy nodded. "Animals can scavenge and carry bones a long way. But someone dug that hole, and I'm guessing they knew there was a skeleton down there."

"I agree," Dad said. "They must have put it there in the first place. That's the only way they'd know where to dig."

My head was spinning. "Why would people dig up a skeleton they'd taken the trouble to bury?"

Then I thought of an explanation.

"Maybe the discovery of Jed's bones made our grave robbers worry the other body they dumped would surface, too. I'll bet they were planning to relocate their victim where animals wouldn't uncover the corpse. If Socks hadn't scared them, we might never have known they'd been here."

Dad nodded. "Possible. But it still begs the question: Why dig up a body that's been in the ground so long there's no flesh left on the bones? It would be next to impossible to prove who was responsible for the murder."

"True," I answered. "But another body might direct suspicion away from Eva—especially if the body turned out to be someone she had no reason to kill."

Dad picked up the thread. "Brie, remember how Paint told us that Kaiser crook disappeared around the same time as Jed? Maybe it's him."

"I can only hope," Billy said. "That damn con man nearly broke my folks. Stole their life savings. They were lucky to hang on to our farm. Lot of my other kin got suckered, too. I might have been as foolish, listening to his promises, if I'd had an extra sawbuck back then."

Eva looked at Billy and nodded. "Maybe those bones do belong to that Kaiser fella, and the killers who shot Jed arranged the same end for him. But if that's the case, why would they bury the bodies a mile apart? Seems like a lot of extra effort unless they shot 'em where they're buried. Hard to imagine why Kaiser would have been on Udderly property."

Billy frowned as he studied his wool socks. He'd taken off his muddy boots and left them by the door. "Don't know about what happened years back, but I have a thought or two about who shot Socks. Sure sounded like a diesel engine that fired up and took off."

He looked over at Andy and Dad for confirmation. Andy was the first to answer.

"Hey, I can tell dog breeds by their bark, but truck engines, not a chance."

"I'm even more clueless about engine noises than Andy," Dad added. "I don't even own a truck."

"Does knowing it's a diesel tell you what kind of vehicle we're looking at?" Eva asked.

Billy scratched his chin and looked at the ceiling. "Given the height and shape of those headlights, my best guess is a RAM pickup." He paused a second. "Hey, you know who drives one of them RAM diesels in his off hours? Deputy West."

Stinky Blue Cheese. Might Deputy West also have samples of my little car's paint on his big fat bumper? I felt certain that snaggle-toothed bologna brain was capable.

"True, Deputy West drives a RAM, but so do a dozen of the farmers I visit," Andy said. "Not exactly conclusive."

Andy was right, though I wanted it to be West, the pig. Of course, calling him a pig was an affront to my porcine friend Tammy. Unfortunately, it was all idle speculation.

Dad stood. "Doubt we can solve this mystery tonight. And since my big sister refuses to let the local law know about our trespassers, we might as well get some sleep. Guess morning's soon enough to ask Iris how we can call in the state troopers without alerting the sheriff."

Eva's shoulders slumped. "Well, we're agreed on one thing. I'm all for calling it a night."

"Want me to stay?" Andy asked. "I have a sleeping bag in the truck. I think Socks will be fine, but it might not be a bad idea to have reinforcements if the idiot or idiots who shot her come back."

Eva chuckled as she shook her head. "Hey, this is a one-holer cabin. We're past capacity now with four occupants vying for dibs on one latrine. Go home. You have your own animals to care for. Thanks again for patching up Socks."

I stood. "I'll walk you out."

As soon as we reached the porch, Andy put his arms around me. "Billy and your dad are good guys, and I love your aunt, but I sure wished we'd had a few minutes—better yet a few hours—alone."

His soft, warm lips found mine. I hadn't bothered to put on a coat to walk him out and the cool air raised goosebumps on my arms. I felt his heat as contact with every part—yep, every part—of his body warmed me up. His fingers massaged my back as they edged downward. Who needed ice cream when apple crisp could come with snuggling a la mode?

Andy's breathing suggested he was excited about more than our gun-toting intruders. Good thing he wasn't spending the night. Knowing his lean, warm body waited a few feet away might have defeated any attempt at meditative chastity.

Breathe in, breathe out.

"I'd better leave before your dad borrows a shotgun and comes looking for me," he said. "I'll be by tomorrow. Must be some way I can help. Eva certainly didn't kill anyone. She won't even shoot a goat-stealing coyote like Mark. She talks big about putting lead in that bandit's bony ass, but I've watched her. Even if she has a clear shot, she aims at the ground a couple feet away. Just wants to scare him."

"Thanks, Andy. Hope you know how much Eva appreciates your help. She thinks the world of you."

He grinned. "Now if I can just get her niece to share that opinion."

Before I could answer, he climbed in his truck.

Well, Andy, you're steadily climbing my opinion ladder. But then so is Paint.

Son of a Porterhouse. They could both make me hotter than a jalapeno without a teaspoon of water in sight. And I was finding meditation had hormonal limits.

TWENTY-SEVEN

"Sunday doesn't mean a day off." Eva's voice broke through my dream. She shook my shoulder again, a tad harder this time. The room was inky black. Were roosters even ruffling their feathers yet?

"Shoulda warned you I don't ask part-timers to help on Sunday mornings. Lilly and I figured folks ought to get a chance to take a pew at church if they had a mind to. Them off means you on."

I blinked, still half asleep. While I'd often spent weekends with my aunts, they apparently gave guests the same sleep-in reprieve as their part-time help. But I wasn't a guest anymore.

"Liverwurst and Limburger. All right, already. I'm getting up." I yawned and threw back the quilt. "Are Dad and Billy up? Can I make a quick bathroom run or is it occupied?"

"Seeing how you're the only one sleeping in, you get a free bathroom pass, even though you're still taking the names of heavenly cheeses in vain."

Sleeping in? What time would my aunt consider early to rise? Four a.m.?

"Billy's gone. Helping a friend patch a barn roof. Howard's in the milking barn. Need you to gather eggs and feed the horses, dogs, and any other critters you find in the barnyard. Once Howard and I finish milking, we'll divvy up chores and call SLED about those bones. You can work the retail counter when we open at one." Eva chuckled. "And don't you go talkin' cholesterol counts to our customers or using none of your 'cheeses' swear words."

In the horse barn, I engaged in my usual do-si-do trying to feed Rita, Lilly's mule. I'd yet to keep her obstinate fat head out of the feed bucket long enough to serve her breakfast like a lady. A chorus of barking dogs broke the morning quiet, followed by the sound of flying gravel. Why were cars fishtailing in our driveway at sunrise?

I ran out of the barn as a second car door slammed. Sheriff Jones and his buddy Deputy West exited one car, and two more deputies climbed out of vehicle number two. What now?

Eva and Dad stood side by side. As the deputies approached, Dad put an arm around Eva's shoulder.

Sheriff Jones strutted to within three feet of my aunt. A growl formed deep in Socks' throat as the injured dog stood guard at her mistress's side.

Cheeses! Had Jones moved his hand to the butt of his gun? The backup lawmen spread and took a couple steps back. One even crouched in a quick draw stance. All of their squinty eyes focused on Socks.

I ran toward my aunt to shift their attention my way and skidded to a stop beside Socks. The hair on the back of the dog's neck formed a stiff warning as her protective growl deepened. Aunt Eva's fists curled as she fought control.

"Down girl," she ordered Socks, her voice calm but stern. I hoped she'd pay heed to her own advice. It didn't pay to mouth off to a bunch of trigger-happy idiots.

She glared at Jones. "What's the meaning of this?"

"Eva Hooker, you are under arrest for the murder of Jed Watson," he answered. "Brought reinforcements in case you want to do this the hard way. I know you got guns and guard dogs. Don't want to kill no dogs, but I will if they give me cause."

"What in hell are you talking about?" Dad sputtered. "You can't tell me you have enough evidence to arrest Eva."

"Oh, but I can." Jones smirked and held up his index finger. "First, the bullet discovered in Jed's skull came from the rifle we found hidden in the attic of her barn."

He smiled and held up his middle finger, easing down his index finger to leave his middle digit proudly alone. "Second, we have motive. Got three sworn statements that Jed Watson learned Eva planned to file for divorce, and he told her she wouldn't get a penny when he kicked her to the curb. Ample reason for the Mrs. to opt for a profitable shotgun divorce."

"You're nuts," Dad snarled.

Eva put her hand on his arm, then reached down to stroke her dog's head. "Socks, stay."

I shook with anger as my aunt held out her hands to be cuffed.

"I'll come peaceful like," Eva said. "Just keep your voice down and don't rile Socks or my brother." She chuckled. "Don't want either of them to come to harm or get rabies from biting the likes of you."

As the sheriff snapped handcuffs on Eva, I crouched to hold Socks' collar. The last thing my aunt needed was some burger brain putting more lead in her dog. Sheriff Jones extracted a wrinkled slip of paper from his breast pocket and began reading Eva her rights. Who knew he could read?

Jones marched her toward his car. One of his ham hands smashed the curls atop her head as he shoved her into the car's backseat.

Eva called to Dad before the door closed. "Call Iris, she'll know what to do. Then finish the damn chores and open the retail cabin at one. We're gonna need all the cash we can get. Bail bonds don't come cheap."

My shell-shocked dad stayed mute until both cars disappeared in a cloud of dust. Socks was the only one talking, her whines plain pitiful.

"Let's go inside." Dad let out an anguished sigh. "Hope to hell Iris knows who to call on a Sunday to arrange bail."

My stomach flip-flopped. "Do they even grant bail to someone charged with murder?"

"Good heavens. Hadn't even considered the alternative. Surely they will. It's not like Eva's been a menace to society the past forty years."

I looked at my watch—8:05. While the sheriff had waited for sunup to make his arrest, he hadn't dillydallied. Thank heavens all the goats were milked. I made a mental list of chores we had to do before we left. Brewing a pot of coffee topped my list. Had the feeling Dad and I needed all the caffeine we could get to keep our wits about us.

By the time Dad received a legal to-do list from Mom, we had less than an hour to get to Boughton Bail Bonds for our nine-thirty meeting with the owner. Mom had already spoken with Bessie, and the widowed owner of the bail bond business was expecting us. We made one small detour to pick up a deed to my parents' house. They were pledging it as collateral until Eva could sign the papers for Udderly. Even with that stop, we pulled up in front of the bail bond office five minutes ahead of schedule.

The drab gray building looked as if some mad dentist had outfitted it with oversized braces. The door and windows bristled with bars and iron checkerboard grills. All that was missing was a guard dog and a rooftop sniper. Understandable given it was a largely cash business in an iffy neighborhood.

Dad hit the buzzer. We heard a series of ka-chunks as someone threw what had to be an impressive array of bolts. A minute later, a large, imposing black woman flung open the door.

"You must be Howard and Brie." She greeted us with a pearly smile and a voice designed to call children from a block away. She seemed to fill the space around her with joy. Despite the reason for our visit, I couldn't help smiling in return. Even her clothes were joyful. All the way up to her oversized purple hat with a spray of lilies on the brim.

"Hello," Dad fumbled.

"Sorry 'bout your predicament," Bessie said. "I was on my way to church when Iris called." She shook her head. "Don't know what Sheriff Jones is thinkin'. Usually I'm meetin' folks whose kids have gone stupid drinkin' and raisin' cane. If'n I decide to bond 'em out, they get a lecture 'bout not causin' good folks more heartache. But I know Eva. She *is* good folk. Always generous when I need help for Haven House. That safe house for abused wives and kids is close to my heart. Eva's too."

"Thanks for meeting us on such short notice," Dad said.

"Not a problem for a friend," Bessie said. "You're good to post bail for up to a million—though I can't imagine the court'll ask that much given the circumstances. Iris said you can write me a check for $10,000, and you said you brought the deed to your house?"

Dad signed papers and our business with Bessie concluded before ten a.m. The deadline she'd set to be off to church so she wouldn't miss too much preaching.

Our next stop—county jail. I'd driven by the facility plenty of times and hardly noticed it. The new plain-Jane institutional building featured no exterior bars, and the surrounding open space was all green lawn, not a single fence topped with barbed wire.

Once inside, an officer ushered Dad and me into what looked like a television viewing room. Three chairs half circled a TV monitor. Huh? A thousand movies had prepped me to expect Aunt Eva to appear on the other side of a pane of bulletproof glass. We'd pick up a phone on our end. She'd look at us until we pointed and pantomimed for her to pick up the phone on her end. Not happening.

An officer quickly disabused us of all our preconceived notions. It appeared we'd subscribed to the jail's very own cable channel. Ardon County had gone high-tech. We'd basically get the same view of my aunt we'd get if we were Skyping with her from some prison in Iran. The officer mashed a button and Eva appeared. When my aunt saw us, she blinked and tried to smile. The effort was fleeting. More sad than reassuring.

"Are you okay?" Dad asked.

"Well, except for the orange jumpsuit. I may wear an orange visor on occasion for Clemson, but orange head to foot has never flattered anyone. 'Course I have a bigger, itchier wardrobe complaint. They took all my clothes. Let me repeat ALL my clothes, including undies, and they don't issue replacements. Can you believe it? I had to buy underwear. From them."

She snorted. "Must have some under-the-counter deal with Dollar General or K-mart. But I'm in no position to protest. You need to put about fifty dollars in an account for me. That'll let me purchase unmentionables, a candy bar or two, and a set of earphones. We can watch as much TV as we like, but only the images are free. Have to buy earphones to listen. Sorta like to hear what the news is sayin' about me."

"My God, this is medieval," Dad sputtered. "I never dreamed. Of course we'll set up an account, and we'll have you out on bail in no time. Already talked with Bessie Boughton. She's more than happy to provide bail. Said you're always mighty generous when it comes to Haven House."

Eva chuckled. "Might not be quite so generous this year if I'm still in the pokey. When will bail be set?"

Dad frowned. "Not till morning. Iris is driving home now. Says she'll handle the bail hearing, but we need to hire a criminal attorney to handle your case after that."

The on-screen Eva's gaze shifted slightly. I could tell she was looking at me. "Niece, you need to hightail it back to Udderly and open the retail shop. Need you to be selling cheese, fudge, and goat soap with more fervor than a televangelist. We need to bring in some cash. If Sheriff Jones and the Watsons succeed in bankrupting Udderly, they'll win even if I spend only one night in jail."

"Don't worry," I said. "We're heading right back to the farm."

My aunt chewed on her lip and ducked her head sideways. A pantomime to let us know anything she said would be heard by unseen ears.

"You know that big bone Socks wanted to chew last night? I'm afraid it might break and stick in her throat. Better make sure it's safely put away."

Cheeses. Eva's arrest had pushed everything else out of my mind. Apparently Dad's, too. We totally forgot about the new bones and Eva's agreement to call SLED.

"Will do," I agreed even though I wasn't sure what she meant by "safely put away." Did Eva want us to hide the presumed gravesite we'd discovered? Mom was en route. Maybe she'd know what was best. We'd hoped to call in state troopers as soon as we completed our early morning chores, but the sheriff derailed our good intentions. Would failing to report our discovery in a timely manner make us guilty of a crime and eligible to join Eva in jail? If so, I wanted a huge spending account for underwear.

TWENTY-EIGHT

We'd just made it back to Udderly when Andy and Paint arrived.

"How's Eva?" Paint asked.

"Still feisty, but she's clearly worried," I answered.

Andy frowned. "The sheriff's off his rocker. Eva's no killer. As soon as we heard about her arrest, we met and talked over how we might help."

"We've both cleared the decks as far as our immediate responsibilities go," Paint added. "If it's okay with you, we'll bed down here for the next few days."

"We hope there won't be any more nighttime trespassers," Andy said. "But just in case, we didn't want Brie here alone."

Mom and Dad seemed to be nodding their approval. Good.

"Oh, wiener warts." I gasped, and then laughed when I saw the startled looks on my would-be heroes' faces. "I can't get distracted again. At the jail Aunt Eva's final marching orders were to keep that bone we found last night safe. Paint, did Andy tell you about our nocturnal adventures?"

"Yep, sorry I missed out on the fun," Paint said. "What do you suppose Eva meant by 'safe'—away from the sheriff's grubby mitts?"

Mom shook her head. "I'm an officer of the court. Not sure I should be listening to this conversation. I understand that Eva agreed last night to bypass the local law and report the find directly to SLED this morning. But now Howard thinks he should hold off contacting SLED until Eva gets home on bail. I'm uneasy about the delay."

"Why don't Paint and I ride up to the property line and take pictures?" Andy suggested. "We can throw a tarp over the hole until Eva gets back."

I turned to Mom. "Do you mind if I go with them? I'll come right back. I'd sort of like to see the scene in daylight. Maybe that'll help chase those spooky images out of my head."

"Sure, go on. Looks like you have capable escorts." She smiled.

"By the way, boys, I don't have a problem with both of you staying the night so long as my daughter doesn't object. Might have worried about Brie's reputation if just one of you bunked here. But both? Nah, you'll keep each other honest."

A look passed between the "boys." Obvious they'd talked it over. Was I a prize in some new buddy competition? Couldn't decide how I felt about that. Maybe I'd work both their butts off to win another kiss.

Only any kissing would have to wait until we cleared Eva's name.

Eva's ATV had two seats and one cargo bed. I jumped in the back. "You two take the front. I want to stretch my legs. Been standing way too long."

I sprawled in the back. A minute later I was hanging on to the roll bar as we bounced our way over Udderly's roller-coaster fields, startling goats along the way. Last night it had taken almost ten winded minutes to run to the property line and reach the injured Socks. Our motorized transport delivered us in a fraction of the time.

"What the...?"

Paint was the first to spot the huge, gaping hole. We jumped from the ATV and walked over to the edge. The hole was now an eight-foot-deep abyss and three feet wide. No dirt piled anywhere. Just a fresh, empty crater. No bones. No anything.

Since I was pretty sure a meteor hadn't slammed into the earth since we'd surprised last night's trespassers, I surmised they'd come back—and arrived better equipped.

Andy knelt beside a wide tread mark imprinted in the damp earth. "Look at these tracks. Can you believe it? A really big backhoe. Construction grade."

Paint walked from the big dig to a decimated portion of the border fence. "They didn't mess around. Looks like they had a dump truck waiting on this side of the fence."

"What on earth? When did this happen?" My mouth hung open.

"This morning you and your dad left Udderly to arrange bail and visit Eva at the jail," Andy said. "They must have snuck back as soon as you left. Given the size of this backhoe, you'd have heard it if you were here."

"Pretty ballsy," Paint added. "Unless they had a lookout." He glanced back toward the cabin. "There's a pretty good sight line from here. With a pair of binoculars I could see anyone coming or going."

I shivered. I didn't much like the thought of someone spying on me. "At least they didn't shoot any more animals."

Andy nodded. "Don't imagine the dogs interfered. I'm sure at least one came to investigate. But it was daylight, and they're used to big equipment and farm hands doing chores. No one was harming the goats they guard."

I shook my head. "What is going on? I sure let Eva down. Keeping that bone safe was her only request. Now it's gone. Along with every other potential clue about what or who was buried here."

Paint frowned. "Have to agree it's bad news. Someone must have thought finding another body would have loosened the noose around Eva's neck. Otherwise the trespassers would have left the bones alone. Somehow that skeleton suggested the sheriff should be looking at someone other than Eva as the killer."

"I agree." The admission turned my stomach. "Not much we can do about it. Another missing puzzle piece."

"There is something Paint and I can do—fix the fence," Andy said. "May not be much help to Eva, but at least we can keep her goats from wandering off."

My task? I put my mind to reclaiming that stolen leg bone and the skeleton that almost certainly went with it. How hard could it be to find who commandeered a backhoe and a dump truck for an off-the-books job this morning? Maybe Mollye, who seemed to know every business and most scoundrels in Ardon County, could give me a heads up on construction equipment and rentals.

TWENTY-NINE

My thoughts seemed to conjure Mollye from thin air. When I walked into the retail cabin, there she was, helping Mom behind the counter. However, a steady stream of customers made it impossible for me to update Mom and Mollye about the missing bones.

While we minded the store, Dad played traffic cop. I'd seen busy sales days at Udderly before, but nothing like this. We had enough cars coming and going to justify a traffic light.

"It's the rubbernecker syndrome," Mom whispered in disgust. "People heard about Eva's arrest on the radio and decided to take a gander at the scene of the crime. Probably figured nobody'd be here so they could poke around."

"On the plus side, they seem to feel guilty enough to buy cheese," I replied sotto voice. "At least we're bringing in cash."

By early afternoon, I felt sure we'd sold a trailer load of cheese—or in vegan speak, three trillion grams of cholesterol. Finally, there was a short break in the action and I filled in my sales associates on our latest setback—missing bones.

Looking worried as well as plain tuckered out, Mom collapsed into one of the retail cabin's rocking chairs. She toed off her shoes, groaned, and rubbed her feet.

"Mrs. H, why don't you take a break?" Mollye suggested. "Brie and I can handle things now that the crowd's thinning out."

Mom sighed. "Glad business was brisk even though I'm dog tired. Given how fast legal costs can mount for a trial, we need all the money we can get."

"You really think it'll go to trial?" I asked.

"Yes, honey, I'm almost certain it will."

Mom decided to take Mollye and me up on the offer to mind the store and left to check on Dad.

Once Mollye and I were alone, she urged me to tell all—including any news bulletins I'd skipped over with my mother tuned in. "Keeping up with the Hookers is proving to be a full-time job," she added.

The short lull in the cheese business continued long enough for me to provide my gal pal with all the gory details. We put our conversation on pause when a batch of customers arrived. As soon as I rang up their purchases and the screen door banged behind them, I nudged Mollye. "Your turn to talk. What do you think's going on here?"

Mollye frowned as she studied a chip in her blood-red fingernail polish. "I think you're right. Someone buried another corpse on the farm, and it sure wasn't Eva."

"Yeah, and now we have no way to prove that second skeleton was ever here. Our only evidence is a hole dug by a backhoe and our Scout's honor that nobody on this farm did the digging. But I do have a theory about Mr. Bones' identity."

Mollye rubbed her hands together. "Oh, boy, can't wait to hear this."

"I think the skeleton belongs to that Kaiser fellow who was reported missing about the same time as Jed. A pretty big coincidence to have two grown men go *poof* at the same time."

Mollye nodded, her earrings jangling like miniature wind chimes. "Makes sense. But why would someone dig up Kaiser's bones now? Why not leave them be?"

"I'm big on theories. It's all I've got. I'm betting whoever killed Jed also killed Kaiser, and he feared Kaiser's body might be uncovered by the same combination of erosion and animal digging that unearthed Jed's corpse. There are plenty of critters around here capable of digging up buried bones—including coyotes and Udderly's own dogs."

"That's one possibility." Mollye nodded. "Or maybe they figured the sheriff would ask SLED to bring in some of those police canines trained to sniff out corpses."

"I seriously doubt the sheriff would ask SLED's help on that score," I scoffed. "Sheriff Jones doesn't need to paint Eva as a serial killer with stiffs buried hither and yon. He's better off sticking with a simple case of domestic homicide. A lot easier to sell to an Ardon County jury."

Mollye's eyebrows rose. "I can see how a second corpse could point away from Eva. It would definitely poke holes in Jones' theory that wifey got fed up with being a punching bag and settled the matter with a little lead. So how are we gonna pursue your Kaiser theory when all you have is a big hole?"

I liked the fact that "we" were going to investigate. I knew I'd need Mollye's help to check out where last night's trespassers might have gone to shag construction equipment. But first I wanted to pick her brain on Sunrise Ridge.

"We have to keep tugging at loose ends like the one attached to Sunrise Ridge. I seriously doubt Jed traded his half of the timberland for shares in Kaiser's gold mine. Even Nancy Watson thought that was a crock."

I took a damp cloth and swiped at a dollop of soft cheese someone had dribbled on the counter. A thought kept buzzing around in my brain, but I had no luck smacking it down. "Can't help but wonder if that property holds a clue about these deaths. Paint took Dad and me to see Sunrise Ridge yesterday. I have a feeling there's a connection."

Mollye shook her head. "Afraid you're barking up the wrong tree. That was forty years ago. I can see how there might be some link to Jed's murder, but how could it possibly connect to the Watsons' deaths?"

The cabin door creaked, and Mom and Dad popped in. My request for sleuthing help on construction equipment would have to wait. No need to worry them with details on my detective plans.

"It's almost five," Mom said. "Only two cars left, and the occupants are packing up. Gawkers not buyers. Let's close up."

"Won't get an argument from me. Dad, you ordered pizzas, right? Want to join us for dinner, Mollye?"

She laughed. "You betcha. I heard you were feedin' five, might as well make it an even number."

Three large pizzas covered most of the surface of Eva's table as we crowded around, elbows touching, to chow down. I chose the seat nearest the veggie pizza, half unadorned with cheese. Since the other two pies were "meat lovers," I reckoned they'd be decimated before anyone paid a call on my veggie-loaded version.

"Howard, why don't you say grace?"

Mom's request surprised me, especially since I'd already shoveled a slice of pie onto my paper plate. Our family wasn't big on saying grace at any meal outside of holidays.

Dad took my left hand, and I reached for Mollye's hand with my right.

"Bless this food," Dad said, "and bless and keep safe the loved ones at this table and our dear Eva, who should be sitting here with us. Amen."

We all added a murmured amen. For a couple of moments, no one uttered a word. We were all thinking about Eva sitting in a jail when she should have been presiding at the head of the table.

Mollye was the first to break the silence. "Paint, I heard you took Brie and Howard on a Saturday drive up to Sunrise Ridge," she said. "Has that deal with the Japanese buyers gone through?"

Smack. That's what had been buzzing around in my head.

"We spotted a group of men at the gate to Phase III, the section that's supposed to be developed next," Paint said. "We figured they were from Tisnomi."

"Guess I should call Kathy and see what she knows," I added.

Mom nodded. "Great idea. Maybe she can tell us where things stand. It's been a couple months since you two talked anyway."

"Who's Kathy?" Andy asked.

"A foreign exchange student who lived with us my senior year in high school." I smiled thinking about all the hijinks we'd pulled. I'd definitely corrupted the quiet, studious Japanese girl. "Kathy lives in Tokyo. Took a job with Tisnomi as soon as she graduated from college."

I looked at my watch. Six thirty at night here. Tokyo was what? Fourteen hours ahead? It would be about eight thirty Monday morning. Kathy would be at work. Probably a bad idea to call her there.

"If I call her when I get up at the crack of dawn, she should just be getting home from Tisnomi."

"Speaking of work, we'd better head home." Mom sighed. "I need to clear my calendar so Howard and I can make Eva's bond hearing."

"Should I come?" I asked.

"No point," Mom said. "The bail arrangements are made, and the hearing itself won't last more than five minutes. You need to stay here and hold down the fort. I'm hoping Eva will join you by early afternoon."

Mollye pushed back from the table. Her eyes twinkled as she glanced from Paint to Andy. "Who's sleeping where tonight?" She wiggled her eyebrows suggestively.

My friend, a definite scalawag, enjoyed stirring the pot. She winked at me, and I felt a blush creep up my neck.

"We're flipping for it, right?" Andy piped up. "The winner gets Eva's bed, the loser gets the couch."

I silently thanked Andy for refusing to take Mollye's bait, especially with Mom and Dad listening. If Eva'd headed the table, the joking would have bordered on raunchy. Bordered? Heck, raunchy would have been the starting point.

Too bad Eva's absence was the main reason Paint and Andy were bunking in the cabin. Well, there was also the fact that Udderly had suddenly attracted a new group of night crawlers. Slimy bastards.

After Mom and Dad left, we cleared the table, and Paint retrieved a few bottles of moonshine from his truck to serve up after-dinner libations. I was happy to see he'd brought flavored, slightly less scorching options. "I'll take a thimble or two of the peach," I said. "Any more and I might sleep right through any exciting visits by those nighttime creeps."

Andy nodded. "Better make mine a short one, too."

Mollye sighed. "Okay, I have to drive home. So I guess I should join the thimble crowd—unless one of you boys wants to share a bed."

Paint grinned. "Long as you don't hog the covers, it's fine with me."

"Dang, Paint, I can't ever shock you into a stutter. You're no fun." Mollye laughed. "Too bad you're not my type."

"And what is your type?" I asked.

Mollye tipped her head sideways as if she had to think about it. "Knows how to take instructions—in and out of the bedroom. Likes to pamper me. Has oodles of money, and laughs at my jokes."

"Have you found anyone who matches all your criteria?" I smiled. I was actually curious. Mollye had teased me plenty. She'd mentioned Deputy Danny McCoy as signing on for bedroom duty, but it sounded like he was a pinch hitter and not a star player.

"Nope," she said. "I'm still waiting for a candidate who checks all the boxes. Meanwhile I'm not averse to auditioning men who can meet even one of my criteria. Though I'm not gonna name names, I have one gentleman right now who does know how to follow instructions."

Andy smiled. "Yeah, Deputy McCoy usually does whatever he's told."

Mollye gasped theatrically. "Cripes, I didn't think anyone knew."

"Veterinarians hear lots of gossip," he answered. "People are so used to talking freely in front of their pets they put me in the same uncensored category."

Paint rolled his eyes. "Mollye, Mollye. You're actually fraternizing with the enemy—a deputy?"

Mollye stuck out her tongue, which made me think again about her licking comment.

"I prefer to think of Deputy McCoy as my own cuddly little mole. I plan to get him panting answers to my questions about backhoes and dump trucks. Tonight, if there's still time."

Paint and Andy were both nodding their approval of Mollye's tactics. I gave the idea a thumbs-up, too. With a loved one in the pokey, all was fair in love and war. And, bless her soul, I hadn't even needed to ask Mollye for help digging up dirt on lessees of backhoes and dump trucks. A friend in "deed."

THIRTY

I closed the door to my bedroom after bidding our two guard dudes goodnight. I chuckled at the fleeting fantasy of both men coming to heel if I whistled. Yes, I'd had more than a thimbleful of peach moonshine.

As I slipped out of my clothes, a breeze from the partially open window whispered against my flushed skin. Hot and bothered. Not a good tipsy combination, considering a pair of handsome gents waited within whistling range. Hmm. I knew their lips shouldn't be on this vegan's menu, but, hey, no animals would be harmed. How did such delicious thoughts keep sneaking inside my brain?

I shook my head to chase away the lust even though I was reluctant to banish my amorous daydreams. They were among the few things that could distract my mind from Eva's horrible plight.

Cashew cuddled up and licked my arm. Not a help in shooing away the image of eager tongues. Dang, Mollye, and her bawdy teasing. Come on, Brie, nekkid men and necking should be the last things on your mind.

I played with the goats. Lilly laughed at their antics. The dogs barked up a storm. Cashew joined the chorus. Right in my ear.

I bolted straight up out of my dream. My mind chugged to process. The night crawlers were back.

A fist pounded on my bedroom door. "Brie, someone's in the barn. Andy and I are going to investigate. Stay here and lock the door."

"Hell I will." I sprang from bed and flung open the door. My mind barely registered Paint's bare chest. Okay, maybe my gaze lingered, but the snarl of dogs reminded me my mind needed to be elsewhere.

Paint's attention stuttered as well. His eyes had a laser lock on my boobs. The long t-shirt that served as my nightgown was worn past the point of peek-a-boo.

"I'm coming with you." I crossed my arms over my chest, and Paint's scrutiny meandered lower, below the hem of my nightshirt. His tongue swiped over his lips.

"Come on, Paint, move it," Andy yelled.

I looked past Paint's nekkidness and spotted Andy at the front door.

"I'm headed to my truck," Andy said. "I'll get my big flashlight and grab something to scare off varmints."

"I'm right behind you," Paint said. "I'll get my shotgun."

I slipped on my Birkenstock sandals and grabbed the heavy sweater I'd flung on a chair. An agitated Cashew circled me, nipping at my toes. Ever since my ill-fated pedicure, she'd been enamored with my pink toenails.

"Sorry, Cashew." I scooted her back in my bedroom, closed the door, and ran to join Andy and Paint.

Before I made it off the porch, two figures ran out of the barn. They sprinted like the devil himself gave chase. Shaking the ground, another much larger form streaked out and slammed into the slower one, knocking him to the ground.

When the larger shape stomped the earth and bellowed "heeeeeeeeoooooowwww," I understood. The intruders had somehow managed to aggravate Rita the mule.

Rita's knockdown victim—definitely a man—scrabbled backwards, trying to get away from her. "Get this crazy bitch off me."

He should never have called Rita the "B" word. She grabbed his coat in her teeth and wrenched him off the ground. Her head waved side to side as she shook him like a stuffed toy. Her foot-long ears flopped up and down and made a sound like a toy helicopter attempting lift off.

When Rita dropped the man, he scrambled to his feet. Still shaking her head, the mule let him get about ten feet before she shambled after him. The man Rita chased was hauling butt. But his butt wasn't fast enough. Despite her ambling gait, Rita easily caught up and nosed the intruder in the middle of his back, prompting another sprawl in the dirt.

Paint and Andy zoomed around the corner from their dash to

their hidden vehicles. Going after weapons caused them to miss the main act of the Rita show.

"Paint, I smell smoke. I have to get the animals out!" Andy yelled as he disappeared into the barn.

Paint looked frantically from the barn to the fleeing culprits and back again. Then he took off, running after the mule and her quarry. "Rita, stop," he called.

The mule braked, but seemed disinclined to return to the barn.

Paint raised his shotgun and a blast echoed across the hills.

When I noticed a flicker of flames in the barn window, my attention shifted. The vision lit a fire under me, jolting me out of my dazed hesitation. Smoke hung heavy in the night air.

"No!" I ran to help Andy save the animals.

All our newborn kids... Eva's horse, Hank. My God.

Andy stumbled out of the barn, dragging a smoking hay bale out to the yard.

"It's okay," he yelled. "Fire's out. Eva keeps a fire extinguisher by the door. Just smoke now."

"You sure? I smell gasoline."

"There's a canister just inside the barn. Our visitors had mega-bonfire plans, but it looks like Rita foiled them."

Rita brayed and snorted on queue. Paint walked at her side as she strutted across the field, looking for all the world like a triumphant gladiator.

"I'll get Hank," I said. Eva's horse occupied the stall next to Rita's. Even with assurances the fire was out, I wanted all the animals in the open away from the gasoline.

"Good. I'll herd the kids outside." Andy turned to Paint. "Did you wing either creep?"

"No. I chased them, but never had a clear shot. Rita was in the way, so I just fired in the air. Before I could catch up, they jumped on a motorcycle and hightailed it out of range. Didn't get close enough to see the make of the bike, let alone who they were."

The riled guard dogs kept barking. I could hardly think with the din.

"Shush, now," Andy commanded, and the dogs fell silent. The dapper vet appeared to be able to whisper to dogs as well as to Tammy the Pig and Brie the Horny.

Paint and I shooed the kids into a large pen. The babes were old enough to scamper on their own and young enough to forget fear in the face of adventure. They play-butted each other, delighted to be cavorting in the middle of the night.

Once all the animals were safe, we collapsed on hay bales a few yards from the barn door. The adrenaline rush had left me shaky and all of us wired.

"Why?" I asked. "Why would someone do this? Try to burn innocent animals to death?"

"They wanted to scare you off the farm and weren't quite ready to roast you," Paint answered. "They didn't count on Rita the attack mule, and I think they were surprised you had company. Good thing we hid our trucks."

I couldn't quit shaking. "I'm so glad both of you were here. Don't know what I'd have done if I'd been alone. So what now? Eva's adamant she doesn't want the sheriff to step foot on the farm. Guess we're back to calling the state police come morning."

"This time we need to video the scene before anything can disturb it," Andy said. "Grab your cell, Brie. Maybe the creeps left some clues."

I grabbed my cell phone and set it to video. Andy led the way, shining his flashlight beam to and fro as we walked into the now empty barn. Our first stop was outside Rita's stall door, which lay in splinters. The mule clearly wanted out, and she hadn't let a few inches of pine stop her.

"Rita drove those thugs off before Paint and I came running. I bet their plans didn't include abandoning a full container of gasoline. Here's where I found the smoldering bale," Andy said.

He bent down, sweeping his flashlight beam across the area in front of the splintered stall. Paint chuckled and pointed to a patch of gooey red on one of the destroyed boards. "They didn't count on an ornery female. Yep, Rita got him good."

"What have you found to laugh about?" I asked.

Andy smiled. "Looks like Rita sent a board flying when she kicked out her stall door, and it slapped one of our arsonists square in the mouth." He bent and picked something out of the dirt and held it up to my cell for a close-up. The jagged remains of a tooth.

"They made a terrible mistake," he continued. "Even trapped in a stall, a thousand pounds of pissed-off mule is nothing to trifle with. This should help us ID the culprit."

"Just need to find out who has one less tooth today," Paint added. "Wish I'd been a little quicker. Between the racket the dogs were raising, our shouts, and a kick in the teeth, the bastards got out while the getting was good."

I shuddered. "Maybe we can ask the sheriff and his deputies to appear in a lineup and smile. I have the distinct feeling at least one of them is involved."

"My vet kit is in the truck. I saw some blood near that tooth. I'll smear some samples on slides for analysis and bag that tooth," Andy added.

"Good." I nodded. "I'm not going to call Mom and Dad in the middle of the night. In fact, I don't want to tell them about this, period. It'll give them one more reason to insist I move off the farm, but we can't keep an attempted arson secret. We need to bring in the law." My shoulders slumped. "Maybe my folks are right. Maybe I have no business staying on Udderly when we haven't the foggiest notion why any of this is happening or who's behind it. Eva's already in jail. What more do they want?"

"They must know you're nosing around and want you to stop." Paint looked at his friend, and Andy nodded his agreement.

"I think Paint and I just made a pact," Andy said. "Doesn't matter who is behind this. We won't let them scare us off. The two of us will stick to you like glue. Nobody's going to hurt you or Eva."

Andy knelt and picked up a barbaric looking pair of giant tongs with chains attached.

"What in blazes have you got there?" Paint asked.

Andy grinned. "A calf jack. First thing I saw in my truck when I grabbed the flashlight. Figured I could use it as a weapon. Swing the chains like one of those wicked Chinese thingies."

"Well, it would scare the crap out of me," I said. "How do you use it?"

"Attach the chains to a calf's legs to wench it out when there's a breech birth."

I shuddered. "Remind me never to recommend you to any friends in need of an obstetrician."

Though I wouldn't mind borrowing Andy's calf jack to make the arsonists wish they'd never been born.

THIRTY-ONE

The alarm startled me. Lord in heaven, could it be five thirty? My eyes burned like someone had dusted them with cayenne. Voices rumbled just beyond my bedroom door. Paint and Andy. In the stingy light of dawn, last night's excitement replayed in my mind like a grainy, old-time movie. Still powerful enough to creep me out.

I smelled coffee. Heaven. The studly duo had me reconsidering my options. Maybe my past relationship problem was monogamy. Having two men around was rather nice. Time for a reality check, Brie. How long would this trio ménage?

I jumped into jeans and a long-sleeved tee and ran my fingers through my unruly curls. Best I could do in the grooming department until I could lay my hands on a washcloth and toothbrush. With three people and one john, there was probably a line. At least I could grab some rescue caffeine.

"IIey, pretty little one. Come on over."

Huh? Tiny toenails clicked across the wood floor as Cashew scampered over to Andy, who was filling my pup's breakfast dish.

I chuckled. "Wondered who you were talking to. Kind of doubted you were calling Paint to breakfast."

"It might have been you." Andy smiled. "You can pull off pretty even while you're yawning."

Somehow the mention of a yawn only made my mouth gape wider. My own breath practically made my eyes water. "Pretty sorry you mean. Is the bathroom free?"

"All yours," Paint answered as he opened the door.

Yikes, bare-chested again, and looking delicious.

He bowed me inside the tiny bath like a waiter. "Want me to pour you some coffee?"

"Lord, yes. As Aunt Eva's prone to say, I'll be back in two shakes of a goat's tail."

I'm not sure it took more than one shake to splash cold water on my face and brush my teeth. Coffee wasn't just calling my name, it was screaming.

A steaming mug waited next to a seat sandwiched between Andy and Paint.

"So tell us what chores need doing," Paint said.

Fortunately, Eva's hired helpers were back on the job this morning, which meant the remaining chores were menial. By the time I'd downed my coffee, we'd divvied up assignments. I promised the guys breakfast—a simple one—as soon as we finished.

I hurried through egg gathering and feeding Rita and Hank. We'd returned them to their stalls shortly after moving the charred hay and gas can. Since Rita's stall no longer had a door, we clipped rope guards in place.

After I finished my chores, I multitasked, phoning Kathy while I fried bacon and eggs and popped English muffins in the toaster. I'd slather my muffin with peanut butter.

"Kathy, it's Brie."

I smiled at her delighted shriek of surprise and the rapid-fire volley of questions that followed. All demanding to know what I'd been up to and if I'd found a leading man for my romance. At first, she thought I was joking about taking up residence at Udderly Kidding Dairy. She quieted quickly as I explained Aunt Eva's plight. Kathy shared what she knew about Tisnomi's pending purchase of Sunrise Ridge and promised to call once she nosed around for up-to-the-minute details.

When my companions returned to the cabin, I quickly plated their breakfasts.

"You can't get eggs any fresher than this," I said. "Fortunately for Tammy the Pig the bacon's not quite as fresh."

Both men laughed.

"Speaking of pigs, do you mind cooking for meat eaters like us?" Andy asked.

"Nope. But if we weren't in such a hurry, I'd try to lure you into the vegan camp with whole wheat waffles with almonds, strawberries, and real maple syrup."

"Ooh, I'm yours," Paint said.

"Me, too," Andy added.

"I'm afraid there's no time today to try and woo you to vegan cuisine." Could I fit wooing into the nighttime schedule?

I filled them in on the tidbits I'd learned from Kathy. Though she worked halfway round the world, she knew more about Sunrise Ridge than any of us sitting twenty miles away. Kathy'd already asked plenty of questions since she was hoping Tisnomi would purchase the property and give her an excuse to visit her American family.

"Tisnomi has set this coming Friday for a go, no-go decision on the project," I explained. "That's when their purchase option expires. Even though a settlement was reached, concerns raised by environmentalists about the undeveloped tract have made them nervous. More importantly, a North Georgia developer is courting them, trying to interest them in a similar project."

Andy's fingers traced the logo on his coffee mug. "Wonder what will happen to our local hotshots if the deal goes south?"

"If Sunrise Ridge goes belly up, Sheriff Jones and Deputy West had better like beans," Paint said. "Imagine that's all they'd be able to afford if they put all their eggs in the Sunrise Ridge basket. 'Course, I still can't fathom how they ever gathered enough eggs to invest in Sunrise Ridge."

"It sure wasn't family money—unless they have relatives in a wealthy crime family." Mollye's booming voice made me jump.

"Hey, Mollye. Didn't hear you drive up."

"Are we great bodyguards, or what?" Andy commented. "I heard a car but figured it was one of Eva's helpers. You'd think we'd be more alert after last night."

"Last night? Do tell," Mollye urged.

Her question shepherded the conversation away from Sunrise Ridge and onto our arsonist visitors. As Mollye digested the news, her plump lips curved upward in a sly smile.

"I had a wee bit of excitement of my own last night, which included a long talk with Deputy Danny—"

"Between pillow fights?" Paint interrupted.

Mollye batted her eyelids. "Pillows may have been involved, but no fights. Danny's a sweet boy. He may not be the brightest bulb, but he accidentally shed light on what Sheriff Jones and Deputy West might be up to. Next time we 'chat' I'll inquire about any co-workers with dentist appointments. I do know West owns a motorcycle."

"What did you learn from Danny?" I prodded.

"One of the sheriff's cousins owns a company that rents construction equipment, and Danny overheard Jones saying something about a backhoe. Since Danny loves big machines, he asked Jones what job he was working on. The sheriff claimed he was helping his cousins dig a pond on the Nelson farm. Wouldn't you know it's just down the road from Udderly Kidding Dairy?"

I tucked that info nugget away. Did the relocated skeleton belong to Kaiser, scam artist extraordinaire? Were his bones destined to be interred at the bottom of a farm pond? How would we ever find out?

"Earth to Brie." Mollye's voice broke through my wool gathering. "Are you going to tell your parents about last night's excitement?"

"Yes, right after the bail hearing. Mom will call as soon as they spring Eva. I don't want to add to our family drama until my aunt's out of jail."

Andy and Paint got up from the table and put their dirty plates in the dishwasher, earning more brownie points. I was becoming quite fond of both men. Too fond.

"I have some furry patients to visit." Andy waved his cell phone. "But please call and let me know what happens at Eva's bail hearing."

"Me, too," Paint said. "As soon as Eva's sprung, tell her Andy and I plan to return on night watch. I'm also going to visit the security guru who put in Magic Moonshine's system. See if he has suggestions to beef up Udderly security with some high-tech extras."

"Like perimeter land mines?" Mollye suggested.

"Nah," Andy answered. "We don't want to harm any innocent four-legged trespassers, just two-legged bastards."

After Andy and Paint left, Mollye dallied to share a bit more gossip and pry into my next-to-nonexistent love life. She had a hard time fathoming how I continued to sleep solo with a handy choice of two hunks bunking a few feet away.

"Come on, Mollye. Can you really imagine sleeping with one when his best friend could hear every creak of the bed?"

"Yeah, maybe it wouldn't be the best timing," she agreed. "So given your seemingly puritan views on threesomes, who's it going to be?"

I shook my head. "You're impossible. New subject. What do you know about the Nelsons down the road, and how can we get on that property to see if they're excavating a new pond?"

"My mom knows Granny Nelson," she answered. "Let me think on it. Keep me posted on Eva's release. I want to welcome her home."

Noon had almost arrived when my cell phone finally rang. "Honey, just wanted to let you know the judge finally granted bail, though that horse's ass of a solicitor did all he could to argue against it. You'd think Eva was a vicious serial killer plotting to assassinate a presidential candidate. Afraid it'll be several hours before we can spring Eva. Even with a half-million-dollar bond, the judge insisted on fitting her with an electronic anklet to track her whereabouts. A deputy is taking her to Greenville for the fitting.

"Dad and I will follow and bring her home. I doubt she's going to take kindly to house arrest. She's only allowed to step off the property to attend church or visit a doctor. Anywhere else and they'll throw her back in jail."

I'd been poised to tell Mom about last night's attempted arson. I clamped my mouth shut. If Eva was going to be imprisoned on the farm, I didn't want her here by her lonesome. I felt certain Andy and Paint would feel the same. Of course, many more bodies sleeping in the cabin and we'd be sharing beds a la Mollye's fantasies. Okay, my fantasies, too.

Stow it. Not the time or place. I needed to dedicate my limited brain power to Eva's predicament and unmasking the a-holes intent on harassing anyone who dared to stay on Udderly.

How hard could it be to find out what ugly Ardon County mug was suddenly missing a tooth? True, a fair number of Watsons were likely to be a few incisors short of a full mouth. They weren't exactly the type of family that flossed together. Still this toothy gap had to be paired with some spectacular black-and-blue bruises courtesy of Rita's vengeful hooves. I doubted the thug was the type to dust his blemish with tinted face powder.

I sighed. I didn't like keeping secrets, and I was already on thin ice with Mom. Withholding news of my Hog Heaven visit hadn't exactly endeared me to her. Still I figured sharing could wait a tad longer. With Eva, Andy, and Paint for companions, I wasn't afraid of spending another night on the farm.

Am I an optimist or what?

THIRTY-TWO

I finished my bookkeeping chores, then weeded the poison patch and Lilly's garden. I'd just carried a scrub bucket into the retail shop when I heard a car drive up. Eureka! Dad's Toyota Highlander stopped next to the cabin. About time. I'd been going nuts waiting for Eva's return.

I heard my aunt grousing the minute the car doors opened.

"Idiots! First they confiscate my underwear and charge me an arm and a leg for unmentionables that were probably made out of potato sacks, and then they clamp this itch-inducing contraption on my ankle. Someone's going to pay. They'll be sorrier than a coyote caught in my hen house when I find out who's behind this mess. If I'm going to jail for allegedly shooting someone, I may as well do the crime and air-condition his hide with a few well-placed bullet holes."

I couldn't see Mom's face, but I imagined her eyes had rolled so far up in her head she could see behind her back. She left it to Dad to talk his sister down.

"Now, Eva, let Iris handle the legal ins and outs. We'll sort this out without any need for a shotgun."

"Legal ins and outs?" Eva fumed. "How can we trust anything legal when Sheriff Jones is trying his dangdest to keep me in the pokey, and old Solicitor Esan Bell a.k.a. Iron Butt appears solidly in his camp?"

I sprinted to Eva and wrapped her in a bear hug. My welcome pushed the pause button on her rant.

"Brie, honey, you're a sight for sore eyes." She swatted at her cheek. I spotted the trail of a tear but pretended not to notice. She'd be peeved if I said a word.

"I hear you've been entertaining men in the evening," Eva continued. "Good thing I'm home to protect your virtue. Did you and your gentlemen friends find time to actually do some chores?"

"A few." I shrugged, and she punched my arm.

Dad bussed Eva's cheek, and gave me a hug. Mom waved from the car. Now that I had a clear view of Mom's face, I could see the toll the stress was taking. For a second, she looked as old as grandma in photos taken right before she died. I looked away.

Dad tugged on one of my flyaway curls. "Afraid we need to get back to town." His shoulders slumped. "I'm hosting a faculty dinner for colleagues from Oxford tonight. Made the commitment months ago. Can't get out of it. I'll call after dinner to check on you two. I can drive back out to spend the night."

"No need, Dad. Andy called an hour ago. He and Paint are on deck again." I glanced over at Eva. "And I'll bet Billy will come over to check out Eva's new ankle jewelry. So we're plum out of spare beds. In fact, Andy's bringing the cot he sleeps on when he's playing nursemaid to an expectant mare. Said he'd sack out on the porch if we ran out of floor space."

Dad attempted a smile. "Not sure I should worry any less with two strapping young men roaming the grounds."

"Don't worry, Howard, I'm here to chaperone," Eva piped up.

"That's what has me worried." His chuckle sounded forced. "I'll call. Love you both."

The dogs had gone crazy hearing Eva's voice. Each big fur ball insisted on a pat on the head and a scratch behind the ears before leaving her side. With the animal welcome home complete, we walked through the milking barn and dairy plant so Eva could make certain everything passed inspection.

I didn't take it personally. She simply needed contact with all these touchstones to believe something was normal. To know she was truly home.

Eva wanted to end her tour at the horse barn so she could check on Udderly's batch of newborn kids and pet and coo over the coltish darlings. I convinced her to come to the cabin first for a much-needed chat. I didn't want her to see the splintered stall door before I filled her in.

I poured us tall glasses of iced tea and set out oatmeal cookies. Cashew seemed as happy to see Eva as me. My aunt scooped her into her lap as I eased into my news report.

Mom and Dad had already filled her in on the unauthorized excavation and missing leg bone. However, last night's attempted arson offered a new shock. Her beet-red face might have frightened me into thinking she would collapse, except Eva managed to suck in enough oxygen to push out a steady stream of swear words. I filed a few of the more colorful combos away for future reference. My aunt had a not-so-hidden talent for cursing.

"You didn't tell your parents about last night?"

I shrugged. "I planned to, but I felt you should call the shots. I know you don't want the sheriff poking around. He has jurisdiction, right? But what about the state police?"

Eva made a sound in her throat somewhere between a retch and a huff. I gathered that was a no. "And what would we tell them? We have no evidence the sheriff's involved. They'd probably call him five seconds after we hung up."

"It might help to verify Mollye's insider info first," I said. "Find out if the sheriff or some of his stooges are really using a backhoe to dig a big hole on the Nelson farm."

Eva snorted. "You plan to pay a social call on the Nelsons? They're related to the Watson clan. All of Jed's blood relatives avoid me and mine like the plague. Up to now, they've never trespassed or tried to do me harm. But I'd say all bets are off now that Jed's been dug up and I'm charged with his murder."

I stared down at my iced tea and the jelly logo etched in the drinking glass. "Mollye thinks she can come up with a legitimate reason to visit."

My aunt's eyes narrowed. "Well, her definition of legit better not be sneaking over the fence. That's a surefire way to get your tail full of lead. I won't have it. Promise me you won't go there uninvited."

"Okay, yes, I promise." I squeezed her hand.

Our exchange seemed to wring the last drop of energy from my aunt. Her eyelids fluttered and her shoulders drooped. Clear advertisements of her total exhaustion.

"Did you sleep at all in the jail?" I asked.

"Not much," she admitted.

"Go take a nap while I start soup for supper. Sounds like we'll have a crowd. Andy, Paint, Mollye, and Billy's coming, right?"

"Yes, Billy wanted to bring me home from jail. He'll be here soon as he quits work. Maybe I should take a little nap. Wake me if there's any excitement. I mean it."

Eva shuffled to her bedroom without further protest—a sure sign she could barely stand. Seeing how the burden seemed to age my young-at-heart aunt made me more determined than ever to see her through this ordeal.

Not knowing the culinary preferences of our dinner guests, I made two vegan soups. One pot of roasted tomato basil and a second of split pea. I rummaged through Eva's freezer and set out a package of leftover ham to thaw. If the carnivores were going into shock, they could pair their soups with thick slices of ham, cheese, and crusty French bread.

I whipped out my cell and asked Mollye to stop by the bakery for a loaf of bread.

"Will do," she answered. "But set those soups on simmer. I'll be at the cabin in fifteen. Got us an appointment with Granny Nelson. A nice-as-you-please invitation."

"What? How?"

Mollye laughed. "No time to explain. See ya in a few. Bye."

Eva was still sleeping when my friend arrived. Since Mollye's idea of a whisper could wake the dead, I intercepted her on the front porch. She was dressed in full pseudo-gypsy attire. It looked like someone had plopped a turban on her head with a loose end that fluttered in the wind. Her jangly bracelets and earrings were slightly smaller than cowbells. A long purple skirt swirled around her ankles as she scampered up the stairs.

"Quite the outfit," I commented.

"It's my woo-woo uniform." Her eyes twinkled. "Folks 'round here find my visions more convincing if I arrive in full regalia. My mom called Granny Nelson and told her I'd had a vision in which she'd played a starring role."

"You had a vision?"

Mollye rolled her eyes. "Course not. I mean I do have the sight now and again, but it's not like I can call up visions on command.

Granny Nelson's an old country woman, superstitious as all get out. Mom figured she'd invite me over if she heard tell of a vision in which she played the lead. Mom was right."

"Does the old lady live alone?"

"No. Two grandsons live on the family farm. Mean bruisers. Went to school with them. Fortunately, they work construction in Greenville. Always stop off for a brewsky. Based on sightings at Hog Heaven, they're never home before dark. Don't worry. We'll have a solo audience with Granny."

"We?"

"Figured you'd want to come along. But we need to hurry."

I hesitated. "Eva's sleeping. I hate to leave her alone. And how would ol' Granny feel about having kin of a hated Yankee invader darken her door?"

"I didn't plan to hand Granny a copy of your family tree. She's old. Probably lumps all young women in the same wanton basket. I'll say I asked you to drive so I'd have a way to get home if I went into a deep trance." Mollye chuckled. "Hell, I'm good at making up shit."

"What about Eva?"

"Leave her a note. We won't be long, and it's broad daylight. Udderly's uninvited guests never come calling when the sun's shining. The Nelson place is right down the road. I'll give Granny a highlights reel of my vision. We just need an excuse to drive up to the homestead. How long can it take to spot a gaping hole or see if there's a honking big backhoe parked on the back forty?"

I was torn. Leaving Eva alone worried me.

"What in the devil are you two up to? Mollye, you look like you're headed to a carnival."

Eva's voice startled me. Apparently the nap had refreshed her. Well, at least it had restored her feisty tone.

"I need to run an errand before supper. Stopped by to see if Brie wanted to tag along. But she says she shouldn't leave you alone."

"Humpf. I'm not an invalid. I have a gun, and I know how to use it. Go on, Brie, git. Or maybe I'll plug you for being a ninny."

I glared at Mollye. My friend could spread lies smoother than frosting on a warm carrot cake. Should I tell Eva where our "errand" would take us?

"Come on, you heard your aunt." Mollye chuckled. "Let's head out before she loads her shotgun and sends us off in a hail of lead."

Eva made a shooing motion. I dutifully followed Mollye to her colorful van. If there was anyone besides Granny on the Nelson homestead, they'd see us coming a mile away.

I sure hoped the old bat was holding down the fort all by her lonesome.

THIRTY-THREE

Mollye's van bumped over a poor imitation of a bad road. My petite car was still in the shop, and I'd passed on the gas-guzzling loaner the auto shop had offered. Good thing. The country lane's deep wallows would have done in either ride.

I rolled down my window for the breeze. Big mistake. Dust flew up in choking red clouds as I stared out at the lifeless fields. It hadn't rained in days.

Not a single bush or tree softened the appearance of the clapboard house, surrounded by a moat of hard-pack clay. I scanned the landscape for some sign of a gaping hole. No luck. A ramshackle shed with canted garage doors stood adjacent to the field. Was it large enough to house a backhoe?

We parked in front of the faded grey farmhouse, the wood so worn it almost looked transparent. If the place had ever seen paint, sun and wind had sandpapered it off. I worried we'd fall clean through the steps on our way to the front door.

I held my breath as we climbed the stairs. Mollye bounced up the five steps, seemingly unafraid of broken legs due to termites or decay. The front porch wasn't exactly a safe oasis. It sagged like an overloaded hammock.

Mollye winked at me, and then knocked on a wooden jamb that looked only slightly more substantial than the cracked door. A cheery yoo-hoo accompanied her knock. "Mrs. Nelson, Mollye Camp here, come to tell you about my vision."

Creaking boards announced a body slowly shuffling our way. The door opened a few inches to reveal a woman's head. Actually, the head looked a lot like a mummified tangerine. Leathery brownish-orange skin puckered around a sunken mouth. Did she have a single tooth? If her grandsons followed her dental regimen, we'd be hard-pressed to tell if one of them had recently lost an incisor.

"Come in. Quick," she muttered. "Doan never leave the door open. Hornet's nest unner the porch. Axed my gran'sons to pour gas inna hole an' light it one night. But they's afraid. Say it's too close o' the house. Might light a bonfire."

I concentrated hard to understand her. Missing teeth gave her speech a sibilant quality. I shuddered. Who would live like this? A rotting house. Killer hornets.

She toddled over to a rocker and waved us toward the couch. A couple of big butts had left lasting impressions in the spongy cushions. Her grandsons? Clearly not the wizened old lady's backside.

We sat. Mollye didn't introduce me, and the woman gave no indication she cared. Seemed she just wanted to hear this vision and go back to whatever she did with her time. Roasting small children? Feeding poison apples to anyone fairer than her?

Mollye didn't wait for a welcome, launching immediately into her spiel.

"Mrs. Nelson, I don't want to frighten you, but Ma thought I ought to share my vision. Since my visions are sometimes warnings, she thought it might spare you some heartache."

Granny didn't comment. She just rocked and inclined her head, maybe an inch.

"I saw the earth open up." Mollye's voice took on a sing-song quality.

Wow, Mollye was good. Bet she could get paid to host séances.

The old lady's chair rocked faster. Her eyes narrowed.

"The hole in the earth was on your farm. I saw it from the air, like I was a hawk soaring overhead. A big mechanical monster chewed at the ground. It put me in mind of a rabid dog the way it growled and tore at the dirt, madly pawing for bones. That's when I saw blood. A man fell in the hole, and the mechanical dog mauled him to death."

The old lady stopped rocking. Her claw hands tightened on the rocker.

Mollye's voice grew louder. "I can still hear his screams as that monster shredded his flesh. Then everything went black. Until you appeared, Mrs. Nelson. I stood by your side as you looked down into the fresh grave. You wore widow weeds. Preacher Jackson mumbled a prayer as a shiny mahogany casket was lowered into the hole."

"Who?" Granny croaked, her voice a coarse whisper.

Jumping Jerky. Mollye's performance raised goosebumps up and down my arms and I knew it was a scam. I'd swear she'd had a vision of a gaping hole, a steel monster, and a forlorn gravesite.

"I'm sorry, Mrs. Nelson. I don't know who died," Mollye answered in her regular voice, not the sing-song chant of her fake vision. "Mom thought if someone was digging holes on your property, you could warn them. Tell them to be careful."

The woman nodded. "I warn my gran'sons. Tell 'em you's here. Tell 'em 'bout your vision."

Uh-oh. Had Mollye thought this through? The old lady might buy into this vision. But I doubted her mean grandsons would be as gullible. The woman fixed Mollye with a stare, her watery blue eyes unblinking inside the mass of wrinkles. Uh oh, had Mollye even taken in the old lady? Maybe her parting words about her gran'sons carried a warning—"I ain't buying your baloney, honey, and I'm going to rat you out to my grands."

"Sees yourselves out," the old lady muttered. "Hard for me to get around. Ain't gettin' up again."

I didn't need to be asked twice. Neither did Mollye. We practically sprinted to the door. As soon as we cleared the stairs, Mollye began speed-walking around the side of the house. I ran after her. I wanted to yell, "What the hell are you thinking?" But I feared ol' granny would hear.

The backhoe was tucked up close to the back porch. Invisible from the front of the house and the dirt entry road. About a hundred yards beyond the house a giant pile of red clay sat like a huge fire ant mound.

"Let's get the hell out of Dodge," I whispered.

"You betcha," Mollye agreed. We ran like screaming banshees nipped at our backsides. I risked one backward glance at the old farmhouse and froze. Nicotine-stained lace curtains had been yanked aside just far enough for beady eyes in a shrunken head to track our every move. The old lady lied. She'd definitely left her rocker.

Yes, and we were off our rockers. Never should have come. No siree.

Was Granny Nelson as accomplished a liar as Mollye? If so, my friend might have just added her own name to the Hooker clan's endangered species list.

Mollye parked her van in front of Aunt Eva's cabin. We were still huffing and puffing like we'd run a marathon.

"She's gonna tell her grandsons," Mollye said. "That old bag knew my vision was a bunch of hooey. We're toast."

I nodded. My friend's fake tale didn't prompt the old woman to gasp and admit there was a mechanical monster and a big hole directly behind her house. She'd seen through the ruse. Missing teeth didn't mean missing marbles. The old bat would rat us out. The only saving grace? The Nelson grandsons wouldn't be home for hours, and Mollye never introduced me. Of course, it wouldn't take a genius to puzzle out my identity.

"Should we tell Eva?" I asked.

"No," Mollye said.

I bit my lip. "We have to. We may have made Eva a target. What if the grandsons are liquored up when they hear about our visit? What will they do? I think we both know. They'll burn rubber speeding down the road to pay the Hookers a nighttime visit. Even if they know Eva has company and Udderly's inhabitants have guns, drunks tend to discount such pesky obstacles."

Mollye nodded. "Guess you're right. I just don't know whether I'm more afraid of Eva or those Nelson thugs."

No contest. I was more afraid of Eva.

THIRTY-FOUR

My aunt handled the news better than we expected. Only two streams of invective followed her verdict that Mollye and I were raving lunatics and ought to be tarred and feathered.

"What were you thinking? Folks here don't take kindly to outsiders snooping on their land. They're doubly touchy if they believe someone thinks they're so plum stupid they can be scammed." Eva sighed. "You didn't just snoop. You insulted Granny's intelligence. If she wasn't so stove up, you'd both be peppered with buckshot. Once upon a time, that old fart was a damn good shot. Her lazy, good-for-nothing husband was a drunk. Often as not she was the one bagging the rabbit or squirrel for the stew pot."

For once, Mollye had no quick comeback. She sat mute and contrite across the table. I zipped my lips, too. Wiser to let Eva run down. A heavy silence followed her rave. The quiet felt like a weight pressing on my chest. The sole sound? Eva's fingers drumming on the table.

"Where'd you say that blasted hole was?" she asked. "How far behind the house?"

"About fifty feet," I answered.

Eva's lips twitched into a conniving smile. "Must be dang near the creek we share. The way our properties line up, Morgan's Creek runs mighty close to the Nelson farm house. Then it dumps straight onto Udderly land. If you're driving down the road, there's a farm between the Nelson and Udderly spreads, but our backlots are cheek to jowl." Eva went silent again. Her fingers rat-a-tatted with increased speed. "Got an idea. A way to get state yahoos to look into the goings on at the Nelsons without the sheriff knowing squat. Hand me that phone book sitting behind you, Mollye. Brie, let me see that smarty cell that puts me in mind of a kumquat growing out of your ear. I'm calling the cops. Environmental coppers."

I glanced at Mollye, who risked raised eyebrows. I shrugged as my aunt thumbed through the white pages. "There's the number for DHEC—the South Carolina Department of Health and Environmental Control—for you imbeciles."

She punched in a phone number, and we kept silent as she frowned and periodically stabbed buttons. I assumed she was running through some automated screening system to keep taxpayers from conversing with humans.

"Yes, this is Eva Hooker. Is Brad Dickey in?" Eva's voice was all business.

Silence. One beat, two. Mollye and I exchanged puzzled looks.

"Hi, Brad. Yes, it's Eva Hooker. Some of my goats got sick right after they drank out of the stream that runs through Udderly. You know the one they call Morgan's Creek. Uh-huh."

Pause. "Yes, I'm sure it's been contaminated, and I'm ninety-nine percent certain I know the source. The Nelson farm. They're digging near that creek. I'm guessing polluted silt found its way into the streambed. They musta dug up something nasty. I'm hoping you can check it out before a thunderstorm makes it too late to save the creek. Be a shame to have to fence my goats off from it."

Pause. "No. I wouldn't call the Nelsons. They'll just try to hide what they're up to. Don't mean to tell you your job, but I'd get whatever document you need to inspect the property. You know that family's not real big on voluntarily cooperating with government."

Eva hung up and laughed. "Brad thinks he'll have his ducks in a row by afternoon. Plans to inspect the site in the morning. Best plan I could think of spur of the moment to get someone looking for our missing bones."

"You're one crafty old coot," I said.

"Don't you forget it. I'm more than a little teed off that you've been keeping secrets and taking stupid risks to save my wrinkled hide. Soon as I hear from Brad, you come clean with your folks. As it is, my brother will want to skin me alive for not letting him know pronto about the attempted arson. Glad I can point out we have an army to protect you tonight."

*   *   *

With six people at Eva's small dining table, we weren't just rubbing elbows. I could feel the heat from Paint's adjacent thigh, and Andy's muscled calf grazed mine every time he readjusted a sneaker. We were seated boy-girl. No place cards involved. Just happened. Billy and Paint bookended Eva, and Mollye sat between Billy and Andy.

All the men dished up servings of the hardy split pea soup, loaded with peas, carrots, potatoes, and onions. Of course, they all tossed cheese and hunks of the ham I'd thawed into their bowls. The women opted for my roasted tomato basil recipe. I was the only hold-out on plunking oodles of cheese on top. Crusty bread was all I needed as a perfect accompaniment.

Before our guests arrived, Eva ordered us to follow her conversational lead at dinner. She'd decide if, or when, we'd discuss the Nelson scouting adventure and tomorrow's DHEC inspection. Her concern was for Billy, who'd already had a mild heart attack. She feared he might stroke out if he knew we'd riled the Nelson roughnecks. That knowledge had raised my own blood pressure more than a skootch.

As a consequence, our dinner chatter seemed rather tame. We discussed Eva's bail hearing, the court system, and electronic anklets. My aunt modeled her new chunky jewelry by hiking up a pant leg and prancing around the room.

Eva confided she was considering going with a public defender. "Hiring what Brie's mom describes as a first-rate defense attorney could bankrupt Udderly." She glanced over at me. "And it could leave Brie's parents strapped as well. Not sure how much difference an expensive lawyer could make."

"How long till the trial?" Billy asked.

Eva shrugged. "Could be months, maybe half a year."

The news dumbfounded me. Would Eva be confined to Udderly all that time? While my aunt spent most days on the farm, being imprisoned here would put an ugly crimp in her lifestyle. No visits to the women's shelter she supported. No poker nights. No evenings at Clemson University for concerts and rodeos. Rooting for the Clemson women's basketball and fast-pitch softball teams were among her favorite pastimes.

Mollye helped me clear the dishes, and I poured coffee for the caffeine fiends. Paint fiddled with his mug, then sighed.

"Don't you think it's time we talked about last night's attempted arson? I'd sure like to know if anyone has some new thoughts about scaring off trespassers."

"Yep, especially if those trespassers include the Nelson boys," Mollye blurted.

"What about the Nelsons?" Billy asked.

"Oops." Mollye glanced over at Eva. "Sorry."

"It's okay," Eva said. "Might as well bring everyone up to speed if we're going to do a little brainstorming."

Five minutes later the entire table knew about the previous night's visitors and Mollye's and my hasty visit to the Nelson farm.

"The upside is that DHEC will do some official snooping at the Nelson place come morning," Eva said, letting us off easy.

Paint smiled. "Well, not much we can do to beef up security tonight, but I did talk to the guy who installed Magic Moonshine's security systems. Since Udderly's size makes perimeter alarms impractical, he suggested placing action-activated sensors near the main buildings. But given that Udderly has all manner of free-range critters roaming about that idea's worthless."

"Sorry you wasted your time," Eva said. "Lilly and I looked at security options early on before there were a lot of fancy-schmancy electronic gizmos. We decided our best bet was to count on our guard dogs and that trusty rifle I keep by the door. Not sure that's changed."

Eva glanced toward the umbrella stand that held her new long gun. "Glad I got me a fast replacement for my .22. That reminds me. Shouldn't that miserable son-of-a-bitch sheriff have to return my gun? Ballistics proved Jed was killed with his own, not my gun. Still can't fathom how someone could have wrestled Jed's weapon away from him and plugged the bastard. Mighty hard to believe that rifle was hidden in the loft for forty years and I never saw it. Don't go up there a lot, but I've visited plenty."

Bet it wasn't there for forty years.

As that thought popped into mind, I wondered why the explanation hadn't occurred to me sooner. Did one of the sheriff's goons plant Jed's gun during the so-called search? If so, where had that rifle been all this time?

Billy patted Eva's hand. "You don't have to worry none about a shortage of guns at Udderly tonight. Paint, Andy, and me all brought artillery to the party. Even those pea-brained Nelsons will think twice about tangling with us."

I shuddered. Somehow the idea of a freakin' arsenal didn't bring me peace of mind. I kept imagining a storm of bullets with us holed up in the cabin, like Paul Newman and Robert Redford in that old movie Mom liked so much.

Could the sheriff somehow convince the FBI we were right-wing militia nutcases who'd taken over a goat farm?

"Hey, Eva, you didn't let me finish my story about my security guy."

Paint's voice stopped my mental spiral into conspiracy land.

Eva harrumphed. "Guess you shouldn't spend so much time yapping about what won't work, Paint. You have something useful to share?"

"Matter of fact, I do." He got up from the table and retrieved a bag he'd stashed by the couch. He emptied the contents on the table. Round, flat micro-discs and what looked like Hobbit-sized radios. "My guy asked if we had any suspects. If so, he said we could plant bugs and eavesdrop or attach trackers to their cars. Not legal but mighty useful to figure out what we're up against. Candidates, anyone?"

"Sheriff Jones and Deputy West are my nominees," I answered. "But bugging the Sheriff's Office would be impossible, and if any of the lawmen are up to no good at night, what would they drive? Official vehicles? Their own cars? Borrowed backhoes?" I closed my eyes to think. "I'll bet it would be easy to bug Victor Caldwell. That banker's involved somehow. He's such a pompous ass. I don't think he'd ever suspect mere mortals would dare bug his office."

Eva drummed her fingers. A nervous tic that popped up more and more often. Had to be the strain.

"Niece, dear, you have a winner. I doubt Victor would soil his hands to join a dig for bones at Udderly, but I'd love to know what's up with that Sunrise Ridge deal. He's clearly in bed with Jones and West. If he's involved in under-the-table dealings with them, maybe we can gain some leverage. How would you propose I go about bugging him?"

I shook my head. "Remember, your little ankle jewelry won't let you go anywhere. But I can visit the bank tomorrow. Not sure he'd invite me into his office, but I think I can finesse his prune-faced secretary if he steps out."

"Ooh, I'll help." Mollye waved her arms like a kindergartener who had to go potty. "We can wait until he goes for his regular afternoon munchies at Abby's Diner. Then I can distract prune puss while you waltz in and plant a bug. What fun."

Andy cleared his throat. "You do recall Paint mentioning that bugging is illegal. If you get caught, Sheriff Jones will throw the book at you—if he doesn't take more drastic action. You know, off-the-books, break-your-legs-type action."

Mollye stuck out her tongue. "Spoilsport. Who could catch this dynamic duo?" She batted her eyes. "Brie and I are stealth warriors. Practically invisible."

I laughed. Mollye was attired in her gypsy-esque costume. I practically needed sunglasses to look at her purple, red, and orange getup. We'd proven quite visible to an old bat with cataracts, and I was betting there were younger, sharper eyes at the bank—not to mention surveillance cameras. Andy had a point. But if we were careful, we could pull it off—or at a minimum talk our way out of trouble.

"Brie, the set of your chin tells me you're going for it," Andy said. "If so, let Paint and me be your posse. We can track your every move on your iPhone. At least we'll know if you've been thrown in jail or abducted."

"Pardon me? Are you planning to become my official stalkers?"

Andy shrugged. "Guess that's one way of looking at it. My granddad's ninety. He's not senile, but sometimes he gets lost. We put a tracker app on his phone. Whenever he goes AWOL, we use the app to locate him. Then we text an SOS to the family. Whoever's closest comes to his rescue."

"You think Mollye and I are going to forget we're in the bank?" I laughed. "Don't think so. And I'm not sure I like the idea of anyone tracking my every move. What if I want to have a secret rendezvous with a hamburger at Sonic? I'd have no secrets."

I was only half kidding. If Paint and Andy could track me, I figured someone else could figure out how to follow the same cyber breadcrumbs.

Mollye knocked on the table to get attention. "Hey, don't you boys want to track my every move, too?"

Paint chuckled. "I'd be too afraid to track your moves Mollye. TMI."

Barking dogs, the roar of a big engine and the sudden screech of brakes saved me from making a decision. We had company. Billy jumped up and hurried to the window. "It's the Nelson boys. Let me handle this."

Billy hefted the shotgun he'd left by the door. Chairs scraped as Andy and Paint scrambled to get up from the table and grab their firearms. The men had stored their favorite weapons inside. Eva, too. She was right behind them, her replacement shotgun in hand. Lord almighty, what had Mollye and I done? Were we in for a firefight?

"Wait," I yelled at Billy just as he reached the door. "Blind 'em so they can't see you. Andy's big flashlight's sitting on the side table."

"Good idea." Andy grabbed the super-powered light he usually kept in his veterinary pack and jumped ahead of Billy. He cracked the door and aimed his quasi-spotlight at the brothers. A "dammit to hell" curse said the light had found its target. That was the cue for our cabin shooting team to step out on the porch, guns raised in we-mean-business poses.

Gunless, Mollye and I scrambled to the window to watch the confrontation and figure out how to help. I considered grabbing a cast-iron frying pan, but, as a weapon, it had severe range limitations. No time to boil oil or Eva's bacon grease to hurl at the gate crashers.

"Git that derned light outta my eyes," a Nelson brother yelled. His slurred speech said he was drunk as a skunk. "We see that little hippie bitch's van's here just like we figered. You tell that lunatic to stay off a our land. That goes for all them Hookers, too."

"Yeah, them Hookers are good for only one thing."

"Get off Udderly, now," Billy yelled back. "Don't have to tell you how South Carolina courts view a killin' when someone shoots a trespasser. Now git afore we air-condition you and that rusty bucket you call a truck."

"We're leavin'," one of the Nelson brothers yelled. "Don't think it's over. Sooner or later, you'll be gone. We can wait."

My heart beat like an overworked tom-tom as the truck roared in reverse. It sprayed gravel as it pivoted one-eighty and flew down the drive, headed back to the main road.

"Hey, did you get a good look at Harry Nelson?" Andy asked. "His cheek was black-and-blue and I swear one of his front teeth was missing."

"Think he was one of the men who tried to burn down the barn?" I asked.

"Maybe. They're kin to the sheriff. They could be in cahoots with him," Mollye added. "The Nelsons both own motorcycles. 'Course, it's quite possible Harry got punched out in a brawl. He's not exactly a people person."

The armed porch brigade straggled back inside. Guns returned to their lineup by the door.

"Think they'll be back tonight?" Paint asked.

"Nah," Billy answered. "But I'd feel better if we had a lookout. Maybe take turns at a watch."

I volunteered, but Eva and the men were only interested in lookouts who packed heat. "Hey," I objected. "You gave me a lesson. I know how to shoot. I can take your rifle."

Eva chuckled. "Yep, you know how to pull a trigger. But none of us are willing to risk your aim. Now, be honest, did you hit a single one of those paper targets I hung?"

I shrugged. Guess I'd better practice more if I planned to live at Udderly and contribute more than cooking and bookkeeping.

After a fair bit of haggling, the gun-toters drew up a sentinel schedule. Much to her chagrin, Eva wasn't given a spot on the rotation either. Billy insisted she was too exhausted. My aunt protested but finally accepted the inevitable. "Men," she muttered. "Stubborn jackasses."

Takes one to know one.

Mollye agreed to join our slumber party. No one wanted our resident hippie-gypsy to return alone to her apartment. While we doubted the Nelson boys were sober enough to drive to her place without playing bumper cars with parked vehicles, they might sober up.

For tonight, I'd share my queen bed. Had to admit Mollye wasn't my first choice for bedmate. However, it would have been a bit crowded if my first two candidates had slipped under the covers.

THIRTY-FIVE

Moonlight streamed through the flimsy lace curtains, serving as a natural nightlight. I glanced at my bedmate. Mollye had stolen the covers and somehow managed to trap all loose edges beneath her ample body. How could she still flounce and bounce the bed like her personal trampoline when she was wrapped tighter than a tamale?

Not going back to sleep. Might as well get up.

I grabbed my ratty robe, slipped my bare feet into a pair of Crocs, and tiptoed from the room. I noticed blankets balled in a nest on the empty couch. Who'd been sleeping there? Paint. Must be his turn on guard duty.

I snuck into the kitchen nook, took a glass down from the cupboard, and shuffled to the sink to run tap water. One sip and I put the glass down. I had yet to get used to the well water taste, a mineral tang that never quite quenched my thirst.

I looked out the window. My breath caught when I spotted a man. A tall one toting a gun. As he walked closer, I recognized shadow man's lean build and casual grace. Paint. Should I keep him company? Help him stay awake? Least I could do since I wasn't allowed to join the armed guard.

Was that my only reason? Nope. Don't go there.

I ventured outside and took a deep breath of the crisp pine-scented air. A perfect antidote to mental cobwebs. The complicated shadows cast by the bright moon lost all menace now that I knew who shouldered the gun.

Paint turned the minute he heard the porch stairs creak. He walked over and slid an arm around my shoulders. An arm that casually—accidentally?—grazed my right boob and brought my nipples to prompt attention beneath my ratty robe.

"Good thing I heard you coming," he whispered. "Don't ever sneak up on a man with a gun. Especially at three in the morning."

I shivered. Maybe it was the contrast between Paint's warm arm and the cool breeze. Somehow the bluish moonlight made me think of icebergs floating in a cold sea. Lonely icebergs?

Paint hugged me tighter. His body heat surged right through his Clemson sweatshirt. "Feels like someone needs warming up."

My brain suggested I pull free. My body vetoed the idea. "Is it really three o'clock?"

"It is. I'm pretty sure the Nelson boys won't be back tonight. I took over for Andy at two. He headed home when I came on. Said he needed to check on his own animals and that sorry pit bull he rescued from the Watson place. He also mentioned he had an early surgery."

"I love watching Andy with the animals," I said. "He's so gentle, so kind."

"Yep, he's my best friend," Paint said. "But I'm not about to spout his virtues when one of our shared interests is in my arms. Come on. Let's go inside the barn and out of the wind. The dogs will let me know if I need to pick up my rifle again."

We walked through the open barn door. Rita huffed. Still uneasy about nighttime visitors after her set-to with the arsonists? Soon as she heard a familiar voice, she settled. I walked to a stack of hay bales, sat down, and pulled my robe closed. If left unattended, the gap would leave my boobs within easy reach if not plain view.

Paint parked his rifle against the wall and joined me on our hay couch. Ready to make hay?

"Now where were we?" Before I knew it, he'd pulled me onto his lap. I might have yelped in surprise but my mouth was occupied. Paint's lips made sure of it. His kisses had definite staying power. His left arm circled my waist holding me tight against his muscled thighs. His right arm wrapped around my upper body. I could feel his heartbeat. His rapidly increasing heartbeat.

I knew he'd release me if I asked. And I planned to. Soon. Very soon. Moonbeams found their way through the barn's high window. Paint looked just as good with a three o'clock shadow as he did at high noon.

"Remember when you told me how you liked to prove you were a good kisser on the first date?" Paint said. "Big mistake. You hooked me. Every time I see you, I want to kiss you."

His tongue slid against my lips. My tongue, that no-good saboteur of my good intentions, proved all too willing to play. It had been too long. Kissing was one of my favorite occupations, right after playing chef.

Paint's tongue went exploring and found my ear. I squirmed with pleasure. That's when I discovered my bottom had made solid contact with another part of Paint's anatomy, one just as hard as his thighs.

Uh-oh. Kisses were bringing us to what the cook in me thought of as the hard-boil stage. You know that moment when you're making candy? The bubbles start to rise and suddenly you risk the pot boiling over if you don't take it off the heat.

Yep, we were there. Any minute now my robe and flimsy nightie would be on the barn floor. My brain insisted I take the pot off the stove. What if my aunt or Billy walked in? Thankfully, I didn't have to imagine Andy interrupting. Still thinking of Andy made me feel like a fickle Jezebel.

Time to call a recess. I gently wiggled free.

"I just came out to make sure you weren't falling asleep," I said. "My duty's done. Time to head back to bed."

Paint loosened his embrace, allowing me to stand. "You're breaking my heart, Brie. But, I can assure you, there's no way in hell I'll fall asleep now." He laughed. "But just to be sure, maybe you ought to come back in an hour."

I bent down and kissed Paint's forehead. "You're a great kisser. I can't begin to thank you for helping Aunt Eva and me. I promise I won't tell anyone your secret—that the heart of a true gentleman beats under that ever-so-attractive chest."

"Speaking of attractive chests."

I stepped back as his hand made a feint toward the sash on my robe.

"See you in the morning, Paint. Good night."

Good night? How would I ever sleep? Every fiber of my body hummed. Five more minutes and I'd have stripped off Paint's sweatshirt, kicked Rita out of her stall, thrown the bad boy moonshiner on the ground, and played Got you! Like a revenuer.

Take a deep breath.

How many other women had succumbed to the same wicked grin and talented tongue? Paint was basically a good guy. But he was a lover, not a keeper. Making love with Paint would be a leap into a five-alarm fire.

Too bad Paint's sizzle was just as seductive as bacon had been when I first turned vegan. Somehow celibacy was proving even tougher than vegan discipline. Especially with constant temptations like Paint and Andy.

I opened my bedroom door and sighed. Mollye hadn't moved. No prayer of prying my share of the covers free. Guess I'd just keep my robe on. Too bad I could still smell Paint's spicy scent on the terrycloth. Or was it my imagination? I inhaled.

Knock it off. Go to sleep.

THIRTY-SIX

I woke with a start. The room was a depressing fog gray, the color I now associated with that unfortunate hour between night and dawn. Time to get up and do chores. Would I ever get used to living on a goat farm? My alarm hadn't sounded. So why was I awake? I'd been dreaming about a train. Probably prompted by Mollye's raucous snores.

I dressed as quietly as I could. Just because I needed to rise and pretend to shine didn't mean Mollye had to stumble out of bed. I heard muffled voices in the main room. Probably Eva and Billy keeping conversation to a whisper.

Was Paint out there, too? I wasn't exactly proud of the kissing my sex-addled brain had encouraged the night before. Paint must think I'm a horrible tease, coming willingly to the plate and then calling the game in the first inning.

I tucked my cell phone in my pocket. What time was it in Tokyo? I hoped Kathy would call as soon as she got home from work. I slipped out and gently closed the bedroom door. Eva and Billy sat at the kitchen table. The smell of coffee made me downright giddy. I poured myself a mug before I joined them.

Eva looked me over and raised an eyebrow. "Hey, sleepyhead. What were you and Paint up to last night? You look as bleary-eyed as he did when he left a couple minutes ago."

Guilt swept over me. Aunt Eva and Billy had a darned good notion what we'd been doing last night. No. Maybe not. Eva was teasing because we both looked like the walking dead. Had she really suspected hanky-panky she'd never have said so in front of Billy, right?

"Paint and I probably shared the same nightmare, imagining the Nelson boys driving their big honking pickup right through your cabin.

What do you need me to do this morning?"

Eva let me off easy. Gather eggs, feed chickens and Tammy the Pig, and make breakfast for our dwindling household, now down to four.

I was filling Tammy's feed trough when I felt the vibration in my pants pocket. Not many people would be calling at this hour. I hoped it was Kathy. Yes!

"Hey, girlfriend. What's the word?"

As I listened to Kathy's report, my mind raced ahead trying to figure out how we could leverage the news that Tisnomi was opting out. Would the bailout cause Victor to panic? How about Sheriff Jones and Deputy West? And did it really matter? Maybe the fate of Sunrise Ridge had nothing to do with Jed's murder or why the Watsons were killed.

"Thanks so much for playing spy, Kathy. You're one heck of a detective. I promise we'll get together soon. In the U.S. or Japan. Or maybe we'll meet in the middle. Always wanted to vacation in Hawaii. I miss you."

No point trying to track down Eva to give my report. It was her first morning out of jail, back on the farm. She'd want to commune with her animals. Have a little normalcy. Besides, I wasn't sure she shared my obsession with Sunrise Ridge and its future. How could it prove her innocence?

I finished my chores and headed to the cabin to start breakfast. Still no sign of Mollye. Lucky girl. I started a new pot of coffee and whipped up a batch of vegan pancake batter. I'd sprinkle in plenty of nuts and chocolates to take my non-paying customers' minds off a missing side of meat.

The smell of fresh coffee proved the right incentive to get Mollye out of bed. In fact, she'd already dressed in her full gypsy regalia. Not that she had a choice. She hadn't planned to spend the night at the Udderly B&B.

"Morning, Mollye. How'd you sleep?"

"Better than you. Woke up once and you were among the missing. Should I ask what you were doing?"

"Just went for a walk," I answered. "No biggie."

She gave me a squint-eyed once-over but let it pass. She'd just poured herself a cup of coffee when the screen door banged, and Eva and Billy returned. I served breakfast and my news simultaneously.

"Kathy talked with a Mr. Isaak, the gentleman overseeing Tisnomi North American operations. Told him she'd love to be considered for a position on a transition team if they made a new acquisition. Kathy's in IT—Information Technology—so she often works on meshing systems after a takeover. Mr. Isaak told her Tisnomi would announce an acquisition soon—in Georgia. Said they'd been considering two properties but decided the Georgia deal was sweeter than the Carolina option. The announcement is set for this Friday."

Mollye's glee was evident in the way she bounced up and down. Her enthusiasm had me a little worried about the old oak chair and its fragile cane seat.

"Ooh, yes. The banker and our local lawmen will mess their britches. Not to mention that other joker Burks-what's-his-name. How do we get the ball rolling? Let them know their greasy gooses are roasted."

"I think we do exactly as planned and plant a bug in that officious little banker's office. A little while later, I'll drop by and casually mention that Tisnomi is a no-go. If I can't wrangle an invitation into Victor's office, I'll make sure my voice carries when I'm talking to his hawk-faced assistant."

"Sounds like a plan," Mollye agreed. "Thanks for breakfast. Got to say if I were vegan I'd want you doing the cooking. Never thought of chocolate chips and pecans in my pancakes. I got to head back to my apartment, take a shower, and change clothes. I'm hoping those a-holes didn't trash my place. Think they were too trashed themselves to do any damage. I do need to open my store this morning. I'm expecting shipments."

"Okay by me," I said. "Afternoon's a fine time for espionage."

Eva stood and gave Mollye a hug. "Behave yourself, and watch out for my Brie. If she's teetering on a high-dive and you think the water's too deep or too shallow, pull the plug. Things don't turn out fine just because you will it. In this old world, plenty of monsters wear suits. Doesn't make them any less scary."

Mollye returned my aunt's hug. "Not to worry. I'll bring Brie back safe and sound."

I walked my friend and fellow conspirator to the door.

"Let's meet in the Bi-Lo parking lot," she suggested. "Say quarter to three. That'll give us plenty of time to find a good spot on the square before Mr. Banker goes for his mid-afternoon pastry fix."

"It's a deal," I answered. "If Eva will trust me to drive her truck that far. I'm still without wheels and a klutz with a clutch."

Mollye skipped down the porch stairs. When she reached the bottom, she turned back. "Oh, Brie. Look for a nondescript tan Camry. Figure my van might be a poor choice for a stakeout. I'll drive Mom's boring car."

THIRTY-SEVEN

Slumped in the front seat of the Camry, we barely blinked, keeping our attention glued on the bank's front door. I considered readjusting my seat but figured it might be set for one of Mollye's tall relatives. The last occupant either had very long legs or was using it as a recliner. I scooted to the edge of the seat to peer through the window.

The Camry sat catty-corner, half a block away from the bank. Nonetheless, we had an unobstructed view. Maybe I'd missed my calling. Snooping and catering. We'll catch your cheating hubby and cater your alimony party.

Mollye squirmed. "Stupid to drink that latte while I was waiting for you at Bi-Lo. If Caldwell doesn't go for his sweet tooth fix soon, I'm gonna have to pee in Mom's AARP trash bag."

"Shh. There he is. Waddling toward Abby's. How long do we have?" I tightened my grip on the door handle. Didn't want a sudden movement to catch the banker's eye before he entered the diner.

"He gets a pot of tea to sip with his pastry. Finds some customer in a booth and wrangles an invitation to sit down. Likes to hear himself pontificate. Imagine we have a solid half-hour."

"Let's be on the safe side. In and out of the bank in ten minutes. Give me two to three minutes after I'm inside. Then you're on."

I power-walked to the bank. I'd dressed in my invisibility suit—the long-sleeve white shirt and tailored black slacks I wore when catering swanky Asheville parties. Just left off the tie that's de rigor for wait staff.

Entering the bank, I casually glanced around to check out the cameras. My friend's recall seemed accurate. Three focused on the teller stations. The remaining two covered the vault area and front door. Caldwell's office appeared to occupy a blind spot.

I marched directly to the desk of the bank president's frumpy assistant. She'd dressed in uniform, too. If it wasn't the same boxy getup she wore when Eva and I visited, today's beige suit was its out-of-date twin.

Her eyes widened. She emitted a wheezy gasp once she realized who cast a shadow over her spotless desk. Yep, she recognized me as one of those loud and dangerous Hookers. Her gaze darted left and right, probably sizing up who she might call to escort me off the premises.

"May I help you?" Those were her words. Frump's tone carried a different message: "What d'you want, bitch?"

My answer? "I'm here to put a bug up your boss's butt." Not that I planned to say that out loud.

I pasted on a demure smile and hoped that didn't seem even more suspicious. "I need to find out if a check has cleared. Number 4053 on the Udderly Kidding Dairy checking account."

She dutifully jotted down the number and hustled over to a terminal one desk away. I checked out the witch's nameplate and almost giggled. Ms. Clod? I'd rather be a Hooker. Whatever her surname, the woman definitely wanted me to breathe air in someone else's personal space.

I caught Mollye's entrance out of the corner of my eye. While I'd pressed the mute button on my attire, she'd dialed up the rainbow volume—if that was possible given her wardrobe. She looked like a living Christmas tree with plenty of tinsel. Santa Claus red top, emerald harem pants, and a sparkly silver belt wide enough to proclaim she'd won a wrestling championship. The dangling silver earrings and clanking bracelets added glitter and sound effects.

Mollye was a walking distraction before she uttered a single syllable. And everyone in the bank seemed to understand that keeping her mouth shut wasn't part of her plan.

Ms. Clod hurried back from a round of furious tapping on her terminal to advise me the check had cleared.

"Thank you." I pivoted one-eighty without another word and sauntered to the stand-up counter a few feet away. I picked up a deposit slip and pretended to write. Ms. Clod's glee at seeing my backside wouldn't last long. Not if Mollye performed as expected.

My friend strode directly to Sour Puss's desk. Her hands-on-hips stance advertised she spoiled for a fight. Mollye flung down her bank statement like a gauntlet. "This is highway robbery." Her near bellow turned every head in the bank. That is every head not already inclined in her direction.

"How can you get away with charging my business thirty-five dollars for a returned check? I know you're making the poor sap who wrote that check pay some ridiculous amount for making a tiny mistake. He told me he miscalculated his balance by a penny!"

I tuned out the rest of the exchange and sidled toward Caldwell's open office. Fortunately, the banker saw no reason to lock his door or even close it for an afternoon donut break. Heck, the safe was down the hall. No money inside.

Of course, I wanted to make deposits not withdrawals. I quickly attached one bug to the underside of his desk. Where to put the second one? I spotted his briefcase. Yes! The soft leather folder had a metal clasp. I fingered the underside of the clasp and pushed the bug in place. Done. Less than a minute. I mentally patted myself on the back.

I strolled to the front of the bank as if I had all the time in the world. Didn't even glance in Mollye's direction. I felt sneaky, cocky, certain I hadn't been made. I heard Mollye's loud harrumph as I opened the door.

I sauntered down the block and admired a window display while I waited for Mollye to join me. Our next act was a duet. She wasn't far behind. She high-fived me before we walked on to Abby's Diner. We entered together, chattering away as friends do. We spotted Caldwell in a booth midway down the aisle. He had his back to us so he hadn't seen us yet, and surprisingly hadn't picked up on Mollye's voice. He must have been holding forth on some arcane subject. The fellow seated across from him had a glazed look that said "How soon can I politely get the heck out of here?"

The booth next to Caldwell's was empty. We slid in, out of Caldwell's sight but definitely within audio range. The diner's rickety bench-style booths were connected. That meant only one shared hunk of fiber board and two thin layers of vinyl stuffing separated me from our target, Banker Caldwell.

I gave Mollye a thumbs-up, indicating it was time to lift the curtain on our little play. The actual time? Three thirty on the nose.

"That's so exciting," Mollye squealed. "Your Japanese pen pal, the friend at Tisnomi, is definitely coming to the States? When?"

At the mention of Tisnomi, the booth at my back violently shuddered, a definite indication we had Caldwell's attention. Either he'd bolted upright or his butt had tightened with cataclysmic force. Yep, he was listening.

"Yes," I answered. "I'd hoped she'd be assigned to Sunrise Ridge so she'd be posted right around the corner. But she says Tisnomi's passing on that property. Instead it's buying some swanky gated community in Georgia. Don't tell anyone though. It's a secret. Tisnomi isn't announcing the deal until Friday."

The waitress arrived to take our order at the same moment Caldwell sprang from his seat. The collision practically knocked her flat. The banker didn't stop to apologize.

"I'm late for a meeting," he muttered as he shoved by. He never glanced in our direction.

Mollye and I shared victory grins as we ordered coffee. The minute Caldwell was out of sight we asked the waitress for to-go cups and plopped our payment and a generous tip on the table.

If we wanted to listen in on any phone calls our Tisnomi news might spark, we had to return to our stakeout vehicle. Our listening devices weren't exactly NSA quality. Our receiver had to be within five hundred feet.

We'd barely popped our takeout in the Camry's cup holders when the receiver burped to life with heavy breathing. Caldwell's squeaking chair provided a background beat. The man hadn't needed that donut. A knock announced a visitor. "Mr. Caldwell, I wish you'd been here. You should have heard—"

"Ms. Clod, I have an important phone call. Whatever you want to tell me will have to wait. Please close the door on your way out."

I smiled. A bonus. If we were lucky, Ms. Clod would be miffed at being cut off and wouldn't confide her travails with Mollye Camp and Brie Hooker. Less reason for the banker to suspect we'd set him up.

Caldwell's call went through. Sticking with his ingrained habits, the banker left the phone on speaker, letting us hear both sides of the conversation. "Sheriff's Office," a woman answered.

"I need to speak to Sheriff Jones. Immediately. Tell him it's Victor Caldwell."

"I'm sorry, he's out of the office and unavailable. Is this an emergency?"

"Uh, no."

"Do you want to leave a message?

"No. Just tell him to call me."

By four thirty, I wondered if Sheriff Jones would ever return Victor's call. Maybe he was testifying in court. Then again, he could be busy organizing a SWAT raid on Udderly Kidding Dairy.

At 4:35 p.m. Victor's phone finally rang.

"What's up?" a male voice demanded when Victor answered.

Definitely the sheriff, and he was in curt, pissed-off mode. I sucked in a breath.

"I need to see you, in person," Caldwell said. "We have trouble with Sunrise Ridge. Big trouble. Those friends of yours up north are going to be very unhappy."

"Shut up," Jones barked. "Not on the telephone. West and I will meet you at Dot's. Leave the bank at your usual time. That should put you there about five thirty."

This was it? Conversation over? Dang. We hadn't learned a blasted thing. Well, nothing we didn't already know. Caldwell was in bed with Sheriff Jones and Deputy West, and they were desperate for the Sunrise Ridge sale to go through.

I turned to Mollye. "Well, pickled pigs' feet, that was a big zero. Who in blazes is Dot?"

"Dot isn't a who, it's a what." Mollye started the car. "It's a failed burger joint out on Highway 11. Went out of business last year. Huge parking lot screened from the road. Teens go there to neck. Ideal spot for Ardon's very own evil axis to meet in secret. We can get there early. I even know a place we can hide our car. Perfecto."

Perfecto? We had no binoculars. At least if they were meeting at five thirty it wouldn't be dark yet. Would spying on the trio from a distance do us any good? I supposed we could tail one of the cars after they finished plotting, but how would that help?

I shared my gloom with Mollye.

She wagged a finger at me. "Ye of little faith. You bugged

Caldwell's briefcase, right? That wanker takes it everywhere. You'd think it was the Presidential football with the nuclear launch code inside. It's a decent bet we'll hear every word those creeps say."

Mollye peeled away from the curb. I buckled my seatbelt and held on tight.

I loved Mollye's optimism. Hoped it was merited. I crossed my fingers her car camouflage skills were as good as her Irish blarney.

THIRTY-EIGHT

"There's Dot's." Mollye pointed at a falling-down building straight ahead. As we skidded into a ninety-degree turn, I gathered Dot's wasn't our destination. We bumped off the pavement and fishtailed up a skinny dirt track. If we lived to reach the hilltop, we'd drive past a weathered red barn. Perched on the ridge, the barn looked directly over Dot's parking lot.

"Do you know the folks who live here?" I asked.

"Yes, before they moved to Chicago. Place has been vacant for months. Not many takers for small family farms these days. We'll stash the Camry behind the barn and park our spy eyes this side of the tree line. They'll never spot us."

I agreed. No one would see us unless they arrived in the next five minutes. It would take that long for the dust we kicked up to settle. At the moment, it hung in low, roiling clouds, an airborne trace of the path we'd traveled.

Mollye parked behind the barn.

"Have to hand it to you, Mollye, it's a great hideaway."

"Did you ever doubt me?" She chuckled.

"Just hope our banker brings his briefcase and everyone speaks loud enough for us to pick up the sound."

The wait proved long enough for our telltale dust trail to vanish. Victor Caldwell's shiny black S-Class Mercedes arrived first. I had no idea what he drove, but ownership wasn't exactly a wild guess. The vanity license plate read BANKR.

I expected Caldwell to leap out of his car and pace while he waited for his sidekicks. Didn't happen. He sat inside, car engine running. Did he suspect he'd need a quick getaway?

Our spyware receiver came to life. Voices. Was he talking to himself? Oh, crap, it was his radio tuned to an all-news station. The five o'clock report.

A sheriff's cruiser pulled in next to the Mercedes. The newscast stopped mid-sentence as Caldwell switched off his radio.

"Why do you suppose Deputy West drove?" Mollye asked as the obnoxious deputy exited the driver's side. The sheriff, who'd ridden shotgun, took a couple more minutes to get out.

"Come on, be good little cheese doodles," I ordered sotto voice. "Climb in Caldwell's car." Might as well pretend I could give stage directions to the doll-size characters below.

I wanted to clap when the lawmen slid their backsides into the rear of the large Mercedes. Guess talking through a cop car's mesh screen would have seemed less cozy. The Mercedes' leather upholstery was definitely a step up from what I assumed was cracked vinyl.

I crossed my fingers and toes. Would we be able to hear the conversation?

"You big asshole," Jones bellowed. "Can't believe you called me at the Sheriff's Office and, like an idiot, you mentioned Sunrise Ridge and my 'friends' up North. Don't you know our calls are recorded?"

"What the hell difference does it make? We're screwed. We promised the family backing Burks that this Tisnomi deal would fly, and, when it did, we'd make them whole, pay back every penny they loaned us to stay afloat. Now Tisnomi's walking away. Not another buyer in sight."

"How do you know the Tisnomi deal's off?" the deputy asked.

"Overheard a conversation. Some Tisnomi employee blabbed. The company's passing on Sunrise Ridge, making a deal on some Georgia property instead. The announcement's Friday. Gives us a little time to make plans."

"Yeah, and who's to say this Tisnomi employee knows his ass from a hole in the ground? You panic too easily, Caldwell."

I was pretty sure Jones was doing the talking, though the sheriff's and deputy's Southern twangs were cured in the same liquor and tobacco marinade.

"You've always been nervous. Thought you'd piss yourself back when we buried Jed and Kaiser."

My breath caught. Had Jones just admitted they'd murdered both men?

"You were so afraid folks wouldn't buy the idea that Kaiser flew the coop with everyone's loot. Told you they would. Worked like a charm."

"Well, the chickens in that coop are coming home to roost." Caldwell's tone dropped into the deep freeze. "They've already dug up Jed. What if someone unearths Kaiser, too?"

"We took care of that." A slightly different voice. The tone almost boastful. "Nobody'll ever find his bones, and there's no connection to Sunrise Ridge."

"I don't like it." Caldwell's voice cut in. "And Nancy. Why her? She was a nobody. You've both gone off the deep end."

"No choice," the sheriff took back the conversational lead. "She just wouldn't stop yammering about Eva faking Jed's signature on that deed. I wasn't gonna risk people connecting that piece of land to Jed's murder."

"This is too much." Caldwell's voice had climbed an octave and acquired a definite warble. "West, think, man. For god's sake, Eli was one of your buddies. I'm out, leaving town tonight. If you're smart, you two will do the same."

"You're not getting a notion to play innocent, are you, Victor? Cozying up to the Feds, maybe? Acting like the deputy and I twisted your arm to launder money?"

Boom! The sound was so loud my body shook.

I screamed. It took a second to realize the scream came in stereo. I shut my trap and clamped my hand over Mollye's mouth.

"Holy shit, I think Jones just offed Caldwell." This was as close to a whisper as Mollye'd ever managed—at least when I'd been with her.

I nodded.

"You think they heard us scream?"

I bit my lip. "No. The blast had to deafen everyone in that car."

I tapped our faithful spyware receiver. Shook it. Not a sound. Audio blowout? Our private broadcast had ended.

My hands shook. Maybe I hadn't seen a murder, but I'd heard one. Not that I could prove it. Our receiver wasn't a recorder.

I jumped up. Mollye grabbed my ankle in an attempt to tackle me back to the ground. "What are you doing?" she gasped. "They'll see you."

I pulled free. "Can't believe I left my phone in my purse." I sprinted to the Camry, grabbed my iPhone, ran back to the ridge, and dropped to my knees. I snapped picture after picture. Jones and West exiting the Mercedes...Jones opening the Mercedes' front door, gun in hand...West wiping down door handles...the cruiser driving away.

When the killers left the scene, Mollye and I collapsed spread-eagled on the grass, breathing like we'd run four-minute miles.

"What now?" Mollye asked. "Do we call the state police? I'm scared to death. Caldwell was their partner, and Jones blew his brains out. It sure sounds like they've offed one boatload of people—Jed, Kaiser, Nancy, Eli, Caldwell. Can you believe it? Half those folks were drinking buddies or their own damn kin."

I shook my head. "Not sure West killed any of them. Looks like Jones has the itchy trigger finger, but the deputy is definitely a willing accomplice. They both scare me. We're way beyond the point where smartass amateur snoops should butt out. It's time to turn this over to real detectives."

I knew who to call. Mom. Had to—even though I dreaded admitting how many secrets I'd been keeping. She'd be furious. She'd also know exactly who to bring in and how to do it.

My fingers were poised above my phone's numeric display when my cell began vibrating. Mental telepathy? Mom?

I looked at the display. Really? Couldn't be.

"It's Eva," I told Mollye. "Good Lord, I hope nothing horrible has happened at Udderly. She never phones anyone unless there's a dire emergency." I answered the call. "Aunt Eva, what—"

Never had a chance to finish. Eva blasted right over my attempts to get a word in edgewise. Guess she figured anything I had to say couldn't compete with her news. If I hadn't just listened to the audio track of a murder, she might have been right.

Eva spit out words like cherry pits in a high-speed processing plant. Soon as she said her piece, she hung up.

"Eva...Eva...damn." Sigh.

"What bee flew inside Eva's bonnet?" Mollye asked. "Why'd she call only to hang up before you could say boo?"

"Wanted to share a news bulletin. Said that DHEC fellow, Brad, phoned. Apparently, it was afternoon when he got to the Nelson place. He showed his authorization to Granny and went around back to look at the pit they'd dug near the creek. Next thing he knew she'd loosed two junkyard dogs on him and started peppering the general vicinity with buckshot. Old Brad made a hasty retreat, then came back with state troopers and a warrant. They found human remains. Old bones, but clearly human."

"That's good news," Mollye said. "Just a wild guess, but based on what we overheard that skeleton must belong to that Kaiser fella."

I nodded. "Eva hung up after she ordered us home. She saw no point fretting over Sunrise Ridge and what Caldwell did or didn't know now that those mystery bones have been unearthed. She was pretty optimistic their discovery would clear her."

"I agree," Mollye said. "Though I'm still more than a little foggy about how and why anyone besides Jed and Kaiser died."

"We won't find any answers here. Let's get while the getting's good. The sun's going to set soon. I want to get as far away as possible before dark. Thank heavens, Jones and West blew out of here as soon as they wiped down Victor's car."

I phoned Mom. It went straight to voice mail. Figuring she was probably in court or with a client, I left a succinct message. "Mom, it's urgent. Mollye and I just saw the sheriff murder Victor Caldwell. Obviously we can't phone the sheriff. Who should we call? What should we do? Call me."

"What now?" Mollye asked as I ended the call.

"Head straight to my folks' house in Clemson. Mom should be back soon."

"I have a backup plan," Mollye said. "Send an SOS to Andy and Paint. Last night when you went to the bathroom, we fixed your phone up with that tracking app Andy mentioned."

"You what?"

"Don't get all huffy. Just text SOS to Paint or Andy. They can see where we are."

"Why didn't anyone tell me?"

"Eva didn't want to hear any guff."

I glared at Mollye but did as she suggested, texting an SOS to both men before we climbed into the Camry.

Having roasted in the late afternoon sun, the car interior was hot enough to bake cookies. Mollye started the engine, and I rolled down my window to let in some air. Too late, I remembered the dust clouds we created on the drive up the hill. Wouldn't be any better on the way down.

We'd almost reached the pavement when we heard sirens and saw the flashing blue lights. What the heck? Two sheriff's cruisers. The first car rocketed into Dot's parking lot and skidded to a stop next to the Mercedes where Victor's corpse was now entombed. The second cruiser initially followed the first into the lot, but then it did a one-eighty and headed for our skimpy dirt lane. The car fishtailed sideways to block our path. No chance of escape.

Hairy Pork Rinds, what now?

"Stop the car." I recognized the voice all too easily as it boomed over some loud speaker contraption inside the cruiser.

"Driver, turn off the motor and put your hands above your head. Passenger, you too, get your hands up where we can see them."

Chipped beef on a shingle, Jones and West had seen our telltale dust trail. They could see exactly where we'd been.

We were dead.

THIRTY-NINE

Car doors slammed. Sheriff Jones and Deputy West weren't wasting any time. I gathered Jones didn't know who occupied our Camry when he barked his hands-up orders. Otherwise he'd have called us something a tetch more colorful than "driver" and "passenger." Sun reflecting off our car's tinted windshield plus the brown smog we'd manufactured were the only reasons we'd been granted a brief reprieve. Any minute Jones would figure out which varmints he'd caught in his trap.

Mollye's hands fluttered above her head. "What are you doing?" she squawked, tilting her head forward to peek around her arm. "Put your hands up or they'll plug us!"

"Shhh. I only need a sec. They won't shoot us in your car. Too big a coincidence to have two car hijackings gone bad. They'll take us somewhere private."

Mollye awarded me a black look. Pretty obvious my prediction hadn't made her feel safe and cozy.

"That SOS you had me send won't do us a bit of good if my phone's off, but we'll be in a worse fix if the sheriff hears it ring. I'm putting it on vibrate."

Jones looked like a Neanderthal and West looked enough like a wraith to play the part of Death. I held my breath as they lumbered to within five feet of our bumper. Both men squinted as they tried to peer through the windshield's glare.

"Damn you, Brie Hooker, put your hands over your head."

Moldy Munster, a positive ID. Now I understood what the phrase "heart in your throat" meant. My ticker pumped blood so fast the veins in my neck twitched like hopped-up junkies. I couldn't swallow.

They'd search us. Tear our car apart. They'd find the receivers.

Not a doubt in the world. They'd go back and search Victor's car for a bug. They'd know we'd watched and listened.

Think. No way to hide the receivers, but I couldn't let them find my cell phone.

Ah ha! Light bulb lit. Good old Dad. He told me one of the cop instructors at the Writers' Police Academy said he learned the hard way where girl gangbangers hid knives. Snug in their undies. A place no man would pat if his mama had pounded a speck of decency in him. Parking a cell "down under" seemed infinitely less perilous than hiding a switchblade near my privates.

Mollye's eyes widened as she watched me suck in my tummy, pry open my slacks and undies, and clear a silken chute for my contraband. Thank goodness, I didn't go for thongs. And I'd thought insidious discomfort was the only reason not to wear them.

I shimmied my iPhone down, down, down until I wriggled it in place. Cold. Yeehaw! Glad I hadn't upgraded to a newer, beefier model. I needed to walk with my pant-a-phone in place. Uh-oh. What if Andy or Paint rang me back? I'd seen a vibrating phone walk itself off a table. Sitting I'd have no problem. But what if a call came in while I was standing? Could it shimmy its way out of my drawers?

"Hooker, did you hear me? Hands up, or I swear I'll shoot."

My hands shot up. I mimicked Mollye's waving routine, making certain my empty hands caught Jones' eye.

Guns drawn, the sheriff and Deputy West bracketed our car. Jones took my side; West the driver's side. Our doors yanked open in unison.

"Out!" Jones yelled.

West herded Mollye over to my side of the car. The sheriff kept his gun trained on us while the deputy patted us down. I figured if West could look the other way while Jones gunned down friends, he wasn't above copping a feel. Still I counted on his need to hurry. The deputy's bony fingers ran down my ribcage and up the inside of my thighs, but stopped short of cell phone territory. Fortunately, there'd been no pulsing phone calls to alert West to the presence of my contraband.

"Cuff 'em," Jones ordered. "Put 'em in the Camry and drive 'em back up the hill. I'll be along. Need to have a little chat with Max first."

Who was Max? Another rotten deputy? Last thing we needed was one more villain.

"What you gonna tell him?" West asked. "Max'll wonder why we didn't follow him into the lot after we got that anonymous tip about a carjacking."

"Got it handled. I'll say we stopped these folks, thinking they might be involved or potential witnesses. Once we discovered they were out-of-towners, I asked you to ride back up the hill with them and take their statements. Doubt Max'll even wonder what out-of-towners were doing on a dirt road to nowhere. If he asks, I'll think of something."

West nodded. "Got it."

"While you're waiting for me, search the girls' car. Take out the seats if you have to. Make sure there's nothing to come back on us. But remember, we need the car later. Everything's gotta go back nice and neat."

A chill slithered down my spine. Whatever Jones had in mind, it didn't sound like we'd be around to refute his version of our meet-and-greet. There'd been so many murders, I didn't think he'd risk shooting us. My bet? Mollye and I would have an "accident." Our car would plunge over a cliff.

"Inside." West shoved Mollye toward the Camry's backseat. She tried to scoot to make room for me but didn't make it past the middle hump. I squeezed in beside her. The front seats were reclined so far our knees grazed the seat backs.

Mollye's cuffed hands found mine. A tear dribbled down her cheek. I wanted to give her hope, assure her all was not lost.

The vibrating gizmo below grabbed my attention. An incoming call. Was it Andy? Paint? Mom? I could only hope. No way to answer.

With West sitting in the front seat, I couldn't risk even whispered conversation. I mouthed the word "Posse." She nodded, but none of the worry left her face. My mind flitted across all the things she may have thought I said. None were good, and one was naughty.

When we reached the barn at the top of the hill, the deputy opened the Camry's back door, ordered us out, and marched us inside the decrepit structure.

"Sit over there." He pointed at a post in the middle of the barn. "Put your backs against the post."

We sat. He unsnapped Mollye's right cuff and my spirits soared. Was he freeing our hands? Then he clicked the just-freed cuff around my wrist. My hopes dashed. He undid one end of my steel bracelet and attached it to Mollye's free wrist. We were now linked arm and arm with the rough wood post in the center.

"It's all your fault, you know?" The deputy's Adam's apple bobbed. "You just couldn't leave well enough alone. You shoulda got the message when I bumped your preppie car into that ditch. Or when the sheriff paid the Nelsons to torch your barn. But no. You just had to push it. You've sealed your fate with Robbie. He'll never let you go now."

Neither Mollye nor I spoke until West's backside disappeared outside the barn.

"What were you mouthing at me? Police?" Mollye whispered.

Police. Of course she'd have thought police. "No. Posse. Someone's been phoning me. Could be Mom, but I'm hoping that tracker app really works, and Andy or Paint got our SOS. If so, they'd know we'd answer if we could. I'm praying they'll just send help. Otherwise I need to be scared for them *and* us."

"What about your mom?" Mollye asked. "What'll she do when she gets your message?"

"What can she do? Call the state police, but she has no clue where we are. Too bad your psychic skills don't include telepathy."

"I wish. I've been directing all my mental energies to making a bucket list and figuring out if there was anything I could cross off while handcuffed. Only thought of one. If I go, I want to take Jones or West with me."

"It's not over, Mollye. Keep your eyes open for opportunities. Anything to delay Jones' plans. Anything to buy time."

Mollye sighed. "You're thinking car accident, right? Bet they pour alcohol down our throats or shoot us up with some confiscated drugs. Make it look like it's our fault. Wild women come to a bad end."

Fried pork rinds, my mind hadn't gone that far. I only figured "accident." Didn't consider that Jones might try to make it look like we were to blame. More heartache for our loved ones.

Damn. Damn. Damn.

They'd pushed me back to my old curse vocabulary. Cheeses and processed meats simply wouldn't cut it.

No way would I let those scumbags get away with making us look like druggies in death.

FORTY

We could hear West swearing as he ransacked the Camry. His expletives went viral when he found our illegal listening devices. Then it got very quiet. He hadn't started the car. Hadn't driven off. What was he doing? Was he lurking within earshot?

I had no idea how long we sat alone and mute. Each minute that passed felt like an hour. The wait unraveled what remained of my frayed nerves. Where were Andy and Paint? Had they received my SOS? What "accident" did the Sheriff and Deputy have in mind?

"Hope you got 'em cuffed so they can't pull any stunts." Jones' voice drifted in from beyond the barn doors. "We should have stuffed something soft inside those handcuffs so their wrists won't look bruised."

"Why? What you planning?" West's tone suggested he was genuinely curious.

Jones sauntered inside as if he hadn't a care in the world. Well, maybe with us in handcuffs, he didn't. West looked a little more hangdog. Probably wishful thinking, hoping one of the two lawmen had a heart or a conscience.

In the low light, it was hard to get a read on their faces even after they came within spitting distance. I looked past them to the world outside. Sky. A beautiful one, with clouds painted lavender and scarlet by the setting sun. Gorgeous. But night followed sunset. Was that what they were waiting for?

"They're so interested in Sunrise Ridge, thought we'd give them one last visit. Not sure they got a good look at Sunrise Lake." Jones' voice had a jokester's lilt to it. Did he really find this funny?

West swallowed and his prominent Adam's apple did a little jig. "You gonna drown 'em? Weigh the bodies down and dump 'em in the lake so they'll never be found?"

"No. The folks that originally bought the property out of foreclosure tried to make it into a fishing camp. Dammed up a mountain stream to fill a big depression and stocked it with bass. Burks kept the lake, perfect way to jack up the price of adjacent lots. But the water's only about thirty feet deep and clear. You can see clean to the bottom when you stand on the bank."

"So what you gonna do?"

"They'll drown all right. We'll try to rescue them, but sadly our efforts will be too little too late. It'll be a shame how they missed the sharp curve on the road that circles the lake. The crash will have knocked 'em out. No chance to escape the car before their lungs filled. Or maybe they'll die of hypothermia first. Who knows? That lake's colder than a witch's tit this time a year."

Jones smiled, apparently enjoying taunting us with his fatal plan. "I thought about pouring liquor down their gullets so the medical examiner could declare it another horrible example of the heartache drunk drivers cause. But those meddling Hookers would raise hell and demand an investigation. I'm afraid some doctor might be able to prove the booze wasn't in their systems long enough to make 'em drunk. No point in taking risks." The sheriff knelt and brought his face even with mine. "You should have learned that texting while driving could be a killer when your aunt bought it." He looked up at West. "You found their cell phones, right?"

West's eyebrows scrunched together. He looked like Jones had asked him to solve a tough algebra equation.

"Found one in Mollye's pocket, but the Hooker broad didn't have no phone in a pocket or her purse. Didn't find one in the car either."

The sheriff grabbed my chin in one of his big calloused hands and squeezed hard. "Where's your cell phone?" he demanded. "I don't know any thirty-something who can draw breath without a cell phone within reach."

I tried my best to look puzzled. "It wasn't in my purse?"

Mollye clutched my hand. "Bet it fell out when we switched cars," she said.

Mollye, bless her, was super-fast on the uptake.

"We were in an awful hurry," she added. "Don't know how many times I've told you not to stick your phone in that open side pocket. It probably got dumped on the ground back at the Bi-Lo parking lot."

Sheriff Jones released my chin and patted my cheek. "Guess it doesn't matter. Mollye will be the one texting since it's her ma's car and she's driving. Let's see her phone. Need to figure out who she'll be texting, and what her last words will be."

"How about 'Screw you, asshole?'" Mollye blurted.

Jones' hand drew back to deliver a slap, but he stopped himself. "No, can't risk any injuries inconsistent with a car accident. Just before we run the car into the lake, we'll knock them out. But even bumps on the head need to look accidental. Have to give some thought to the how of that."

I fought my sudden nausea. I'd underestimated the sheriff. He was no dummy. Guess he'd investigated enough accident scenes to know how to stage one so it looked authentic. Still I saw a few flaws in his plan. Sunrise Ridge had a security gate, and the guards kept track of who came in and out. How were they going to get Mollye's Camry through the gate so both of us were registered visitors?

Oh, Limburger on a Ritz. Not exactly a puzzler if the sheriff had a security guard in his pocket. Is that why he'd picked Sunrise Lake as our last resting place?

FORTY-ONE

Jones and West perp-walked us to the Camry.

"You've been very naughty girls." Jones squeezed my upper arm hard enough to leave a bruise. Guess his concern about leaving mystery injuries had momentarily escaped him.

"We found your two-bit listening devices. They're long gone."

He shoved me in the back behind the passenger's seat. West bundled Mollye in from the opposite side. I expected the car to show some evidence it had been torn apart. It looked neater than mine ever had. Jones reached across to buckle me in. For a fleeting moment, I thought he wanted to keep me safe. Then I realized it was another form of restraint. Safer for them, not me. At least they'd cuffed our hands in front of us. No arms torqued behind our butts for the ride up the mountain.

The deputy took the wheel; our crooked-toothed chauffeur from Hades. Standing outside the car, the sheriff leaned in to give West his orders. The deputy might be our driver, but Sheriff Robbie Jones was clearly in charge of deciding how our ride would end.

"I'll take the lead," Jones said. "Stay right on my tail. I radioed the gate. My nephew's on duty so it's cool. Told him we'd be there in about twenty. He'll put a note in the log that a Mrs. Ellis called to say she was expecting visitors. Justification for letting our young ladies in. He'll give us a guest pass to hang on the mirror before the Camry goes for a swim."

Jones ducked lower and turned to look over the seat at Mollye and me. He raised a hand next to his pock-marked puss and waggled his fingers in a cheery wave. "See you soon, girls."

The Camry purred to life. No duct tape slapped over our mouths or hankies stuffed down our throats. Not a slip up. How would they explain gummy residue on our cheeks? Besides gags weren't needed. We were in the boonies; they were in total control. Screaming wouldn't do a thing except further annoy the jerk in the front seat.

Had my posse gotten our SOS? Were they riding to the rescue?

"Deputy, how about a little entertainment?" I heckled. "Given the Camry's swan dive will be our swan song, why not give us the lowdown on how you and your boss Robbie got launched on your crime spree."

I hadn't a clue if West would bite, or if it would make a whit of difference if he did. But my curiosity was real. Besides, if Paint and Andy actually managed to rescue us, knowing how many bodies the lawmen had buried could come in handy.

While the deputy didn't utter a word, I caught the strange look on his face as his gaze flicked up to the rearview mirror to meet mine. Did he have regrets? He didn't look exactly happy about killing us.

"Come on, tell us. Why'd you kill Jed Watson? Wasn't he a buddy?"

"Didn't kill him," West mumbled. "Jed got the whole ball rolling. Just his bad luck he took a bullet."

"What the frick?" Mollye joined the conversation. "You saying it really was Eva who shot him?"

"No, stupid. Kaiser shot Jed."

Huh?

"So how did Kaiser end up dead?" I wanted to know. "A shoot-out at Udderly corral?"

West snorted. "Not quite. Once Jed found proof Kaiser was a con artist, he convinced Robbie and me to help him rob the Yankee scumbag, steal back some of the money he stole. Figured Kaiser couldn't exactly file a complaint with the cops."

"What went wrong?" Mollye asked.

"We ambushed Kaiser, but that slick bastard was faster and meaner than we bargained. Somehow he grabbed Jed's gun, and it went off when they tussled. Bullet went straight into Jed's brain. Don't think he even blinked before he died. 'Course it didn't do Kaiser no good. Jones offed the Yankee slimeball a minute later."

"So why bury their bodies half a mile apart?" I asked.

Though it was getting darker by the minute, enough twilight remained to see West's crooked alligator smile in the mirror. Okay, he wasn't sorry about everything that had gone down.

"Robbie came up with one heck of a fix. We'd pot Kaiser near where we ambushed him, carry Jed's body back to his house, and shoot Jed's wife. Make it look like what they call a domestic dispute. Jed had told us he thought his wife was fixin' to leave him. Robbie said it would be plain wrong for some Yankee witch who wouldn't stick by her man to inherit Jed's farm, Watson land. Normally I don't go in for killing women, but Robbie's mind was made up. No point arguing with him."

West paused and shook his head. "Only we couldn't find the damned woman. Waited till three in the morning. When she didn't show, we dug a grave for Jed. Robbie figured if she ever came back and the body got dug up, he'd investigate. No matter when that happened, she'd be the prime suspect." West chuckled. "Damned if he wasn't right. It worked like he said. Just a little late."

The fog in my brain was lifting, but I still had a dozen questions. Act one in this little drama took place forty years ago. How did the banker and Sunrise Ridge connect with the current murder spree? Might as well try to keep the deputy running off at the mouth.

"What does any of this have to do with Sunrise Ridge?" Mollye asked.

Good. We were on the same wave length.

"The way Jed originally planned it, he'd sign over his share of the timberland so it would look like Kaiser conned all of us. Wanted it to look like we were all victims who'd lost somethin'. That way nobody'd suspect us when Kaiser disappeared. Jed figured a few acres of next-to-worthless timberland wasn't a big sacrifice considering what we'd pocket. Only Jed didn't get around to attaching his John Hancock to the deed before he got shot."

I nodded. "So you forged Jed's signature and talked Victor into witnessing it for a piece of the action? You used the banker to launder the money, too?"

West clamped his mouth shut and shifted sideways to glare at me. "Yankees. This is why you're in the mess you're in. It's your own fault. You never stop pushin', do you? Yack. Yack. Well, I've said all I'm gonna say. I'm tired of your yapping. You've given me a monster headache."

He switched on the Camry's radio, dialed in a local country

western station, and cranked the volume to an eardrum-splitting level. Apparently, the last song I'd hear would be about a cheating spouse, a bender, a truck, a dog, or time in the pokey. Goody.

I glanced over at Mollye. Her head was bowed, lips moving, hands clasped. Praying. Didn't know if it was for our salvation or to make good on her wish to take these idiots with us.

Me? I was still praying for inspiration.

Even though I hoped Andy or Paint would send help, I knew we couldn't count on it. There had to be something we could do to cheat a watery grave.

I love to swim. In fact, I'd been on a synchronized swim team in high school. Didn't mean I wanted a burial at lake.

Think. A memory tugged at my mind. *Mythbusters.* Adam underwater. In one episode of *Mythbusters*, Adam buckled himself in a sinking car. He was trying to prove a person could get out of a submerged vehicle if he didn't panic. Easy for him. Adam had a diver in the backseat with a spare tank of air.

I didn't think the lawmen planned to give us a diver or a tank of oxygen.

Focus. The *Mythbusters* episode did demonstrate that you needed to wait until the inside filled almost completely with water to open a submerged car door. Something about equalizing pressure. Okay, if Adam can do it, so can we. Of course, his water wasn't freezing, and he had a diver standing by. Easy-peasy.

Fat back and sausage links! How far down would we sink before the water climbed high enough to open the door? Then there was that big, couldn't-be-ignored hole in my Swiss cheese thinking. We'd be knocked out cold. Jones and West had already let that little secret slip. They'd conk us before the tires left dry land.

FORTY-TWO

I looked out the window, searching for landmarks as I tried to track our progress. All too soon, darkness cloaked the landscape. No streetlights on the winding rural road. The Camry's headlights flashed on pines, pines, and more pines as we slalomed up the mountain. I'd lost count of the hairpin turns.

Now and again, I glanced behind us, hoping to glimpse headlights. Nada. Not a moonshiner or veterinarian in sight. So much for a rescue posse.

Our car slowed, and then stopped. Up ahead, the sheriff's cruiser cozied up to Sunrise Ridge's well-lit gingerbread guard house, and Jones stepped out of his car. He chatted amiably with a twenty-something, presumably the nephew, who probably had no idea he was about to become an accomplice in the murder of two thirty-somethings.

West exited the car to join the confab. Before closing the door and walking away, he leaned in and shook a finger at us. "Now don't you two go anywhere. Nice how cars these days have newfangled safety features like door and window locks to keep kiddies safe."

We heard the click. The skinny deputy ambled up the road. He shook hands with the baby-faced creep. The guard hut's spotlight offered good visuals of the trio but no audio. They kept their voices low. We couldn't hear a dang thing.

Hmm, if we couldn't hear them, maybe they couldn't hear us.

"Hey, Mollye," I whispered. "How you doing?"

"How do you think? I'm freaked. How can you sound so calm?"

"I have an idea. Hey, it's worth a shot. A long shot. But we don't exactly have hundreds of options. For our 'accident' to look legit, they have to put us in the front seat. I have my fingers crossed they're as lazy as they are overconfident. If so, they won't want to strain themselves hefting two unconscious bodies. I'm hoping they'll wait till we're up front to knock us cold. That'll give us a chance."

Mollye rolled her eyes. "If you're trying to cheer me up, you're failing miserably, girlfriend."

"Well, if we know what's coming, maybe we can hand them a surprise. As soon as we're in the front seat, you push the pedal to the metal. We'll zoom into the lake before they have a chance to conk either of us over the head."

"Hey, I saw *Thelma and Louise*. I don't recall there being a scene after those broads drove off the cliff. The dang credits rolled."

"True. But our car's gonna be pointed at a lake, a shallow lake. Water means a lot softer landing than plummeting into a canyon a mile down."

"Not sure it's better for me," Mollye muttered. "I can't swim. Won't even take a bath without a snorkel handy."

I stifled a giggle. "Hey, I was a certified lifeguard. Just promise me you won't panic. If you fight me, neither of us is likely to make it. We stand a good chance of living through this if we go into the water conscious. Getting out of the car's the only tricky part."

I saw no need to mention the possibility of hypothermia or the likelihood our escorts would take potshots at us if we ever surfaced.

I heard footsteps. West coming back to the car.

"Will you do it?" I asked.

Mollye nodded and squeezed my hand. "You know my mom can't swim either."

Given the goofy smile on her face, I worried her mind had snapped. Was she retreating into some fantasy?

Mollye dug her nails into my wrist to focus my attention. "Listen up. Mom always worried about driving off a bridge and being trapped in what amounted to a steel coffin. She keeps one of those doohickeys that break car windows in the glove box. That's our escape hatch."

West arrived within earshot, and Mollye and I both zipped it. He climbed in, slipped a visitor hang-tag on the rearview mirror, and cranked the motor.

"Not long now, girls. Just had a few details to work out. Jeff's gonna place a couple temporary roadblocks. Most of the houses built so far are second homes, getaways for rich Yankees. It's pretty quiet in March since most vacationers wait for warmer weather. But Jones didn't want to risk a nosy neighbor happening by while we're setting up your accident."

An underlying melancholy warred with the adrenaline rush buzzing in my veins. Would Aunt Eva go to jail? Would Mom and Dad forgive my snooping? My brain detoured from family to Andy and Paint. Would have been fun to discover where their tantalizing kisses might have led.

I stifled a sigh. Didn't want to give West the satisfaction.

FORTY-THREE

The deputy piloted the Camry through the open gate and headed down the road. Lights proved rarer than Ardon County vegans, but moonlight glistened on the water.

Water? *Braunshweiger!* We'd arrived at the lake. As the old maxim goes, time to sink or swim. I was pretty sure about the sinking part. The swimming part seemed up in the air. Or water. Oh, Bratwurst.

The deputy stopped the car, then twisted in his seat. He bit his lip, putting his yellowed teeth in plain view. He looked nervous.

"Brace yourselves. Robbie says we need to leave authentic skid marks. So Mollye's about to begin an 'out-of-control' skid toward the lake."

"Do you do everything the sheriff tells you to do?" Mollye muttered. "Kiss his ass when he bends over?"

"Shut it, Mollye. We'll wind up just shy of the embankment. Nose down, but dry. Need to stuff you two up front before the actual plunge."

He swallowed again. I had the feeling he shared a tiny bit of our abject fear. "You ain't gonna see it coming. We'll knock you out soon as we haul your asses out of the backseat and get a good swing at ya. Robbie don't want no last-minute squirmin' and fightin' once you hear Porky Pig sayin', 'Th-th-th-that's all folks.'"

Swell. I knew two porky pigs. Too bad they were smarter than I reckoned and not near as lazy.

West stomped on the gas pedal. The car rocketed ahead maybe two hundred feet, then shimmied sideways as he mashed the brakes. His high-pitched cackle told me that despite the whiff of fear I'd smelled on him, the deputy'd always wanted to play NASCAR. My eyes scrunched shut as my head whipped forward, then snapped back. For a fleeting second, I hoped the front airbag might engage and punch our idiot do-whatever-he's-told driver in the nose. I opened my eyes. No white bag. No bloody nose. No luck.

"I think Thelma and Louise might want to come up with a Plan B," Mollye mumbled.

Couldn't agree more. There had to be something. Maybe the cold water would revive us? Mom always claimed I was an optimist.

West exited the car. The dinging open-door alarm announced he hadn't switched off the motor, hard to tell with these quiet hybrids. The Camry's reflected headlights, now aimed at the inky lake, glowed like hot embers. The car perched on tilt; the front wheels plopped over the edge of the bank, poised for a downhill run. The show-off deputy had cut it mighty close.

Out of the corner of my eye, I spotted the sheriff peering into the backseat. As he yanked my door open, I jerked away from his hammy hands. A glint of metal. He had the key to my cuffs in one of his hands. Let him uncuff me. It'd give me a better chance to put up a good fight. I'd claw his eyes out, land a swift kick in the *cajones*, follow that with a head butt. Maybe I'd knock us both out.

Jones unlocked the cuff on my left hand.

"What the..."

I never heard the end of Jones' surprised yelp. It was drowned out by the piercing blare of a truck horn. Someone trying his audio best to wake the dead. Yes! Headlight beams barreled our way.

I swung my freed left hand at Jones. Swiveled sideways as far as my seatbelt allowed. Since the seats were set for long-legged front seat passengers, I had zero space to maneuver. But the sheriff was distracted. I squirmed sideways to lash out with a crippling kick.

Yoowww! A solid hit...on a very solid door frame. All portions of the sheriff's stocky bod had shifted out of range.

What the Feta?

Jones had jerked his butt—and fat head—out of the car. And he was hot-footing it to the driver's side. "Out of my way, West." He shoved the deputy, dove into the front seat and jerked the gearshift into drive.

"Go round to the other side," Jones ordered West as he braced his arms against the front door frame and grunted. His face contorted, looking all the world like some out-of-shape weightlifter in a hernia competition. His cartoon-red cheeks puffed out like balloons. Maybe he'd pop an artery. A girl could hope.

"For chrissakes, help me shove the damn car in the lake," Jones yelled at his deputy. "We need these two out of the way so we can deal with our uninvited guests."

My head whipped toward my side of the car. The skinny deputy had joined in the push-'em-down-the-hill contest, a new luge-sport.

Cheeses!

The car pitched forward. It rolled, then raced. Goodbye, Jones and West. So long solid ground.

I fumbled with the seatbelt. Come on, come on. Snap. Precious seconds wasted.

I lurched toward the space between the front seats. Stretched my arm toward the buttons to open the windows. Where was the danged child safety lock?

We hit the water. A graceless belly flop.

My body slammed forward. I saw the gearshift just before my head hit.

FORTY-FOUR

Screams. Deafening.

Mollye's and my shrieks overlapped in ear-splitting disharmony.

"Stay open!" Molly screeched.

I felt dizzy. I was on my back. How? I'd flipped.

I blinked. Where was Mollye? Why was a red sandal wedged against the backseat arm rest? Water gushed in over the sandaled foot at the center of my cockeyed view. The red sandal disappeared.

Blast. The outside rush of water slammed the car doors shut, locking us in tighter than any Ardon County jail cell.

"Are we floating?" Mollye, still handcuffed, frantically pawed at her seatbelt.

Floating? Sort of. Looking backward I could see most of the car's rear-end still bobbled topside.

"Yeah, but it won't last more than a few seconds."

The windows. I'm supposed to open the windows.

I squirmed to pull free. What was holding me? I yanked. The empty handcuff was stuck, trapped between the seat and the gear console. I yanked. Nothing. I stretched my uncuffed hand toward the driver's side window controls. My fingers scrabbled over the buttons. *Push.* Nothing. Moved to the next button. *Push.* Nothing.

Too late. The liquid vacuum sucked down the Camry's hind-end. Water covered the outside windows.

Sobs wracked Mollye's body. "The water's already past my ankles. It's freezing."

Her teeth began to chatter, or maybe I was hearing my own doing the la cucaracha imitation.

The stuck handcuff finally popped free, and I struggled to sit up.

"Mollye, turn around and kneel on the seat. Put your mouth near the rear window. That's where the air bubble will stay. We have loads of time."

A few minutes anyway. Five, ten, fifteen? I hoped we wouldn't run down the clock.

"What makes you an expert? You a former submarine captain?"

"Nope. Didn't stay at a Holiday Inn last night either. I just like *Mythbusters*. Don't be a wimp. Us Yankees go skinny-dipping in water colder than this."

Mollye snorted.

I hoped humor would take the edge off our terror. It kinda worked. For me.

"I'm gonna go for your mom's window-breaking thing-a-ma-jig. What's it look like?"

I could barely understand my friend's reply what with the steady interruption of chattering teeth and hysterical hiccups.

"Just stay put, Mollye. Keep breathing nice and steady. Don't panic. That'll use up oxygen faster."

She nodded and gulped air. Suggesting calm to someone afraid of water and trapped in a sinking auto was about on par with asking Eva to give up cheese.

The car's downhill hurdle seemed to slow. But the murky depths screwed with my internal compass. Was the car still moving or did the rippling water provide the illusion? If Jones was right, the lakebed resembled a shallow bowl and not an impact crater. Shallow would keep the surface within a swimmer's reach.

"Mollye, trust me. We'll get out of here."

Icy water crept past my kneecaps. The cold sent frosty shoots up my spine and wrapped around my chest like some glacial form of kudzu. *Frozen frankfurters!*

I'd lied to Mollye. Not even Canadians were daft enough to dive into lakes fed by mountain streams. A balmy fifty degrees? If we were lucky. How long before hypothermia set in?

Nope, don't ask, don't guess. Focus.

Past time for me to find the thing-a-ma-jig in the glove box. The relentless invasion of frigid water already covered the front seat cushions. The dashboard was totally submerged. Its triangular hazard light glowed bright red. I could even read the well-lit gas gauge. Nice to know we had three-quarters of a tank inside our fish tank.

No light arrays to direct me to the glove box, but I knew where it was. The car's headlamps helped. Water diffused the beams, creating a twinkling cocoon that wrapped the car. What lay beyond? Our own black hole in space.

How long before the lights winked off? Another question better left unasked.

My head was still above water, but it wouldn't be when I tried for the glove box.

A pep talk. That's what I needed. Go girl. Just take a deep breath and go for it. It won't be bad. Your face will numb up in seconds. After your heart clocks out from shock, you won't feel a thing.

"What you waiting for?" Mollye's tone managed to convey panic, irritation, and skepticism.

"I'm going." I sucked in so much air I almost burst the buttons on my blouse, then plunged headfirst into the water.

Perhaps thrashed might be a better descriptor. With seemingly millions of tiny icicles tattooing my cheeks, I fought a gasp reflex. Knew it would only give the arctic river a fast track to my tonsils. Oh, and a gasp would also end my lifelong love affair with oxygen.

My Popsicle fingers found the dash and danced along its contours searching for the glove box latch. The water served as liquid Novocain. A mittened toddler had more dexterity than I could claim. Hard to believe the frozen marbles that had replaced my eyeballs could actually see.

I spotted the outline of the latch. Pushed. Nothing. Water pressure? I banged the compartment with the flat of my hand, hoping enough water would seep in to equalize the pressure. I bashed the dash again, and hit the latch. Sprong!

My fingers scrambled inside. Thank heaven, the car was new and Mollye's mom had yet to stuff the glove box with maps, tissues, extra napkins and all the other crapola that nested in mine. My fingers touched something besides paper. Oblong, plastic. I'd never seen a window-smashing thing-a-ma-jig, but this matched Mollye's description. I searched again, just in case there were other candidates. Nope. The smooth plastic doohickey seemed the only choice. Besides my lungs were fixing to burst.

I crawfished, wriggling back through the watery tunnel between the seats. When I rose up, it took forever to reach air. Water had climbed within two feet of the backseat roof. I sputtered and gasped, guzzling oxygen like I'd been water boarded. I'd been under sixty seconds, maybe ninety. My old synchronized swimming buddies would be ashamed of me.

"Did you get it?" Mollye asked.

"Think so." I raised my manacled right hand to show her the puny-looking plastic prize. "Glad you told me it could pass for an obese key holder. Otherwise I'd have looked for a hammer."

"Hand it over," Mollye said. "I'll do the honors. Mom showed me how. Just press this gizmo against the window to release the spring-loaded steel point."

"You sure? I can do it. The water's gonna pour in as soon as the window cracks, and I haven't a clue what happens to the shattered glass."

"I'm dead sure. If I bust open the window, I'll know when to take my last breath."

"Won't be your last," I promised. "Wait! Take off your shoes and that scarf."

"My scarf? Why?"

"Hey, I'll buy you a new one. We can't afford extra baggage. With my luck your scarf would wrap around my head like a blindfold. I need to see the Camry's headlights to tell which way is up."

"Okay, I'll shuck the shoes," Mollye nodded. "But not the scarf. Danny gave it to me. Don't worry, it won't flutter." She whipped off the sodden scarf and stuffed it inside her pants.

"If you don't save me, I'll come back and haunt you," she added. "I have experience with the spirit world, you know. Take a big breath. Here goes."

I'd barely gulped a mouthful of air when an exploding wall of water flung me backward. If there was broken glass, I never saw it in the liquid hurricane. Mollye put her shoulder to the door. I breast-stroked through the opening.

Mollye's eyes were wild and every appendage she owned thrashed at the surrounding water. I jived left, snuck up behind her, and clamped my right arm with its clunky unwelcome jewelry across her ample chest. Had to muster all my strength to pin her tight to my body. Couldn't let her turn and hang on me. A death sentence for both of us. I kicked and stroked. Mollye, bless her, quit thrashing.

The flow of water caressed my body as we edged higher. Adrenalin fueled my strokes. I no longer felt icy pinpricks; they'd merged into a raging bonfire that licked at every scrap of exposed skin. Exhaustion lurked. My lungs burned. Keep going!

We broke the surface. I gulped air. Thank God.

Mollye sputtered and choked. "I'm drowning!" Her head bobbed under.

I'd loosened my grip as soon as I felt air on my cheeks. Bad mistake. Mollye couldn't swim, didn't know how to float. Her panic ignited a tornado of agitated motion. She flung herself at me and tried to lock her handcuffed arms around my neck. I ducked, took a big breath, and dove. I ambushed her from behind and once again locked her against my body.

"Stop fighting," I gasped. "Or I swear I'll knock you silly."

Bang! Bang!

Gunshots. Fear ignited a new interior chill. My heart stuttered. Were they shooting at us? Were Andy and Paint up there in the dark? Were they still breathing?

FORTY-FIVE

Bang! Bang!

This time I heard metal pings after each shot. Ricochets off either the sheriff's cruiser or the rescue truck. Was it Andy's or Paint's ride? I hadn't seen anything except headlights prior to our baptism.

I tried to block out the gunplay. Getting out of the frigid lake was priority number one. I swam as fast as I could, given I had a fidgeting, swearing friend clamped to my side.

With my body on autopilot, my mind whirled. Did the shots suggest a gun battle or a shooting gallery with Paint and/or Andy as clay ducks?

The shore looked reasonably close, maybe one hundred feet. Cupcake swim for even a back-of-the-pack triathlete like me. In normal times. Not in cold water dragging a sodden, fully clothed body.

The truck's headlamps served as a lighthouse beacon. I kept them to my left as I angled toward shore. Beaching in the sheriff's lap wouldn't help our posse—or us. Once ashore we'd make an end-run to the truck. If our luck held, we could all flee the mountain together.

First, reach shore. The clock was ticking. My arms possessed all the strength of stretched-out rubber bands. I hoped Mollye wouldn't recall she had me by two inches and forty pounds. If she panicked and set her mind to it, she could twist me into a pretzel and sit on my head.

A clump of bubbles rose from below and airbrushed my arms. I flinched. A fish? No. Mountain lakes didn't boast anything bigger than trout.

A geyser shot up beside me. *Holy Havarti!*

A scream tore from my throat. Jones or West had come for us. We hadn't escaped.

Mollye screamed, then gagged on the geyser's falling spray.

A man's large hand clamped over my mouth.

"Shhh. Sound carries."

I tried to bite, then torqued my neck enough to take a gander at which monster the lake had spewed up—Jones or West.

"Andy! You scared the deviled ham out of me. What are you doing?"

A brief smile flicked across his face before his need to gulp air took priority. The veterinarian was definitely down a quart or two on oxygen.

I struggled to tread water and keep Mollye's head high and dry as we waited for Andy to suck in enough air to talk.

"We flipped for it…" The need to gasp air pushed the pause button on Andy's answer. "I got to play Jacques Cousteau. Paint got Rambo. He's keeping the sheriff busy."

He paused to take two quick breaths. "We called state troopers as soon as we figured out Jones snatched you." Andy panted. "I snuck past the sheriff. Swam out. Dove on the Camry's headlights. Empty. You'd rescued yourselves."

"Not quite. We haven't made shore. We need to swim now, talk later."

"Want me to tow Mollye?" Andy asked.

"Hey, I'm not a barge," she sputtered.

Relief at having a new ally helped restore my humor. "Could have fooled me. Andy, you can tote this barge soon as you get your breath back."

My sidestroke sliced through the water. Again and again. I kicked, too, though a budding cramp pulsed in my calf.

My strokes got shorter. My nerve endings grew indifferent to the cold. Numbness, cramps, exhaustion. A depressing trifecta. Time to swap. Let Andy lug Mollye a while.

I reached to tag him, when my foot scraped something ragged. A rock? A tree stump? Had I touched bottom? "Mollye, I'm gonna loosen my grip. Don't go crazy. I think we've reached the shallows."

I quit stroking and let my legs feather down. Yes! I could stand. Sort of. Fear and exhaustion turned my legs to Jell-O.

Andy stood, the water little more than waist deep on him. He took Mollye's arm to steady her as she found her feet. "We can wade in.

Quietly," he said. "Can't give Jones and West our position."

Mollye let out a relieved whoosh of air. "Thank the Lord. I swear I'll never take a bath again. Only quick showers, maybe spit baths. Had enough dunking for a lifetime."

Her whisper was barely audible. Either she'd taken Andy's admonition seriously about the need for quiet or she was too hoarse to boost her volume.

Slimy rocks lining the bottom of the lake made walking a slip-and-slide adventure. But driven forward by the promise of dry land, we slogged from waist-deep to knee-deep in no time.

"Let's head toward that stand of pines." Andy motioned to a spot about twenty feet farther left. "The embankment's real shallow and the trees offer a little cover."

We clambered ashore and fell in a sprawl on the soft pine needles. For long minutes, we engaged in a communal wheeze-a-thon, hoping to inhale enough oxygen to find that elusive second wind. Dry land hadn't brought total relief. A slight breeze snuck beneath the pine boughs and tried its best to turn us into human Popsicles.

Andy sat up. "Imagine Paint could use a little company. No sirens yet. Hope the state troopers get here soon."

"What about that baby-faced killer on the gate?" Mollye whispered. "What if he called in reinforcements? Heck, he could be sneaking up on Paint right now."

"He won't sneak up on anyone any time soon." Andy's white teeth flashed in the moonlight. "I shot him with my tranq gun. Same dose I'd use to knock out a bear. Left him on the floor of the guard hut and the gates wide open for the cavalry."

"Will they come—the state troopers?" I asked. "This is the sheriff's bailiwick, right? What if the troopers call Jones to see what's happening? The sheriff has a radio, and he can spin convincing yarns. He could say your call was bogus, and he'd handle things. Cheeses! Maybe more of his deputies are on the way."

Mollye shook her head. "Don't think so. Danny's introduced me to other deputies. They're not dirtbags like West. Remember? After Jones murdered Victor he made up a cock-and-bull tale about us to keep Max, that other deputy, in the dark."

"What?" Andy looked back and forth between Mollye and me.

"Jones killed Victor?"

"We saw him do it," Mollye said.

"Oh, pickled pigs' feet." I suddenly remembered the cell phone wedged in my undies. Andy's eyes grew bigger than Frisbees as I began a foray into my panties. Probably looked like I'd picked an inopportune time to scratch an itch. Awkward, too. My right hand with its dangling handcuff wasn't in play. Had to pretend I was a leftie.

Eureka. I snaked my mitt back out of my sodden panties and waved my iPhone in victory. "Hid it after I texted you. Hope we can save the pictures we took of Jones and West wiping down Victor's car after they smoked him."

Andy's mouth hung open. "You are certainly the most interesting woman I've ever dated."

"Enough lovey-dovey crapola," Mollye grumped. "Let's make sure our friend Paint remains 'unleaded.' We need to haul ass to the truck and boogie on out of here."

Andy slid a knife out of a sheath on his belt. "Paint has my gun, but I have a little something to give Jones or West if they jump us."

We trekked through the woods single-file—Andy, me, Mollye—trying our dangdest to lurk in the shadows and avoid twigs that might snap-crackle-pop under our bare feet. Not a single gunshot since we reached shore. That scared me. Could it mean the sheriff didn't need to waste any more bullets because he'd already killed Paint?

A pine branch snapped. So loud it sounded like a gunshot. In the woods just ahead. My heart tripped as Andy's knife hand flew up. He'd heard it, too. An animal or a two-legged critter?

A hand shot out from behind a tree and grabbed Andy's forearm.

"Easy with that knife, partner. It's me."

A whoosh of air escaped Andy's lips as Paint released his arm.

"You 'bout gave us all heart attacks." Mollye thumped Paint's chest with her handcuffed fists. "Why'd you leave the truck?"

Paint shrugged. "Seemed like a good idea. Ran out of ammo. Maybe you ought to stock more firepower in your vet-mobile, Andy."

Andy looked my way. "When I saw the SOS, I swung by and picked Paint up at his store. Knew Mollye must have clued you in on your phone's new feature. When you didn't answer our calls, we figured we'd better hurry. Didn't think to grab an extra box of shells."

"Glad you hurried," Mollye said. "Five more minutes and we'd have been primed for a permanent sleep in Davy Jones' Locker."

"What now?" Andy asked. "Hide until—"

A wail of sirens interrupted. We started stumbling toward the road.

Paint stopped short and we almost tumbled like a row of cascading dominoes. "Stop at the edge of the woods," he warned. "Let's make sure our new arrivals are really the white hats before we put our hides in plain sight."

"Agreed," Andy said. "Even if they're troopers, there's no guarantee one of them won't have a jittery trigger finger. Running at them in the dark would be plain dumb."

We stopped five feet short of the clearing. The moon was high, and my eyes had become accustomed to the dark. The two new vehicles were clearly state patrol, not Ardon County Sheriff's cruisers.

Four troopers exited the cars, but stayed behind them for protection. A bright spotlight lit up the sheriff's cruiser like it was mid-afternoon.

"Sheriff Jones, please come out where we can see you with your hands up," the lead trooper yelled. "We need to sort this out. Maybe you can explain everything that's going on. Maybe you're just doing your job. But the calls we got, well, we have to investigate, have to take it seriously."

Jones stepped into the light, holding his empty hands high, and started talking a mile a minute. "Glad you're here. We thought we were dealing with an ordinary trespassing complaint. But the gate-crashers—two women—fought us like alley cats. Had to handcuff 'em. We put 'em in the backseat of their car while we decided our next move. That's when their car rolled into the lake. We wanted to dive in and try to get 'em out but then this truck barreled up. Someone opened fire. I'm guessin' they called their boyfriends. They're hiding around here somewhere."

My anger boiled up like a volcano. The weasel had spun the truth a complete one-eighty. Well, he wouldn't get away with it. I opened my mouth to scream, "He's lying!" when Andy clamped a hand over my mouth. This was getting to be a bad habit. If we ever got out of this mess, I'd explain his big fat paw was not one of the parts of his anatomy with a permit to access my lips.

Andy's eyes pleaded. "Jones thinks you and Mollye are dead and can't contradict him. He's discrediting Paint and me as deranged boyfriends. But he's got a surprise coming—you two are alive. Let's see what else he's got up his sleeve. And West hasn't shown himself. That worries me."

The sheriff sauntered toward the troopers like a total innocent. "Can I put my hands down now?"

Instead of answering, the lead trooper asked another question. "Who's the 'we' doing the arresting? Sheriff, tell whoever's with you he needs to come out with his hands up."

Jones hollered, "Come join us, Deputy. These troopers can see we were just defending ourselves."

Nothing happened. West didn't pop up.

"Come on, Deputy, hustle it up," the trooper ordered. "Don't make us come get you."

I held my breath. Why didn't West show himself? Was he going cowboy or planning a suicide by cop?

A minute went by, then two. Nothing.

"Oh, God," Paint whispered. "Maybe I killed West. I aimed high, over the truck. I just wanted to keep them pinned down."

Jones lowered his hands as he stood beside the troopers.

"Jenkins, stay here with the sheriff," the lead trooper said. "Swihart and I will go collect the deputy. Maybe he's injured."

The leader motioned Swihart to go to the right of the sheriff's cruiser, while he took the left wing. I prayed West wasn't planning to shoot his way out of this.

The troopers disappeared behind the cruiser.

"Call an ambulance," the leader yelled. "The deputy's dead. It's a crime scene."

"Dammit," the sheriff raged. "Those peckerheads murdered my deputy. Hunt 'em down before they kill one of your men. Those assholes are still out there, and they've got guns."

FORTY-SIX

"We don't have guns," Paint yelled.

He stretched his hands high above his head as he stepped out of the woods. "There's one shotgun in the truck, empty. I only fired a few shots over the sheriff's cruiser, way over their heads. We're unarmed. Didn't want to come out till we were sure the sheriff wouldn't gun us down."

Andy, Mollye, and I lurched out of the pines to join Paint.

"Damn you, Jones, you lying scumbag," Mollye yelled. "Thought we were dead, didn't you? Too bad. We're alive to tell what a lowlife murderer you are."

"She's right. Don't listen to anything that dirtbag sheriff says," Andy shouted. "We asked you to come. Why would we invite state troopers if we were trying to gun down the sheriff and his deputy?"

Assuming the posture of what we figured was I-give-up protocol, we all waved our empty hands on high. The clink of handcuffs provided audio accompaniment to Mollye's and my waves. Her hands-up gesture lasted maybe two seconds.

"Look, guys, that freakin' sheriff tried to drown us," she said. "We've been soaking in ice water for half an hour. You'd dern well better get us someplace warm and dry before we croak."

That's when things became a blur. The troopers patted everyone down and administered breathalyzer tests before removing Mollye's and my handcuffs and handing out blankets. Trooper Swihart shepherded Mollye, Andy, and me—the water-logged trio—into the back of a patrol car, cranked up the heat, and told us not to talk. He kept watch from the driver's seat.

Since Paint was an admitted shooter—and wasn't drenched—they led him to another patrol car. Guess they didn't want us conspiring to fabricate a common story. Imagine they also wanted to avoid accusations of using hypothermia as a torture technique to elicit confessions.

The sheriff slumped in the back of his own cruiser. He'd been assigned a front-seat minder, too. Encouraging. Guess the state cops hadn't swallowed Jones' story hook, line, and sinker.

More sirens. More troopers. Two ambulances.

A gray-haired paramedic peered in the window at us, then opened the car door. "I'm Steve," he said. His intense blue gaze roamed over us, assessing, yet concerned and kind. "First, let's get you out of those wet clothes. You girls can undress behind the ambulance doors."

As we scooted out, he handed us beach towels. As I peeled off my wet duds, their odor seemed to intensify. A piquant mélange of mold and sweat with a dash of algae or dead fish. More clothes to burn.

After we emerged in our towel-wrapped birthday suits, Steve and his colleague—the nametag read Gary—wrapped us in thermal blankets, checked our vitals, and tsk-tsked when they discovered our temperatures hovered around ninety-five degrees. Before I knew it, I was on a stretcher, and they'd poked me with an IV. I hate IVs and complained. Steve's eyes twinkled when he suggested there was an alternate—using a catheter to pump warm water into my kidneys.

Cheeses.

I fell asleep. Exhaustion trumped anxiety.

I woke as they rolled my stretcher into the ER. When I opened my eyes, Mom, Dad, and Trooper Swihart were jockeying for prime bedside positions.

I looked at Mom. "You got my message?"

She nodded. "We were worried sick. Phoned the state police. Good thing Andy and Paint called them, too, so they knew where to head. Friends in EMS let me know when they got word an ambulance was bringing you to the hospital. Are you okay?"

"Ma'am, I'm sorry but you can't be in here," Swihart interrupted. The trooper had hopped into the ambulance for our trek down the mountain. Apparently he wasn't going away any time soon.

"I'm her lawyer," Mom huffed. "And I'm advising her not to speak with anyone until we talk. So maybe *you* should leave."

A man in a white coat cleared his throat. "How about this? I want everyone to exit except the young lady. I need to examine her. Please take your custody battle outside."

The doctor declared me dehydrated—sort of ironic since I'd soaked in lake water for at least thirty minutes. The doc prescribed more fluids—external ones, thank you very much—and said I was good to go. He smiled when he handed me a bundle of clean, dry clothes. "Your 'lawyer' asked me to give these to you."

When I left the curtained examining area, Mom and Dad hugged me. Swihart had vanished. Mom Esquire had won temporary custody of the suspect.

"I informed Trooper Swihart I was also legal counsel for Paint, Andy, and Mollye," she said. "No one is to speak with any of you unless I'm present. They're keeping Mollye overnight for exhaustion, but she'll be fine. Now tell me what happened and don't you dare leave anything out this time." She paused and lasered me with her sternest stare. "I hope you've learned it's a very bad idea to hold out on your lawyer. Before we head to the SLED office, you need to tell me everything— including anything stupid the four of you did. They're holding Paint at SLED now. He'll be the first to be deposed."

I confessed all, including our—in hindsight potentially dangerous—plan to unhinge Victor with the news the Sunrise Ridge sale was kaput. I continued with a report on how we'd eavesdropped on the banker's chat with the sheriff and deputy. When I got to my eyewitness report of Victor's murder and the efforts of Jones and West to make it look like a carjacking gone bad, Mom's hand flew to her mouth.

"Oh, my God. You are so lucky to be alive."

I handed Mom my waterlogged iPhone. "We can prove we're telling the truth if someone can salvage the photos we took."

Dad snatched my phone. "I'll take it to Hal. He teaches computer engineering. If anyone knows how to retrieve those photos, he will."

Mom shook her head. "No, honey, we have to give the phone to SLED so Jones won't be able to argue we tampered with the evidence. If it's possible to save the photos, SLED can do it."

*   *   *

I fell asleep as Dad drove Mom, Andy, and me to the SLED office in Greenville. Dad had gone looking for Andy and found him just as he'd been given his walking papers.

Andy wore scrubs a doctor friend scrounged up. I remember getting in the backseat of Dad's SUV with Andy, whose truck was still at the crime scene. Besides he probably wasn't in any condition to drive. I sure wasn't.

Not sure how Mom convinced Swihart it was kosher for her to let her two "clients"—Andy and me—travel in the same car without the officer's butt planted between us. Maybe Swihart was as tired as we were.

I woke when the car stopped. I was snuggled against Andy. His arm held me close to his chest. I could feel his steady heartbeat—a heartbeat the sheriff would have ended if he'd had the chance. Andy and Paint took quite a risk to come to our rescue. I sincerely doubted my ex-fiancé would have put his life on the line like that.

Limburger and Liverwurst. I was wildly attracted to both Andy and Paint. How could that work out? Not.

"We're here," Dad said. "I'll park the car and be in as soon as I call Eva. Promised I'd give her an update. She wanted to come, but I told her to sit tight. Nothing she could do, and who knew what vengeance other Watson relations might have in mind. She needs to keep watch on her animals. 'Course I'd love the chance to 'interrogate' the sheriff. Water boarding seems more than appropriate. That cold-blooded killer needs to hang. I'd do whatever it takes to make sure he pays."

Wow. While Dad writes murder mysteries, his heroes rarely do more than tiptoe over a legal line to get their man. Having a killer target his daughter and older sister seemed to change where he was willing to draw the line.

Inside the SLED facility, Andy and I were escorted to a waiting area, while Mom was whisked to the interview room where officers waited to talk to Paint.

After Dad joined Andy and me, we sat in uncomfortable silence. An hour went by. Then another hour slipped past. What was taking so long? Didn't they believe Paint? Were they charging him with murder?

Finally Mom appeared with Paint at her side. Andy jumped up and gave Paint a brotherly hug. "Hey, man, looks like you're free. Did they believe you?"

Paint's lips quirked up in a grin. "Iris Hooker, Esquire, is one heck of an advocate. Think I'll owe her free moonshine for life, or my first born." He winked at me. A gesture that prompted Andy to roll his eyes.

"Iris made sure they asked all the right questions," he added.

Mom patted his arm and gave us a quick summary. "Brie and Andy, you still need to give statements, but SLED now has sufficient evidence to charge Sheriff Jones with the murders of both Victor Caldwell and Deputy West."

"What?" Andy, Dad, and I sang out in a fair imitation of a trio.

Mom nodded. "West was shot in the back with a small-caliber bullet. They believe it came from a throw-down gun Jones kept in an ankle holster. Max Weaver, a deputy, confirmed Jones always carried it. The gun was found in the water a couple feet from shore."

"How did Jones think he'd get away with killing West?" Andy asked.

"Imagine he planned to claim Andy or Paint snuck behind them and killed the deputy," Mom said. "Jones just didn't plan on troopers patting him down, finding an empty ankle holster, and asking one of his deputies about it."

"Why would the sheriff kill his partner in crime?" I asked. "They were in this together. From the beginning—forty years back."

"Suppose it's the same reason Jones killed Victor," Andy said. "The sheriff didn't trust West to keep his mouth shut. He didn't want any loose ends that could unravel and contradict whatever story he spun."

Mom smiled. "You go to the head of the class, Andy. None of you are suspected of wrongdoing. Brie's pictures told the real story of how Victor died. Deputy Weaver, who the sheriff tried to dupe into believing Victor was carjacked, confirmed that Jones and West stopped Mollye's Camry—the one now at the bottom of the lake."

Mom paused and cut a look my way. "With the possible exception of illegally planting listening devices, you're off the hook. Given the circumstances, I doubt there'll be charges. Let's get your statements taken, and maybe we can get out of here before dawn."

FORTY-SEVEN

When I woke, sun streamed through the lacy curtains in my new bedroom. I glanced at the clock: 4:02 p.m. Holy Swiss Cheese. Eva'd let me sleep away the entire day. I rubbed my eyes. Tried to shake off that logy feeling that comes when you've been totally zonked out. 'Course I'd only slept twelve hours.

It was four a.m. when Mom and Dad deposited me at Udderly. They wanted me to come home with them, but Udderly was my home. Wow. The realization made me chuckle. Who'd have thunk it? A vegan chef calling a goat cheese farm home. Lots of kidding around. Pun intended.

I threw on jeans and a t-shirt. I heard Eva bustling about in the kitchen and headed her way. She squeezed me in a hug that would do any wrestler proud. When she returned to face down the onions and celery on her chopping block, I took a second look at the kitchen counter and barked a laugh.

"What the deviled ham?"

My loose-leaf cookbook lay open next to a lineup of vegan essentials—tofu, walnuts, oats, and beans. Eva was making my moatloaf. Would wonders never cease?

My aunt gave me her best steely eyed stare. "Don't you say a word. This is a one-time deal. A thank you. Never gonna happen again. I'm convinced tofu is Lucifer's evil version of slimed cream cheese, and I hope I never have to stick my hands in it again."

I laughed and kissed her cheek. "Want me to finish?"

"Don't need to ask me twice." She turned on the kitchen faucet and scrubbed her hands like they'd been exposed to deadly toxins. "Your folks and all your fellow troublemakers—Mollye, Paint, and

Andy—are coming to dinner. I already fixed lasagna loaded with meat and cheese for us normal folks. "

The troublemakers arrived within a few minutes of each other. Mollye drove up in her psychedelic van, and Andy and Paint came together in Paint's truck.

"You still without wheels?" I asked Andy as he climbed out.

"Till morning, supposed to get my vet-mobile back before noon. They impounded it to photograph and measure the bullet holes. Imagine that'll give my customers a new conversation topic. Not sure my insurance covers shoot-out repairs."

Mollye piped up. "Hey, your truck may have a few holes, but Mom's Camry is now a moldy fish tank. I'm praying the Sheriff's Department has to cough up the money for a replacement since Jones and West pushed it in the lake. Mom would be doubly mad at me if buying new wheels comes back on her or ups her insurance premiums."

Mom and Dad pulled in while all members of the newly formed Udderly gang of thirty-somethings stood on the front porch. Dad brandished two bottles of champagne—a definite signal of good news.

"Let's go inside, you scallywags." Mom made shooing motions to move us into the cabin. "Take a seat so we can tell you all how this story ends—a happy ending for a change."

Due to repeated interruptions from her audience, Mom needed almost an hour to unwrap the layers of a conspiracy that lasted four decades. The insider details had come from an unexpected source— Deputy West's wife.

"Deputy West may have been a scumbag, but he loved his wife— and trusted her," Mom began. "Told her everything he and the sheriff had ever done. Where all the bones were buried. Soon as she heard the sheriff would be charged with killing her husband, she spilled all. The solicitor was kind enough to share the information with me—sort of an apology for trying his dangdest to deny Eva bail." Mom turned to Dad. "It would make one heck of a murder mystery. But who'd believe it really happened?"

Thanks to Deputy West's monologue, Mollye and I knew most of the backstory, but Mom provided a synopsis of the original crime for our tablemates. Her tale began when Jones, West, and Jed, Eva's unlamented late hubby, planned to rob the Yankee scam artist, Kaiser, and run him out of town. To appear as innocent victims, the trio agreed they'd make it look like they'd all lost money to Kaiser. That meant the sheriff and Jed would forfeit Watson timberland to the scam. Wasn't worth much, and they could always buy it back down the road. They simply had to wait long enough that people wouldn't wonder where they got the dough.

When they ambushed Kaiser, he tussled with Jed and shot him with his own gun. Jones returned the favor and shot Kaiser.

Now West and Jones had two bodies to explain. They buried Kaiser and planned to give Eva a starring but dead, non-speaking role in a staged murder-suicide. Only Eva flew the coop. Not knowing if she'd ever come home, they buried Jed at Udderly, figuring if his body was ever found, Eva'd be the prime suspect. The sheriff kept Jed's gun, knowing it might come in handy later in a frame-up. It did.

While Victor wasn't present at Kaiser's ambush, he was in on the plan. His job was to launder the money so they could cash out in their early forties and retire to the good life. That way their newfound wealth could be explained by shrewd investments. Victor hooked them up with Burks and Sunrise Ridge.

The killers didn't anticipate two things. They didn't know Burks, the presumed head of the posh development, fronted for much bigger and nastier crooks, and they didn't plan on an environmental group delaying development for more than a decade.

At this point in Mom's story, Mollye interrupted. "But why did they murder Nancy and Eli Watson?"

"They were desperate for the Tisnomi sale to go through," Mom answered. "They couldn't afford to have Nancy caterwauling, saying Jed never really sold that timberland. If there was a question about the title to the land, they knew Tisnomi would walk. Jones hanged Eli to keep anyone from asking why Nancy was killed. Went back to his original murder-suicide playbook."

Eva nodded. "And Jones killed Victor because he panicked and he thought the banker would do something stupid, get caught, and sing like a canary."

"That's right," Mom said. "Jones also figured West might turn into a chatty Cathy, given how messy things had gotten with the truants at this table. With West gone, the sheriff could spin any tale he wanted, and there wouldn't be a soul around to contradict him."

"So am I in the clear?" Eva asked. "When can I get this itchy electronic spy contraption off my ankle?"

Dad smiled. "Your favorite attorney got all charges dropped and made you an appointment to have your ankle jewelry removed tomorrow. 'Course your legal bill is going to be mighty steep."

"Put it on my account." Eva smiled. "And pour the champagne, little brother."

Dad poured—vegans have no problems guzzling, uh, sipping champagne—and the toasts began.

Eva was the first to raise her glass. "To my favorite niece, Brie Hooker. Without her snooping and roping in her friends, I might well be headed to jail. Thank you, love."

I looked around the table. I'd lived on Udderly Kidding Dairy such a short time. But I loved everyone at this table, including outrageous Mollye and the two handsome men sitting on either side of me.

I almost spit out my champagne when Paint's active fingers snuck under the tablecloth to give my knee a squeeze. A fraction of a second later, Andy played his hand, slightly higher.

Holy ham hocks. Life at Udderly was going to be interesting.

LINDA LOVELY

Linda Lovely finds writing pure fiction isn't a huge stretch given the years she's spent penning PR and ad copy. Linda writes a blend of mystery and humor, chuckling as she plots to "disappear" the types of characters who most annoy her. Quite satisfying plus there's no need to pester relatives for bail. Her newest series offers good-natured salutes to both her vegan family doctor and her cheese-addicted kin. She's an enthusiastic Sisters in Crime member and helps organize the popular Writers' Police Academy. When not writing or reading, Linda takes long walks with her husband, swims, gardens, and plays tennis.

The Brie Hooker Mystery Series
by Linda Lovely

BONES TO PICK (#1)
PICKED OFF (#2)

Henery Press Mystery Books

And finally, before you go...
Here are a few other mysteries
you might enjoy:

FIXIN' TO DIE

Tonya Kappes

A Kenni Lowry Mystery (#1)

Kenni Lowry likes to think the zero crime rate in Cottonwood, Kentucky is due to her being sheriff, but she quickly discovers the ghost of her grandfather, the town's previous sheriff, has been scaring off any would-be criminals since she was elected. When the town's most beloved doctor is found murdered on the very same day as a jewelry store robbery, and a mysterious symbol ties the crime scenes together, Kenni must satisfy her hankerin' for justice by nabbing the culprits.

With the help of her Poppa, a lone deputy, and an annoyingly cute, too-big-for-his-britches State Reserve officer, Kenni must solve both cases and prove to the whole town, and herself, that she's worth her salt before time runs out.

Available at booksellers nationwide and online

Visit www.henerypress.com for details

I SCREAM, YOU SCREAM

Wendy Lyn Watson

A Mystery A-la-mode (#1)

Tallulah Jones's whole world is melting. Her ice cream parlor, Remember the A-la-mode, is struggling, and she's stooped to catering a party for her sleezeball ex-husband Wayne and his arm candy girlfriend Brittany. Worst of all? Her dreamy high school sweetheart shows up on her front porch, swirling up feelings Tally doesn't have time to deal with.

Things go from ugly to plain old awful when Brittany turns up dead and all eyes turn to Tally as the murderer. With the help of her hell-raising cousin Bree, her precocious niece Alice, and her long-lost-super-confusing love Finn, Tally has to dip into the heart of Dalliance, Texas's most scandalous secrets to catch a murderer...before someone puts Tally and her dreams on ice for good.

Available at booksellers nationwide and online

Visit www.henerypress.com for details

PUMPKINS IN PARADISE
Kathi Daley

A Tj Jensen Mystery (#1)

Between volunteering for the annual pumpkin festival and coaching her girls to the state soccer finals, high school teacher Tj Jensen finds her good friend Zachary Collins dead in his favorite chair.

When the handsome new deputy closes the case without so much as a "why" or "how," Tj turns her attention from chili cook-offs and pumpkin carving to complex puzzles, prophetic riddles, and a decades-old secret she seems destined to unravel.

Available at booksellers nationwide and online

Visit www.henerypress.com for details

FIT TO BE DEAD

Nancy G. West

An Aggie Mundeen Mystery (#1)

Aggie Mundeen, single and pushing forty, fears nothing but middle age. When she moves from Chicago to San Antonio, she decides she better shape up before anybody discovers she writes the column, "Stay Young with Aggie." She takes Aspects of Aging at University of the Holy Trinity and plunges into exercise at Fit and Firm.

Rusty at flirting and mechanically inept, she irritates a slew of male exercisers, then stumbles into murder. She'd like to impress the attractive detective with her sleuthing skills. But when the killer comes after her, the health club evacuates semi-clad patrons, and the detective has to stall his investigation to save Aggie's derriere.

Available at booksellers nationwide and online

Visit www.henerypress.com for details